DARKMAGE

The Mage Chronicles: Book 3

LISA CASSIDY

Tate House

National Library of Australia Cataloguing-in-Publication entry

Creator: Cassidy, Lisa, author.

Title: Darkmage / Lisa Cassidy.

ISBN: 978-0-9953589-4-2 (paperback)

Series: Cassidy, Lisa. Mage Chronicles; 3.

Target Audience: For young adults.

Subjects: Fantasy fiction.

First published 2018 by Tate House

Cover artwork and design by Jeff Brown Graphics

Map artwork by

This book is dedicated to the two other members of the Tate House team—Kathy and Sarah—without whom I would never have gotten to a third book! Amazing supporters and the most generous of friends. Thank you.

CHAPTER 1

A bird swooped low overhead, screeching loudly, but Alyx barely noticed, her attention firmly focused on trying to convince a stubborn Bluecoat to do things her way. She hadn't missed the glances the twins were shooting each other though— if their amusement became any more blatant, she was going to give serious thought to beating them about the head with her staff.

"Lord-Mage Casovar booked us ship passage for a reason. It's safer." Irritation leaked from Dashan's voice, and he wore that stubborn look on his face she hated.

"I'm aware of that," Alyx said, keeping admirable hold of her temper. "But I think it's important that we go overland instead."

"So you can see your brother." It wasn't a question, and the cocky assurance in his voice almost tipped her over the edge. Damn his need to be right about her all the time.

"You don't think it's important we talk with him?" she asked. "If we go overland, we can head east and cross Shivasa to the north of Widow Falls. You yourself said it only takes a day or two to cross there because it's so narrow. We'd be in Rionn inside a week."

His eyebrows shot upwards, voice rising an octave to match. "You want to cross Shiven territory with a unit of Bluecoats? Why don't you declare war on them while we're at it?"

Alyx caught another look shared between the twins—more amusement—and gritted her teeth. Her patience was wearing dangerously thin, and she blessed Tarrick's silent presence at her side. If it wasn't for his characteristic steadiness, this would have become a shouting match much sooner.

"You're being dramatic." She tried for calm and mostly managed it.

"I'm not," Dashan said flatly, crossing his arms and staring her down. "I'm responsible for your protection, and the safest way to get back to Alistriem is via ship."

"You're responsible for my protection, but that's it," she snapped, his high-handedness finally shattering her hard-won patience. "You're forgetting who's actually in charge here."

An icy silence fell, Dashan's expression hardening into real anger. "You're pulling rank on me?"

A retort was ready on her lips, but Tarrick spoke up before it could leave her mouth. Clearly he'd decided it was time to step in.

"Dash, I'm concerned about Alyx's protection as much as you are, but Dawn is with us," Tarrick said. "Unless the territory we're planning to cross is absolutely infested with Shiven warriors—doubtful, given how far east it is from the rest of the country—she will identify any patrol well before they see us. We should be able to get across and into Rionn without them ever knowing we were there."

"And I think getting back to Alistriem sooner rather than later is a good idea," Dawn added. "Even allowing for a stop at Widow Falls, we'd get there much faster than if we go by ship. Don't you want to find out why we were so precipitously ordered home? What if something is wrong?"

Dashan levelled a stony look on Finn, who gave a sheepish shrug. "I agree with Alyx. Sorry."

"Fine." Dashan spoke through clenched teeth. "We'll do it Alyx's way."

She sighed as he stalked away to pass on the news to the other Bluecoats— Dashan's temper was never enjoyable to experience, and she was just as irritated with herself for failing to keep calm. Now she faced a long trip home with a moody Bluecoat who would make a point of continuing to test her patience. Not exactly what they needed while trying to safely cross Shiven territory.

"At least you tried being patient with him," Tarrick said dryly.

"For at least a whole minute," Finn chimed in.

"You're both hilarious," she said. "I'm going to get something to eat."

ALYX RUMINATED on Dawn's words as she chewed on a piece of stale bread by the fire. They were two days out from DarkSkull, a mysterious summons from the Rionnan king via Lord-Mage Casovar resulting in Alyx, her fellow apprentice mages and her Bluecoat escort leaving weeks ahead of the official end of the study year. She hoped there was nothing seriously wrong. There'd been no indication of it in the note.

Inevitably her thoughts turned to her fight with Dashan. There was another complication she didn't need. She'd been slow to realise the powerful attraction growing between them, but now it was impossible to ignore. And each time she thought of how he'd kissed her, how she'd wanted him to, a horrible surge of guilt followed.

Cayr. Her best friend since childhood. The man she loved. Planned to marry. Even though they were technically apart while she was away at DarkSkull, that hadn't changed the fundamental understanding between them. They loved each other, always had and always would.

Finn wandered into her eyeline, snapping her from the never-ending circling of her thoughts. She offered a smile as he settled himself beside her. "Dawn says the east route is clear as far as her magic extends."

"Not surprising." Alyx nodded. "But we need to make sure she gets enough rest before we hit Shivasa."

"I'll keep a close eye on her." He gave her a pointed look. "You need rest too."

"I'm fine."

Neither of them said it, but they were both thinking of the nightmare she'd had the night after leaving DarkSkull. It had been the worst so far, and had left them all uneasy about what it meant. The feeling that she'd forgotten something important continued to niggle at her... but each time she tried to remember, there was nothing there. The harder she tried, the vaguer her memory became—and the more her head ached. It was a familiar sensation.

"Do you think he took memories from you?" Finn seemed to pick up on her thoughts.

Alyx gave a sharp nod. The mere thought of it made her feel sick, and she silently begged Finn not to pursue it.

"Is that why you don't seem overjoyed to be going home?" He smiled, changing the subject. "Not that I'm not grateful you haven't mentioned Cayr's name a thousand times in the past few days."

She chuckled, but it rang hollow. "It's hard to be excited about going home after everything we learned this year, knowing Taliath are being hunted and wondering why a dark mage is haunting my night-mares." And Brynn. What would happen to him? As angry as she still was about his role in hunting Taliath potentials, she counted him amongst her dearest friends. She'd managed only a quick letter—left in the hands of Rodin to deliver—as they passed through Weeping Stead, but wasn't confident it would reach him anytime soon, especially if he was away on council business.

Finn hesitated. "It's not just that, is it? Alyx, the fight between you and Dashan before, it felt like it was more than just about which way to travel home. And you've both been maudlin ever since."

"Dashan is mad because he hates it when anyone tells him what to do, especially me," she said sharply.

He lifted an eyebrow. "All that may be true, but are you forgetting what I stumbled into at the dance?"

"I've told you that was nothing but a moment of confusion. And even if it were different, it's none of your business!" He'd poked at a sore spot, and she reacted without thinking in an attempt to shut him down.

Finn's mouth tightened. "Dashan isn't the only one who hates it when you talk down to people like the high and mighty noble girl you used to be."

"Finn—"

4

But he was already gone, having risen to his feet and walked away. Alyx tossed the remains of her bread away in frustration. She'd apologise later.

SILENCE WEIGHED over the group for the four-day journey down through Shivasa and into northern Rionn, and not just because of the potential danger around them. Dashan remained uncommunicative and distant, often assigning himself to patrol duty, and Finn's annoyance with Alyx lingered in his cool words and lack of conversation. Tarrick went into his usual protector mode, focusing on nothing but ensuring they stayed clear of the Shiven, and while Dawn may have noticed the tension, the burden of keeping them safe lay with her magic, and she had no energy for anything but that.

Some of the tension left as they crossed safely into Rionn, as if a giant breath had been exhaled. That first night Alyx approached Finn with a peace offering while he stood sentry some distance from the fire —the chance at an intellectual conversation.

"Do you think Shakar turned dark because he became invulnerable?" It was a thought that had been weighing on her mind since the revelations in Carhall, as she tried to reason her way to an understanding of why the council was murdering innocents, or even some idea of why they were so afraid of a mage of the higher order absorbing invulnerability.

Immediately Finn's eyes lit up, his lingering coolness towards her vanishing. "Not literally, I wouldn't think. But power corrupts, and a mage of the higher order being invulnerable too? That is power at its most pure."

"How?" She frowned.

"It gave him the ability to do whatever he wanted," Finn said simply. "Who or what was going to stop him once he set his mind to it?"

"Isn't that overly simplistic? We all have an innate sense of right and wrong—just because we can do something doesn't mean we do. And from all accounts Shakar was a rational man."

"But that's just it, most people can talk themselves into anything if they think it's for the right reasons. What wouldn't you do, for example, to save your father? Or one of us? And there lies the problem... once you'd rationalised it to yourself, who could stop you?"

Alyx bit her lip, mulling that over. It made a certain chilling sense. She'd killed a man last year—something she'd never ever thought she would do—to protect Tarrick. What wouldn't she be willing to do, if presented with the same situation again? At least now, if she went too far, there were those who could stop her.

Finn's warm hand landed on her shoulder, and his cheerful smile dispelled some of the darkness of her thoughts. "Just don't go taking any Taliath lovers and we'll all be fine."

She tried to smile for him, but couldn't. "Killing Taliath potentials can't be the answer, Finn."

He sighed. "I think if the council had been able to come up with a better one, they wouldn't be doing what they are."

"They could kill their own," she murmured, mostly to herself. But no, the council was far too wrapped up in the importance and power of mage blood. They'd probably never even thought of the fact that killing a handful of mages of the higher order would mean a lot less death than killing every Taliath potential they could hunt down.

"The council might argue that trying to kill a mage of the higher order with multiple magical abilities could result in more deaths and attention than killing an untrained young Taliath potential." Finn seemed to have heard her anyway. "Council aside, someone is taking out the most powerful mages anyway. You, Casovar and Galien are the only mages of the higher order remaining, and next time Tarrick gets overly protective, you might remember that until we go back to Dark-Skull, you're away from the protection of the council, and cut him some slack."

Fear trickled through her, and she tried to ignore it by turning her thoughts to Casovar—how had he stayed alive this long, especially since leaving the council? Was it just that he was in Rionn, away from the mage world, or was there something else?

Dashan remained stubbornly distant as he led them unerringly

6

through the rugged terrain of Widow Falls to Ladan's estate, and Alyx let him be. By the time they reached the gloomy fortress of Ladan's home, she was utterly sick of the tension, and hoped seeing her brother would help her focus on something else.

She reined in as they exited thick forest, emerging onto the cleared ground around the walls to find the arched gates wide open. The Blue-coats looked around uneasily, probably remembering their previous visits. It couldn't be easy for them riding in without their weapons—an order Alyx had chosen to allow Tarrick to convey to Dashan had resulted in all swords and knives being stored away in saddlebags.

"This is odd." Finn was the first to say it out loud.

"Where are the fearsome warriors and hunting wolves?" Dawn added.

"He obviously knows we're coming," Dashan said tersely, looking at Alyx. "Is there any reason we're sitting out here gaping like fools?"

Refusing to react to his tone, she kicked Tingo forward, leading the group through the open gates and into the circular cobblestoned yard beyond. Romney waited at the top of the steps, his sword sheathed at his waist. As she brought Tingo to a halt, the lord himself appeared from inside, boots rapping sharply on the stone. He came down the steps quickly, concern filling his voice. "Alyx, is everything okay?"

"We're all fine," she said quickly, smiling at the worry in Ladan's green eyes as he stopped by Tingo. "We were ordered home to Alistriem early, and I wanted to pass through on the way. Is that all right?"

"It is." His hard face softened slightly, and he reached up to touch her knee in greeting. Then he stepped away from Tingo, sharp gaze scanning those with her. Unbelievably, a tiny smile tugged at the corners of her brother's mouth when he spotted Dashan. "Lieutenant. Romney's scouts informed me your unit was escorting Alyx. Welcome back to Widow Falls."

"Thank you, Lord Mirren. My boys and I won't be a bother. Is it all right if I take them through to the barracks you provided us last time?"

"Please do." Ladan nodded. "Aly-girl, bring your friends inside. Food has been made ready for you. Romney, make sure a meal is provided for the Blue Guard officers also."

"My lord." Romney bowed his head and strode down the steps, gesturing for the Bluecoats to follow him towards the barracks.

"I don't believe it," Alyx said in mock wonderment as she joined her brother and they walked inside, Tarrick and the twins trailing a wary distance behind. "You've made a friend."

"What are you talking about?" he muttered.

"'Welcome back to Widow Falls, Lieutenant'," she echoed his words teasingly. "Ha! You've never welcomed me to your home."

He scowled.

THEY GATHERED in Ladan's private study after dinner, Romney joining them at Ladan's insistence. "He's my second, Alyx, and I trust him with my life."

The grizzled warrior should have looked out of place with his fierce features and assorted weaponry, but he was a quiet, solid presence as he refused a seat and took up a position by the door.

Dashan had arrived with him, taking a seat on the couch furthest from Alyx. She sighed inwardly. Keeping her distance hadn't worked. The tangle of emotion between her and Dashan would continue to rise to the surface if they didn't deal with it one way or the other. She just wasn't sure how.

"Why has the lord-mage summoned you home early?" Ladan's voice drew Alyx back to the present. They'd deliberately not discussed anything important over dinner, with Ladan's servants coming in and out serving food and wine.

"We were hoping you might be able to give us an idea," she said. "Have you heard about anything happening in Rionn that would warrant the summons?"

Ladan shared a glance with Romney. "The disputed area has become almost an open battle zone in the months you've been away, particularly in the region around Port Rantarin. I'm not kept apprised of all the developments, but I'm aware the king walks a fine line. Rionn is in the weaker position, and if we complain too strongly about the Shiven forces' behaviour, we risk sparking outright war."

Finn frowned. "It sounds to me like that's what the Shiven are hoping for. By behaving with increasing aggression in the disputed area, they may be trying to push Rionn into initiating a fight. That way they can't be blamed for starting a war."

"I believe the king sees that same danger," Ladan said. "But if we don't put up any resistance in the disputed area, Shivasa will see it as weakness and an invitation to come and take what they want."

"Shivasa may want to avoid blame for starting a war, but that won't hold them indefinitely, not if they're truly intending invasion," Dashan pointed out.

Ladan nodded. "But it will hold them a while. If they invade without cause, they know they'll have the Mage Council to deal with, and likely Zandia and Tregaya too. King Mastaran has to be aware if Shivasa takes Rionn, they'll look to his country next."

"I don't see how any of this explains Casovar summoning us home from DarkSkull early." Dawn spoke into the ensuing silence. "Three second-year mage apprentices aren't going to help with any of that. In fact, we'd be more use against the Shiven if we were left to finish our training."

Agreement registered on all their faces. Disappointment joined the unease Alyx was already feeling—she'd been hoping Ladan might have some answers for them.

"Whatever it is, it seems we can rule out anything dire having happened," Tarrick said, rising to his feet. "I'm exhausted and we really should get going as early as possible tomorrow."

Exhausted, all Alyx wanted was to follow them as they drifted out the door, losing her troubles in the comfort of a warm bed for a few hours. But there was more she needed to discuss with Ladan. He was standing by the fire, his look pensive, and she wished she didn't have to give him more difficult news.

He spoke suddenly. "Spit it out, Aly-girl."

"I'm sorry," she said softly. "About what I learned in Carhall. Learning that the council is hunting Taliath... it can't have been easy news to hear."

He made a sharp gesture. "I had suspicions, particularly after Master Howell's warning. I do appreciate you and Dashan warning me as quickly as possible. It's allowed me to take certain precautions."

"You're my brother. I worry about you."

He smiled slightly. "It's been a while since I've had anyone other than Romney worry about me."

"There's more you should hear." She hesitated. "Finn and I think we've worked out why our mother really ran away with you and went into hiding. We don't have proof, but it makes a lot of sense."

Ladan resumed his seat, waving her to the chair opposite. "Tell me."

She explained as succinctly as possible; that their mother had found out—or at least suspected—the council was hunting Taliath, and had left to keep both Ladan and their father safe from the council. When Alyx had finished, the room fell silent while Ladan processed it all. His gaze had turned distant, the fingers of one hand curling against his leg. The crackle and pop of the fire filled the empty space and weariness tugged at Alyx's bones. It had been a long day.

"She was so obsessed with staying hidden," he murmured eventually. "After we left you and Papa, we never went to any big towns and the places we stayed before Widow Falls were remote. I remember that. She was a mage of the higher order, yet I never saw another mage apart from my stepfather."

"I think she was deliberately keeping you out of the council's sight," Alyx said softly. "And herself, too."

"If you're right, then why did she write the letter to Romas before her death?" Ladan finally looked up, meeting her gaze. "Why would she go back to the council?"

"You said she left suddenly, in a rush," Alyx said. "And the half-written letter in her study indicates she met with an old mage contact around the same time, a man named Terin. I think she found out something, either from Terin or elsewhere, that prompted the letter to Romas."

"Something big or important enough to breach her self-imposed exile?" Ladan frowned, rising to his feet. "But she disappeared over ten years ago. If you're right, then what could it have been?"

"The missing mages," Alyx said. "It has to have been that. Someone or something has been causing the most powerful mages to disappear for years. Despite the full weight of the council's resources being put into finding out what's going on, they've found nothing. Whoever it is, they're powerful, well-organised, and well-resourced."

Bitter knowledge flashed over Ladan's face as he looked at her. "Right. An organisation like that... who else would have the capability to kill a mage of the higher order who learned their secrets?"

"Exactly." Alyx swallowed around the sudden lump in her throat.

Eventually Ladan shook his head. "No matter what happened, my focus has to be Widow Falls right now—my forces are increasingly stretched with each week that passes. And you can't go chasing whoever is behind the missing mages until you are fully trained yourself. It's too dangerous."

His words were sensible, but she couldn't accept them. "I understand why your priority is Widow Falls, but I'm not letting this go," she said firmly. "How do we know what happened to our mother isn't connected to the danger Rionn is facing now?"

"Shivasa is Rionn's problem," he said dismissively. "Not some missing mages. We need to deal with Shivasa and leave the Mage Council to look after itself."

"You don't mean that," she said softly. Ladan had loved their mother. She saw the emotion in his green eyes every time he spoke of her, despite his hard face and cold words. "You adored her like I adore Papa. They were all we had after the separation. And all three of us deserve to know who killed her and why. More than that, I need to know, Ladan, and I think you do too."

His jaw tightened at the emotion in her voice, and he wouldn't look at her, but eventually he gave her a sharp nod. "What do you want me to do?"

"Try and find out what you can about Terin. I'll use the opportunity of being home to talk to Papa and Astor—they might remember something useful. I can't shake the thought that what happened to our mother has some connection to what's happening now, and if so, the sooner we find it, the better."

"I'll do what I can, if you promise me you'll be careful." His stern gaze was almost a physical weight. "I won't have you putting yourself in unnecessary danger for this. You are still only a half-trained mage."

"Rionn is in trouble, and I will do whatever it takes to protect it," she said quietly. "But I won't be stupid, I promise. Will you come to Alistriem while I'm there? I know Papa would love to see you, and it will be almost two months before I have to go back to DarkSkull."

Ladan's hand curled around an ornament on the mantle as he took several moments before speaking. "While I understand logically why our parents did what they did... especially with what we've found out... it would be hard for me to leave here. This is where I feel safe, it's the place that nourished me when I had nobody but Romney and my warriors. It's the place my stepfather made me feel welcome in. It's my home."

"Believe it or not I know exactly how you feel." She stepped up to his side. "But would you consider it, for me? I would like to see you. And so would Papa. Don't forget that he lost a son in all this."

"I'll consider it, I promise."

No LONGER FEELING like sleep despite her weariness, Alyx went downstairs after leaving Ladan, seeking fresh night air. The main yard was clear, the sentries on the walls visible only as shadows in the faint moonlight.

Her wandering feet brought her to the barracks alongside the main building, part of her hoping to find Dashan. And there he was, sitting alone on the steps by the door. His jaw was clenched and he wore that hardened look on his face she knew so well.

Alyx hesitated, half turning back in the other direction, but it was impossible to walk away from him when he looked so alone.

"This seat taken?" she asked softly. He shook his head, eyes on his boots. She took that as assent and settled on the step beside him. "You're still mad at me, huh?"

"Not really." He let out a long breath, reaching up to rub his forehead. "I'm worried, that's all. The council, Shivasa, these nightmares of yours, the summons from Casovar. It has me on edge."

"Me too." She hesitated. "Listen, Dash, I know we haven't had a chance to talk since what happened at the dance, and now we're suddenly going back home, and I—"

He raised a hand, cutting her off. "There's no need to re-hash it. We're friends. Whatever else happened was a mistake."

The misery his words caused took her aback and her voice was sadder than she'd meant it to be when she spoke. "I hope you know that the last thing I ever want is to hurt you."

"I do. I'm not a fool, Alyx," he said gently. "I've always known how you and Cayr feel about each other."

She swallowed. "Is something wrong? The fight we had... there's more going on than you just being annoyed at me."

A sad smile flashed across his face. "Thank you."

"For what?"

"You noticed," he said. "Nobody else ever does. It's like most of the time I'm invisible to everyone. I'm just the half-Shiven loser who is good for nothing."

Alyx winced. "Don't you think that's a little dramatic?"

He huffed a laugh. "I suppose it is. Ignore me, I'm being especially maudlin tonight."

She touched his hand. "This past year... you've helped me through some of the most difficult times I've ever experienced. I wish you would let me help you in the same way."

He squeezed her hand briefly, but his eyes were far away. Despite her better judgement, she tangled their fingers together, hoping that it would help.

"Are you worried they'll send you back to the disputed area?" she guessed.

He gave a sharp nod. "There's a good chance. At least until you go back to DarkSkull."

"I won't offer false promises, but I will do absolutely everything I can to ensure you come back with us," she told him firmly. "And not only because I don't want to go back there again without you, but because you made such a difference. You made the militia better and you made DarkSkull safer."

He squeezed her hand again, almost painfully tightly. "Thanks."

They fell into a comfortable silence for a long while. Alyx began to truly relax for the first time since the nightmare, falling into a light doze against Dashan's shoulder.

"What about you?" he asked, waking her. "You must be upset about Cario. None of you have mentioned his name since you told us what he did."

A bitter mix of sadness and anger welled up at the mention of Cario's name. He'd been her friend, and he'd betrayed them. The whole time he'd been with them he'd been reporting to the council on her.

"I don't want to think about it," she murmured. "I'm pretty sure the others feel the same way."

"They're angry," Dashan said just as softly. "But you're hurt."

She nodded. He understood her better then she understood herself sometimes. There was comfort in that, but also pain and guilt. Because in this moment, she wanted Dashan, not Cayr. And that knowledge tore at her heart. How could she do this to Cayr?

"I need time." Alyx deliberately separated herself from Dashan, untangling their hands and standing up. Soon she would see Cayr, and he would once again be the one she talked to about everything. That thought felt both right and wrong at the same time, her guilt and sadness inextricably linked so that nothing was clear.

"I think we both do," Dashan said, dark eyes glimmering with too much understanding as he looked up at her.

CHAPTER 2

Their first sight of Alistriem came as the glow of the mid-afternoon sun lit up the golden spires of the palace perched above the city. A smile crept over Alyx's face—she'd missed the sheer loveliness of her home. Tregaya was rugged and green, but Rionn was beautiful.

The road grew busier as they approached the eastern city gates, and as they maneuverer around a heavily-laden cart, the part of Alyx that wasn't revelling in the sight of her home after so long experienced a sudden flash of foreboding that chilled her to the bone.

Why?

The city appeared unchanged from the outside, although the fact there were now six well-armed City Guard officers monitoring those coming through the eastern gate was likely reflective of an increased security posture following the Shiven attack on the palace earlier in the year. The guards seemed awed by their group—the majority of Rionnans had gone their entire lives without seeing a single mage, let alone five of them riding into the city accompanied by a unit of elite Blue Guard—but waved them through after a brief exchange with Dashan.

"Straight to the palace?" Tarrick asked.

Alyx shook her head with a frown, not sure where her sudden unease was coming from. "I know we're all anxious to learn what Casovar wants, but I think it might be a better idea to talk to my father before seeing him. Besides, a hot bath, clean clothes and some sleep before dealing with whatever it is would be nice."

"That does sound appealing." Dawn sighed. "My skin itches."

Alyx grimaced in sympathy. "How about we meet at my estate early tomorrow morning and ride over to the palace together. Dash?"

"Fine with me." He shrugged. "As soon as we report in to barracks it will filter up to the palace, though. Lord-Mage Casovar will know you're back sooner rather than later."

"Sooner, I think," Tarrick muttered, looking around them at several staring citizens. "Our arrival certainly hasn't gone unnoticed."

"Casovar can wait a single night," Alyx said. "Tarrick, will you stay with me? There's plenty of room, and the twins put you up all last summer. I think it's my turn."

"Thank you," he said, looking pleased. "I'd like to make sure Dawn and Finn get home safely first, though."

She chuckled, sharing a warm look with Dawn. Some things never changed, and Tarrick's innate protectiveness was as fundamental to him as breathing. "Absolutely."

"A'ndreas home it is." Dashan gestured to the Bluecoats and they set off again, more slowly now they were in the busy city streets.

The familiar sounds and smells of Alistriem swamped Alyx's senses as they rode deeper into the city; the salty smell of the sea overlaying a veritable smorgasbord of scents, from fruit and vegetables in the markets, to horse manure, freshly caught fish and the incense stores in the rich quarter. She breathed in deeply, the familiarity of it soothing the edges of her recent anxiety.

"What...?" Finn reined in suddenly. "Dashan, who are those soldiers wearing red?"

Catching the strange note in Finn's voice, Alyx looked where he was pointing. Five men marched down the wide avenue towards them. They wore scarlet long-sleeved tunics despite the warmth of the day, and were heavily armed—one had an axe slung over his back, another a crossbow, while the others wore

16

swords. From their stride and bearing, it was obvious they were soldiers, but she didn't know any Rionnan military unit that wore red.

"I've never seen them before." Dashan was frowning, as were the Bluecoats.

Tijer kicked his horse forward. "Lieutenant, we have the authority to ask them their business."

"What are they doing?" Dawn asked.

The five men had abruptly crossed the street and entered a small jewellery shop. Moments later they emerged, two of the soldiers dragging an overweight middle-aged man behind them. Once in the street, they dropped him unceremoniously into the dust, and one of the soldiers kicked him hard in the stomach.

Shock flared, freezing Alyx for a moment as she tried to process what she was seeing. This sort of violence didn't happen on the streets of Alistriem, not at the hands of soldiers. She was snapped from her daze by a sharp movement at her side. Dashan had dismounted and was striding towards the soldiers. Concern rapidly replaced her shock. This isn't good.

"Dash, wait!" She slid down from Tingo's back and went running after him, but he reached the scene before she could catch up.

"What's going on?" Dashan's voice was sharp and loud enough to catch the attention of everyone nearby. A hush fell over the street, most people doing their best to appear like they weren't watching with morbid fascination.

"Lieutenant." A man with captain's stripes on his chest stepped forward. He was much shorter than Dashan, with a stocky build and a belly running to fat. Sweat beaded on his forehead in the warm sun. "This is no business of the Blue Guard."

"I'll decide that for myself. Who are you?"

"Captain Dunnat of the Mage Guard."

"I've never heard of any such thing," Dashan said coolly.

Dunnat's eyes moved to Alyx as she stepped up beside Dashan, surprise flashing on his face when he took in her attire, clearly recognising what it meant. His beady eyes shifted their gaze behind her, narrowing, and she glanced back to see the other Bluecoats had ridden up with Tarrick and the twins. Her concern increased at the potential for the situation to turn nasty in a hurry.

At least the Bluecoats seemed content for the moment to let Dashan speak for them. Finn was casting worried glances at Dawn, who'd paled, while Tarrick seemed uncertain how to respond to what was happening.

Dunnat's gaze returned to Dashan. "Lord-Mage Casovar created the Mage Guard three months ago. We're responsible for hunting Shiven spies and keeping Alistriem safe."

"Last I checked, keeping Alistriem safe was the job of the City Guard," Dashan said.

"Then you must have checked a long time ago, Lieutenant." Dunnat's eyes lingered insultingly on Dashan's chest, which was bare of any markings identifying him as a commanding officer.

A nerve ticked in Dashan's jaw. "No matter what your remit, no Rionnan soldier has the authority to beat citizens in the street. Help that man up at once."

"As I said, this is not Bluecoat business," Dunnat said, his tone warning Dashan to back off. The other red-cloaked soldiers were all watching the standoff in fascination, but one of them had his boot firmly planted in the jeweller's back, keeping him prostrate on the ground. The jeweller was red-faced, gasping for breath. The sight turned Alyx's stomach. No citizen of Rionn—no person— deserved to be treated that way, not until a crime had been proven.

At Dunnat's dismissive tone, Dashan stiffened. Alyx laid a calming hand on his forearm, hoping he wasn't about to lose his temper and physically attack the captain.

"What is he supposed to have done?" she asked, gesturing to the jeweller.

"He was seen talking to a Shiven spy."

"I don't know any Shiven spies!" the jeweller cried out. "I swear it. You have to believe me. I'm just a jeweller. I don't know any spies. Please."

Tears trickled down his face, smearing the dust from the road on his skin. He gave a grunt of pain as the boot on his back pressed down harder, forcing him further into the dirt.

Alyx's hands curled into white-knuckled fists at the sight and she channelled her anger into the icily-arrogant tone of the very rich. "Captain Dunnat, what exactly do you think a jeweller knows that would be of interest to a Shiven spy?"

He stiffened. "That is none of your concern. You and your pet Bluecoats should be on your way."

She stepped closer. "You should be more polite when speaking with your betters, Captain Dunnat. What will Lord Egalion think when he hears how you behaved towards his daughter?" She waited for that knowledge to ripple across his face, then spoke again, coldly. "You will order your soldiers to help that man up at once. Am I clear?"

Dunnat flushed a deep red, one hand dropping to his sword. A low murmur swept through the growing crowd, a palpable tension settling over the street. In the same moment, the other red cloaks moved to stand behind their captain, echoing his gesture. At the implicit threat to their charge, the Bluecoats drew swords, the sound of ringing steel echoing sharply in the street. They'd dismounted without Alyx even realising, their jovial expressions gone, replaced by the dangerous focus of veteran fighters. A couple of the red-cloaked soldiers visibly quailed at the sight and took a step back.

Dashan held his hand up in a sharp gesture, stopping the Bluecoats in their tracks. As well-disciplined as they were, Alyx worried over how long he was going to be able to hold them back.

"Don't be foolish," Dashan warned Dunnat. "Lady Alyx Egalion is under our protection. You take a step closer, and there will be a fight that you won't win."

Fear added to the tension in the crowd now and those on the periphery began slipping away, having no desire to get caught up in a fight between Bluecoats and Mage Guard.

Dunnat's gaze flicked between Dashan and Alyx before an expression of determination settled over his face. He didn't care who they were.

"The Blue Guard has no authority here. Leave us to our business."

"The Blue Guard reports directly to the king via Lord-General Caverlock." Dashan's voice was rock hard, but he was holding his temper. "And the king outranks Lord-Mage Casovar, no matter what pretensions he holds."

"I—"

"Pick that man up. Apologise. Let him go," Dashan warned. "Now."

Dunnat's flush deepened to an angry purple. "I will not be spoken to in such a manner by a Shiven half-blood."

Alyx's temper snapped. Dunnat's soldiers were behaving like street thugs, and it horrified her to see any citizen of Alistriem crying in terror on the ground. The fingers of her right hand flickered, summoning her mage knife to her hand with a quick burst of magic. In one move she shifted forward and placed the tip of the knife against Dunnat's throat.

One of his men made as if to step forward, and suddenly Tarrick was at Alyx's left side, a mother-of-pearl glow shimmering from his raised fist. Dashan's sword point joined the blade already at Dunnat's throat. His eyes had darkened further and he looked dangerously angry.

"You will do exactly what I told you to," Alyx said slowly. "Now."

Dunnat's jaw clenched, hatred flashing in his eyes. She was making an enemy here, but couldn't bring herself to care. After a moment he nodded and gestured to his men, who reluctantly backed off. Alyx stepped away and sheathed her knife. Nario and Josha ran forward to help the jeweller up and back inside his store. Dunnat snapped an order and the red cloaks marched off. He hesitated a moment to shoot a furious glare at Alyx and Dashan before turning and stalking after them.

"Nicely done, Lady Egalion," Tijer said respectfully as they watched the crowd that had gathered slowly disperse.

She nodded, angrily swinging herself back into the saddle. "I want to know what is going on."

"You're not the only one." Dashan's brown eyes still snapped with fury.

"Calm down, Dash." Alyx touched his arm again. "We'll deal with it."

Dawn shuddered, still white. "If you had heard what they were thinking. I wasn't prying but their thoughts were so strong... so much violence."

"It's going to be fine," Alyx said, burying her own concern so it didn't reflect in her voice. "We'll address the situation first thing tomorrow with Lord-Mage Casovar. He can have those men disciplined once we explain what happened."

This seemed to reassure the Bluecoats, who remounted and formed a protective escort around Alyx, Tarrick, and the twins as they made their way towards the A'ndreas residence. Dawn kept shooting worried looks at Alyx, though, and Finn's forehead remained creased with a frown the entire way there.

CHAPTER 3

Alyx didn't linger at the A'ndreas home, staying only long enough to hug the twins goodbye and confirm their plans to meet the following morning. The noise and smell of the city faded behind them as she, Tarrick, and her escort rode up into the forested hillside above the city. The light along the road grew dim as the sun began to set over the hill.

Dashan rode stiffly, determinedly uncommunicative, and his Blue-coats were in a similar mood. The joking and camaraderie that had characterised their trip from Widow Falls was gone. Tarrick was quiet too, his thoughts appearing to be far away.

"We'd best head back to the barracks." Dashan broke his silence as they reached the gates to the Egalion estate.

Alyx nodded. "I'll see you soon?"

He nodded tersely. "If you have the time."

He really is in a mood. Ignoring his tone, she turned and called a farewell to the other Bluecoats. They chorused back in a way that made her smile.

"Bye, Dash."

He tipped the brim of his hat, then turned his stallion and rode off, the rest of the unit falling in behind him. Alyx kicked Tingo forward through the gates. Surprised by her vehemence, the big stallion skittered into a canter, spraying small white pebbles everywhere as he galloped down the driveway.

Tarrick reined in beside her at the front of the house, dark eyes scanning the graceful mansion with approval. "Will your father be home?"

"I'm not sure. He could still be over at the..."

Her words died off as a tall figure emerged from inside the house. His short-cropped greying brown hair framed a serious but handsome face, one that lit into a smile at the sight of her. An answering smile tugged at her mouth, and she swung down out of the saddle to meet him.

"Papa!"

"Alyx?" he asked in astonishment, sweeping her into a hug. "I couldn't believe it when Safia told me you were riding in."

She hugged him back tightly, soaking in his warmth and steady presence. She adored her father, always had, and always would. It eased a knot of worry deep inside her to see him safe and sound.

"What are you doing back so soon?" he wanted to know.

She frowned. "What do you mean? Lord-Mage Casovar ordered us back from DarkSkull early."

Something flickered in his eyes, quickly hidden. "I see."

Her eyebrows shot up. "You didn't know, did you?"

"I confess I didn't." Garan acknowledged with a sigh, but continued speaking before she could question him further. "You've brought a guest?"

She nodded, turning to where Tarrick waited awkwardly at the bottom of the steps and waving him up. "You remember Tarrick, Papa? I hope you don't mind if he stays with us, we have a lot more room here than the A'ndreas family does."

Garan offered his hand. "Be welcome in my home, Tarrick."

"Thank you, Lord Egalion." Tarrick shook the hand firmly. "I appreciate your hospitality, although I'm not surprised. Alyx always speaks highly of you."

Alyx couldn't stay quiet any longer. "Papa, we just ran into some soldiers in the city claiming to be a Mage Guard. They were beating a man in the street."

Something unnameable flashed across her father's face. "You didn't intervene, I hope?"

She frowned. "Of course we did. Papa—"

He stepped closer, gripping her shoulders. "Let's discuss this inside. Go and freshen up and I'll see you at the dinner table."

Alyx shared a confused look with Tarrick. "All right."

"That's my girl." He kissed her forehead. "Go on. Tarrick, Safia will show you to one of our guest rooms."

Safia appeared from where he'd been hovering inside the doorway and ushered

Tarrick inside. Alyx looked back at her father, who remained on the top step, one hand rubbing at his forehead. "Are you all right, Papa?"

He turned, the troubled look on his features replaced with a smile that mingled pride and a touch of sadness. "Last year when you came home, an overly thin and exhausted young girl came rushing out of a carriage and straight into my arms. This year a self-possessed young woman rode through my gates. I've never seen you look more like your mother, Alyx."

Tears pricked at her eyes. "I did better, this time."

ALYX'S FATHER waited until servants had finished carrying dishes to the table and the kitchen door had closed behind them to speak again. "Tell me what happened this afternoon."

"When we ran into the Mage Guard, they were dragging a jeweller out of his shop." Some of her anger returned at the memory of it, her appetite vanishing. "When the Bluecoats instructed them to stand down, they refused. It almost came to a fight."

Her father's face tightened. "You shouldn't have intervened."

She stared at him, confused. "They were mistreating the man without any evidence of wrongdoing."

"And risking starting a fight in the streets was the best solution?" her father asked sternly. "You cannot go throwing yourself about as

Lady Egalion whenever you like. Not when you've been away so long."

"It wasn't about that," she said, taken aback by his vehemence. "And I think the beating of an innocent man does concern me. Are you telling me you would have walked away from that and done nothing?"

Alyx was dimly aware that Tarrick was glancing between the two of them, his expression caught between awkwardness and fascination. The food so far lay untouched on their plates.

"The Mage Guard fall under the remit of the lord-mage," Garan explained. "I have no authority where they are concerned, and neither do you or the Bluecoats."

Alyx shared a look with Tarrick. "So we were supposed to sit idly by while an innocent citizen was beaten?"

"You don't know that he was innocent, that the Mage Guard didn't have proof," Garan pointed out.

"That's true, sir," Tarrick said carefully. "But their behaviour... it wasn't consistent with my experience of your Blue Guard, whose level of professionalism and skill rivals that of the Leopards in my country."

"I acknowledge what both of you are saying," Garan said. "But you've just arrived home after several months away. You'll be speaking with Lord-Mage Casovar tomorrow, and no doubt he can answer some of your questions. In the meantime, you must not do anything else like you did today. I ask you to trust me on that."

"Okay." Alyx nodded hesitantly. "Papa, is everything all right? Has something
happened here that would warrant our early summons home?"

Garan sat back, lifting his hands into the air as if to ward off her questions. "I don't know why Lord-Mage Casovar ordered you home early. But the situation with Shivasa has grown steadily worse. There are reasons those men behaved as they did this afternoon."

She opened her mouth to push harder, but the words died when she realised how weary her father looked. "We'll talk to Lord-Mage Casovar in the morning. I'm sure he'll be able to explain things to us."

"Thank you." He smiled and leaned over, touching her shoulder affectionately. "I am glad to have you home, Aly-girl."

The pet name made Alyx think of Ladan. She missed him, wished he could be in Alistriem too—at the very least he'd be able to help her make sense of all the changes.

"Lord Egalion," Tarrick spoke. "Can I ask if you had any problems returning to Alistriem from Carhall?"

Garan shot a considering glance in Alyx's direction. She gave him a slight nod.

"None. Lieutenant Caverlock's unit escorted me safely to Tennan, and the worst I can say about the ship journey back to Rionn was the storm we had two nights in. Another unit of Bluecoats was awaiting me in Turatin when I docked, and the trip back to Alistriem was uneventful."

"I'm glad to hear it, sir." Tarrick spoke politely, but Alyx hadn't missed the way his hand clenched briefly around his spoon. Learning the Mage Council was hunting Taliath had affected Tarrick as much as it had her—he idolised the council and everything it stood for, and he'd struggled with accepting what they were doing.

Garan seemed to sense some of Tarrick's ambivalence. "We may have been worrying about nothing in Carhall."

"Maybe," Alyx said, trying to sound sincere for Tarrick's sake. "Have you had any issues managing the king's knowledge of what the council is doing?"

The troubled look crossed Garan's face again. "No. In fact he seems to have forgotten about it entirely. He hasn't raised it with me since we returned."

Alyx glanced at Tarrick, who gave a little shrug. Shaking her head, she returned her attention to her food. Inevitably, Garan began asking about their time at DarkSkull. She and Tarrick were careful to keep things general, and not mention the attacks on DarkSkull or being part of a combat patrol. Her father's reaction to their intervening with the Mage Guard suggested now wasn't the best time to tell him the extent of her activities at DarkSkull.

Instead they regaled her father with tales of the hot springs, working in the fields, and the endless monotony of mage lessons. Garan appeared to take a liking to Tarrick, and soon they were laughing and joking like they were old friends.

Alyx left them in the middle of Tarrick telling Garan about his family in Zandia and went out to check on Tingo and Tarrick's mount. Henri had cleverly stabled the two highly-strung stallions next to each other, and they seemed calm enough despite the new surroundings. She lingered a little while to feed Tingo some sugar cubes and stroke his silky nose before heading back to the house.

Her father was rising from his chair as Alyx re-entered the dining room, but Tarrick was nowhere to be seen.

"He was tired and went upstairs to get some sleep," Garan said in answer to her raised eyebrow.

She smiled a little. "The two of you seemed to get along well."

"He's an impressive young man, and very protective of you." He hesitated. "He speaks glowingly of your Bluecoat escort. Dashan in particular."

"I'm not surprised, they're friends," Alyx said, unsure what her father was getting at.

"Now that you're home, I think it would be wise for you to keep your distance from Dashan." He was avoiding her gaze, the fingers of one hand idly tapping the tabletop.

Alyx frowned. While her father had never been entirely comfortable with her having Dashan as a friend, he'd never said anything like this before. "Why?"

"You know his reputation as well as I do."

"I also know the man. Which, if you bothered to do, might change your opinion of him," she said. Her puzzlement deepened—this didn't sound like her father. "Have you forgotten he was the one who got you safely out of Carhall?"

"His abilities as a Bluecoat don't change who he is." Garan's voice had an edge to it now. "You need to start being more conscious of your position, and your role here in Alistriem."

"What is my role here in Alistriem?" she challenged. "I'm an apprentice mage—you decided that for me when you sent me to Dark-Skull two years ago."

Something in her words made him angry, and his next words came out sharply. "Your tune has certainly changed."

"So has yours," she countered. "You've tolerated my friendship with Dashan since childhood. Why are things suddenly different?"

"Dashan Caverlock is a wastrel and a fool." Garan was avoiding her gaze again, his hand on the table curling into a fist. Something was making him angry, but what? She didn't understand any of this. "His Shiven blood ensures he'll never become anything more than a lieutenant in the Blue Guard."

Alyx stared at her father in shock. "Why would you say that?"

"Alyx—"

"No, Papa, where is this coming from?" she insisted. "You've always judged people on their merits."

"Exactly," Garan said the word sharply, as if it explained everything. "You forget how much older I am, and how much more experience I have. You might consider listening to me for once rather than deciding that you know better than everyone else."

Alyx stiffened in affront. Her father had never reprimanded her so severely, or so unfairly. She stared at him for a long moment, trying to contain her shock, then turned and walked out of the room without another word. He didn't try and call her back.

On the other side of the door she hesitated, half of her wanting to go back, to demand answers for why her father was behaving so unlike himself and why her home was so different from when she'd left. But they were both angry, and she didn't want to say something she'd regret.

By the time she reached her room, hurt was trickling in under her anger and shock. Why hadn't her father shown more faith in her and how she'd changed? Her mouth thinned with determination. If he wouldn't see it, then she'd show him. And at the same time, she'd use the opportunity of being home early to find out what had caused all these changes in her home.

Then she could fix it before she went back.

HER OLD ROUTE to the palace hadn't changed a bit, although tonight Alyx made the journey on foot rather than horseback. Her anticipation grew with every step, her telepathic magic making it easy for her to avoid the Bluecoats on patrol and slip into Cayr's bedroom window without being seen.

The prince was in his sitting room, reading by the light of his fire, completely absorbed in the book in his lap. Delight bubbled up in her as she regarded him, temporarily replacing the shock and anger that still lingered from her fight with her father.

"Good to know you still leave your bedroom window unlocked."

He looked up, the astonishment on his handsome features so strong it made her laugh. "Alyx?"

"It's me."

Cayr jumped to his feet and crossed the space between them to throw his arms around her. She chuckled at his enthusiasm, returning his bear hug. "It's so good to see you," she murmured against his shoulder. "I missed you."

"Oh Alyx, you have no idea." They rocked back and forth for a long moment, neither wanting to let go.

Eventually they parted and she beamed up at him. "I can't tell you how good it is to see your face."

"You look different," he murmured. "I can't quite pin it down, but you really look different. You look great."

"So do you." And he did. His features had changed subtly, reflecting those of a young man rather than a boy. His golden curls were neatly cut for once, enhancing his looks. A moment later they both broke into sheepish chuckles as they realised they were staring at each other.

"You're back more quickly than I expected," he said, then frowned a little. "Don't tell me you came through the disputed area rather than by ship?"

"Neither. We... wait, you're aware of Casovar's summons and my father isn't?" Alyx stepped away, shaking her head. "It's like the world has turned upside down since I left."

"It's not as odd as you make it sound. My father approved the summons, and I spend most of my time with him these days." Cayr said. "Things have happened while you were away, but no doubt you'll be meeting with the lord-mage in the morning and he can explain."

Alyx sighed, accepting the logic in his words. "You're right. I am glad to be home. I missed you."

"I missed you. It's hard not having my best friend around. How are you?"

"I'm okay," she said honestly. "This year wasn't as bad as the first. I didn't expect to be back so soon, though."

"I assume Dawn and Finn came with you?"

"And Tarrick, too."

"What about Dash?" Cayr asked eagerly. "My life has been utterly boring since he left. Father has been thrilled that the entire source of frivolity and pranks in my life has been away."

She smiled automatically, but Dashan's name caused her to wonder where he was—he'd been so angry earlier. She hoped he was okay, then shook herself in frustration for dwelling on it. She was with Cayr, and she had missed him. Her smile grew wide and genuine. "Remind me to tell you about the incident he caused with the baby spiders."

"I swear I could hear the two of you bickering from here in Alistriem." Cayr laughed.

A sharp twinge of guilt twisted in her chest. Cayr saw her look and misinterpreted it. "Come on, one day you and Dashan are going to have to learn to get along. I know what good friends you are despite all the arguing."

"He riles me," she grumbled, which was true enough, then sought to change the subject. "I'd like to say our return home was wonderful, but we ran into this new Mage Guard of Casovar's in the city on our way in."

Interest flashed over Cayr's face. "I'm glad. They've been doing some excellent work ferreting out Shiven spies in the city. You'll be working with them while you're here, I think."

She frowned. Cayr's enthusiasm was at sharp odds with what they'd seen. "When we came across them, they were dragging a jeweller out of his store and beating him in the street. You haven't heard of them doing anything like that before?"

"I'm sure they had good reason for it." He gave a little shrug. "But I don't want to talk about the Mage Guard right now, you've just come home. Can you stay a while?"

Irritation with him flared so strongly it took her by surprise. Cayr's tendency to gloss over things he didn't want to deal with had never really bothered her before, but now she found herself wishing he'd grown past it. Then she felt bad—he was right, and this was her first night home. The last thing she wanted to do was start nagging him after months apart. So she let it go and shook her head regretfully.

"I should get back before my father realises I'm gone."

"Or you could stay," he murmured, stepping closer and taking her hands. "He doesn't know you're here, right?"

She raised an eyebrow at him. "If anyone knew we were alone in your rooms right now both of us would be in a lot of trouble. Serious trouble."

He shrugged, and she didn't step away. So close to her, he was warm and safe. His fingers curled around hers, but instead of the fission of delight his touch usually roused, an odd despair began to unfold inside her. It wasn't the same. Nothing was.

"Nobody needs to find out," he said.

He leaned closer, his intention to kiss her clear as day. When she shook her head slightly, disappointment flashed over his features, but he didn't push.

"Like you said, I just got back," she said, squeezing his hands. She needed time to settle back in, that was all. Everything would go back to normal then. "We need to talk properly before we... go back to where we were."

"All right." He let go of her hands. "But soon. I don't want to waste any more time."

She managed a smile for him before changing the subject. "I really do need to go. Thank you for looking after my father. Coming home to find him safe and well was a wonderful relief."

"I'd do anything for you," he said softly. "I'm so glad you're back."

She gave him a final brief hug. "Night, Cayr."

Out in the darkness and the cool night air, Alyx walked briskly, sneaking out of the palace gardens and into those of her own estate. She fought the despair curling through her, pushing it down and out of her mind. Things would be all right. They would.

She just needed time.

CHAPTER 4

Breakfast the next morning was eaten in strained silence.
Tarrick was shown into the dining room by a servant not long
after Alyx had sat down with her food. Garan appeared only
moments later. He greeted Alyx coolly, but always the polite host, was
warm in his greeting to Tarrick.

She ate in silence. Sleep had been difficult to come by—fear of
another nightmare warring with unease over what had happened with
the Mage Guard and shock over her confrontation with her father had
kept her from relaxing enough to rest.

Judging by the wary looks Tarrick began shooting at her and her
father, it hadn't taken him long to realise they had argued.

"A fight about Dashan," she sent Tarrick a brief explanation. "Papa
is angry about something, but I'm not sure what."

The tense silence remained, broken occasionally by the rustle of
paper as Garan finished reading each page of the small stack of parchment sitting before him. Once she'd finished, Alyx rose, glancing at
Tarrick with raised eyebrows. He nodded and finished his last few bites
before standing too.

"Papa, we're going to see Lord-Mage Casovar."

"Good." He glanced up briefly from his papers. "I'll be heading over to the palace myself soon, so I won't see you again until dinner."

"I... " She wanted to say something, but wasn't sure what. Before she could think of anything, his attention had returned to the papers. Shaking her head, she turned and followed Tarrick out of the room.

Their boots echoed as they crossed the marble floor of the entrance foyer, then escaped out into the early morning air. It was warm already with a hint of the heat to come later. The twins rode in as Alyx and Tarrick were exiting the stables. Alyx lifted her eyebrows in surprise when Tarrick gestured for Dawn and Finn to dismount.

"Is something wrong?" Dawn asked as they clustered together on the pebbled drive, leaving the horses to graze on the lawn nearby.

"Did your father tell you anything?" Finn jumped in before Tarrick could respond.

"Not really." Alyx cast a glance at the house. "He says the situation with Shivasa has grown worse, and that's why the Mage Guard was created. He's got no authority over them apparently—they report directly to Casovar."

"That fits with what Ladan told us about things being worse," Finn said.

"Is there something else?" Dawn asked, her eyes on Alyx's face.

"I think so," Alyx said. "My father isn't himself. He got angry with me last night over an issue that... something is off."

"It's possible Casovar will have an explanation for it all," Tarrick said. "But until we have a better idea of what's happening, my instinct tells me to keep Alyx's ability from him."

Dawn's eyes were distant, but her voice was firm when she spoke. "I agree."

"It's now widely known at DarkSkull what I am," Alyx said, casting a worried glance at her friend. "Surely he already knows."

"I wouldn't be so sure," Finn disagreed. "The masters protected the knowledge from him before."

"Too many people know for it not to leak out eventually. For a start, the king would have told him we were in Carhall for the council meeting," she pointed out. "He's going to wonder why."

"If he does, we tell him Cario's grandfather pulled strings to get us on the trip," Finn said. "We should get rid of our patrol stripes too. If Casovar knew we'd been part of a combat patrol, he'd want to know why. And given a large part of the reason was that Alyx is a mage of the higher order, it's best if he doesn't ask questions."

Tarrick frowned in disappointment as he considered Finn's words, but then gave a shrug. "It's all right. We'll be getting new stripes next year anyway. Don't First Patrol members wear blue?"

They busied themselves taking off their robes and cutting off the three green stripes. Alyx was unaccountably sad as she slid her green fabric into the pocket of her breeches; it felt like her last link to the past year at DarkSkull had just been severed.

"Ready to face the beast?" Finn joked as he tucked the cotton strips into his pocket.

All of them chuckled.

THE SIGHT of the picturesque sandstone palace and gardens had always calmed Alyx. Today though, the strange dread that had gripped her on entering the city returned in full force. Instinctively, she looked for Dashan, then immediately felt guilty. To distract herself, she urged Tingo up beside Dawn's horse.

"Is everything okay?" Alyx asked. "You seemed like something was bothering you back there."

"I'm probably just being silly." Dawn sighed. "But those soldiers yesterday... if you could have heard what was leaking in their thoughts. It was awful. I can't shake it."

"I should have heard it," Alyx said wryly. "But I haven't put nearly as much practice into my telepathic magic as I have to telekinesis and concussion force. I still can't pick up thoughts unless I actively try."

"It's not always a comfortable ability to have," Dawn said softly.

"It's going to be all right," Alyx said with more confidence than she felt, wanting to try and ease some of the disquiet in her friend's blue eyes. "Whatever the situation here, we'll adapt to it like we always do."

Dawn mustered a smile at her words, but Alyx got the distinct impression her friend wasn't reassured at all.

· · ·

AT THE PALACE, Tarrick and the twins fell in behind Alyx as she led the way through the maze of palace corridors towards the wing set aside for the lord-mage.

They were walking along a lushly carpeted corridor that housed the offices of many of the king's senior advisors and staff when a door ahead opened, and an older man emerged wearing the green uniform of the Rionnan army.

"Sparky!" Alyx called out in genuine pleasure.

The man looked up with a surprised smile. Rionn's most senior general and commander of their army was of medium height, with short-cropped reddish grey hair and beard. He was also a close friend of both the king and Alyx's father. Alyx and Cayr were the only ones besides her father and the king allowed to call him by his nickname.

"Hello, Lady Alyx. What a surprise! I thought you were away at DarkSkull Hall?"

She smiled widely and allowed him to kiss her hand. "I'm back for a short time. It's good to see you. Will you meet my friends?" She waved them forward. "This is Dawn and Finn A'ndreas, and Tarrick Tylender from Zandia."

"You must be the apprentices training with Lady Alyx," Sparky said politely.

"Yes, sir." Finn managed an awkward bow, Tarrick a much smoother one. "It's a pleasure to meet you."

"Are you here meeting with the king?" Alyx asked.

The general's smile faded, and for a moment a deep weariness flashed in his eyes, stunning her. Sparky was renowned for his appetite for a challenge—when she was growing up, he'd always vibrated with an energy that filled whatever room he was in. What could be causing him to suddenly look tired and old?

"I had a meeting with the lord-mage this morning and was just popping in to speak with Lord Raffison on my way out." His smile returned. "I'd love it if you came to dinner while you're home, Lady Alyx? My wife would love to see you."

"I'd love to."

"Wonderful. I'll speak to Greta this evening—how long do you plan to be in Alistriem?"

Alyx glanced at Tarrick. "We have about seven weeks or so before we have to go back to DarkSkull."

"We'll organise something soon then." The general smiled, some of the life returning to his features, and left them.

At the end of the hall, Alyx pushed through the doors to the lord-mage offices. The first thing she saw was Dashan and Cayr, standing over by the window and laughing. Both young men turned at their entrance, Cayr immediately crossing to Alyx and leaning down to kiss her cheek. "Good morning."

"Hi." She smiled up at him, trying not to let her gaze shift over to Dashan, despite still being worried about him.

"Dawn, Finn, it's good to have you home." Cayr shook their hands. "Tarrick, welcome back to Alistriem."

They exchanged pleasantries for a moment, Tarrick and the twins more comfortable with the prince now. Dashan wandered over to join them and Cayr grinned as he slapped Dashan's back. "I have to admit, I'm astonished to find this one returned all in one piece. I felt sure he'd have an army of angry Tregayan husbands chasing him with pitchforks!"

"Are you insinuating I might exhibit a less than innocent behaviour towards the opposite sex?" Dashan said in injured tones. While all four others laughed, Alyx winced, guilty knowledge making her sensitive to anything that might let Cayr know what had happened between them.

"Not all of them, just the blonde and curvy ones," Cayr said.

Dashan chuckled, his grin only widening at Alyx's scowl. She opened her mouth, ready with a retort to put him back in his place, but Cayr read her perfectly and spoke before she could.

"Not much has changed in nine months, I see," Cayr noted, glancing between them with a long-suffering smile that was reflected in Tarrick's rolled eyes. Dashan chuckled, but it had a false note to it, and he looked away. She hadn't missed the brief flash of emotion in his eyes, and part of her suddenly wished she wasn't in this room with both Cayr and Dashan together. She cleared her throat, changing the subject before Cayr picked up on anything. "What are you doing here anyway, Dash?"

"Orders from my commander, who apparently received them

directly from the lord-mage himself." Dashan's cheerful mood vanished completely. "Commander Hawkwerst was less than impressed to receive orders from a man he doesn't even report to."

"He is the lord-mage of Rionn," Cayr interjected. "Hawkwerst is overreacting as usual."

"Since when does the lord-mage of Rionn order about members of the Blue Guard?" Dashan demanded.

"Since now," Cayr said as if it were the most obvious thing in the world. "When he's in charge of the defence of Rionn. And when do you take anything Hawkwerst says seriously—you've spent the last four years complaining about how he's more obsessed with maintaining his power base and preparing for a luxurious retirement than having a functioning command."

"Cayr!" Alyx jumped in before a real argument could develop. Dashan's expression showed he was sinking towards true anger at his friend, and Cayr's cheerful blitheness was only going to make it worse. "You weren't there yesterday when—"

Her words were forestalled by the door opening to admit Lord-Mage Casovar. A tall, lean man shrouded in his black mage robe, his dark hair was cut severely short in a way that over-emphasised his prominent cheekbones and thin face. The grey eyes were what she remembered most—they pierced her in the same way Rothai's ice-blue ones often did, but that was where the similarity ended. Rothai's were full of hidden intensity; Casovar's were cold as an iceberg.

"Good morning, Your Highness." He bowed towards Cayr, his voice smooth, without any hint of emotion. "Apprentices. I understand you arrived back in the city yesterday, and appreciate you coming to see me straight away."

Unlike their previous interactions, Alyx now had ready access to her magic, and it instantly picked up on the power hovering around Casovar like a cloak. It intimidated her in a way that Galien no longer did, and this made her angry with herself, and him. The anger made her lash out.

"You're welcome, Lord-Mage Casovar," she said coolly. "Now that we're here, perhaps you could explain the reason for our arbitrary summons home."

His expression tightened at her high-handed tone. Cayr shot Alyx a warning look, which she refused to acknowledge, instead meeting Casovar's gaze. He smiled a little before responding. "I will be happy to address that in a moment. First,

Lieutenant Caverlock, I understand you were in charge of Lady Egalion's protection detail?"

"Yes, sir."

"Then it was you who accosted my Mage Guard soldiers while they were carrying out their duties yesterday afternoon?"

Dashan flicked a glance at Alyx, his shoulders stiffening slightly. "Yes, sir. They were behaving unreasonably towards the owner of a jewellery store."

"You had neither the right nor authority to interfere with the duties of the Mage

Guard," Casovar said crisply. "I will address the matter with your commander, although I am inclined to be lenient given you have been away. From now on you will stick to your duties as a Blue Guard officer and that is all, am I clear?"

"With all due respect sir, I take orders from Commander Hawkwerst, not you."

Alyx winced, the echo of it flashing over Cayr's face. Dashan's tone had been deliberately provocative, and no matter how wrong Casovar might be, he was still a Bluecoat addressing Rionn's lord-mage. Casovar smiled slightly, crossing the room to stand in front of Dashan. Alyx's breath caught at the subtle menace the mage exuded, and she wondered if anyone else in the room could sense it. A quick glance at Dawn's set expression confirmed that at least she had, and Tarrick had discreetly shifted to stand closer to Dashan. Finn was frowning, eyes darting between all of them.

Needing to break the tension, she spoke up. "If I may, Lord-Mage?" She waited a beat until he shifted his attention to her before continuing. "Perhaps you were not given all the information. I supported Lieutenant Caverlock's intervention with the Mage Guard. They were behaving violently towards a citizen without any proof of wrongdoing."

"It is not the Mage Guard's job to explain themselves—or provide evidence—to

Bluecoat lieutenants or mage apprentices." Casovar's voice dripped contempt. "They report directly to me, and you can be assured I am fully across their activities."

What? Was Casovar overstating his involvement with the Mage Guard, or did he truly know the depth of their activities and not care? Alyx opened her mouth, but at a discreet nudge from Cayr, closed it again, allowing him to speak instead.

"Lord-Mage, perhaps as a favour to me you'll ensure your Mage Guard understand they must behave in a way that befits their status as soldiers of Rionn. I know my father would not take kindly to news that his people were being mistreated in the name of hunting Shiven spies." Cayr concluded his mild words with a slight smile, and Casovar had no choice but to concede, nodding his head in the prince's direction.

"Of course, Your Highness. I will speak with the Mage Guard captains today."

"Thank you, Lord-Mage."

Alyx frowned. She'd hoped Cayr would be firmer with Casovar— even if the lord-mage didn't know the extent of his soldiers' activities, he should. Still, the prince's reasonable tone and words had de-escalated a tense interaction.

Casovar turned back to Dashan. "You're dismissed, Lieutenant. Expect to hear from your commander soon."

Dashan's face hardened, and he glanced from Cayr to Alyx, dark eyes burning,

before eventually giving a stiff nod and striding from the room. The door slammed so loudly behind him that Finn jumped.

"Lord-Mage, I have a meeting to attend with my father," Cayr spoke into the ensuing silence. "Thank you for your time this morning."

"Your Highness." Casovar bowed his head as the prince left the room much more

quietly. Alyx's eyes stayed on the closed door—she wasn't certain why Cayr had chosen to leave, but suspected he wanted to make sure Dashan calmed down before reporting to his commander. She and

Cayr had intervened to save Dashan from himself enough times growing up to recognise the instinct.

Dawn suddenly stiffened at her side. The telepath's gaze was firmly fixed on Casovar, who was staring at Tarrick with a look that reminded Alyx of a predator sizing up its prey. She shivered slightly.

"You were here last summer too," Casovar said smoothly. "What is a Zandian apprentice mage doing back in Rionn?"

"I'm Apprentice Tarrick Tylender, sir, and I'm part of Lady Egalion's study group at DarkSkull Hall. Our master granted me an exemption to finish the study year early and travel here with them."

"Tylender." Casovar frowned in thought. "I recognise the name. You're the younger brother of Hinga and Loren, the two mage bodyguards to the Zandian emperor?"

"That's right, sir." A hint of pride filled Tarrick's voice.

"I was going to ask what possessed a Zandian of your background to leave school early and spend a summer in Rionn, but that clears things up." Casovar smiled thinly. "An embarrassment to the family, I gather, given you've managed to align yourself with three arguably lesser mages. I don't suppose spending the summer in Sandira holds any interest for you."

Before Tarrick could respond to the insult, Casovar turned back to Alyx, dismissing him. "In answer to your question, Apprentice Egalion, the situation with Shivasa has become such that I judged you would be of more use to me here than staying an extra couple of weeks at Dark-Skull to finish the year."

He'd deliberately dropped her title and a small smile hovered at the corners of his mouth, as if he were daring her to challenge him on it. The fact he so obviously wanted her to was the only thing that held her back.

"My father has told me of how serious the situation has become." She struggled for calm and won. "And we want to help."

Good, Alyx. Dawn's whisper of thought in her mind was so subtle it was barely there, and it was gone just as quietly. She fought the urge to look at her friend.

"I'm glad we're in agreement." Casovar turned brisk. "You've had a long journey, so take the day to rest. I expect all of you back here tomorrow morning to begin work."

"Yes, sir," Alyx agreed on their behalf.

"Apprentice Tylender, I won't have rogue mages in my city. If you stay, you will

follow my orders the same way the others are expected to."

A slight tightening of his eyes was the only thing that betrayed Tarrick's sense of

insult at Casovar's condescending tone. "I understand, Lord-Mage."

"Good. You're all dismissed. I have things to do."

CAYR WAS HEADING down the hall towards them as they exited, one hand running through his tousled hair.

"Where's Dash?" Alyx asked immediately.

"I couldn't catch him." Cayr fell into step as they turned into a wide walkway that joined two wings, heading into a more isolated section of the palace. "How did the rest of your meeting go?"

The scent of flowers wafted up on the breeze, normally something that would make Alyx smile. But now her attention was distracted by what had just happened.

"It wasn't great. I'm worried about his cavalier attitude towards what we saw yesterday." She shook her head. "In fact none of what happened back there sits right with me."

Cayr frowned. "What do you mean?"

They slowed, clustering around a railing that looked down over a small garden with a bubbling fountain in its centre. Alyx raised an eyebrow at Dawn, who concentrated a moment then gave a little nod. "We're alone."

"Casovar is different," Alyx said. "More confident in his power and authority. He had no compunctions treating me like an inferior, despite the fact he doesn't have a drop of noble blood in him outside his title, and my family goes back generations. He should be tip-toeing around me and he wasn't."

"Worse, he was baiting you," Dawn added. "He wanted you to lash out at him."

41

Finn lifted an eyebrow. "Why would he do that?"

"I don't know. I didn't dare try and read his thoughts, but his desire to push Alyx was practically vibrating from him."

Alyx, disappointed she hadn't picked up the same thing, none-theless trusted Dawn's ability implicitly. Another trickle of concern went through her.

Cayr leaned back against the railing, his casual posture a direct contrast to the rest of them. "I think you're overreacting. Casovar is a little high-handed and arrogant, yes, but he's been working extremely hard these past few months both in strengthening our borders and increasing Alistriem's security. Don't forget the Shiven attacked us here in the palace almost a year ago—Casovar is critical in ensuring that never happens again."

"I'm aware of that," she said evenly, not liking the faint hint of condescension in his tone. "And we want to keep Alistriem safe as much as you do. But that doesn't mean we should be dragging citizens into the street and beating them."

"That was one incident, and Casovar already promised to speak to his captains about it. Besides, he was right—the Mage Guard had no obligation to show you what information they possessed. That jeweller may not have been as innocent as he looked." Cayr pushed away from the railing. "I have to run, I'm sorry—meeting with my father. Drink tonight down in the city?"

"Cayr, what you're saying is logical, but we know what we saw." Beside her, Dawn nodded firmly at Alyx's words. "It wasn't right."

"You're seeing issues where there aren't any." He huffed out a breath. "My father thinks, and I happen to agree, that the safety of Rionn belongs best in Casovar's hands, given how strong a mage he is. What isn't right about that?"

"Cayr, I—"

"I'm sorry, I really have to go," he apologised, leaning down to kiss her cheek. "See you all later down in the city. I want to hear all the stories from DarkSkull!"

"He hasn't changed much, has he?" Finn chuckled as Cayr disap-peared around a corner. "I'm not sure whether to be glad or worried to have such a cheerful prince and heir. Reassure me that he takes some things seriously, Alyx."

"Not seriously enough," she muttered to herself—it was like a betrayal to say it, but it was how she felt. Pushing her disappointment with Cayr out of her mind, she straightened. "Casovar having full control over the defence of Rionn explains some of what's going on with my father. The balance of power at court has changed."

"Particularly if—Cayr's assurances aside—the Mage Guard aren't always doing the right thing, and your father has heard about it," Finn said.

Alyx nodded sharply. "Casovar said we'll be working with the Mage Guard, so let's use that opportunity to see the truth for ourselves."

And if her instinct was right and something was off, Cayr would have to listen to her.

"I'm starting to think it might be a good thing we came home early," Dawn said pensively.

A troubled expression flickered over Finn's face. "I think you might both be overestimating how much we can do."

Tarrick chuckled and clapped him on the back. "I have no shame in admitting you're the smartest of all of us, Finn, but sometimes you overthink things. Alyx is high nobility, and she's practically betrothed to the future king. We're not at DarkSkull anymore—here, she has all the power and influence."

Alyx caught Dawn's glance in her direction, and they shared a moment of silent communion. Tarrick was right—so why did it feel like there was something they were missing?

CHAPTER 5

Alyx stepped into the bustling inn, a wave of overly-warm air sweeping over her. All the fireplaces were lit despite the balmy evening, giving the place a bright glow. Her shoulders relaxed fractionally at the sight of Dashan sitting alone by the bar. She'd come early in the hopes of talking to him before the others arrived, when he would inevitably mask what he was truly feeling beneath his easy grin and humour.

A few curious glances flicked her way as she headed towards him, and it took her a moment to realise it was the light dress she was wearing—too fine to belong to the usual customer in a place like this. She wasn't in Weeping Stead anymore, where she was merely a faceless mage apprentice. Back home, she was Lady Egalion again.

Or at least part of her was. The two selves coexisted uneasily inside her. At DarkSkull it was easy to be the mage apprentice and nothing more. Here she couldn't escape the other part of her, nor could she ignore how easy it was to slip back into that person.

Dashan looked like he'd been there a while. His sleeves were rolled up, and there were two empty ale glasses sitting next to a third that was only half full in front of him. He glanced up at her approach, then gestured to the barman to bring her a drink. "You're early."

"Your powers of observation are outstanding." She settled onto a stool beside him. They were the only ones at the bar, though that would soon change as evening deepened into night.

"How did the rest of your meeting with our delightful lord-mage go?" Dashan spoke in a low voice.

"He says he wanted us back early to help with the Shiven threat. He insulted Tarrick, then tried to bait me into lashing out at him." She shrugged. "It wasn't fun, but we'll only have to put up with him for a few weeks until we go back to DarkSkull."

He regarded her for a long moment. "And?"

She sighed. "Casovar has been placed in full control of the defence of Rionn. Cayr didn't say it outright, but I got the distinct impression he has a lot more influence over the king's decisions than when we left for DarkSkull."

His jaw tightened, and he was silent a long moment before he said, "When I left the palace earlier, I went looking for an old contact from the City Guard, invited him out for an ale."

Dashan had gone looking for answers. She shifted closer to him, wishing she'd thought to do the same thing, that she hadn't let Cayr talk her into doubting her instincts. "What did he have to say?"

Instead of replying, he gave her a little smile, a genuine one that curled up her insides with a happy glow despite her refusal to acknowledge it. "There was a time you would have assumed I'd spent the afternoon on a bender and made some rude comment about my drinking habits."

"Now I know you better." She kept her voice brisk. "Are you going to tell me what your friend said or what?"

"It wasn't good." His eyes darkened, and her warm glow vanished. "According to him, what we saw yesterday wasn't an isolated incident. There have been increasing patrols through the poor quarter, targeting households where those with Shiven blood live. He told me similar stories of what we saw yesterday—only most times it's those of Shiven blood being dragged out of their houses. There have been occasions where City Guard on patrol have come across young men beaten half to death and left in the streets. There's no proof it was Mage Guard of course, the victims are too scared to say."

Her heart dropped—this was what she'd feared, what Dawn had feared too. Anger quickly followed on the heels of her dismay. "If Casovar thinks he can target the Shiven community just because of some spies that may or may not exist—"

"I don't care who it is!" The words came out raw and intense. "I don't care if they are half-blood Shiven or Lord Darden's eldest son. The Mage Guard are invading people's homes, hurting them. That doesn't happen here, Alyx. It shouldn't happen anywhere, not to anyone."

"I agree," she said softly, strongly affected by his declaration. It matched how she felt so closely, and yet that was partly his influence. Two years earlier and she'd have been just like Cayr, brushing off anything that threatened her happy bubble and attending a fancy dinner with her court friends rather than worrying about any of it.

"What did Cayr have to say about it all?" he asked.

Irritation surged. "As usual, he's insisting everything is fine," she muttered. "Casovar promised to talk to his captains about the behaviour we saw, and that was enough for Cayr."

"Give him time. We both know he prefers to see things in black and white terms, good and bad." He gave her a little smile. "He listens to you, though."

Warmth spread through her chest, and she couldn't help meeting his eyes with a soft smile. "You've always made such an effort to see the best in us, even when that must have been damnably difficult at times."

He shifted on his chair, his arm brushing against hers. Her heart was suddenly lodged firmly in her throat, and she was glad he spoke next, because she didn't think she'd be able to summon words if she tried.

"These past couple of years haven't been easy ones for you, mage-girl, and to your credit you've used that to try and become a better person. I have faith Cayr will too. You both have good hearts underneath the privilege and arrogance."

"I... " She cleared her throat. "Thanks, Dash."

He swung away from her then, abruptly changing the subject. "We're not going back to DarkSkull, are we?"

"Why would you say that?" she asked in genuine surprise. "Four half-trained mages aren't going to be any use to Casovar if the Shiven threat escalates." She paused. "What did Hawkwerst say when you reported to him?"

His shoulders stiffened. "I haven't reported in yet."

"Dash—"

"Don't start, Alyx."

Recognising one of his moods, Alyx took a sip of her drink and said nothing further, offering silent companionship. Eventually, he broke the silence.

"I went to see my father, tell him I was home. Casovar had already spoken to him about the incident yesterday." Dashan lifted his glass, draining its contents in two swallows. "I was told in no uncertain terms that I should apologise to Captain Dunnat, and until I did, I would be placed on suspension."

"Dash, I—"

"I tried to explain to him what had happened. I was calm, didn't lose my temper. But my father stood there, listened to what I had to say, then told me that if I didn't apologise to Dunnat and get myself reinstated I was done." He chuckled bitterly. "So much for supporting your own son. Father doesn't even like Casovar, yet he still takes that man's side over mine."

"What are you going to do?" she asked quietly.

He turned his burning gaze on her. "Do you know the last time a Blue Guard commander took orders from Rionn's lord-mage? Never, that's when. And now I'm being told to apologise for stopping a bunch of louts beating a citizen on the streets. I won't do it."

As angry as his voice was, there was only pain in Dashan's dark eyes. She wanted to help, but didn't know how. Everything in her yearned to reach out to him, offer what comfort she could, but that was a dangerous path. And it wouldn't make things any easier for him. So she settled for the only words she could think of. "I'm sorry that your father can't see what sort of man his son has grown into. He's a fool, a blind one."

Dashan's hand lifted to cover his face, and he took a deep breath. Then he stood, rummaging in his pockets for coins to leave on the bar.

"You don't need or deserve my self-pity tonight, mage-girl. I'll see you later."

"Hey—" She reached out to stop him, but he cut her off.

"You were right when you said we both needed time. Give me that. Please."

Her arm dropped back to her side and he turned away without another word. But she couldn't leave it like that.

"Dash, wait!" she called after him but he ignored her, pushing his way through the crowd to the door. Alyx rose to follow but instead ran into Cayr and her friends at the door.

"What did you say to Dash this time to run him off?" Cayr joked. "He looked in a foul mood."

"I... " Alyx hesitated, eyes on Dashan as he disappeared into the crowded street. "Nothing."

"I wish you could have restrained yourself for once," Cayr said good-naturedly as he ushered her back inside. "I haven't seen him since Carhall."

"Sorry," Alyx muttered, still glancing back as she was pulled into the bar. "Where's your Bluecoat detail?"

"Stationed discreetly at every entrance." Cayr pulled the cap he was wearing further down over his curls, no doubt hoping he wouldn't be recognised. Eventually someone would notice all the Bluecoats and wonder why they were there, but that usually took a while. Finn found them a table while Tarrick offered to fetch the first round.

"You drink these days?" Cayr asked with an amused smile.

"Sure," she said.

"I bet that was Dashan's influence." He chuckled. "Don't tell me I'm going to have to start carrying you home from the party district every night."

"No, it wasn't," she said shortly, taking a seat beside him at the table. Again, her eyes were drawn towards the door that Dashan had left through.

The light in his blue eyes dimmed. "Alyx, I was just joking."

"I didn't know you highborn types even knew about the party district." Finn grinned.

"What's that?" Tarrick placed a mug of ale in front of Alyx. She thanked him with a smile.

"It's an area in the southwest of the city," Finn said. "All of the rowdier inns are there, as well as most of the city's theatres and clubs and several brothels of varying levels of quality. If you took a poll of all the fine citizens of Alistriem who have spent a night sleeping off overindulgence in the city's inns, you'd probably find that the majority of them had been in the party district."

"We've never actually been there," Alyx admitted.

"Neither have we," Dawn said pointedly, causing her twin's superior smile to fade quickly. They all chuckled.

"Sandira has places like that too," Tarrick said of his home city. "But more than one. My brothers took me to one once, right before I started at DarkSkull. It was a night to remember."

The men shared a conspiratorial glance while Alyx and Dawn made a show of rolling their eyes. In the following silence, Alyx opened her mouth to bring up Casovar, wanting to try and push Cayr to talk about it more, but the inn had filled to bursting and people were crowded all around them—it wasn't the place to discuss state business. She'd have to wait until she could speak with him more privately.

"Tell me about DarkSkull," Cayr said instead. "Alyx, you said something about an incident with spiders in someone's beer?"

"That was one of Dash's finest hours." Finn laughed.

"Now there's someone I bet has been to the party district many times," Tarrick said.

"You're not wrong." Cayr smiled easily. The cavalier words irritated Alyx—all anyone ever focused on when it came to Dashan, even his friends, was his less ideal behaviour. He was so much more than that. "So who ended up with spiders in their ale?"

"Only the most powerful apprentice at DarkSkull, and he has a nasty temper, too." Finn grimaced.

While Finn and Tarrick eagerly recounted a slightly-embellished version of the story, Alyx leaned over to Dawn. "Your parents must be thrilled to have you home early."

Dawn smiled. "They were. It was hard to separate ourselves from them to come here tonight. What about you?"

"My father was happy to see me," Alyx said.

"But?" Dawn asked, sensing her unspoken thought.

"He seems different. He reprimanded me last night, like I was a child. I didn't react well, which made it worse, but even so... he hasn't spoken that way to me in years."

"He's probably under a lot of stress," Dawn said. "Think about it from his perspective—being forced to send his daughter away and learning where his son is, all in the space of a year. Then add the increasing threat from Shivasa, finding out the Mage Council has been hunting Taliath and now having his influence at court eroded by Casovar."

"When you put it like that..." Alyx sighed. She got so caught up in herself sometimes, she didn't think what other people might be going through. The past year must have been just as awful for her father as it had been for her. Speaking of others, Dawn's smile wasn't as bright as usual. "Is everything all right with you?"

Her friend made a visible effort to shake off her disquiet. "I'm struggling to forget what happened yesterday is all. But I'm determined to take advantage of the extra-long break from DarkSkull."

"I want to as well, but... " Alyx hesitated, then shook her head and straightened her shoulders, forcing a smile to her face. She didn't want to ruin Dawn's night, and what Dashan had told her could wait until morning. "You're absolutely right."

"There's something I've been wanting to tell you." Dawn leaned closer, pink tinting her cheeks. "Rickin kissed me at the dance."

Alyx's eyebrows shot up, and she was so surprised it took her several moments to work out what to say. "What?"

"Shh." Dawn giggled.

"Right, sorry." Alyx lowered her voice to a whisper, astonishment colouring her tone. "I can't believe you didn't tell me!"

If possible, Dawn turned even pinker. "I wanted to, but we were so busy with Third Patrol after the festival, and then the sudden summons home. Besides, I kind of wanted to keep it to myself for a little while, you know? My own little happy secret."

"I know exactly what you mean." Alyx reached out to squeeze Dawn's arm in excitement. What had happened was obviously making her friend happy, and she wanted to share that. "Tell me everything. At once!"

Dawn turned in her chair to face Alyx, her blue eyes alight. "After you left early, Rickin asked me to dance, and we ended up dancing for ages. And it was so romantic with the candles in the garden, and he was being so sweet." Dawn sighed, her expression turning dreamy.

"I take it this was a good kiss, then," Alyx teased.

"It was wonderful." Dawn sighed again. "But you already know what I'm talking about. Your first kiss must have been just as wonderful."

"It was." Alyx glanced sideways at Cayr, who was still engrossed by the spider tale. The sight of him made her spin back to Dawn. "Wait, I thought you liked Dash?"

"That was just a silly crush." Dawn chuckled. "And Dash made it clear in his own charming way that he wasn't interested."

"Oh." Alyx swallowed, suddenly fascinated by the table top in front of her. Dawn wasn't really interested in Dashan. I wouldn't be hurting her if... and there she cut her thoughts off ruthlessly, forcing herself to pay attention to Dawn.

"Rickin is different. I think I might really like him. He wants to spend more time together when I go back." Dawn gave a little smile. "You know, he was so great with the Galien thing, supporting us, and he really helped Finn this year in sparring class."

"I like Rickin. I'm really happy for you." Alyx found a smile and leaned over to give her friend a hug.

Cayr laughed loudly as Finn and Tarrick came to the end of their tale, jostling into Alyx and breaking the hug. She and Dawn shared a secret smile before re-joining the main conversation.

"Everything all right, Alyx?" Cayr asked, leaning closer to her and lowering his voice. "You seem a bit down this evening."

"I'm all right. It's really good to see you again." She meant those words.

His smiled widened. "Me too. Welcome home."

"Thanks." She leaned into him slightly, feeling comforted by his presence beside her. Despite that, her eyes were continually drawn to the door Dashan had disappeared through and she had to keep fighting the urge to go and look for him, make sure he was all right.

"What fun things have we missed while we were gone?" Dawn asked Cayr. "Any more scandals with Lord what's-his-name and the kitchen maids?"

"Lord Ragarn?" Alyx grinned, glancing at Cayr. "I told them what you wrote in your letters about him. They're even more invested in the story than I am."

"I have a great story to tell you about him," he promised. "After this last incident, my father had to send him back to his estate in the south. I don't think he'll be welcome back in Alistriem anytime soon."

The story about Lord Ragarn was juicy, and Alyx laughed as loudly as the others during Cayr's exaggerated telling of it. But as the night passed, she couldn't help her continued glances at the door. She tried not to wonder where Dashan had gone, tried not to want to be wherever that was, but it was impossible. He was hurting, and that meant she was hurting too.

CHAPTER 6

Cayr rode in as Alyx headed out to the stables the next morning. Tarrick was inside finishing up his breakfast and she expected the twins to appear any minute. As tempting as it was to be deliberately late to get under Casovar's skin, Alyx had resolved to keep the peace. At least until they went back to DarkSkull. Antagonising the lord-mage wasn't going to help Rionn against the Shiven.

"Morning!" Cayr greeted her as he swung down from the saddle. His blue eyes sparkled with pleasure at the sight of her, and she couldn't help but feel the same way—it was so nice to be able to see him so regularly again. Even better, it was an opportunity to talk to him about what she'd learned from Dashan the night before. She waved a greeting, but he was in an energetic mood and started talking before she could.

"I know Lord-Mage Casovar wants to see you this morning, but Mira and Lissa are planning a welcome home picnic for you this afternoon," he said. "I wanted to come and tell you straight away—it's such a beautiful day."

"Oh, I was actually intending to ride out and visit Astor after we finish with Casovar." Alyx headed towards the stables and he fell into step beside her. Beyond wanting to see her godfather after so long, she was keen to get his take on the changes in Alistriem. "And then I've already made plans to go swimming with Tarrick and the twins."

"Really?" Cayr stopped walking, a frown creasing his forehead.

"Sure. The weather is getting warm enough. It will be fun." She hesitated. "Why do you look so shocked? I'm sorry for upsetting your plans, but I didn't know about the picnic."

"I just... Mira and Lissa are your friends, and you haven't seen them for months."

Alyx laughed and continued walking. "If Mira and Lissa have planned a picnic for me, then it's only to look good in front of you. I remember well the delight they took in gossiping about you and Jenna behind my back. They weren't my friends, not truly."

Silence greeted her words, and she glanced back to realise he hadn't kept walking with her. She stopped at the concern written in his blue eyes. "What is it?"

"You never used to talk like this. You loved picnics with Lissa and the other girls—you all used to conspire against Luden to get out of lessons early so that you could go on picnics, or shopping in the city."

She sighed. It was too easy to forget that Cayr hadn't been there to see how her time at DarkSkull had changed her, changed her perspective on things. "If I truly thought they'd missed me and wanted to see me, of course I'd go. But my absence was simply fodder for their gossip. That's fine, really, but I don't want to go to a picnic and listen to them chatter for hours on end about the latest court scandal or what the new fashion in gloves is."

His frown deepened. "You used to enjoy that chatter as much as you did buying a new dress. Is... is this about Jenna?"

Alyx smiled. "No, it's not about Jenna. I'm not jealous of her anymore, and while I doubt I'll ever like her, I don't want to hold a grudge."

"You don't?" Hurt flashed on his face.

Sudden panic tightened her stomach. She'd spoken without thinking, but the words were truer than she realised. Now when she thought of Jenna, she felt only a mild dislike. There was not even a flicker of jealousy, not even at the thought of her kissing Cayr. That acknowledgement was too dangerous to pursue, and she ruthlessly pushed it out of her mind.

"I've been away for months," she tried to explain, to herself as much as to him.

"What happened with you and Jenna is in the past as far as I'm concerned."

"All right." He sighed. "I'll tell them you're busy. They'll probably still have the picnic anyway."

"Exactly," Alyx pointed out. "And if you'd like to escape their mindless chatter this afternoon, you're more than welcome to come swimming with us. I was planning on inviting you."

Instead of the smile she'd been aiming for, the concern on his face deepened. "I can't simply walk away from social engagements like you seem to have suddenly decided to. My behaviour reflects on my father and my future as king, and those people you're calling mindless will be my future allies at court. I can't afford to offend them."

His words stung, and forced a disturbing realisation on her. She'd changed in her time away, but he hadn't, or at least not in the same ways. Two years ago she'd have been spouting the exact same sentiments.

"You do know that you're not just going to be king of Alistriem's court, right?" she said sharply. "You'll be responsible for many other people, including the Shiven half-bloods the Mage Guard have been dragging out of homes in their 'search' for spies."

He took a step back. "What are you talking about?"

"Dashan told me last night—he spoke to a friend of his in the City Guard. What we saw with the jeweller wasn't an isolated incident, Cayr."

"So now you're taking some City Guard officer's word over that of Rionn's lord-mage? Over mine?"

The genuine hurt in his voice drained her anger as quickly as it had come, leaving her weary. She hadn't wanted this, hadn't wanted to come home and find herself at such odds with the most solid, constant person in her life apart from her father.

"Cayr, we both grew up in the same world, and it took me leaving to see how narrow and small that world is. I miss it—I miss the simplicity and ease of it, of delighting over beautiful dresses and going to picnics and being the girl everyone admired." She took a breath, the words coming easier now. "But I can't ever go back to that, not anymore, because that would mean leaving behind people like the twins and Tarrick, and even Dashan, eventually. It would mean treating people according to their wealth and power instead of how they stood unflinching at my shoulder in the most terrifying moments of my life."

His eyes were fixed on her, at once both intense and bewildered. "And you think because I haven't experienced 'real life' like you have, I don't care about anyone outside my friends and those of my social standing?"

"I didn't," she said simply. "And it wasn't even a choice. I simply didn't think about anything outside my own world."

"You sound so... " He stumbled to a halt. "I've known you my whole life, known you better than anyone else in the world, and I never imagined I would hear anything like that come out of your mouth."

"Going away changed me," she said simply. "I won't go back to what I was."

"No," he said, voice aching with sadness. "You shouldn't."

The moment held, their wordless communication as easy as it had always been despite everything. A flicker of movement in the periphery of her vision caused Alyx to step back. "The twins are here. I need to fetch Tingo, and then we really have to go." She hesitated, reluctant to end their conversation. "But we really need to talk about the Mage Guard. I don't think Dashan's friend was lying."

Cayr's expression remained pensive as he nodded. "I'll do my best to meet you for swimming later. We can talk more then."

"We'll look out for you." She held her smile a moment longer, trying to convey reassurance, before turning away and heading to the stables.

LORD-MAGE CASOVAR GREETED them at the door to his offices. "Please come through."

Alyx followed the others down a short corridor that led into a much larger, rectangular space. Arched windows lined the wall to her left, allowing in the morning sunlight and providing a view into a neatly-tended garden. The sounds of horses and stable-workers could be heard drifting through a partially opened window—

the palace stables were on the other side of the garden wall.

Long tables covered with parchment and maps filled the space, chairs scattered around them. Two soldiers wearing dark red leather tunics stood studying a particularly large map hanging on the opposite wall, their scarlet cloaks discarded nearby in the warmth of the room.

"This is where I spend most of my time," Casovar explained. "As will all of you, going forward." He waited for their nods before continuing. "I realise that I may have come across as... overbearing yesterday. I was merely attempting to establish, from the beginning, that I am in ultimate charge here, of you and the Mage Guard. Provided you can accept that, I believe we can make an effective team. Do you agree?"

"Yes, sir," Tarrick spoke for them. At his side, Alyx nodded and smiled, keeping her hands relaxed at her sides. Nobody owned her, but she'd grown accustomed to swallowing her pride at DarkSkull, and she could do that here for the short time until they returned.

A cool smile flickered over Casovar's face as he regarded Tarrick. "You're the designated spokesperson, are you? I suppose that makes sense, given you're a Tylender."

"We can all speak for ourselves, sir." This, surprisingly, from Dawn, the edge to her voice barely hidden.

"Good." His gaze lingered on her for a single, intense moment, then he lifted his head. "Firstly, then, I'd like to have a brief discussion with you about your talents. Finn, you're a healer, yes?"

"Yes, sir."

"Dawn, you're a telepath, and Tarrick a warrior mage with concussive power?"

"That's right," Tarrick spoke again, perfectly polite.

"And Alyx?" Casovar turned to her. "I recall you didn't develop much in your first year, have you made any progress?"

Irritation surged at being addressed on a first name basis, but she pushed it away. "I've had some success doing what Tarrick does. I haven't actually managed to create a concussion ball yet, but I can create the light."

The lie came easily off her tongue, and at her side, Dawn's shoulders relaxed.

"That's not promising, and I'm surprised the masters let you back for a second year. Perhaps I can help develop you further," Casovar said briskly. "I'm hoping your lessons at DarkSkull have at least given you a grounding in rational and strategic thinking."

A door at the opposite end of the room opened and a member of the Mage Guard entered. Alyx's heart sank when she recognised Captain Dunnat. He looked equally displeased to see her and the others.

"Good timing, Captain," Casovar said crisply. "You've met my apprentice mages, I understand?"

Dunnat's gaze flickered over them in distaste. "Yes, sir."

"You'll be working together closely," Casovar said.

"What will we be doing exactly?" Alyx asked, avoiding Dunnat's glare and trying to remain polite.

"I created the Mage Guard to track down and arrest the Shiven spies I believe have infiltrated Alistriem," Casovar said. "You will work alongside Captain Dunnat to assist in that endeavour. Dawn, your telepathic powers will be especially useful."

"Is that all?" Tarrick frowned.

Casovar gave him an appraising look. "For now. Once I have had time to assess your abilities, your duties will expand. Is there a problem with that, Apprentice?"

"No, sir." Tarrick's voice was neutral.

"Good. Let's all sit. I'd like to discuss in some more detail the training that you undertook at DarkSkull this year. Captain, you're dismissed for now."

ALYX KICKED Tingo into a gallop out of the city, hoping the ride to Astor's property would clear her head. Casovar had left them at midday in the hands of Dunnat, instructing the captain to brief them on the structure and activities of the Mage Guard. Contempt had dripped from his every word as he addressed them, and the feeling was mutual.

Where Tarrick and the twins were respectful enough of Casovar's rank and power to swallow their dislike around him, they seemed to have no such compunctions with Dunnat. Their briefing had ended after one particularly scornful comment from Tarrick—Dunnat had flushed red, his hand dropping to his sword momentarily before he'd thought better of it.

"Do you have any further questions for me?" he'd asked stiffly.

"No, I think we're done for today," Tarrick had replied, just as cold. Alyx's mouth twitched in a smile at the memory of it, although the incident had her seeing for the first time that Tarrick was no longer a youth on the cusp of manhood. At eighteen, he was very much a young man, not only an imposing physical presence with his height and muscle but with a confident and sure manner that inspired instant respect.

Eventually she left the main southern road and headed out on the private road that led to Astor's estate. The gates were open and she galloped through, bringing Tingo to a rapid halt in a whirlwind of dust at the end of the paved driveway.

Astor was holed away in his study, thick tome in his lap, cup of tea steaming at his side when Alyx was shown in. A smile spread over her face at the familiar sight, widening at the look of astonishment on his face.

"Alyx!" He rose to hug her in greeting. "What are you doing back?"

"You haven't heard?" she asked.

"No, I didn't think I would see you until the end of the DarkSkull year, another couple of weeks at least."

"Lord-Mage Casovar ordered us back early."

"He did?" Astor lifted an eyebrow. "Would you like a cup of tea?"

She chuckled at the abrupt segue. "I'd love one."

He rang a bell, and they chatted idly about the book he was reading until one of his maids had brought Alyx a steaming cup. She studied him while taking a sip. He was as sprightly and sharp looking as ever. In fact, he looked even better than before she left. Retirement certainly agreed with him.

"You're not pleased about the lord-mage's summons," Astor noted, finally turning the conversation onto serious ground.

"I'm not pleased about the lord-mage," Alyx said.

"May I ask why?"

"He's arrogant, condescending and ambitious."

Astor chuckled. "At least two of those three descriptors have applied to your own character at some stage or another."

"I know," she conceded. "And I do realise that, personal feelings aside, his job is to help protect Rionn. I'm trying to keep reminding myself of that."

"You seem different." Astor studied her. "A little older perhaps, or wiser?"

"Older, definitely." She smiled faintly. "Not quite wiser, I don't think."

He shrugged. "From what I hear, Casovar seems to be doing a fine job protecting our borders."

"Does he?" Alyx asked. "I mean that as a genuine question."

"I don't know anywhere near as much about the goings on of Rionn since I retired," Astor said. "But I would have heard if he was mismanaging his job. I still speak regularly with the king and your father."

"What about the Mage Guard?" She described what had happened with the jeweller. "And I've heard that wasn't the only time they've been overly rough, particularly in regard to those with Shiven blood."

"I can't claim to know much detail on Mage Guard activities," Astor conceded. "But I do know for certain that the spies exist. Our soldiers have died as a direct result of information being passed on troop movements in and out of the city and our barracks in the region."

That was interesting to know, but didn't make her feel any better about Dunnat and his louts. "That's not an excuse for violent behaviour. Every Rionnan citizen has the right to be treated with respect until they are proven guilty of a crime."

"Come now, you've seen enough now to know that in times of war we can't always do the right thing," He gave a little shake of his head. "Sometimes a little bad is required in aid of the greater good."

Her shoulders sagged a little at that bitter truth. "From what you've said, I'm guessing you don't take issue with Casovar being placed in ultimate charge of Rionn's defence?"

He gave her a sympathetic smile. "It's Casovar's DarkSkull training and powerful mage abilities that make him a key part of our security. With the Shiven looming ever closer, I'm not surprised the king is relying on him more."

Alyx sat back in her chair, conceding that her intense dislike of Casovar might be clouding her judgement. Astor was a wily old man —if he didn't sense anything amiss, then perhaps there wasn't anything majorly wrong going on. "I'm glad to hear it. I just want to help keep Rionn safe, that's the whole reason I went back to DarkSkull."

"Good. Now, tell me everything." Astor leaned forward. "What have you learned in the past nine months?"

"Ugh, too much." Alyx rolled her eyes. "If I never have to put another sentence together using Zandian verbs I'll die a happy woman."

Astor laughed. "Languages was one of my favourite classes. What about your magic?"

"I..." Alyx hesitated, though she wasn't sure why. She loved and trusted Astor, as much as she did her father, but Tarrick's voice in the back of her head warned her not to declare what she was unless she truly had to. "I struggled in that as much as anything else."

"You'll get there," he said reassuringly, although she didn't miss the tiny frown that flitted across his face. "And I'm glad to have you back home. I've missed our visits."

"Me too." Alyx stood. "I have to go, but I'd like to come back for a longer visit. I'd like to talk about my mother... I learned some things about her this year."

"You know that you're welcome here any time."

"I'll be back soon." She hugged him, then left.

ALYX RODE back to the city at a gallop as the sun lowered on the horizon—she was already late, and still had to return home to change out of her mage attire. The city streets were thronged with people, slowing Tingo to a walk.

As she waited at a busy cross-roads, she spotted the Blue Guard barracks and recognised Tijer as one of the guards on the front gates. Making a split-second decision, she turned Tingo and rode up to him.

"Lady Egalion." Tijer straightened sharply, a warm smile belying his formal manner.

"Hi, Tijer. How are you settling back in?" she asked.

"It's nice to be back," he said. "Although all of us would be pleased to form your escort when you return to DarkSkull."

"I'm pleased to hear it," she said. "I'm looking for Dash. Can you point me to where he's quartered?"

Tijer's smile faded, highlighting the narrowness of his features. "Lieutenant Caverlock has been suspended from duty. We haven't seen him since late last night."

Her heart sank. He really had refused to apologise to Dunnat. She wondered how long it would be before he was thrown out of the Blue Guard entirely. Irritation and worry mingled in her—why couldn't he just get over his damn anger for once?

"The orders came down from Lord-Mage Casovar," Tijer continued. "If you see the lieutenant, please encourage him to come back. Commander Hawkwerst wants to speak with him. It isn't good, him disappearing like this."

"I'll certainly talk to him if I see him." She frowned. "While I'm here, have you heard anything more through the Bluecoats about the Mage Guard? I'd really like to know if what we encountered two days ago was an aberration. Dashan heard that maybe it wasn't."

"None of the Bluecoats like them much, Lady Egalion." Tijer glanced at the other guard, just out of hearing distance on the opposite side of the gate. "But we don't have much interaction with them. There's a... well, I'll be blunt. The Bluecoats are the elite guard of Rionn—soldiers from other commands tend to be beneath our attention, if you know what I mean."

"People thinking they're better than others for no particularly good reason?" she said tartly. "Yes, I know too well. I'd appreciate it if you could let me know if you hear about anymore overzealous spy hunting."

"Yes, my lady." He saluted sharply, then hesitated. "Lieutenant Caverlock, he's a good leader and a great soldier. It took being posted to the disputed area with him for some of us to see it, and that's our shame. None of us like what's happening here. Tell him that we want him back."

"I will."

"My lady... " He hesitated again. "That's not just me talking. The lieutenant has more support than he realises."

Her regard for Tijer increasing rapidly, Alyx smiled. "I look forward to seeing you in a month or so, when we head back to DarkSkull."

A smile crept over his face. "We'll be ready, Lady Egalion."

"You don't plan to swim?"

Alyx looked up at Cayr from where she lay out on the sand. She'd been contemplating her conversations with Astor and Tijer, but had yet to come to a clear resolution. "These evening breezes are still a bit too cool for me."

"You'll be remembering them fondly when summer hits properly."

"At which point I shall dive into the ocean with joyous abandon."

He smiled and held out a hand. "Come for a walk with me?"

"I'd love to."

The breeze, while making it too cool for swimming, was pleasant as it ruffled the skirt of Alyx's light sundress. It was nice—freeing—to be in something other than apprentice attire.

The glow of the setting sun cast an orange glow over the water, almost like it was on fire. Shouts of laughter made her look back to where the twins were ganging up on Tarrick in the water. Dawn spotted Alyx and waved. She returned it with a laugh.

Thanks to Cayr's Bluecoat detail, they had a section of the public beach to themselves—though none of them were unaware of the curious looks tossed their way by those outside the cordon set by the Bluecoats. It was either that or they went to the private beach below the palace, but Alyx would never again subject her friends to the sneering gazes of the other highborn youth, many of whom would be enjoying the private beach on such a fine evening. She ignored the part of her that wished her life was back amongst that world.

As she and Cayr began walking, two Bluecoats discreetly fell in behind them. A firm look from the prince had them dropping back out of earshot.

"I feel like we argued this morning, and I hate thinking you're angry with me." Cayr squeezed her hand. "I'd like to talk, starting with what happened with Jenna before you left."

"Jenna is not what we need to talk about," she said.

"The Mage Guard again?" A touch of incredulity filled his voice. "I've explained that to you, and I spoke to Casovar like you asked."

"I talked to Astor this afternoon, and I agree that maybe I've been making a bigger issue of things than I should," she acknowledged. "Even so, what Dash told me is concerning. I think we should do more to make sure the Mage Guard isn't hurting innocent people."

He ran a hand through his hair, a sure sign he didn't want to talk about something. "I think we need to let Casovar do his job and focus on us."

"This!" She stopped suddenly, forcing him to turn and face her. "This is our problem, not Jenna. Last year when I came home you hid things from me because you wanted to pretend everything was fine. I—"

"I hid it from you because it was nothing, it meant nothing, and I didn't want you to—" Matching irritation flashed over Cayr's face, his voice rising an octave as he cut over her.

"What about Dashan?" She threw the words at him, unable to keep the anger from her voice. "He was hurting, Cayr. You promised him he wouldn't be posted to the disputed area, even though you shouldn't have, and what happened to him up there hurt him. You ignored it, you didn't tell me about it, and we are his best friends. We should have been there for him."

He nodded sharply, mouth forming a tight line. "You're right, I did hide things from you. It was wrong. I don't know how many times you need me to apologise for it before you forgive me."

"I forgave you for Jenna a long time ago." And it was true. "But you're doing the same thing now. I've come home and you won't talk to me about the Mage Guard, or even acknowledge there's a problem. Instead you want to go back to how things used to be between us. It's like you're hiding from everything going on."

He took a step towards her, blue eyes blazing with determination. "I'm not hiding. I love you, Alyx. I'm trying to talk about us because I am willing to do whatever it takes to move past what I did to you last year and build our future. I will be king, and I want you as my wife and my queen. Is that clear enough?"

"How can you be so certain?" she asked, shaken and confused. Because she wasn't—even though she'd been telling herself she was over and over. Too much had happened.

His determined expression faltered. "You're not?"

"Cayr..." She hesitated. "While I admit I'm glad that nothing happened with Jenna, I told you when I left that we should both take the opportunity to be sure of each other and what we wanted. I didn't just mean you—I needed the time too."

He frowned. "The way you just said that... did something happen for you?"

She swallowed, hating the surge of guilt and confusion that came at the thought of Dashan. For the briefest of seconds she considered lying, brushing his question off. Her certainty about Cayr, about what she wanted, had been shaken, but she loved him, that was still true. But that meant she couldn't lie—because otherwise she'd be doing to him exactly what he'd done to her with Jenna. Summoning her courage, she forced herself to meet his eyes. "Yes," she said softly.

Hurt suffused his features. The expression tore at her, and she swallowed, struggling for the resolve to continue.

"Who?" he demanded.

"It doesn't matter." The last thing she ever wanted to do was ruin Cayr's friendship with Dashan. Honesty was one thing, but there was no need for him to know this.

"What does that mean?"

"It was something like what happened with you and Jenna." Alyx winced as the words tumbled out of her mouth before she thought them through; Dashan was no Jenna. But she couldn't take them back, and saying anything else would only hurt him more. "Nothing came of it, and it won't happen again."

He swallowed, blue eyes darkening with pain. She wanted to make it right, to erase the hurt, but the words were out now and she couldn't take them back.

"Is being with me still what you want?" he asked. "Because it's what I want more than anything."

"I've always wanted a future with you in it," she said. "But so much has happened and we've both changed. I would like to take things slowly and see what happens."

"I would wait forever for you," he said earnestly. "And I'll do whatever it takes, I promise you."

She reached out and took his hand, starting to walk again. "Thank you."

Silence fell, and she sensed he was chewing over what she'd told him. She thought about saying something, trying to explain better, but in the end decided just to let him think it through for himself.

Eventually he broke the silence, changing the subject. "Will you tell me something about your time away? Last year you were so reluctant."

"I was," she admitted. "And I'll do better this time. There is one big thing I've really wanted to tell you."

His soft smile returned, and some of her guilt eased. "What is it?"

"I have an older brother." She smiled at the confusion that settled over his face. "It's true, and he happens to be the lord of Widow Falls."

"You're joking with me," he accused.

"Nope." Her smiled widened and she squeezed his hand before turning serious. "It's a long story, and not a happy one."

Cayr listened patiently as they strolled along the shoreline and Alyx related everything she'd learned in the past year about her parents and her brother. Telling him relaxed the both of them, easing the tension that had built up from her admission. It felt easy again, like things had always been between them. After she finished speaking, a long silence fell.

"That must have been difficult news to hear," he said eventually. "Yet in telling me, you sound very calm and accepting."

"It was more than difficult," she said. "Had I been two years younger and still in Alistriem, it would have been one of those times I came running to you, and you would sit by me and hug me until I stopped crying."

66

"I wish I had been there this time," he whispered.

"I wasn't alone." Alyx's heart ached as she thought of Dashan, and the reassurance she'd felt with his arms around her. Guilt returned, tangling her stomach in knots and killing the momentary contentment she'd felt.

"I'm glad," Cayr said. "And I'm sorry I was upset with you this morning for wanting to spend time with your friends from DarkSkull instead of Lissa and the others. They've clearly been good friends to you."

"They were very supportive," Alyx said, the knots in her stomach twisting further as she allowed Cayr to assume it had been Tarrick and the twins who'd been there when she was most alone. And they had been, at least for some of it.

"I... " Her words trailed off as she caught sight of four red-cloaked soldiers walking along the main street above the beach. They were moving too determinedly to be on a simple patrol, and her first instinct was to go and follow them, see where they were going and what they were up to.

"Alyx, wait!" Cayr caught at her arm. "Where are you going?"

"The Mage Guard are headed somewhere." She pointed.

"Right. Doing their jobs." He sounded mystified. "Come on, keep walking with me. I've missed you."

Still she hesitated, wavering between her desire to walk with Cayr along the beach on a beautiful evening and her instinctual distrust of the Mage Guard. The temptation to use her telepathic magic to try and learn their intensions was close to overwhelming, and she was about to give in to it when Cayr tugged sharply at her hand.

"Alyx!"

A flare of annoyance went through her and she yanked her hand free. "Stop pulling me."

More hurt and confusion flashed over his face. "What is wrong with you?"

Dawn's laughter filtered along the beach; she and the boys had drifted closer in the course of their water fight. They were clearly having a lot of fun, and Alyx made the decision to let go of her concerns and join them.

"I'm sorry," she apologised. "Captain Dunnat and his soldiers really got to me the other day, that's all. Come on, let's go and help win that water fight."

She ran towards the shore before he could protest, and was relieved moments later as his splashing footsteps joined hers.

"Where's Dash tonight?" Tarrick asked a while later as they trooped wearily back to their towels, dripping cool ocean water.

"I don't know," Alyx admitted, explaining what Tijer had told her. The subject of Dashan brought her concern for him rushing back, and all she felt when Cayr slung an arm around her shoulders was confusion.

"Is there anything we can do?" Finn asked.

"No." She sighed. "Dashan is his own man. He needs to accept the consequences of his actions. We can't always step in to protect him from himself."

"I wouldn't do it if I thought he was acting from a bad place." Cayr looked torn. "But all you say about him is right, and I can understand the way he acts because of the awful life he has had."

And she'd only compounded that, spurning him for Cayr, even though she wasn't even sure... Enough! Alyx took a firm hold of her wandering thoughts. Dashan was hurting, but she couldn't be the one to help. That wasn't fair to him or Cayr.

Deep down, where she boxed her deepest fears away, she buried the growing realisation that nothing was ever going to go back to the way it had been.

CHAPTER 7

The remainder of their first week back was spent in Casovar's rooms at the palace studying reports about suspicious activity in the city and its surroundings. These came from several different sources, including private citizens and the City Guard, and most were anonymous.

The majority seemed dubious at best and vexatious at worst—in one case a blatant attempt by a struggling merchant to get his main competitor arrested—but Casovar insisted they carefully review each report. Any that weren't obviously fabricated or completely lacking in usable detail were passed on to Dunnat and the Mage Guard to investigate.

Alyx had dreaded being sent out with the Mage Guard, certain she wouldn't be able to stand by and do nothing if they crossed the line in their behaviour, but so far Casovar kept them in the palace reviewing the reports.

"Your studies at DarkSkull make you better equipped to understand how valuable the information is than Dunnat's men," Casovar explained when Tarrick asked. "Not to mention your language skills."

That seemed plausible enough—the odd report came in written in Zandian or Shiven—but Alyx wondered if Casovar was hesitant to have his apprentices work too closely with the Mage Guard given their evident dislike for each other.

On the third day, Casovar began taking Tarrick and the twins out to the adjacent garden; initially to observe their ability to use their magic, and then to continue their training. When Alyx rose to join them the first time, Casovar waved her back to her chair, remarking that being able to summon a green light was useless, and there was no reason for her to accompany them.

The words had stung and she'd sat fuming at her desk until she became aware of Dunnat's beady eyes watching her, a smirk on his face. Turning away from him, she'd continued reading through the pile of reports before her, and as her anger slowly faded, logic reasserted itself. It would have been difficult in the extreme to hide her powers under Casovar's direct scrutiny, and being left out of the sessions was the best thing that could have happened.

That night the apprentice mages walked down to the city together to share dinner, a routine they'd quickly fallen into. On this occasion Cayr accompanied them too, his Bluecoat detail setting up a discreet cordon around the café they'd chosen.

It was sheer coincidence that Cayr and Alyx were leaving, lagging behind the others, as Casta and a group of friends strolled past the café, presumably off duty in their civilian clothing.

"Lady Egalion." Casta waved cheerfully, leaving his friends to jog over. It took him a second to recognise Cayr as her companion, resulting in a sharp salute and much deeper bow.

"Lieutenant," Cayr sounded amused. "You know Alyx?"

"He's part of my protective detail," Alyx explained.

"I wouldn't have interrupted you, except Tijer and I have been trying to work out a way to come and talk to you." Casta's glance flicked between Alyx and Cayr, making it clear he didn't want to say much in front of the prince.

"Do you mind?" Alyx gave Cayr an apologetic smile and waited until he'd gone to catch up to the others. "What is it, Casta?"

"You asked Tijer to keep his ears out for any information about the Mage Guard, and if they were crossing the line again." His mouth tightened. "Two nights ago they raided three homes in the poor district—all residents were of Shiven blood. One lad was beaten half to death when he tried to stop them arresting his mother."

The poor district. A large corner in the southwest of Alistriem where its poorest citizens—and criminal elements—lived. It began only a few blocks back from the public beach. She tried to keep her growing anger from her voice when she responded. "How sure are you of this?"

"An off-duty Bluecoat was at a brothel nearby with some friends," Casta admitted. "They were leaving when the raid happened. Tijer and I spoke to him directly."

"Alyx, is something wrong?" Cayr had wandered back over. "Tarrick and the twins are headed home."

"Those red-cloaks we saw the other night at the beach were on their way to a raid," she told him, voice seething despite her best efforts. "A Shiven youth almost died trying to protect his mother from being arrested."

Cayr stiffened. "If his mother was spying on our army, then he shouldn't have tried to stop the arrest."

"Are you confident they had proof of that? After what I saw when we arrived back in Alistriem, I'm not confident at all," she snapped. "Damn it! I knew I should have gone after them!"

"If I may, Your Highness." Casta cleared his throat. "Word amongst the Blue Guard is that the red-cloaks often become overly violent when conducting their activities. At the very least, their professionalism is questionable."

"I'm not surprised to hear the Blue Guard hold such a low opinion of the Mage Guard given the rivalry between the two units," Cayr said icily. "And I don't appreciate you bringing rumour and innuendo to Lady Egalion in the middle of the street like this."

"Cayr, enough!" Alyx said, horrified. "Casta, please go back to your evening. Thank you for bringing me the information."

Casta gave a much stiffer salute to Cayr, flashed a quick smile at Alyx, then turned to run after his friends.

She spun back to Cayr, the anger and regret swamping her so strongly her hands trembled with it. "What possessed you to talk to him like that?"

71

"Since when is it all right for a Bluecoat to accost you in the street with dramatic stories about Mage Guard raids?" He seemed genuinely confused by her reaction.

"Casta is a friend who has protected me on multiple trips to Dark-Skull and back," she said evenly. "I asked him and the others to keep an ear out for the Mage Guard doing anything like what they were doing to the poor jeweller when we arrived. And now they've gone out and raided three homes, almost killing a youth," she said. "One of your citizens. What are you going to do about it?"

"Rionn is at war!" Cayr stepped towards her, anger vibrating from him. She'd finally broken through his determined pretence that everything was fine, and a quick jolt of satisfaction speared through her. "It might not be official, and it might not be an open battle, but Shivasa wants us. I will do whatever it takes to keep my country safe."

"The citizens in the poor quarter are part of your country." She searched his face. "All you see is the court and the nobles in it. And I know you love Rionn, and you want to protect it, but think about what that means."

"They attacked us in our own home!" His chest heaved with emotion, blue eyes snapping. "They tried to kill my own father. They tried to kill you. I don't care how old they are or whose mother they are, the Shiven are—"

"Your best friend is half-Shiven!" She cut him off ruthlessly, desperate to make him see. "You've never seen him as anything other than your friend. Being Shiven doesn't automatically make Dashan a spy, or a bad person. Why is it different for those living in the poor quarter?"

"I... " Cayr's anger faltered, and he lifted a hand to run through his hair. "I don't know."

"I'm not trying to hurt you, Cayr." She searched his face, looking for a glimmer of understanding. "I'm trying to make you see that just because you have good intentions, it doesn't make what you're doing right. It doesn't make what the Mage Guard is doing right."

He turned away from her, his gaze distant as he watched the people walking by them, oblivious to the curious stares his Bluecoat detail caused. She let him think, hoping her words had gotten through to him.

After a moment he turned back, an expression of focused determination on his face. "I will undertake a personal review of the Mage Guard activities to ensure they are acting appropriately. But Alyx, if I find they are operating within the parameters of their role, and are simply finding and arresting those putting our soldiers in danger, I will do nothing. Is that clear?"

"Thank you," she said.

He gave her a shaky smile. "Do you plan on challenging me like this when you are queen?"

"Cayr, come on, that's a long way in the future." She sighed. "Maybe you won't want to marry someone who challenges you like I just did." Like Dashan always challenged her—to be better, stronger. She ached at his absence, but pushed the emotion away. It wasn't fair to Cayr.

"I can take being challenged," he murmured, pulling her closer as they started walking. "But we've never fought like this before."

"I think we see the world differently now because of the different experiences we've had."

"Those differences will make us stronger," he said determinedly. Alyx nodded agreement, ignoring the doubt worming its way through her heart.

THREE NIGHTS LATER, the doorbell rang as Alyx left the dining room. She'd parted from Tarrick and the twins after finishing her reports, hoping to spend some time with her father over dinner. That hope had been dashed when he'd stayed late working at the palace.

They hadn't spoken properly since their angry words on her first night back. He wasn't home often, and they usually only saw each other for a few moments at breakfast. She didn't like the way things were between them, and wanted to fix it. She resolved to try again the next day.

The ring of the bell was a surprise and, curious, Alyx waved away one of the servants going to answer the door. A familiar figure stood on the step.

"Dash!" Her shoulders sagged in relief. "I've been looking for you all week! Where have you been?"

He shrugged. "Oh, you know me. I get around."

She gave him a searching look. He was out of uniform, wearing only brown breeches and a worn, blue shirt under a black jacket. His eyes met hers, dark and unreadable. Alyx was about to give in to her utter relief at seeing him and throw her arms around his neck when her telepathic magic tinkled a warning.

"I tracked him down at the barracks." Cayr stepped out of the shadows, and she guiltily tore her eyes from Dashan. "He wasn't doing anything but polishing his sword."

Like Dashan, Cayr was dressed in worn, understated clothing and a cap concealed his golden curls. Her gaze narrowed. "What brings you both here?"

He grinned. "We've come to take you out with us for a night on the town. It's time to properly celebrate your return."

"Do you really think that's a good idea?" Alyx glanced back at Dashan, whose expression remained closed. "Besides, I've been home a week already."

"And yet the three of us still haven't spent any time together," Cayr urged. "Come on. Don't tell me you're still mad at me?"

They hadn't spoken since their fight over the Mage Guard, largely due to Cayr's commitments with his father.

"You two had a fight?" Dashan snorted. "About time for pigs to start flying, I suppose."

Alyx ignored Dashan's baiting. "I wish you'd take the situation more seriously."

"What situation?" Dashan asked.

"I'm doing as I promised I would." A cold soberness flashed over Cayr's face for the briefest of moments before his carefree grin returned. "But tonight is about finally having some fun. No serious talk. Come on, Alyx."

"Are you sure about this?" Alyx directed her question at Dashan.

"Absolutely." Dashan grinned, but she recognised it for what it was, the shield he held up to the world to hide what he was really feeling. For a moment she considered trying to pick up his thoughts, but quickly dismissed the idea. She could never breach his privacy like that. "It'll be fun."

"Come on." Cayr reached forward and grabbed her hand, pulling her out of the door. "Tarrick and the twins are waiting for us down below. We're going to introduce them to the party district."

"I was hoping for a quiet night at home," she said, resisting him.

"Why, is everything okay?" Dashan's eyes bored into her.

"We can talk about it over ale," Cayr said. "Come on."

"What about your Bluecoat detail? I'm not sure they'll be too pleased at you going to the party district." She looked behind them, searching for the tell-tale blue.

"I lost them back at the palace. Dash created the perfect diversion for me to sneak out." Cayr shrugged. "They think I'm safely ensconced in my room, reading."

That explained their clothing. Her sense of unease deepened. This was going to be one of the rare occasions where they went completely incognito. She glanced down at her attire, relieved she'd changed out of her mage robes into a summer dress after arriving home earlier.

"They'll be waiting for us. Let's go." Cayr tugged at her hand.

"I have a feeling I'm going to regret this," she muttered, but followed.

ALYX SPENT most of the walk down into the city trying not to look at either Dashan or Cayr. The confusion that arose from how glad she'd been to see Dashan and the realisation of how much she'd missed his absence from her life didn't help matters.

Tarrick and the twins waited for them inside the city gates. All were dressed in an understated fashion, so clearly Cayr had warned them what was planned. All three were pleased to see Dashan, and he was as charming and jocular as usual as he greeted them, slapping Tarrick on the back and giving Finn a little shove.

"You look worried." Dawn noted as she and Alyx linked arms.

"You don't think the idea of the prince of Rionn loose in the city without his protective guard is something to be worried about?"

"Cayr won't be in danger when he's surrounded by mages, even half-trained ones," Dawn said. "And I know the three of you have done this before. That's not what is really bothering you."

Alyx cursed Dawn's powerful mage power, and briefly re-focused the mental shield that Howell had taught them. It was something she maintained constantly now, particularly around Casovar. A mage's mental shield was far more about their ability to summon and maintain a strong mental focus than actual magic, and both Finn and Tarrick were confident her skill at shielding wouldn't give Casovar any indication of her magical strength. Her fear and intense dislike of Casovar gave her more than enough motivation to achieve that mental focus.

"Dashan's in one of his moods," she explained reluctantly. "And that's never a good thing."

"He's probably just still upset about what happened with Casovar," Dawn said. "He'll be fine."

Alyx wasn't so sure, but she smiled and allowed herself to be drawn into a conversation about where they should go once arriving in the party district. The delineation between the few square blocks which made up the district and the city around it was clear. Inside, it was brighter, louder and filled with people. Light spilled out from inn doors, extra lamps lined the streets, and the sound of laughter, music and the more chaotic tenor of inebriated conversation filled the evening air.

The inn Dashan chose was already loud with lively music, its patrons crowding out the doors and filling the tables lining the pavement. Dashan and Tarrick shouldered their way through to the bar to order drinks, while Cayr and Finn took care of finding them a table near the edge of the room.

Alyx tried to let the music and upbeat atmosphere relax her, but the level of disquiet she felt made that impossible.

"Cheer up." Cayr nudged her arm. "It's not that bad. Surely you're glad to be home?"

"Absolutely," Finn answered for her. "There's nothing like the inns of the party district on a warm summer's evening."

Alyx had to laugh at that. "We've never been here before!"

"We have in my imagination," he said gravely, making them all roll their eyes.

Cayr leaned back against the wall, throwing a casual arm around Alyx's shoulders. Dashan chose that moment to reappear with Tarrick and the drinks. Nothing showed on his face, but when he put the glass of ale in front of Cayr, it slammed into the table with more force than was necessary. Alyx jumped, barely avoiding having ale splashed on her lap.

Finn cleared his throat loudly, barely suppressing his amusement. Alyx shot him a glare.

"What is with the two of you?" Cayr raised his eyebrows. "Moods both as dark as thunderclouds."

"We're supposed to be having fun tonight," Tarrick added, taking a long swig of ale.

"Don't tell me your noble blood is still all in a twitter because you're suddenly not as important as you used to be?" Finn teased.

"I thought you'd been coping remarkably well in that respect," Dawn added.

"It's not that." Alyx took a deep breath. "I'm sorry. I do want to have fun."

"In that case, you'll be willing to dance with me?" Finn stood and offered his hand.

She agreed with alacrity, glad to escape the tension of the table, and for a while she really did enjoy herself. The music was fantastic, with an energetic beat, and Finn made her laugh with his outrageous dancing. He'd obviously taken her words from days earlier to heart, because he didn't bring up Dashan or Cayr once.

By the time they returned to the table she was thirsty, and gulped down her glass of ale. That left her with a pleasant buzz, and she and Dawn proceeded to laugh themselves silly over Finn tripping over his own feet and falling on the floor.

A little later, Cayr grabbed her hand for a dance. They swung and twirled with all the others on the crowded floor for a while, then he took her hand and led her to a small alcove off the main bar.

"I wanted a little quiet time with you," he explained.

"It is rather loud in here isn't it?"

"And crowded." He grinned. "You look like you're finally starting to relax."

"I am," she agreed. The presence of her friends, not to mention the alcohol, had finally served to relax her. "Thanks to you and the others."

"I didn't realise how much I truly missed you until you came back," he said. "It was like a part of me was missing."

"I missed having my best friend around, too," she admitted.

Cayr shifted closer, one arm reaching over her shoulder to lean against the wall. "You are so much more beautiful than Jenna could ever be. You've changed, Alyx, and in the best way possible. You're stunning."

"Cayr..."

"Shh," he whispered, leaning down to kiss her.

His kiss was as she remembered it, warm and sweet. It took her back to the days before she'd left for DarkSkull, where her happiness had been pure and unaffected. Her eyes slid closed as she clung to that memory and tried to ignore the sadness rising in her.

He pulled back after a long moment, smiling softly down at her. "I've been wanting to do that ever since I saw you again."

Alyx opened her mouth to reply, but as she did, her glance shifted and fell on Dashan. He clutched a glass of ale in his hand, newly purchased from the bar, and the raw hurt that spilled from his dark eyes made it obvious he'd seen everything. A dancer bumped into him, partially spilling the ale. He didn't notice, his entire attention on her.

Her breath caught. Tears threatened, and she couldn't understand how Dashan's pain affected her so powerfully. Before she could move, he was gone, melting back into the crowd.

"Alyx?" Cayr's voice turned her attention back to him, and only sheer willpower kept her tears from falling and becoming obvious to him.

"Cayr." She paused, realising with sudden clarity that she shouldn't have allowed him to kiss her. "I told you we needed time."

He shook his head. "You know how I feel about you. We talked about this."

"And I should have said more." She looked at him steadily. "We've both grown up, changed. We need to take things slowly, get to know each other again."

"I know, and I agreed, but... I'm going to marry you," he said suddenly, fiercely. "I haven't changed that much."

Had she? Alyx found she didn't have the answer to that question, and that scared her. She forced a smile, and reached down to take his hand. "Come on, let's go and dance."

"ARE YOU ALL RIGHT?" Cayr asked a short time later, after he noticed she wasn't paying complete attention.

She nodded. "I'm getting a little thirsty."

"Back to the table we go, then." He led her over.

Alyx stopped dead in her tracks as they approached the table, and someone behind bumped into her when she obstructed their path. She completely ignored the man's protests—her eyes were fixed on Dashan and the pretty young woman in his lap. She was giggling as he nuzzled at her neck. Dawn and Tarrick sat huddled in conversation on the other side of the table, likely trying to give Dashan some privacy.

"What do you think you're doing?" The words were out before Alyx thought about them, born of the sudden, overwhelming jealousy clawing at her chest. The woman broke off her nuzzling at Alyx's sharp words, her gaze bleary with drink as she tried to focus in Alyx's direction.

Dashan seemed equally inebriated, words almost slurring when he spoke. "Isn't it obvious?"

"If you're going to put on a display like that, please do it somewhere else." Her voice was icy.

"Hey, I got another jug!" Finn's voice broke the bubble of tension that had fallen around them following Alyx's words. He took in the situation immediately, concern replacing the merriment that had been on his face. "Maybe we should just call it a night?" he said, glancing between Alyx and Dashan. "It's getting late, and we have to meet with the lord-mage early tomorrow."

"You can do as you like, I'm sticking around for a while." Dashan tightened his arm around the woman's waist, making her giggle into his ear.

"Mate, don't do this," Cayr said with a sympathetic smile. "Let us walk you back to barracks." Like Alyx, he recognised exactly what sort of mood Dashan was in. If he stayed, he would keep drinking and his behaviour would only get worse.

"Get your filthy Shiven hands off my girl!"

The words were bellowed loudly enough to cut across the noise, and Alyx turned as a man near double Dashan's size pushed his way through the crowd towards them. He had others behind him, all strapping farmers by the look of them.

"This is not good," Finn muttered under his breath.

"She's your girl?" Dashan mocked. "Doesn't look like it to me. Maybe you should find yourself a woman you can keep."

Alyx winced, disgust at his behaviour quickly rising to match the searing jealousy twisting her stomach. As the girl scrambled away with a drunken shriek, the man roared and swung his fist at Dashan, who dodged, but not quite quickly enough. He took the fist on the edge of his jaw and fell backwards with the chair. The jilted man kept coming, aiming kicks at Dashan's prone form.

The man's friends joined in then. Part of Alyx—the furious part—was tempted to leave Dashan to his well-deserved beating, but Cayr leapt into the fray before she could stop him, jumping onto the big man's back and trying to pull him off Dashan.

With a sigh, she threw herself sideways into a man that was trying to drag Cayr off his friend, sending them both staggering. A beefy arm wound around her neck, and she gasped for air. Reluctant to use magic in such a crowded, public place she struggled to release herself from the fierce hold.

A moment later the man's arm suddenly loosened, and she dropped to the floor. Gaining her feet, she saw Tarrick wrestling on the floor with her attacker. She looked for Dashan and Cayr, caught a glimpse of them between Finn and a strange man's wrestling figures, and tried to force her way through.

The brawl quickly escalated out of control, involving more and more patrons of the inn. Somebody slammed into Alyx from the side, and she lashed out with a foot, kicking his shin hard, then swearing at the pain that shot through her toes. Dashan and the farmer wrestled on the table top, rolling straight toward her. She dodged aside as they crashed into the floor, just in time for Cayr to come stumbling backwards from a punch and land on top of the pile.

She went to help, but found herself being dragged backwards as two hands grabbed her shoulders. Looking around, she recognised the uniform of the City Guard, and immediately stopped struggling. More City Guard officers moved in to break up the fight, grabbing and holding those fighting.

"Damn," she muttered as she and the others were dragged from the inn. "Casovar is going to love this."

CHAPTER 8

Somewhere down at the end of the hall a cell door clanged. A man's voice swearing came next, followed by the fading echo of booted footsteps and another door closing. The man swore a few more times before subsiding. Silence fell.

"What did you do in your first week home after a long absence, Alyx?" She spoke loudly into the silence. "Oh, I spent the night in the city jail after getting arrested for being in a bar brawl. It was great fun."

"Could you pipe down?" Dashan groaned. "My head is killing me."

She gave him an icy look. The six of them were arrayed on hard wooden benches that ran the length and width of the barred cell. The place stunk of vomit and unwashed prisoners. Alyx had been breathing through her mouth as much as possible, but that technique had so far proved fruitless. At this moment she would give anything for clean clothes and a hot bath.

"Your head wouldn't be killing you if you hadn't drunk so damned much." Cayr had worked himself into an uncharacteristically foul mood—perfectly understandable since at some point soon, he was going to have to inform his father, the king of Rionn, that he'd been arrested for drunken behaviour. He also had a lovely, vivid bruise colouring his jaw.

"Spare me another righteous moral lecture," Dashan muttered.

"I've always wanted to see the inside of an Alistriem jail," Finn spoke, presumably attempting to defuse the tension. "It's a childhood dream."

Nobody responded. Dawn sat quietly in the corner opposite Dashan, eyes on the floor. Alyx wouldn't be surprised if her magic was picking up the turmoil in several minds around her. Being battered by emotional thoughts often caused her to withdraw into herself. Tarrick seemed wearily resigned to their predicament and was staring at the bars across from him, no doubt thinking along the same lines as Cayr. She wondered if a Tylender had ever seen the inside of a Zandian jail.

"What is your problem, Dash?" Cayr could be stubborn at the best of times, and it seemed he wasn't going to let this go. "You've been in a sour mood all night, ogling women and starting brawls. Is it really so hard to get over yourself and apologise to Dunnat?"

"I don't want to hear it." Dashan waved a dismissive hand. "You think you know me, up there in your pretty palace with your pretty clothes, but you know nothing."

"Cayr supported you back there. He jumped into the fight that you started," Alyx said angrily. "So maybe you could try being a little nicer."

"Well, excuse the drunken lout in the corner. I don't know what I'm talking about, right?"

Cayr straightened. "Quit the tone, Dash. I won't tolerate you speaking to Alyx like that."

"Hey!" she snapped. "I'm right here."

"That's enough!" Tarrick rose to his feet. "If I hear one more piece of bickering, I will loose an energy ball into this roof and hope a falling piece of rock knocks you all out!"

Finn rose to his feet, stumbled to the bucket by the wall, and illustrated Tarrick's words nicely by vomiting copiously into it. Dashan, the closest to him, patted the mage sympathetically on the back until he finished and slumped down to the floor with a groan.

Alyx tried not to look at Dashan in the tense silence that enveloped the cell, but found it impossible. As furious as she was about his behaviour, she knew the cause of it and it was time to stop pretending she didn't.

Cayr's kiss. It had taken her back to a time when she'd been happy. But that happiness had been a façade, borne of her innocence and naïveté. Cayr was her friend, and he was handsome, but everything had changed so much since she'd come home. She'd been feeling uneasy and off-centre, and she finally acknowledged the reason. Beyond Casovar, beyond the new Mage Guard.

It was Cayr.

"Cayr?"

Alyx started from her thoughts as Dashan spoke, rising to his feet. He looked steadier, his eyes alert.

"What is it?"

"I'm sorry. I acted badly tonight. The things I said were insulting and wrong. You've always been a good friend to me, despite everything. You didn't deserve my behaviour."

"Why, Dash?"

"I have no excuse." Dashan held out his hand. "Someone told me recently that I might be a good man, beneath all the swagger and the drinking. I messed up tonight, but I'd like to try and prove that person right."

Alyx tried not to let the tears welling in her eyes fall as Cayr smiled and took Dashan's hand. "You've always been a good friend to me too. You kept me grounded, kept me true to who I was. I accept your apology."

"Then we're good?"

"We're good."

"I'm glad." Dashan gave Cayr a sad half-smile before returning to sit in the corner of the cell.

Alyx couldn't take her eyes off him. She was angry and disappointed over how he'd behaved, but he knew he'd been wrong, and pride echoed through her at how he'd acknowledged it with Cayr.

"Praise the gods," Tarrick muttered, eyes turning heavenward.

They laughed, loudly and uncontrollably, as the tension that had been lying between them cracked into a million pieces.

THEY WERE FINALLY LET out just after midnight. The jail watch

84

changed, and one of the young men on the new shift was an old unit-mate of Dashan's. He instantly recognised the people Dashan was with, and informed his superiors that Cayr's story of being the prince was indeed true, and not a drunken fabrication. The poor watch commander almost tripped over himself in his rush to set them free.

By then, Alyx was tired, hungry, and uncomfortable. She and Cayr found themselves under Bluecoat escort straight back to the palace. Tarrick elected to remain in the city and stay with the twins for the night rather than walk all the way back up the hill, and so it was only Cayr, Alyx and Dashan left to make the long trek. The streets outside were emptier than they had been earlier in the night, though the air was still warm.

Cayr was silent on the walk. Alyx felt for him—he was no doubt dreading the coming confrontation with his father. Hopefully word wouldn't spread about what had happened, though it seemed doubtful one of the guards wouldn't tell the story.

"Are you okay?" Dashan ventured after a long silence.

Alyx snorted, determinedly not looking at him. "I don't want to talk to you right now."

"I owe you an apology."

"Your behaviour was appalling."

"It was," he said. "It won't happen again, I promise you that."

"I believe you." She sighed.

Dashan glanced ahead to where Cayr walked. "Do you think he's forgiven me?"

"I can hear you." Cayr's voice floated back. "And yes, I've forgiven you, although I'm going to think twice next time you try and convince me to spend a night out with you."

"Noted," Dashan called back.

Another short silence fell, and this time Alyx broke it. "You went sailing this past week, didn't you?"

"Yep, up the coast and back."

"I went looking for you at the barracks. Tijer told me you hadn't reported in like you were supposed to—that you were still suspended because you refused to apologise to Dunnat."

He shrugged, features set in his most stubborn expression. "I have nothing to apologise for. None of us do. And I needed some time to myself. The ocean soothes me."

"I think you need to learn to swallow your pride."

"This coming from you?" Dashan raised his eyebrows.

"It's what I've been doing this past week," she said. "And it galls me, but it's the right thing to do. As much as I might dislike Casovar, he's working to protect us."

Dashan looked away, jaw clenching.

"What good are you to anyone if you get kicked out of the Guard?" she went on.

"What good am I to anyone in the Guard?"

"Stop it," Alyx said angrily, forcing him to halt beside her. "I know that nobody has ever thought much of you, but you need to rise above that. You are a good man and a skilled warrior, so behave like it."

The hardness melted out of Dashan's face and he smiled down at her. "You think I should apologise to Dunnat?"

"I do."

"I'll think about it," he promised.

"Alyx is right." Cayr had slowed up without them realizing. "You're a worthwhile man, Dashan. I hope one day you start believing that."

"Thanks, my friend." Dashan clapped him warmly on the back.

Comfortable silence fell, and lasted until they arrived at the gates to the Egalion estate. Dashan lingered with the Bluecoats, leaving Cayr and Alyx a moment alone.

"Good luck with your father," she told him.

"He'll be angry, and so he should be." Cayr shrugged. "It means he'll keep me busy for a while so it could be a few days before I see you again."

"Do what you need to do. I'm not going anywhere yet."

He kissed her on the cheek. She leaned into him, despair uncurling in her stomach and spreading through her veins like heavy lead. His touch was warm but it didn't make her feel. She didn't initiate anything further, and he accepted that with a resigned smile before walking away. The relief she felt at that only sent the dread flying into guilt. She gathered up the emotion and fashioned it into resolve.

It was time to stop hiding from the truth.

. . .

ALYX'S FATHER was in the foyer when she came in, the wide space lit only by two lamps. In the shadows cast by the nearest lamp he looked drawn, with faint shadows under his eyes. She wondered if he'd been waiting for her.

"Safia told me you came home early for dinner tonight so we could eat together, so I thought I'd wait up for you," he answered her unspoken question. "I'm sorry I wasn't here."

"It's all right. I know you have a lot on your mind." She paused. "I don't like fighting with you, Papa."

"Me neither." He came closer, serious face creasing into a smile. "Did you have a good night, Aly-girl?"

"It was... interesting. Tarrick decided to stay down with the twins rather than walk all the way back up here." Telling him what had happened probably wasn't the best way to resolve the tension between them. He would find out soon enough on his own. "Is everything all right with you?"

He sighed, and her heart sank at the weary note in it. Her father was having a bad time, and she wished she could help somehow. "It's been a long day, after a whole series of long days. I missed you while you were gone, and now you're back I've barely seen you. I'm sorry."

"I understand how difficult things are for you." Maybe if she made him see that she truly did understand, he might confide in her, trust her more. "There's no easy resolution to the tightrope we're walking with Shivasa, and Lord-Mage Casovar is encroaching on the influence you once had with the king. On top of that, you've had to send your daughter away to a place where you can't protect her and learned that your son has been in Widow Falls all these years."

"You've really been thinking about this." Approval filled his voice, warming her.

"Not when I first came back," she admitted. "Dawn helped me see things from your perspective. I wish you would let me help you."

"You can help by not being at war with Casovar." He smiled a little, drawing her towards him. "And by giving me a hug occasionally."

"I can do that." She wrapped her arms tightly around him and held

87

on for a long moment before stepping back. "And I can hold my temper for a few weeks before we go back to DarkSkull."

"I'm glad to hear it," he said dryly. "Not that it makes me feel any better to know that you'll be going away for another year. You must be enjoying your extended time back at home?"

He framed it as a question, obviously seeing something in her face. When she didn't immediately say anything, he waited patiently, giving her space.

"While I was away, I had certain expectations about how things would be when I came home, but... " She stopped, shaking her head. "Can I ask you something?"

"You can ask me anything. I hope you know that."

"When you met my mother... when you married her... how did you know that she was the one for you?"

He rocked back on his heels at her question, which had clearly not been what he was expecting. "That has a long and complicated answer, I'm afraid."

"Can you try?"

"I can." He was quiet a moment, eyes cast skyward as he thought it over. "I suppose the best way to explain it was that whenever your mother was around, I felt alive. It was this noticeable thing—whenever we were together, or even if she was just in the same room, I felt more energised, happier somehow. And then when we were apart, the world went quiet. It's been quiet for so long," he added sadly.

His pain was a tangible thing, and the echo of it whispered through her as his words resonated strongly. "Thank you," she whispered, reaching out to squeeze his hand. "I'm so sorry that you had to go through that."

He gave her a little smile. "Hearing the news that your mother was dead was the worst thing I've ever experienced. But I've had you all these years, my darling girl, and I wouldn't give that up for the world."

"I'm here for you, if you ever want to talk, or if you just want company."

"Thank you," he said, then frowned as he studied her face. "Are you all right, Aly-girl?"

"I know you've been worried about Cayr and me, and about my expectations there."

Once again he seemed taken aback by the change in subject. "All I want is to prevent you being hurt. A courtship—a marriage—with a future king is no easy thing."

"I know." Her voice turned bleak despite her best efforts. The despair was back, weighing down her shoulders so that she had to take a deep breath to get enough air. She hadn't cared that it would be hard, she'd only wanted Cayr. But now she didn't, not anymore, and admitting that to herself was harder than anything she'd ever done. Even now she clung to it, trying to rationalise, to tell herself she did love Cayr, that he made her happy. Sadness welled—but he didn't make her feel alive. Someone else did.

"Alyx?" Garan seemed to sense her emotion, his voice laden with concern.

"I don't think you need to worry about that anymore," she whispered. The words loosened something in her, a final honest acknowledgement to herself that she would never marry Cayr. She couldn't. The Alyx that had spent the last two years at DarkSkull, that had suffered and struggled and made it through stronger... she wasn't in love with Cayr Llancarvan.

Her father's frown deepened, but she leaned up to hug him before he could speak. "I'm really tired, Papa. I'll see you in the morning."

He held her tightly before letting her go, and she could sense his troubled gaze on her back as she walked up the stairs and down the long corridor to her rooms. Once the door closed behind her, she leant back against it and allowed the tears to fall.

She wasn't sure whether the intensity of her sadness was due to her father's grief or her no longer denying the fact that the final part of a dream that had once made her so happy was gone, and that future along with it. Whatever it was, her tears fell for a long time that night.

CHAPTER 9

The storm of emotion had mostly passed by morning, and she'd even managed a few hours of bone-tired sleep before dawn. As she'd sobbed until her head and chest ached, she'd worried that she might not recover, that this disappointment and grief wouldn't end. But when she did wake, she almost felt lighter at no longer denying the truth to herself, even though the grief at letting go formed a still-tender scar in her chest.

Her father looked up when she joined him at breakfast. "I didn't expect to see you up so early given how late you came in last night."

"Lord-Mage Casovar will expect us at the usual time." Alyx smiled wryly, robbing the sting out of her next words. "I'm following orders like a good girl, Papa, don't worry."

Garan sighed and put down his spoon. He pushed his bowl of porridge away and turned to face her. "You know I appreciate that, but last night you looked... down. Is everything all right?"

"There are some things I've been working through," she admitted.

"Anything I can help with?"

"You already have." She hesitated, about to say more when Safia appeared, carrying a sealed note for her father.

Alyx turned to her food while her father took the note and broke the seal. A frown passed over his face—so quickly if she hadn't been glancing at him at the right moment she'd have missed it—before he put it aside and returned to his breakfast.

"Who was that from?" she asked lightly. Demanding direct answers from her father wasn't working, so she decided to try a subtler approach.

"The prince." Garan spooned up another mouthful of porridge, and if Alyx hadn't noticed the frown, there'd have been no way for her to tell something in the note had bothered him.

She summoned a teasing smile. "Since when does Cayr write to you instead of me?"

"When it's something on behalf of his father." Garan chuckled, again giving no indication anything was wrong.

"So it was a message from the king then?"

"Not really. Our prince is going away unexpectedly. We've been working on a project together and he was asking me to keep an eye on it while he's gone."

For a moment she wasn't sure which part of that sentence to pursue first. Cayr leaving? And what project?

"I don't suppose you know why the prince is heading south so unexpectedly?" Garan asked before she could. "You were with him last night. Did he mention anything?"

"No." She cleared her throat. There was an excellent chance the king was sending Cayr away as punishment for being arrested, but the less her father knew about that the better. "Is it really that unexpected?"

"Not entirely. The king has been wanting him to visit the southern lords, and apparently there's some minor issue with the Brennan counting houses he wants the prince to deal with." Garan flashed her a smile. "It's just that usually there's a lot more planning that goes into these official trips."

Alyx smiled in shared amusement. "Yes, it does take time for the Bluecoats to polish their swords to a bright-enough sheen."

They ate in companionable silence for a little while, her father looking more relaxed than she'd seen him since returning home. As much as she hated to change that, it seemed like the best opportunity to talk to him about the Mage Guard.

"Papa, can we talk about Casovar and the Mage Guard?"

His relaxed air immediately vanished and she could tell from the look on his face as he opened his mouth to reply that he was going to give her another non-answer.

"You have to know about the raids," she said softly. "And no matter what you tell me, I know you, and you can't agree with what they're doing."

"The situation is complicated."

"Then explain it to me." When he began shaking his head, she pushed. "I'm doing what you've asked me to do, despite how hard it is, but I think I deserve to know why. Why are you standing back and allowing Casovar so much influence? Why haven't you done something about the Mage Guard?"

"You're assuming I'm standing back," he said quietly. "I ask you to trust that whatever I'm doing, it's in your and Rionn's best interests."

Alyx leaned forward. "There was a moment, during the last year at DarkSkull... I was on the ground and I was hurt. And in that moment, I had to decide whether I would continue to take the punishment and accept whatever happened to me, or whether I would stand up and fight back." She took a breath. "I chose to fight back, Papa, and in doing that I found a strength inside myself I didn't even know was there."

He reached over to take her hand, worry filling his face. When he opened his mouth—surely another useless apology—she shook her head. "I need you to understand that I can't put away that strength I found. It burns in me. And if something is wrong here, if there's something I can do about it, you have to let me help."

"You are helping," he assured her with such vigour she truly believed him. Even so, she couldn't help thinking about what was happening to those in the poor quarter.

"You're asking me to stand by and do nothing while people are getting hurt. I don't know if I can do that."

His gaze bored into hers, firm and steady. "I'm asking you to trust me, to trust in who I am, even though it's difficult. Will you do that, Aly-girl?"

She sat back with a sigh. "Part of me thinks you just love the fact I have to bite my tongue on a daily basis around that man," she grumbled. "Teaching me a lesson?"

"Me, never!" He gave her his innocent face.

She chuckled and pushed back her chair. "I should go. Lord-Mage Casovar doesn't appreciate tardiness."

ALYX RODE TINGO across the palace grounds and left him in the stables, noting that the others' horses weren't there yet. Her choice to ride instead of walk to make up time had worked better than she'd thought. Or maybe Finn's hangover had led to a late departure for Tarrick and the twins as well. She smiled in amusement at the thought.

As she approached Casovar's offices, she spotted a familiar tall figure leaning over the balustrade, looking out into the gardens. No longer instinctively ignored, delight curled in her stomach at the sight of him, followed quickly by a spark of anticipation that accompanied a flutter of nerves. For so long she'd denied the possibility of anything more than friendship with Dashan, but now it was hers if she wanted it. And despite the nerves turning her stomach into knots and the guilt over Cayr still lingering, there was absolutely no doubt in her of Dashan's feelings. It was part of what made her feel so safe around him —that despite their differences and bickering, he never gave her cause to doubt that he would always stand by her.

"Hello stranger." She joined him at the railing.

He returned her smile, and her heart did a lazy flip in her chest. "Good morning, mage-girl."

"What brings you to this dusty old corner of the palace?"

"I came to apologise to Captain Dunnat. One of his soldiers said he was on duty here this morning, though he doesn't seem to have arrived yet."

Alyx smile widened. "You did, huh?"

"It doesn't solve anything." His fist curled on the stone, shoulders stiffening. "I know you spoke with Tijer and Casta, what you asked them to do. And they told me what they found out."

"We'll make it right, Dash. Somehow. I promise you." And she reached out to cover his hand with hers. It was an unconscious gesture, but once she'd done it, she made no effort to take her hand away. His fist uncurled at her touch, their fingers tangling together. Dashan had gone still at her side, but all the stiffness had melted from his shoulders. Unconsciously, they'd shifted closer to each other, so close their arms were pressed together and it would only take an infinitesimal movement to kiss him.

"I think we should stop pretending there's nothing between us," she murmured, her heart flipping again at the look of warmth and surprise that flared in his dark eyes. "Because I've stopped pretending that I want to be with Cayr."

"Lady Egalion?"

Alyx yanked her hand from Dashan's and spun so quickly she almost tripped, grateful that their posture had hidden their joined hands. Jenna stood a short distance off, wearing a polite smile. Dashan turned more gracefully, but a quick glance showed a slightly dazed expression on his face. Alyx cleared her throat, rapidly trying to regain clarity of thought, and finding that rather easy to do at being faced with Casovar's beautiful adopted daughter. Her ability to make Alyx feel like an ungainly clod in her presence hadn't faded at all with time.

She wondered if the young woman remembered their last encounter, where Alyx had threatened to burn Jenna's golden hair to cinders. Judging from the sharp look in Jenna's blue eyes, she remembered it perfectly.

"Lady Casovar." Alyx spoke just as politely. "Hello."

"I apologise for interrupting your conversation," Jenna said. "But it's nice to see you. We organised a welcome home picnic for you, but you didn't come. In fact, you haven't come to see us at all."

Alyx summoned an equally polite but utterly insincere tone. "Yes, I know, and I'm sorry for that. Your father has kept me very busy."

"I understand." More polite falseness, this time with a sickly-sweet smile added for good measure. "The protection of Rionn is a serious matter."

"It certainly is."

"Lieutenant Caverlock." Jenna tilted her head. "This is a strange place to find an officer of the Blue Guard."

"Not one who needs to speak to your father's captain," Dashan said easily. "I'm waiting for him."

"I see." Jenna dismissed him from her notice. "Lady Egalion, you wouldn't happen to know where Prince Cayr is, would you?" Her smile took on a superior quality. "We had planned a breakfast together this morning, but he's late and I thought he may have been caught up with my father."

"Actually, my father received a note this morning to say he's left the city for a trip to visit the southern lords," Alyx said, ignoring Dashan's start of surprise beside her.

Jenna frowned. "That's sudden."

"Yes." A smile curled at her mouth. "He must have forgotten to let you know in the rush to leave."

"Oh." Jenna exuded disappointment.

Unable to help herself, Alyx widened her smile and added a touch of superiority to her voice. "I suppose you haven't seen much of him lately, what with him spending most of his time with us."

Beside her, Dashan cleared his throat in suppressed amusement, while Jenna's gaze turned wintry cool. "Indeed. Have a nice day, Lady Egalion."

They were both silent as Jenna rounded the corner and disappeared. An amused smile lit up Dashan's face as he turned to her. "You really can be a superior snot, Lady Egalion."

She shrugged. "She brings out the worst in me."

There was a momentary awkward silence as they stared at each other, then Dashan gave a little smile. "She kinda killed the moment, huh?"

She laughed, awkwardness entirely broken, and lightness filling her. This was what she wanted, what she needed—Dashan always, always making her mood brighter no matter how awful she felt. Reaching out for his hand, she murmured, "Come with me."

She led him, unresisting, down into the garden and over to a small alcove shielded from prying eyes by the vibrant green leaves of a weeping tree. The expression of dawning hope and adorable confusion on his face gave her the courage to be completely honest.

"I meant it," she told him steadily. "I was going to talk to Cayr today, but now I'll have to do it as soon as he gets back. Cayr's not who I want."

Dashan took a step closer, voice aching with restrained joy. "Alyx, are you telling me you want us to be together?"

Instead of replying, she leaned up to press her mouth against his. He didn't hesitate for a second, returning the kiss with a passion that had her heart racing and heat flooding her body. This was nothing like the kisses she'd shared with Cayr. This was so much more that she didn't even have words for it.

Part of it was how real it all was. This wasn't a fantasy built up in her head over years about her best friend, this was dropping her walls and allowing someone in who knew her better than anyone else in the world—the woman she'd become, not the one she'd once been. And it was easy, because she'd never had to be anything or anyone else other than herself with Dashan.

His hands slid up her back, then entangled fiercely in her hair. She gasped, arching her neck so he could trail kisses down her skin before returning his mouth to hers. Eventually they broke apart, panting softly, their foreheads gently touching. Alyx took both his hands, squeezing softly, eyes slipping shut at the sensation of his warm skin enclosed in hers.

"Are you sure?" Dashan breathed, his words dancing over her cheek.

"I'm not in love with him," she whispered the painful truth. "I want to be, but I'm not. I've changed, I don't know if I was ever really in love with him, or if I mistook friendship for love."

"And me?" His shifted back slightly, eyes searching her face, lighter than she'd ever seen them.

She huffed a laugh. "I don't even know how this is possible. You irritate me, I irritate you. We argue constantly."

"You know that's not true anymore."

A small smile curled her lips. "I like fighting with you."

"In case it's not clear, I want this," he said with such sincerity her heart lurched. "Yes, you irritate me, but you also challenge me, make me want to be better. You have no idea how strong and smart and beautiful you are."

She smiled, turning her head up to capture his lips again. They kissed more slowly, taking their time. She wondered whether she'd ever get enough of this wonderful feeling, like she was floating and falling all at the same time.

Eventually she had to pull back for air, smiling up into his handsome face. "Can it just be the two of us, just for a short time?" she asked. "I mean, I know we'll have to tell people eventually, but I need some time to let this... how I feel ...settle."

He smiled, brown eyes soft and warm as he regarded her. "I think that can be arranged."

Alyx stepped away as her magic warned her that Dawn was approaching with the others. Her irritated thoughts were leaking out loudly. "Go and apologise to Dunnat—he's arriving with Tarrick and the twins. I'll see you tonight?"

"I'm looking forward to it." He winked at her, then walked away.

Alyx stayed where she was, needing several deep breaths to calm her heated skin and racing heartbeat. And like she had when first waking, she felt lighter, almost weightless with a slowly uncurling happiness.

She was smiling as she went to face Casovar for the day.

CHAPTER 10

A whisper of unshielded thought coming from the gardens behind her house had Alyx reaching instantly for her staff. It was late, and she was halfway back from the stables after checking on Tingo before turning in for the night. Her first instinct was to send her telepathic magic out to warn Tarrick, but by then she'd recognised who the thoughts belonged to.

Curiosity and anticipation mingling, she turned away from the front doors, her boots crunching on the pebbled drive as she walked around the side of the mansion and through a gate into the back gardens.

"Brynn?" Why was it he was always showing up when she least expected it?

The blond mage stepped out from the shadows of a large tree, grinning at the look on her face. "Fancy meeting you here!"

Alyx stared at him for a moment. She wasn't entirely sure whether she was still angry at him, or genuinely pleased to see him. In the end she decided it was a mix of both. Learning he'd been hunting Taliath potentials in his job as a council spy had horrified her, but she believed him when he'd told her he hadn't known the council was planning to murder them.

"Are you going to stand there staring at me all night?" he inquired eventually.

"I don't even know where to start," she said dryly. "What are you doing here?"

"That's an easy one." He brightened. "By fortunate coincidence, I was visiting my family when Captain Rodin delivered your hastily written note to Sarah."

"I didn't think you'd get that for months, or that you'd make sense of it if you did." Alyx made a face. "Dashan wouldn't give me more than a few minutes in Weeping Stead on the way out."

"I did understand it, and I went to see Romas the next day. I told him that all the travelling the council had me doing was wearing me down and I needed a break, a new assignment." Brynn's mouth quirked. "I had to use every inch of mage power I possess to convince him."

"Are you sure he was convinced?" she asked sceptically. Brynn's magic was in his voice, but even so, Romas was no fool.

"Not completely, but it's plausible enough. I've been travelling nonstop for almost two years tracking... well, you know what I was doing." Brynn's face turned momentarily dark. "I exaggerated how exhausted I was, how I needed to be in one place, even if just for a little while. I even implied I was thinking of leaving the mage order because it was getting to be too much."

"And what did they say to that?" Her scepticism deepened. Romas wasn't exactly one to care about individual mages' wellbeing.

"Here's where it gets weird. They asked if I'd be willing to come here and work for the council as a spy in Alistriem."

"You're telling me Romas not only believed you about wanting a break, he then suggested you travel to Alistriem where I just happen to be?" She scoffed. "What are they up to?"

"I swear, I don't know." He raised both hands in the air. "But here are some things I do know. Galien will pass his trials soon—within weeks he'll be a fully-fledged mage warrior spending all his time working for the council. I imagine that means there is less need for what I was doing, because Galien will be able to hunt and track himself, and will probably do it more efficiently given the number of magical abilities he possesses."

Alyx's stomach turned at the thought of Taliath potentials being killed more efficiently, but Brynn was right. "Go on."

"I also know the council doesn't have good coverage of Rionn. And I know that the council is aware that we're good friends." He gave a bitter smile. "I've been authorised to tell you I'm alive."

Alyx laughed, but there was no warmth in it. "They think your friendship with me will give you better access into Rionn."

"That's where logic takes me." Brynn sighed.

"How long have they posted you here? I'll be heading back to DarkSkull in a few weeks."

"They told me it could be months, but weren't any clearer than that."

"I'm glad," she said. "Despite all the council's machinations, I feel better knowing that you'll be here after I'm gone. I worry about my father, and Cayr."

"You know I'll do my best to look out for them." Brynn craned his neck as he studied his surroundings. "Nice place you have here. A little larger than mine."

"I liked yours better."

"Really?"

"It was warm, and cozy, and filled with people who love you. I love my home, but this place is big and, at times, cold."

Brynn grinned again and held up a hand, revealing a bottle of cider that had been hidden in his robes. "I've got something that will make us warm and cozy. Want some?"

She glanced up at her bedroom window, where her large, comfortable bed and thick quilt awaited her. It was dark in there though, and empty. Tarrick had already gone to bed and her father was still at the palace. And while weariness tugged at her, she'd missed Brynn.

"I'd love some."

They settled down at the base of the tree, leaning against it and stretching their legs out before them. Brynn took a swig from the bottle and passed it to Alyx, who did the same. The cider was an equal mix of sweet and bubbles, and the alcohol warmed her from the inside out.

"How's Dashan?" Brynn asked casually.

"Why do you have such a fixation... " Alyx spun towards him, mouth falling open as she caught a tendril of his thoughts. "You knew!"

"It was bloody obvious." He beamed unabashedly. "What about Cayr?"

"He's a subject I don't plan on discussing with you, apart from saying he's away from the city right now."

"But you and Dashan are..." He waggled his fingers.

She raised her eyebrows. "What does that mean?"

"You know." He waggled them again.

"I don't. Nobody knows what that means," she said primly.

"Ha! I don't need you to tell me, anyway. You have that look on your face."

"What look?"

"The look I had after the first time that Sarah and I..."

"Dash and I haven't gotten anywhere near that far yet," Alyx said hastily.

"Yet?" He raised his eyebrows in amusement. "So you plan for it to happen?"

"No! I mean..." She glared at him. "Shut up."

He looked away. "That's probably a good thing."

Alyx frowned at him. Brynn sounded unusually sober. "Can we please stop talking about Dashan?"

"Sure. Tell me what's been happening here? I only arrived yesterday."

Alyx related everything, giving him a rough overview of their experiences of Casovar and concern about the Mage Guard.

"Hmm."

"That's all you have to say?"

"I haven't spoken to the lord-mage yet, and probably won't, so I'll take your word for what he's like."

Alyx was confused. "Why won't you be speaking with Casovar?"

"I'm here as a council representative, and Casovar is no longer a council mage." Brynn shrugged. "My mandate isn't the protection of

Rionn, it's the protection of the mage order. Which reminds me, there's another thing I have to tell you."

"Do I want to know?" she asked sourly.

"You might like this piece of news." Brynn rolled his eyes. "My priority here is to carry out tasking for the council and report back. However, I have been told that when I have capacity, I'm to undertake any tasking that you may have for me."

"You're kidding?" Alyx stared at him in astonishment.

"I'm very serious."

"Then I want you watching the Mage Guard," she said without hesitation. When he raised his eyebrows at her eagerness, she gave him a more detailed accounting of the situation. "Cayr promised he was looking into it, but he's away from the city indefinitely. My father insists he's got the situation under control, but if we can get proof of the Mage Guard going too far, he could take it straight to the king. I'll talk to Tarrick tomorrow, but I'm sure he'll agree."

"You can't." He was already shaking his head. "Romas was very clear on that. We're to tell nobody else of my existence."

"I can't keep lying to them about this. Do you have any idea how happy they would be to know you're alive?" The longer she kept the secret, the more pain she caused her friends.

"You have to," he said helplessly. "I'm only useful as a spy if nobody knows I'm here. Do you really want word getting to Casovar that the Mage Council has a spy in Alistriem? Particularly since you clearly don't trust him yet."

Alyx sighed, letting her head fall back against the rough bark of the tree. "Great. More secrets. More lies."

ANOTHER SEVERAL DAYS passed before Casovar broached the topic of their summons again. They'd been home just over two weeks and apart from reviewing reports and training with Casovar, no other work had eventuated. While having extra eyes to get through the high number of reports that came in each day was no doubt useful for the lord-mage, Alyx wondered whether it really had warranted summoning them home early from DarkSkull.

Part of her didn't care. As condescending and arrogant as Casovar was, having the longer break from the harsh learning environment at DarkSkull wasn't the worst thing in the world. At least she didn't have to study for tests every day and face Rothai every morning. And being so far away from the council was a relief she hadn't anticipated. Not feeling the bitter tide of anger that twisted in her chest every time she had to deal with Romas or think about how the council operated was a heavy weight off her shoulders.

The door opened, breaking Alyx from her thoughts. Casovar walked through carrying a large rolled map under his arm. He gestured for them to join him at the map table as he spoke. "I'd like to discuss further the reason I recalled you back here early."

Alyx and the twins glanced at each other in surprise as he unrolled the map onto the table and took a seat. Tarrick instantly leaned over it, frowning slightly as his eyes ran over the detail.

"My decision to bring you home from DarkSkull was prompted by information I received indicating the Shiven leader has appointed a new commander for his army, and that they are planning to annex the disputed area," Casovar said.

"Information from where?"

"How credible is the information, sir?"

Alyx and Tarrick spoke at the same time, and she cast a rueful glance in his direction. Unsurprisingly, Casovar chose to answer Tarrick's question.

"Initially, I questioned the source," he said. "But I subsequently received complementary information in a different report. I am confident it is accurate."

"If Shivasa tries to take the disputed area by force, that will be tantamount to a declaration of war," Finn said.

Casovar's thin eyebrows drew together as he frowned. "Not quite. The disputed area is after all named that way for a reason. Shivasa will insist they are merely reclaiming their own territory."

"Maybe so, sir, but that can't be all they want," Tarrick said.

"You are right, Apprentice. If it were just the disputed territory they were after, then why the attacks in Tregaya over the last twelve months?"

"You mean the attacks on DarkSkull Hall?" Dawn said carefully.

"Yes, King Mastaran apprised the king of them when he was in Carhall," Casovar agreed, giving no indication he knew they'd been involved in defending against the attacks. Alyx gave a small sigh of relief. "No doubt Shivasa's end game is to expand its territories, and Rionn is in the weakest position. Our army does not match the might of Zandia, nor do we have the same strength in mage power that Carhall possesses. They will come for us first."

This was the first inkling Alyx had had of why the king had grown to rely on Casovar so much. As a mage of the higher order, he was worth an army of mage warriors. He also clearly had good information sources.

"Do you know anything about the new army commander, sir?" Finn asked.

"No," Casovar said quickly, looking down at a point on the map. "I have my sources trying to obtain any information they can."

"How can we help?" Dawn asked.

"Since your return, I've been developing a better understanding of your skills and abilities. I will be deploying you to the disputed area to help in holding the Shiven back. If they annex the disputed area completely, Rionn will be in serious trouble. You will be my mage force in the field, similar to the way that the Zandian emperor deploys his trained mages."

Shock flared on all their faces, and Alyx spoke up before thinking. "Sir, we're not even close to being fully trained. We technically haven't even finished our second year."

"You don't need to be at DarkSkull to continue your training," he said brusquely, rolling up the map. "I am a mage of the higher order with many years' experience. There is no better teacher for you."

"I don't see how you can teach us if we're deployed to the disputed area," she pushed.

Irritation clouded his features. "You won't be permanently out in the field, Apprentice."

A silence fell. Alyx wanted to look at the others to see their expressions, but controlled herself. It was Finn who broke the silence, speaking aloud what they were all starting to realise.

"You never intended for us to go back to DarkSkull at all, did you, sir?"

"No. The sooner you accept that you belong to me, Apprentices, the better off you'll be," Casovar said, letting the words resound through the shocked silence.

Alyx's fury at his claim of ownership literally made her hands shake. She kept her eyes downcast as she fought for control, fists white-knuckled at her sides, doing everything she could to keep from showing him her anger. This was what I chose, she told herself determinedly. I chose to go back to DarkSkull to be a mage.

When none of them protested, Casovar gave a satisfied nod. "You'll be leaving tomorrow for the disputed area. Please pack a bag and be down on the military dock at least a half hour before dawn to meet the army captains travelling with you. The ship will leave on the dawn tide."

"Sir, I understand that we're here to help you in defending Rionn," Tarrick said quietly. "But I have to emphasise that we are not trained warrior mages."

"And I'm not sending you into battle, Apprentice, not yet," Casovar said. "You're going up there to familiarise yourselves with the area and integrate with the army. You'll only be there a few weeks, then I'll bring you back to continue your training. If and when the Shiven move in force against the disputed area, I'll reassess your role."

"Yes, sir." Tarrick nodded.

"Oh, and one more thing," Casovar said as they stood. "Any more drunken incidents like the one last week, and you'll regret it severely. Am I clear?"

Alyx took a step forward without thinking, her fists clenched so hard at her sides that her nails dug painfully into her palms. Casovar's glance caught hers, mocking her, daring her to make a move against him. Her anger screamed to be let out, making her stomach roil as she held it in. But by responding, she'd be letting him win.

"Something you wanted to say, Alyx?" he asked politely.

"No, sir." Her voice came out admirably calm. "I'll be at the docks tomorrow morning, as you requested."

"It won't be necessary for you to bring a bag," Casovar said coolly.

"There's no point in deploying a useless mage to the borders. You'll stay here and continue working with the Mage Guard."

Fury at the insult to her pride flared so strongly it was on the tip of her tongue to admit what she was, put him back in his place, but the challenge in his grey eyes stopped her. A reaction was what he wanted... and until she understood why, she refused to give it to him.

She hated it, was disgusted with herself for doing it, but bowed to his authority. "Yes, sir."

And on the heels of her impotent frustration came worry for her friends. They were going away into danger without her power there to protect them. Her stomach sank and she had to bite her lip and force a smile as Casovar left. As soon as he was gone, she turned and headed for the door, muttering something about needing air. None of them tried to stop her.

She couldn't keep doing this. Not indefinitely.

CHAPTER 11

Outside it was mid-afternoon, a hot sun and still air shrouding the palace in a heavy listlessness. Alyx's feet took her on a well-trodden path through the gardens, at first pounding in angry strides, then gradually slowing. Maybe it was the heat of the day, or the walk, but her anger began to fade, her thoughts instead turning to Casovar's revelation.

He wasn't sending them back to DarkSkull. They were potentially never going back to DarkSkull. Part of her thought this was the best news she'd ever gotten. No more Rothai or Romas, no more Mage Council. No tasteless breakfasts at dawn or tedious language classes.

Not having to leave home again.

It was always going to be this, after all. Eventually she and the twins were going to be back in Alistriem, trained mages and working for Casovar and the king. Only this way it would be Casovar completing their training, not DarkSkull. That fact would infuriate the council, of course, but that hardly bothered Alyx—in fact it gave her a spark of amused satisfaction.

But that meant Casovar completing Alyx's training. And there was the rub. She'd have to tell him what she was. Until the council learned who was behind the disappearing mages, being a mage of the higher order was an extremely dangerous thing to be. And to willingly reveal herself to someone who she wasn't certain had her best interests at heart... no, it was too risky.

Her feet slowed further as she reached the garden leading to Cayr's bedroom window, her troubled mind having taken her there without thinking. Guilt merged with a kind of panic at the thought of the conversation she would have to have with him when he returned. One good thing about going back to DarkSkull was that he would have time away from her after she... wincing, Alyx forced herself to finish the thought—after she hurt him badly. And wouldn't she only be adding to the pain if she continued a relationship with Dashan in Alistriem, right in front of Cayr?

Shaking her head to try and dispel the confusion of her thoughts, Alyx turned around and headed back towards the mage offices. Hopefully Tarrick and the twins would be finished with their work and they could head into the city for a drink and a meal. A cold ale and the company of her friends seemed like the perfect antidote to the chaos in her head.

The rooms were empty of Mage Guard or anyone else, but the door to the garden stood ajar, and the faint murmur of voices trickled through in the sluggish afternoon air. Alyx followed the sounds, hoping she wasn't about to run into Dunnat and his men taking an afternoon break.

Instead she came upon Tarrick and the twins. Finn and Dawn stood opposite each

other, voices low but clearly engaged in an argument. Tarrick watched, a concerned frown on his face.

"I don't know why you're both making such a big deal of this." Finn's long-suffering tone indicated he'd made this point several times. "So he's unlikeable and rude. He's also a mage of the higher order charged with the defence of Rionn. That happens to be our job too. What did you think we were signing up for when we went to DarkSkull?"

"You're being as literal as always." Dawn's voice bled matching frustration. "What are you going to do when he sends us out to harass some innocent jeweller in the poor quarter? You really think a man who encourages behaviour like that is someone we should be following?"

"What are our options?" Finn challenged. "Leave here and sign up to work for the Mage Council? No, I didn't think so. Quit being mages? After everything we accomplished and learned at DarkSkull you want to give up now?"

"I'm not suggesting we—"

"Is everything all right?" Alyx cut over Dawn's furious rejoinder, hoping to end the argument.

All three pairs of eyes snapped to her. Dawn's were smoky with anger, Finn's determined, Tarrick unsure.

Finn huffed a laugh. "Tell me, Alyx, are you thrilled at this development because it means you never have to step foot in DarkSkull or deal with the Mage Council again, or are you horrified because your noble blood can't bear the thought of bowing down to Casovar?"

"A mix of both actually," she said mildly, refusing to allow him to bait her. "What's got you so riled up?"

"I'm so sick of pretending that being mages is going to consist of being pure and righteous and morally right all the time. It's not. The Mage Council is corrupt and far too concerned with holding onto its power. Casovar is just as hungry for power and arrogant and cold along with it. We have to work with one of them, and that's going to mean doing things we don't like."

Alyx stared, completely taken aback by the passion in his voice. She'd been unaware how deeply he felt about this. Nobody seemed to know how to respond, and the tense silence was thankfully broken by the appearance of Dashan.

"This is where the party's at, huh?" he said cheerfully. "Not the location I'd pick."

She couldn't help her smile at the sight of him. "What brings you here?"

"If you cast your minds back to last night's conversation, we agreed I would meet you all here after my shift ended so we could go out for a drink..." Some of the laughter in his face faded as he took in the scene. "Did someone die?"

"No. We got some interesting news from Lord-Mage Casovar," Alyx responded when no one else did.

Dashan opened his mouth to ask the obvious question, but then shook his head. "This isn't the best place to talk. Come on, let's get a drink and you can fill me in."

They filed back inside to find Dunnat had returned. He was standing over the map table, pointing out something to another one of his soldiers. He looked up at their entrance, face tightening in dislike.

"Captain!" Dashan lifted his hand in a jaunty wave.

"Lieutenant." Dunnat's face tightened further.

"Good to see you as always." Dashan's smile widened as he opened the door to let the others out. "We should do this again sometime. What do you think, some jugs? I hear the Foxhole is popular with you red-cloaked lot. It's a little... well... cheap for our tastes, but don't let it be said we Blue Guard can't get down in the gutter with our comrades every now and then."

"Get out of here, Lieutenant, before I do something you'll regret."

"Oh, Captain, we both know I'd take you in under ten seconds. Best keep that pretty sword of yours where it belongs, inside its pretty sheath."

Dashan smoothly swung the door shut as Alyx was the last to pass him, and an instant later all four of them were erupting into poorly-concealed giggles. For a precious few moments their shared mirth dispelled the tension that had enveloped them.

As the laughter finally died and they reached the palace gates, heading out and down into the city, Alyx tugged on Dashan's arm. "Nicely done."

He winked. "Any time, mage-girl."

"I'm sorry for getting so worked up." Finn muttered the apology before taking a long swallow of his ale. He'd sat stewing in silence while the other three filled Dashan in on the meeting with Casovar.

"I see the truth in what you're saying," Dawn said. "I struggle with it, that's all. I'm not convinced that Casovar is entirely on the right side of this. What about what the Mage Guard is doing? A man that allows his soldiers to behave like they do isn't to be trusted. And he lied today—when Tarrick asked him whether he knew anything about the new Shiven commander, he lied."

Alyx straightened in surprise.

"I thought you said his mental shield was seamless?" Finn said.

"It is. I didn't pick up his thoughts, only a whisper of emotion behind them.

It's hard to be certain, but he was momentarily uncomfortable," Dawn said.

"Maybe he was just upset that he doesn't have more detailed information?" Finn raised an eyebrow.

She scowled. "Fine. Yes, or maybe he had a sudden pressing need to use the privy."

Dashan snickered. Alyx shot a glare at him. The amusement on his face deepened.

"While I wholeheartedly agree with you Dawn, Finn is right, we can't disobey Casovar when he is so important to Rionn's security," Alyx said regretfully. "Particularly if he's right about the Shiven's invasion plans."

"What about the Mage Guard?" she pressed.

There was a moment of silence, nobody really sure how to answer her. Impotent anger continued to surge through Alyx whenever she thought about them hurting innocent citizens, and Cayr's sudden departure meant his promised review was on hold indefinitely. There was hope Brynn might come up with something, but she couldn't tell them about him.

"She's right," Dashan said. "If we do nothing about it, pretend nothing is wrong, we're as bad as they are."

"I'm not sure what we can do." Alyx sighed. "I've spoken to both Cayr and my father. But until we come up with something, we should continue to question whatever Casovar has us doing. And Tarrick, you should go back to DarkSkull. You need to finish your training."

He didn't reply immediately, contemplating the ale before him. He was torn. Becoming a warrior mage was what he wanted more than anything else, and by not going back to DarkSkull, he would be delaying that indefinitely.

"There is one way we could all go back," he suggested eventually. "We could choose to work for the council rather than your king."

"I will never work for the council," Alyx said with quiet finality. Neither of the twins gainsaid her.

He nodded, unsurprised. "Then I stay. Your protection is more important to me than anything, and it's not just because you're a mage of the higher order."

Tears pricked her eyes. Surely she didn't deserve friendship like that?

"You're not the only one who's learned what real friendship is," Dawn spoke into her mind.

Alyx swallowed and gave her friend a grateful look before turning back to him. "Tarrick, you continue to sacrifice what you want and what you believe in for me. It's time to stop. Your mage training is too important. I have protection already, not the least of which is another mage of the higher order. I would miss you terribly, but I want you to do what's right for you for once."

"You would be better protection for Alyx if you were fully trained," Finn pointed out. "After your trials you could come back here if it's what you still wanted."

Tarrick's face tightened. "I don't feel comfortable leaving you all here with Casovar, not yet. Dawn has a point about him."

"We're about to leave Alyx behind in the city," Finn said. "There's not much protecting you can do from the disputed area."

For a moment he didn't reply, the truth of Finn's words resonating into the silence. Tarrick's shoulders sagged, and he gave a little shake of his head. "The truth is, I don't know what I want. Since I can remember, I wanted to grow up and be like my brothers, a powerful warrior mage. Only I was going to work for the council rather than the emperor, establish myself, maybe one day even be on the council. Make my family proud." His voice trailed off. Alyx had never heard such raw emotion from Tarrick, and judging from the silence at the table, none of the others had either. "You're all my friends, and so I want to stay with you. It feels right. But I don't know if I'm ready to let go of my dream yet."

When he glanced up and saw them all staring raptly at him, he instantly stiffened, a hard expression closing down the openness that had been there. Recognising the depth of his discomfort, Alyx changed the subject.

"The bigger question is what to do about me?" She lowered her voice. "Casovar can't train me if he doesn't know what I am."

"He should be told," Finn said bluntly, earning a dark look from Tarrick. "If a bunch of murderous, corrupt council members know she's a mage of the higher order, why shouldn't Casovar know?"

"Will you keep your voice down!" Tarrick hissed.

"Sorry." Finn raised his hands in the air. "You know I'm right."

"I'm uneasy at the idea," Dawn admitted, giving her brother an apologetic look. "Something about Casovar makes me reluctant to tell him any more than he needs to know."

"While I appreciate you all looking out for me," Alyx interjected dryly. "It is my decision to make."

"What will you do?" Dashan asked, eyes dark as he regarded her.

"Wait a little longer," she said, raising a hand as Finn opened his mouth. "Your time in the disputed area will give you a better understanding of what he's up to, how he's going to use us. And while you're away, I'll make more of an effort here to work with him. I'll also do what I can about the Mage Guard. Once you return, we'll make the final decision together."

"The time will give us an opportunity to think about what we really want, as well," Dawn said thoughtfully, and although she was looking at Tarrick, her gaze seemed far away.

"For what it's worth, I agree with Alyx and Tarrick," Dashan offered. "We need to learn more before making any firm decisions."

Tarrick's smile flashed. "We?"

"Yeah." He shrugged slightly, glancing around the table. "We're a team, right?"

"Right." Alyx smiled across the table at him, warmed by the light in his brown eyes. He grinned back.

Conversation segued to Dashan's recent sailing trip, and news of the goings on amongst the Blue Guard. Alyx leaned towards Dawn and deliberately lowered her voice.

"How are you doing? I mean, I know this isn't just about Casovar for you. Not going back to DarkSkull means not seeing Rickin again anytime soon."

Dawn sighed. "I'm trying not to think about it too much. I miss him, and I looked forward to seeing him again, but it's not like we had a serious relationship."

"You could write to him?" Alyx suggested. "I'm sure Dashan wouldn't mind getting a letter to Captain Rodin—I know they agreed to stay in touch."

Dawn's face lit up. "That would be wonderful, thank you! Being able to explain why I'm not coming back would ease my mind."

"Good." Alyx smiled and leaned back. "Write the letter and I'll make sure Dash sends it."

A SHORT WHILE LATER, Alyx rose, claiming tiredness and stating she planned to go home for an early night.

"Sure, I'll see you at breakfast tomorrow." Tarrick smiled.

"You'll come and farewell us at the docks?" Finn asked hopefully, all his earlier anger seemingly gone, or at the very least smothered by several glasses of ale.

"I'll be there," she promised.

"I'm on duty tonight, so I'll walk you halfway." Dashan rose too, grabbing his jacket.

Alyx caught Finn's knowing look and summoned enough magic to spear a thought into his head strongly enough to make him wince. "Finn, we are friends, but some things are private."

He looked towards her, slightly shamefaced, and nodded. "Night, Alyx."

ONCE THEY WERE WELL clear of the inn, Dashan caught her hand and she leaned in to his side. "How does a night-time sailing trip sound?" he asked. "I promise to get you back early enough to sleep before tomorrow."

She smiled at the thought of having him all to herself, just the two of them for a few hours—those moments were so rare and precious—

but then heaved a regretful sigh. "It sounds wonderful, but I have a meeting."

"With who?" He frowned.

"I've been wanting to tell you—Brynn is here. The council has assigned him to Alistriem."

"I thought we were going to spend some time together?" He eyed her with amused impatience.

"We are." She grinned up at him. "We're going to spend time together at a meeting."

He scowled, but it was half-hearted. "Where are we going then?"

"The Cuttlefish Inn. I assume you've heard of it?"

"I dislike your tone, young lady." He sniffed. "I am not aware of every single drinking establishment in Alistriem."

"So you don't know it?"

"Well... "

Alyx laughed. "Sot."

"Snob," he shot back.

She chuckled and he dropped her hand, wrapping his arm around her shoulders instead and pulling her closer. Alyx pondered on the delightful strangeness of it as they walked; as much as she'd grown and changed in the past year, she was still very young when it came to men and courting. And Dashan was no boy, he was a grown man who'd had plenty of women in his bed before. She wondered how much he would want from her, and how soon.

"What's troubling you?" His voice broke through her thoughts.

"Nothing."

"You've got your thinking face on." He stopped them near the inn's entrance. "Talk to me."

"I'm not troubled," she explained. "I was thinking about us, and well... how different we are... in our experience."

It didn't take Dashan long to work out exactly what she was talking about, and when he did, he grinned openly. "Alyx, we've only been – whatever we are now – for a week. I'm hardly planning to push you up against that wall there and ravish you in full view of the public."

"I know that." She scowled at him.

"Hey." He caught her hand, turning serious. "I'm not looking for anything more than you're willing to give. I'll wait until you're ready. It doesn't matter to me how long that takes."

"I trust you," she told him. "I honestly was just thinking things over."

"Good." He leaned closer, his breath hot in her ear. "However, I am very much looking forward to the day when I can ravish you at a place of your choosing."

Alyx's heart thudded and she flushed hotly from head to toe. Dashan brushed his lips against her cheek, his grin telling her he knew exactly what effect he had on her.

"So cocky," she muttered, taking his hand as they went inside. They were halfway to the back room before her composure began to return.

Brynn's thoughts, deliberately left open, led Alyx to a small room at the back. A lamp hung from the ceiling, casting a flickering glow over the proceedings. The man himself sat in the room's only chair.

"This is all very mysterious and secretive," Alyx commented dryly as she entered.

"I am a spy." Brynn sighed, his green eyes brightening as Dashan came through the door behind her. "Hello, Dashan."

"It's good to see you again, Brynn." Dashan settled himself against the wall by the door. "And I approve of the room choice. Lovely waft of urine in the air."

Alyx looked around the dingy room with distaste and resigned herself not to touch anything. Who knew what she might catch. "I thought conducting secretive meetings in back rooms would actually make it pretty obvious you were a spy?"

"It was the best I could do at short notice. Next time we'll meet in the palace gardens in full view of your Blue Guard," Brynn said impatiently. "Now, why are we meeting?"

"Lord-Mage Casovar told us this morning he's not sending us back to DarkSkull," she said. "So firstly, I need you to get a message to Romas to let him know."

"Romas will be livid." Brynn frowned. "Not that I'm pleased about the idea either. Did he give you a reason?"

Alyx relayed the conversation they'd had with Casovar, her tone betraying her feelings on how he'd spoken to them.

"Apparently Alyx almost lost her temper and pulverized him with her fancy mage powers," Dashan added once she'd finished.

"Because he ordered me around like I was the servant who cleaned his shoes." She scowled.

"Well, lucky you're not, because I've seen you try to clean shoes before and it wasn't pretty."

"I can clean shoes just fine, Dashan."

"Sure you can."

"At least I know how to dress neatly. Have you seen your shirt lately? It looks like your horse ran over it, numerous times."

"My shirt is fine, thank you very much," Dashan said indignantly, one hand smoothing the material down his chest.

Brynn raised a hand. "Back to the subject at hand, why isn't Casovar sending you to the disputed area with the others?"

"He thinks I'm useless."

Dashan snorted and Alyx glared at him again. No matter how good it felt to kiss him, he was still horribly annoying.

"You haven't told him what you are?" Brynn considered that. "Probably a good thing if you don't trust him, but Alyx, enough people know now that he's going to find out sooner rather than later."

"I know. I'm surprised he hasn't already, to be honest."

Brynn's eyes narrowed. "I wonder if the fact the council hasn't told him is connected to why they want me here in Alistriem."

"This mage of the higher order thing, it really puts Alyx in that much danger?" Dashan was frowning.

"Yes, it does," Brynn said soberly.

"Why, exactly?"

"The council wants to harness her power for their own ends, but at the same time, they fear that she will become another Shakar. If they ever begin to think she's heading down that path, they'll kill her—hence murdering a bunch of innocent potential Taliath to prevent that possibility. On the other hand, something out there is killing powerful mages in increasing numbers. Nobody knows who yet, or why, but Alyx is a prime target because of how powerful she will be one day."

The words hung in the air, all the more shocking for their bluntness. She'd never heard the threat to her life spelt out so starkly before, and a shiver ran through her. Dashan straightened and reached out to Alyx in one movement, taking her hand and pulling her into his side. He wrapped both arms tightly around her.

"Hey," she said quietly. "I'm okay."

"I'm going to protect you," he swore fiercely. "They have to get through me before they get to you."

"Tarrick and the twins will protect her too, me included," Brynn said from his chair. His words were filled with sincerity, but his gaze was on Dashan as he spoke.

"I can protect myself," Alyx replied, trying to reassure the deep concern she read in Dashan's eyes. Gently, she pulled away from him, but stayed close, comforted by his warmth at her side.

He wasn't reassured. "What about these nightmares you've been having? We said we'd get help back in Alistriem but it's been over two weeks and we've done nothing."

She sighed, stepping away and rubbing at her suddenly throbbing temples. "The Mage Guard and all the changes here have distracted us."

"What nightmares?" Brynn asked.

"Alyx thinks someone is causing them," Dashan said flatly. "She had one on the way here and it was so bad she woke vomiting and shaking."

"Whoever it was spoke to me," Alyx said. "Warned me destruction was coming and I couldn't do anything to stop it."

Brynn glanced between them, face turning bone-white. "Who could be doing that?"

"We don't know." She shook her head.

"Okay." He took a breath. "How can I help?"

"One problem at a time." Alyx gathered herself. "Anything on the Mage Guard yet?"

"In two days?" He raised an indignant eyebrow. "No. It's at the top of my list though."

"Good. We also need to work out whether Casovar can be trusted. Can you find his sources and corroborate his information?"

"I'll do what I can."

Dashan shifted, his hand lightly touching her cheek and turning her to look at him. "And you'll talk to Lord Astor about your nightmares." He was wearing his stubborn expression, and a glance at Brynn showed similar insistence in his raised eyebrows and pointed look. No help there.

"Fine, yes, I'll talk to Astor," she relented. "Now, we'd best go before one or more of us catches something disgusting."

Brynn's mouth quirked. "I'll get a message to you when I find a better place to meet. Take care of yourself."

CHAPTER 12

I t was still dark outside when Alyx headed down for breakfast the next morning, and she was surprised to see her father already up. He was distractedly chewing on a piece of toast while studying the papers in front of him.

"Isn't it too early to be awake and working already?" she asked.

"Sleep was elusive, so I decided to get an early start." Her father frowned. "What's your excuse? Safia tells me Tarrick was up and out with a bag before I woke."

She poured milk into a cup of steaming tea and stirred it. "Did you know Casovar isn't planning to send us back to DarkSkull? He wants to finish our training himself."

Garan put down the paper he was reading and eyed her speculatively. "I didn't."

"He's sending Tarrick and the twins north to the border this morning, to help out in the disputed area. I didn't have to get up quite as early, but I'm going down see them off."

The look of unease on her father's face deepened. "Why isn't he sending you?"

"We haven't told him what I am—he thinks I only have a little magic, and am therefore useless," she said carefully, studying her father's face for his reaction. Either she was about to get a stern telling off, or...

"That's sensible, I suppose." He sighed, rubbing at his eyes.

"I knew it!" she said in triumph. "You don't trust him either. Otherwise you'd be reprimanding me severely right now for lying to Rionn's lord-mage."

His face tightened. "Maybe I'm just glad my daughter isn't being sent away into danger. No matter what you are, you're a long way from completing your training. I certainly wouldn't be sending a handful of half-trained mages barely out of childhood to fight on Rionn's behalf."

Her hand tightened on her teacup, but she fought hard to keep her voice even when she spoke. "When are you going to start believing that I'm not the spoiled, sheltered girl who left here two years ago? If there's a problem with Casovar, I deserve to know."

"And I've asked you to trust me!" The sharp words reverberated through the room. Garan's hands were curled, white-knuckled, on the table top—and all at once it was like they were back to her first night home, when he'd been full of an anger she didn't understand. It hurt that he wouldn't confide in her, wouldn't understand what she'd been trying to tell him ever since she got back. But getting angry with him wouldn't help him understand that, and it wouldn't help whatever it was he was going through.

So she let the words echo around them without responding, drained the last of her tea and pushed back her chair. Garan's eyes were fixed on the table before him, his look distant.

She walked to the door in silence, pausing at the threshold. "Maybe you might try trusting me, Papa."

IT WAS A BEAUTIFUL, cool morning and Alyx decided to walk and take the shortcut from the palace down to the docks rather than riding all the way through the city. The gardens of her home were silent and empty, a light mist hugging the ground and giving the world a hazy beauty. Dashan waited for her at the gate leading into the palace grounds, and the sight of him dispelled the mood of sadness and frustration that her encounter with her father had caused.

"What brings you here?" She arched an eyebrow, unable to help the smile that spread over her face.

"Tarrick asked me last night if I would mind escorting you down to the docks given he would be up and out earlier than you."

"Did he really think I was going to get attacked somewhere between here and the docks?" she said in mild irritation.

"He hates that he has to leave you here unprotected. But I am more than happy to take on those duties while he is gone." Smiling, Dashan leaned down to kiss her, and she wrapped her arms around his neck, pressing herself against him and losing herself in the joy of it all. When they finally parted, her breathing had quickened and his eyes were dark and full of the same happiness she felt. "Morning."

"Morning." She laughed.

After a moment, he took her hand and they started walking. It seemed as if they were the only two people in the world as they walked hand in hand through the misty gardens. Neither of them said much, content to be in each other's company.

"Can I ask you something?" she said.

"Always."

"I realised last night that I haven't asked how you feel about not going back to DarkSkull." She hesitated, searching his face. "It's what you wanted, isn't it?"

He squeezed her hand. "Yes, but mostly because that's where you would be."

"It's not only that. You were useful there. I know you loved being able to train the militia. You disappeared for a week after we got back because you were so upset at the idea of staying here and being confined to the Blue Guard."

"We both know there were other reasons I went away," he murmured.

She leaned into him, the echo of that pain flashing through her. "I'm sorry."

"Don't apologise, mage-girl." He smiled again. "And you know, it's not all bad. Commander Helson from Weeping Stead wrote a glowing letter to Commander Hawkwerst about our conduct in Tregaya. He mentioned me specifically. They're going to promote me to captain."

She stopped walking and regarded him with delighted surprise. "Dash, that's wonderful! Congratulations. Why didn't you mention it?"

He shrugged. "I didn't want to jinx it."

"It's not really what you want though, is it? You feel trapped in the Blue Guard."

"I've been thinking on that too." He started walking again and she fell in beside him. "If I keep my head down and work hard, there's a good chance I could reach commander level in a few years. Especially if I start behaving better towards my father."

She lifted an eyebrow. "That doesn't sound like the Dashan I know."

"I figured... " He cleared his throat, and this time it was him who stopped walking, his eyes firmly fixed on his boots. "A commander in the Blue Guard might be a more acceptable consort for... well... the daughter of a lord."

Alyx stared at him in shock, her mouth falling open before she realised it. "Dash, I—"

"I'm not trying to put pressure on you or assume anything," he said hurriedly. "I don't have any expectations, I promise."

She swallowed, her vision suddenly blurry from the tears in her eyes. He huffed out a surprised laugh when she threw her arms fiercely around his neck. "At least you're not yelling at me and running away," he murmured.

"Far from it," she said softly, holding on tightly a long moment. "But no matter what happens with us, I want you to be happy. I don't want you living a life you don't want just for me."

"I will take that under advisement. It's a long time in the future anyway." He took her hand again as they began walking. "Nothing we have to worry about now."

It was a long way off. She couldn't practically think about marriage until her mage training was done, even though a marriage to Cayr had been her single goal since the age of twelve or so. But this wasn't a young girl's innocent fantasy. Marriage to Dashan. The thought was both too big to wrap her head around and tantalising at the same time. Then a laugh burst unexpectedly from her chest. Dashan lifted his eyebrows at her and she grinned.

"We'd never stop fighting, Dash."

He laughed aloud and wrapped an arm around her shoulders. "The poor servants."

Neither of them mentioned the less amusing reality of a future together, that the daughter of Lord Egalion marrying a Bluecoat of any level was unlikely to ever be acceptable in the eyes of the court.

Soon they reached the narrow path down to the city worn away by the three children that they'd been with Cayr. The docks were busy; most of the fishing boats were coming in from the sea and unloading their morning catch. Dawn was breaking, and a pink glow cast a hazy light over the area.

They made their way to the army dock out to the west of the warehouses, and as they approached where they would meet the others, Dashan let go of her hand.

"Sorry," she said. Their relationship was still so new she wanted to wait a little longer before telling her friends. Not that she could imagine not wanting to be with him anytime in the near future—and that in itself was a scary thought.

"It's fine." He shrugged, appearing genuinely unconcerned.

Tarrick and the twins were waiting with their horses on the open jetty, each carrying a single large bag. Behind them, a long row of soldiers was slowly making its way across the gangplank and onto a moored ship. Alyx caught sight of a few red cloaks, indicating some of the Mage Guard were also travelling.

"Alyx, you came!" Dawn waved at her approach.

"Of course I did." Alyx hugged her.

"Dash! I need your input on something." Tarrick called out eagerly as he spotted Dashan.

"He can't decide whether to take his mage knife and a dagger, or just his mage knife." Dawn rolled her eyes. "I think I should go and pay attention or Dash will have him taking a whole arsenal."

Finn approached Alyx as Dawn left.

"Looking forward to your trip?" Alyx asked him. "Circumstances aside, you must be thrilled to be travelling somewhere you've never been."

"It should be interesting." The gleam in his eyes belied his casual shrug.

"I'll miss you all," she said. "Make sure you use that genius brain of yours to keep them safe."

"I will," he said, before clearing his throat awkwardly. "Look, Alyx, I'm sorry I keep poking at you about Dashan. You were right, some things are private and it's not my business. Accept my apology?"

"I could have been nicer about it," she apologised. "And it's not that I want to hide anything from you. Do you understand? I have a few things I need to work out, and it will take time."

He couldn't help himself, and a smirk crossed his face. "So if anyone asks, Lady Alyx Egalion is unattached and free to court whomever she pleases?"

"Exactly," she said firmly.

He sobered. "I'm truly sorry things didn't work out with Cayr. I sense that it's been your decision, but even so, it can't have been easy."

His sincerity demolished her defensiveness. "Thank you, Finn." She hesitated. "About yesterday—are you all right? I don't know if I've ever seen you so worked up about something that didn't involve Galien."

She regretted her question as soon as she saw the shadows return to his green eyes, but his tone was mild. "Sometimes I see things so clearly, more clearly than anybody else seems to. I try and explain, but you all resist so firmly to doing anything even remotely wrong, even Tarrick. I don't think it's sustainable, and I'm truly afraid of any of you getting hurt because of it."

"I can't speak for the others, but I resist because I refuse to be trapped into a certain way of things." Alyx shrugged. "I realise that's part of my arrogance, but sometimes I think it's the right thing to do."

"Maybe," he mused.

"I'll keep listening to you, though." She reached out to squeeze his arm. "Promise."

The shadows in his eyes vanished and a small smile crept over his face. Casovar appeared then, striding along the dock towards them, and all conversations died.

Alyx and Dashan stood back while the lord-mage gave Tarrick and the twins their final orders. They would be sailing north along the coast to the town of Gosper. From there, they would ride out to the border, escorted by a unit of Mage Guard the entire trip.

Alyx hugged them all as they stepped on board, even Tarrick, much to his embarrassment.

"We'll only be gone for two weeks," he snapped as he extricated himself from her hug.

"You'll miss me." She chuckled.

"Keep them safe, Tarrick." Dashan clapped him on the back in a far more manly and acceptable manner, and then the ropes were being untied and the boat was moving out into the water.

As the boat slowly disappeared from sight, the sinking feeling from the day before returned, and not even Dashan's steady presence at her side could dispel the worry that clawed at her chest, or the impotence she felt at them leaving without her and going into danger alone. She desperately hoped that she'd made the right decision in not telling Casovar about herself, and that by the time her friends returned she would have learned that he could be trusted.

CHAPTER 13

Alyx yawned, looking up from the spidery handwriting before her to glance out the window. Dusk was falling and that meant it was time to go home. She'd just finished compiling her completed work into a neat stack when Casovar entered the offices. Surprisingly, he had Astor with him.

"Good evening, sir," she said. "I was just finishing up for today. Hello, Astor."

"Alyx." Astor smiled a greeting, but Casovar didn't speak until he'd sat down opposite her. Astor took a seat between them.

"Please roll up your sleeves to your elbows," Casovar instructed Alyx.

As usual, she pushed through her instinctive reluctance to do anything Casovar told her to and laid her bare forearms on the table. "Why?"

"I'm going to test your magic," he said. "I thought Lord Astor's presence might improve your ability to access it. He's a familiar face and should help you relax and concentrate better."

Alyx glanced at her godfather. Hiding her magic from Casovar was one thing, but Astor was one of the people who knew her best. Damn. She wasn't sure she was going to be able to pull this off. Turning back to Casovar, she tried stalling. "Can I ask why you didn't do this when you were testing the others?"

Casovar's grey eyes flicked to hers. "I didn't want them covering for you. Do as I ask, Apprentice. I don't have all night to babysit you."

She nodded and took a deep breath, summoning enough of her magic to illuminate her hands in a pearly-green glow. Keeping it under such tight control wasn't easy, and if it hadn't been for the hours of practice she'd put in that morning, it might have been impossible— she'd noticed that if she didn't use her mage power for a length of time, it tended to burst out of her like a flooded dam over a levee wall.

"Now try and separate your magic from your hand into a ball of energy."

Puzzlement flickered over Astor's face, and Alyx cursed inwardly. She'd told him last year after first coming home from DarkSkull she had minor telepathic talent. Why hadn't she remembered to tell Casovar the same story?

"Alyx!" Casovar snapped, sensing her distraction.

"Sorry, sir." Alyx frowned as if she were concentrating hard. After a moment, she allowed her mage light to flicker.

"Try harder," Casovar said. "Focus."

She frowned harder, clenching her jaw and staring hard at her forearms. The mage light flickered again, more brightly this time, but then faded back to its usual colour.

"I'm sorry," she said. "I can't do it."

Casovar frowned and sat back in his chair. "You really are a lesser mage. Lord Astor?"

Alyx's gaze shot to him, her breath catching. Would the act she'd just put on fool him as it had Casovar?

"I concur with your assessment, Lord-Mage." The older man stroked his beard. "She doesn't seem to be able to do much more than summon a mage light."

She let out the breath, feeling as if she were walking on the ledge of a very high window. Maybe Astor had forgotten what she told him. Or maybe she could fudge with him later, pretend she'd been wrong about her mage talent.

Casovar turned back to her. "How is your skill with a staff?"

Alyx shrugged and tried to look sheepish. "Mediocre at best, sir."

"I want to see. Come with me."

Casovar stood abruptly and moved to the door. She followed, her stomach sinking—she'd passed her first hurdle, but had another coming. They walked the short distance down to an empty Bluecoat drill yard in silence, Astor trailing behind. Casovar had brought his own staff and gestured for Alyx to draw hers. She did so, eyeing him warily.

A glance at Astor wasn't helpful. He'd assumed a blandly interested expression but was avoiding looking at her. Great. Either she revealed to Casovar her competency or take a beating. Briefly she considered telling him everything, but just as quickly discarded the idea. Not without talking to Tarrick first, not when Casovar continued to make her so uneasy it often set her teeth on edge.

Inwardly Alyx groaned. She thought she'd moved past being beaten in sparring practice.

The lord-mage moved quickly and efficiently with his staff. Alyx blocked and counter attacked as she had been taught at DarkSkull, but deliberately left her blocks a little too late, her attacks just off target. Casovar battered two of the fingers on her right hand, bruised her right shoulder and delivered a smart blow to her left ribs before giving up.

"You were right," he said, stepping away from her. "Mediocre. You've learned the moves, but you can't implement them properly."

"I'm sorry, sir."

Casovar shrugged. "I needed to be sure you wouldn't be of any real use to me, particularly given who your mother was. I'll see you in the morning, Apprentice Egalion."

As soon as the gate to the yard closed behind him, Alyx let out a curse and tossed her staff angrily across the yard before cradling the fingers of her right hand to her chest. "Damn, that hurt!"

"Hmm, it certainly looked painful." Astor wandered over. "You have some internal fortitude, young Alyx."

"What does that mean?" she grumbled.

He arched a single eyebrow. "Please tell me you're not taking me for a fool in my dotage?"

"You're not in your dotage," she scoffed.

An amused smile flickered across Astor's face. "Arrogant bastard, isn't he? Assuming you're useless just because you told him so."

So Astor had guessed some of it, at least. Alyx sighed. "You can be very superior at times, Astor."

"I can," he agreed. "I also love my goddaughter. I hope you know you can trust me with anything."

Alyx went over to pick up her staff. "I'm just like my mother. And yes, I can use a staff well enough when I need to, much better than you saw."

"Temari." Sadness flashed on Astor's face, followed by something she couldn't name. "If you truly are like her, then Casovar is probably the best teacher you could have."

"I don't trust him yet."

"I can see that," Astor said dryly. "With you preferring to be beaten rather than telling him the truth."

"It's not so different to being at DarkSkull." She chuckled.

"Come on inside. I'll strap those fingers for you and get a poultice for your shoulder."

"No, it's okay. I'll go down and see..." Alyx stopped as she realised that she'd been about to say Dashan's name. But he wasn't here, he was away from the city for a week on patrol. A shaft of disappointment shot through her, startling her with its strength.

"See who?" Astor inquired.

"Oh, nobody." She shook her head. "This poultice better be good. My shoulder is killing me."

"How have you been?" Astor asked as they sat in a corner of the mostly-empty palace kitchens, sharing hot tea by the great fire.

"Fine," she said. "It's difficult, acceding to Casovar's high-handed orders every day, but Papa tells me it's necessary, and I trust him."

"You're right to do so," Astor said. "What about Cayr? You must be missing him. It's a cruel blow to return from months away only to have him depart Alistriem almost immediately after."

"I do miss him, but..." She sighed, toying with her mug. "We were always so close, you know that. I wanted to marry him. He tells me he still wants the same thing."

"And that doesn't make you happy?" He smiled. "I'm astonished you're not doing cartwheels right now."

"I don't want it," she said quietly.

Silence filled the room, and when Alyx looked up Astor was staring at her with a contemplative expression on his face. She'd expected surprise, but there wasn't a trace of that in his eyes. "You expected this to happen."

He gave a little shrug. "Not specifically, but I'm the one person here that understands what DarkSkull Hall does to a person, Aly-girl. You're not a child anymore, and I'm not surprised that you're questioning what it is that you want, the things you feel."

It was a relief, talking to an adult in her life who did understand. It also made her remember Dashan's insistence that she discuss her nightmares with him. She put her tea down.

"Astor, can I ask your advice on something?"

"Anything," he said earnestly.

"I've been having these nightmares." Alyx explained them in detail. "I haven't had one since the night after leaving DarkSkull, but I know it's inevitable. I don't know what to do about it. My master didn't have any answers. Dashan thought you might have some ideas."

"I have to admit I've never heard of another mage causing nightmares. It would have to be a telepath, and a powerful one. Powerful indeed if they can reach you both here and at DarkSkull."

She shivered at that thought. "Whoever it is knows who I am, too."

"They would have to know you to some degree, to be able to target you so specifically," Astor said absently, face indicating he was deep in thought. "You can't use telepathic magic at such a distance on a mind you've never met."

That was chilling. She hadn't even thought about it that way. "Why would they be targeting me? And who?"

"Key questions. You said the nightmares started in your first year at DarkSkull, so perhaps it's someone you met there. Or someone in the mage world who learned of your existence when you arrived."

Alyx tried to hold back the fear that trickled through her and forced herself to ask the question that had been niggling at her. "Do you think it could be whoever is behind the missing mages?"

"It's as good a guess as any. But why torture you with nightmares? To scare you?"

"If that's the motive, it's succeeding," she said dryly.

Astor's eyes fixed on her, the blue in them intense. "I see."

"I wish it would stop," she admitted.

Astor rose with a smile. "I promise to do some research to see if I can help. After all, I have plenty of time on my hands now that I'm retired. In the meantime, I'm sure I can find marshmallows here somewhere. What say we roast them over the fire and make some hot chocolate?"

"Like we did when you minded me when I was little?" She smiled.

"Exactly."

Alyx rose. "I'm in, but only if you promise to—"

"Put the whipped cream inside the hot chocolate instead of on top." Astor laughed. "Yes, Aly-girl, I remember."

The hot chocolate was sweet and rich on her tongue, and it momentarily warmed her body. But she couldn't dispel the shiver that went down her back at the thought of her nightmares, and when she glanced up at Astor, seeking comfort, his gaze was distant, his mind a long way away from her and her problems.

CHAPTER 14

Alyx looked up, smiling in pleasure as her father came through the door of the mage offices.

"Have you come to take me to lunch?" she asked hopefully.

"Sorry, no." His return smile lightened his too-serious face. "I'm here for Lord-Mage Casovar. The king wants to see him."

"Oh. He just left to see the king."

Garan chuckled. "We must have missed each other on the way."

"Is it something important?"

"The Tregayan ambassador sent a message to Darien this morning indicating he had some important news to share. The king has asked the lord-mage and I to be there for the meeting." Her father looked apologetic. "I'd offer to take you with me, but—"

"I'll come," she said with alacrity, eager for a chance to hear what the ambassador had to say.

"Really?" Surprise filled his voice. "You'll be bored."

"Not at all," she said. "Especially if the ambassador's news concerns the trade agreement that Tregaya and Zandia have been working on. If the negotiations have gone well, it would give us an easier time bringing in weapons from Zandia for the army."

The astonishment on her father's face deepened. "You know about that agreement?"

Alyx couldn't help but roll her eyes. "For goodness' sake, Papa, it wasn't just magic I learned at DarkSkull. We had a test on the subject. Only Finn got better marks than me."

"Is that so? All right then, it's up to you."

She piled together the papers she'd been working on and rose from her chair, wincing as a jolt of pain shot through the shoulder she'd dislocated in the fight against Fengel. Casovar's 'sparring' the previous night had tweaked the old injury.

"Something wrong?" He narrowed his eyes in concern.

"An old sparring injury," she said. "I'll be fine."

"I remember the time you hurt your other shoulder," he said wryly as Alyx shrugged on her mage robe and they went out into the hallway.

"I was ten." She chuckled. "And it was all Dash's fault."

"He dared you to climb the tree as high as he had, and you weren't tall enough to do it." Her father's eyes twinkled down at her. "Cayr told you not to, but of course you never conceded defeat when Dashan was daring you."

"I could hardly back down," she told him. "I'm an Egalion."

He gave her a look. "You fell, of course. Lucky that bush was there at the bottom or you would have hurt more than your shoulder."

"Dash felt guilty though." Alyx grinned. "I was able to play on that for a week before he realised I wasn't really that badly hurt."

"I was furious," Garan observed.

She winced. "Yes, I remember that too."

The conversation made her think seriously for the first time about how her father was going to react to news of her relationship with Dashan. Although she might never have to tell him—if things with Dashan didn't work out, there'd be no need for him ever to know.

But they were working out. Oddly, against all logic and reason, being with him was making her happy. If she was honest with herself, the major factor in her ability to concede to Casovar on a constant basis was the happiness she was experiencing in the other parts of her life. Being home was one of those things, but Dashan was a bigger one.

"Alyx!"

Her head shot up as she was wrenched from her thoughts. Garan stood by the door of the audience room, one eyebrow raised. The Blue-coats on guard had already stepped away.

"Sorry, coming."

The king was inside, along with Lord-Mage Casovar and Captain Dunnat. Sparky was nowhere to be seen. Casovar didn't look pleased to see Alyx there, but said nothing, for now presumably not willing to gainsay her father in front of the king.

"Hello, Alyx, it's nice to see you again." Darien Llancarvan was in a good mood, and his anger at Cayr had either been forgotten or faded in the weeks that had passed since their arrest. She was tempted to ask when Cayr would return, but didn't want to push it.

"Your Highness." She bowed low instead, keeping her voice polite.

"Alyx has some knowledge of the new trade agreement from her studies at DarkSkull, Darien," Garan spoke casually. "I hope you don't mind her being here—she's interested to learn of any developments."

She looked at her father in surprise. He rarely addressed the king by his first name in the presence of others; it was a privilege he used only when the two men were alone. Darien didn't seem to notice, he merely waved Alyx to a chair, but Casovar stiffened perceptibly. She held back the smile that wanted to creep across her face—it seemed Garan was deliberately reminding Casovar of his close relationship with the king. Maybe she hadn't been trusting her father for no reason after all.

Lord Rostan Dunkeld came through the door a moment later. A short, wiry middle-aged man, he'd been the Tregayan ambassador to Rionn for fifteen years, his tenure extended due to the genuine friendship that he'd developed with the king. Alyx had met him only on a couple of occasions growing up, but her father had always spoken well of him.

"Everyone is here." The king waited until Rostan had seated himself. "What is your news, Lord Dunkeld?"

"Insurrection in Shivasa," the man said succinctly.

Alyx sat up straighter in her chair. What?

The same surprise filled the king's voice. "What do you mean?"

"Our southern militia bases have sent several reports over the past weeks. They've been brief and sketchy but there have been enough of them to give us a rough picture of what is happening," Rostan said. "It seems to have started in a large town in southern Shivasa; by all accounts the district administrator was rather a nasty sort. The good townsfolk started protesting, then rioting. The man was forced to step down, but when the people saw that their protest had worked, the riots began spreading throughout southern Shivasa. As of right now, the whole region is seething with unrest."

Garan frowned. "How violent is it?"

"Nothing beyond a spot of looting or burning for now. As far as we can tell, there isn't yet any organised resistance, mostly just patches of rebellion throughout the south. Interestingly, some of our reports indicate parts of the population are going out in protest in support of the Shiven leader and his local representatives."

"If it continues to spread, the unrest could result in a lessening of Shivasa's forces along the northern border of the disputed area," Garan mused. "They've been steadily building up troop numbers for months —in preparation to annex the area, we've judged. This could slow that down."

Alyx's eyebrows rose. She hadn't known about the increasing number of troops, although it made sense. It wasn't surprising Casovar hadn't told them, but it was hard not to be irritated that her father hadn't.

"I consider it unlikely," Casovar disagreed. "Shivasa has a large army and their leader prioritises resourcing the military over most other things. If the unrest isn't yet organised or overly violent, they still have plenty of soldiers to throw at us."

"But in the long term, we could expect that to happen," Garan pushed. "Particularly if resources going to the military lead to food or other basic supply shortages."

"Not if the Shiven leader gets the unrest under control. Their military is frighteningly efficient at putting down dissidents."

Alyx hated to agree with Casovar, but what she'd learned in Master Alaria's class indicated he was likely right. "Are there mages involved?" she asked Rostan.

"We don't know." Rostan shrugged.

"You think that might be the case, Alyx?" the king asked.

"There are Shiven mages." She nodded. "And not all of them are trained at DarkSkull Hall by the council."

"Those are uncorroborated reports," Casovar dismissed her.

"With all due respect, sir, they're more than uncorroborated reports."

"How so?" the king asked as Casovar's frown deepened.

She ignored the lord-mage and focused on the king. "During my time at DarkSkull, there were several attacks on the school. Most of them involved conventional weapons as well as mage power. The mages involved were Shiven, and hadn't been trained at DarkSkull. Logic would imply they were trained in Shivasa."

"King Mastaran mentioned the attacks when we were in Carhall," Darien said, glancing at Garan. "Lord-Mage Casovar feels that the council was exaggerating the danger they face."

"It gives them excellent reason to charge more for their services," Casovar said smoothly.

Alyx opened her mouth to rebut him, but her father's hand shifted to rest lightly on her forearm. Instead of speaking, she simply nodded in Casovar's direction.

"Thank you, Alyx, Lord-Mage," the king said. "Rostan, can your militia scouts determine whether mages are involved? If the Shiven army has to devote resources to subduing mages, then they'll have to commit a lot more troops than if they're just dealing with unhappy farmers, which might mean relief for us in the north."

"Of course, Your Highness." Rostan nodded.

"Garan, speak to Sparky and ensure our scouts are doing what they can to learn about what's happening in Shivasa also."

"I'll do it today."

"Your Highness, whatever the case, I don't think we can afford to relax our vigilance in the disputed area," Casovar said.

"I agree." The king waved a hand in dismissal. "Let's pick this up later when we have more information."

Casovar gestured for Alyx to follow him as they left. She gave a little wave to her father, comforted by the fact he was remaining in the king's audience chamber while the rest of them left.

"In the future, please refrain from offering unsolicited opinions in formal meetings, Apprentice."

She took a breath, swallowed. "I apologise, sir. It won't happen again."

"I want you to go back and write a message to your friends. Given this development, I'll need them to remain where they are a few extra weeks. They can be of assistance in ascertaining what effect the unrest in Shivasa has on their troop build-up."

A sharp slide of disappointment went through her. She'd been looking forward to her friends' return. They'd been gone almost two weeks already and she missed them. "Yes, sir."

"Something wrong?" he snapped.

She schooled her face to calm. "Not at all. I'll write the letter now."

"Make sure it's done by this evening."

He left then, mage robe swirling around his ankles as he moved with quick, decisive strides in the opposite direction of his offices. Slowly she uncurled her fists, taking deep breaths to calm her restrained anger. She wasn't sure how much longer she was going to be able to swallow her temper around him. Whatever her father was up to, she hoped it happened before she lost it entirely.

WHEN THE NIGHTMARE inevitably came again it grabbed her from a sound sleep. The dark mage's power held her effortlessly, but this time there was no attempt to cause pain. Alyx stilled in his grasp, everything inside her balled up tightly, waiting for what horror would come next.

"*The destruction I showed you... have you ever considered that it might be necessary?*"

Confusion stirred. The voice was the same, a whisper of thought that raked over her mind, but he was holding back, not actively trying to cause pain. Was he trying to have a conversation with her? That thought was somehow more terrifying than if he'd just been trying to hurt and scare her.

"*I know you heard me.*"

Somehow she summoned the bravery to reply, and stunningly he

138

allowed her enough use of her magic to do it. *"Destruction on the level you showed me is never necessary."*

"That is a naïve point of view. You've learned better than that."

"Why is it necessary?" Her voice remained tentative, expecting the pain and fear to be unleashed any second. But if she humoured him, maybe he'd tell her something useful.

There was a considering silence, although Alyx was left in no doubt of his dominant hold over her. His magic suffocated hers, allowing only enough for a trickle of telepathic magic.

"You've seen the true face of the Mage Council."

"You want to destroy the world because of the council?" Surely not.

He laughed then, and she winced as it reverberated through her skull. *"Foolish girl. I don't want to destroy the world. I want to destroy the Mage Council and everything it stands for. I want to protect those the council wishes to destroy."* A beat of silence, then: *"Think about that. Then think about which side of this fight you'd really like to be on."*

He was gone then, catapulting Alyx into wakefulness. She sat up in bed, gasping, sweat plastering her nightdress to her skin. Instinctively she summoned magic, using its green glow to dispel the shadows in her room. It was a long time before her rapid heartbeat settled and she'd calmed enough to curl back under the covers.

Who was this mage? And could he really want the same thing she did?

CHAPTER 15

Alyx made her way to the Cuttlefish Inn, taking the long route and ensuring that she wasn't followed. It wasn't quite midday, and the inn was mostly empty as she entered, ordered herself a cider and sat at a table in the corner of the room.

"Where's that big hulking warrior of yours?"

Alyx jumped at the sound of Brynn's voice—despite the fact that she had a full view of the inn from her table, he'd still managed to arrive without her noticing.

"Away from the city," she said. "Nice mental shielding."

"I'm a spy," he said in an exaggerated whisper.

"One with a notoriously sloppy shield," she said grumpily, annoyed he'd gotten the best of her. "You're also late. Why are we meeting here?"

"You said no secretive back rooms, so here we are at a table in full public view," Brynn said, taking a sip of his ale. "Have you ever read my thoughts?"

"Only when you've deliberately left them open to me."

Brynn appeared to consider this. "I don't know if I would have that sort of self-restraint."

"I don't think you would either," she said dryly. "You don't seem to have any problems using your power to force people to do what you want."

"Ouch." He winced. "My power isn't that strong, you know. I can only influence people to do what I want, not force them."

Alyx shrugged. "I don't want to know what people's private thoughts are. I imagine how I would feel if someone read my thoughts, and that's what makes me hate the idea of doing it to others."

"I hadn't thought of it that way."

"I'm glad we've cleared that up." She tried to keep the impatience from her voice. "Do you have anything for me, or are we meeting for fun?"

"I have nothing," Brynn announced. "Which means I have a lot."

She bit back her annoyance with an effort. "What is that supposed to mean?"

He grinned at her, then turned serious. "I can't find any of Lord-Mage Casovar's informants. I don't know who he is getting his information from, and therefore I don't know where they are getting their information from. So I can't tell you how credible his information is."

Alyx stared at him. "It's been two weeks since I asked you to do this."

"I know, and I've been working hard, I promise you."

"What about the Mage Guard?"

"There I've had marginally better luck." He leaned closer. "I've followed them on two night patrols through the poor quarter. On the first, they were rude and rough—don't ask me how they think anyone is going to give them information when they behave like poorly trained thugs, but—"

"Brynn!"

"Right. Sorry. The second time was more interesting." His voice lowered. "This patrol was heavily armed and they were more determined and focused than the other lot. I was preparing to see something like what you've described, but when they entered the street that looked to be their destination they ran into a unit of city guard."

"And?"

"That was it. The City Guardsmen claimed to be undertaking an investigation into a smuggling ring—they thought one of the houses in the street was a storage location for illegal goods. From what I overheard, the Mage Guard captain was irritated, but agreed not to interfere with the City Guard investigation and called his unit back. They left and went back to barracks." Brynn took a sip of ale. "Interesting thing was, not long after they left, the unit of City Guard cleared out too. All of them."

Alyx's eyes narrowed as the implications of that hit her. "If the City Guard thought there was a smuggling house in that street, there would be a constant watch on it. A discreet one, but they wouldn't leave it unguarded."

"Exactly what I would have assumed, so I checked. That street was empty. I went back the next day—same thing, no guardsmen anywhere, not even any hidden ones keeping an eye on the house."

"So they were lying to the Mage Guard. Why?"

"Not a clue." He took another sip of ale. "Stopped whatever the Mage Guard were about to do though, didn't it?"

It certainly had. And it had stopped it without a direct confrontation, or any implication that someone might have been trying to do just that. Her father. She rubbed at her eyes—or maybe it was just sheer coincidence. "Keep looking into it, will you? And Casovar as well. He has to be getting his information from somewhere."

He nodded, then hesitated. "You should know. I've passed all this on to the council."

"That's fine," she said. "As little as I trust them, I don't think it's a bad thing if others are looking into Casovar as well."

"I agree," he said, then changed the subject. "Any more of those nightmares of yours?"

She winced. "Last night, actually."

"I thought you looked a little pale. What happened?"

"He... " She hesitated, reluctant to say it out loud. "He talked to me."

Shock filled Brynn's boyish face. "About what? The weather?"

"It was all a bit vague. One thing was clear—he wants to destroy the Mage Council. The hatred I felt in his thoughts... it was corrosive, bitter." Alyx swallowed, her stomach turning at the memory.

"That's good. It's a piece of information on him. We had nothing before."

"That's true," she admitted. "But I think I preferred it when he was just trying to scare and hurt me. I don't want to be holding conversations with a presumably crazy and incredibly powerful dark telepathic mage." She shuddered involuntarily.

"Darkmage," Brynn murmured, mostly to himself.

"What?"

"Nothing." He shook his head. "Your words reminded me of the theory you said Finn had come up with, that maybe Shakar had the ability to cause nightmares. They used to call him Darkmage, you know?"

"Shakar?"

He nodded. "Not the council. But it was a nickname used by survivors in villages and towns he'd destroyed. In most accounts written by people at the time who weren't mages, that's how they referred to him."

"Maybe this mage has read those accounts—maybe he idealises Shakar somehow because he fought the council too?" Alyx suggested. "Whoever it is, Astor thinks he must know me to be able to reach my mind here and at DarkSkull."

"Not a warming thought." Brynn made a face. "But if it happens again, try to focus on using the nightmare as a way of getting information. The more he tells you, the closer we'll be to working out who he is, and where."

She nodded—he was right. "I'll try."

"And we could try making a list," he suggested. "Everyone we know from DarkSkull who would have reason to travel in this region or is strong enough to reach further with their telepathy, or both."

"We could," she said, dubious, "but I don't know how helpful it would be. The only telepath we know at DarkSkull strong enough to reach me here is Romas, and we don't even know if he is that strong."

His face fell. "Right. And you talked to Howell about this too? So if he knew of a telepath that powerful, he would have told you."

"Maybe."

Brynn finished his ale and rose. "I'll keep thinking on it. I still believe this could help us. Be careful, Alyx. Same time, same place, next week?"

"I'll be here."

ALYX TURNED over the paper she'd just finished reading and added it to the ever-growing pile. Letting out a bored sigh, she began reading the next page. The words started to blur after two sentences, and she looked up, rubbing at her eyes.

The room was momentarily empty of Casovar and Mage Guard members, and her eyes fell on her left arm. A silly smile crossed her face as she pushed up the sleeve of her shirt, revealing the silver bracelet on her wrist. Her fingers traced over the delicate filigree, pausing on the tiny charm of a mage staff that had been attached to it.

Dashan had returned from patrol the day before, and they'd gone for a night sail together. It had been peaceful and relaxing, the loveliest couple of hours she'd experienced in weeks. He'd given her the bracelet and muttered something about seeing it in Gosper and thinking she'd like it.

"Look at you being romantic," she'd teased, loving his discomfort and the slight flush in his cheeks.

The door opened, heralding Casovar's return. Alyx shoved her sleeve down and returned to reading the paper before her.

"Anything?" he asked her.

"No sir, I—"

The rest of her words were forestalled by the door opening and one of the Mage Guard appearing.

"Lord-Mage, you have a visitor," the soldier reported. "He says he's a representative from the Mage Council."

Alyx was as surprised as Casovar looked, and for once was glad to be in his offices—she didn't want to miss finding out what the Mage Council wanted. Brynn hadn't mentioned anything a week earlier when they'd met, so she assumed he knew nothing about the visitor.

"Show him in, Tordren."

Tordren disappeared briefly and voices sounded outside before a familiar figure came striding in. Her jaw had dropped before she realised what she was doing, shock flooding her. A moment later came a twist of pain and anger that choked up her throat.

Why is he here?

Cario Duneskal looked coolly confident in his impeccably tailored mage attire, his jaw clean-shaven and blonde curls neatly cut. Exactly as she remembered him, except now he wore a black mage robe, marking him an apprentice no longer. His gaze flicked over Alyx before settling on Casovar.

"Lord-Mage Casovar, hello. My name is Cario. I was sent here as a representative of the Mage Council."

Casovar's lip curled slightly. "You don't look old enough to be more than a third-year apprentice."

"I passed my trials a month ago." Cario was unmoved by Casovar's contempt. "And perhaps I should have elaborated. My name is Cario Duneskal—grandson of Councillor Rawlin Duneskal."

"The picture becomes clearer," Casovar said thinly. "What brings you here, Mage Duneskal?"

"The council has been monitoring the situation between Rionn and Shivasa, and although you have not requested mage assistance, we feel that it is time to offer what help we can. I'm here as a liaison to offer that support."

"It's a shame that you travelled all this way for no reason," Casovar said. "You're not invited, Mage Duneskal, and you're not needed."

"I don't answer to you, Lord-Mage, only to the council," Cario said amiably. "If you have a problem with my presence here... well, that would be odd, wouldn't it? Since I'm only here to assist your efforts. Indeed, once Shivasa learns of the Mage Council's official interest in Rionn, it might cause them to be little more cautious."

A charged silence hovered between the two men. It was as if Casovar's menace merely encircled Cario's affectation of calm, unable to pierce it. Alyx saw the moment Casovar decided not to openly flout the council; his shoulders relaxed slightly and he gave a faint nod. It was an interesting lesson for her in the reach and power of the council —even uninvited in a country with little involvement in the mage order they could impose their presence. Not a comforting realisation.

"You may assist, Mage Duneskal, not take over. Is that clear?"

"I wouldn't dream of it." A slight smile flickered over Cario's face. "I've had a long journey, Lord-Mage. I'll return tomorrow and you can fill me on the situation, if that suits you?"

Casovar nodded sharply, and Cario smiled once more before turning on his heel and striding out. He didn't even glance at Alyx. She was up and after him before Casovar had time to realise what she was doing and stop her. Outside, Cario's long strides were carrying him down the hallway leading to the main palace entrance.

Anger building, she went after him. "What are you doing here?"

Cario slowed and turned, his expression still unreadable. "Hello, Alyx. I would have expected a warmer greeting from a friend."

"We're not friends."

A shutter fell over his eyes, and he nodded. "I suspected that you had overheard my conversation with Romas. Especially when I never heard from you. Not even a letter."

Her shoulders stiffened. "I don't write letters to those who betray me."

Something like scorn flashed over Cario's face. "You think you know so much, but in fact you know very little."

"What is it I don't know? That you're a council spy who pretended to be my friend so that you could spy on me for months?" Alyx pushed back the tears that threatened. "I counted you as my friend."

"And I counted you as mine!" he snapped.

"Right. You spy on all your friends, do you?"

Her raised voice caught the attention of a passing servant, and they both fell silent while the startled-looking young man quickened his pace down the hall. It was Cario who broke the silence. "Perhaps you might give me the chance to explain?"

She stared at him for a moment, then spun on her heel, pushing open a nearby door that led to the gardens. His footsteps sounded behind her as she led him to a more private area before eventually stopping by a bubbling fountain.

Cario spoke before she could. "I am no more a council spy than you are."

"Then I suppose Tarrick and I imagined what we overheard," she mocked.

"In what conversation between us over the past year did I ever sound like I want to be anything like my family? When did I ever do anything to suggest being a spy for the council is something I would do?"

"You were spying. Clearly whatever you said to me was a lie."

"The council thought I was spying on you. They were wrong."

That momentarily gave her pause. His eyes were bright with intensity, an emotion she'd rarely seen in the cool and unaffected Cario Duneskal. "What does that mean?"

"After our first year at DarkSkull... well, I was slated to join Galien's group for second year. It made perfect sense—he was the most powerful student, and I had the most powerful mage connections." Cario sat down by the fountain, shoulders slumping. "It was the last thing I wanted. I hate everything Galien stands for. I wanted nothing to do with combat patrols or being a warrior mage. I thought if I could get into your group, I could escape everybody's notice. I had no idea you were a mage of the higher order."

"How does this end in you being a spy?"

He looked up at her, and for the first time she saw Cario stripped bare of any masks. His rawness tugged at her on a visceral level. "I knew of the council's interest in you, even though I didn't know why. I went to my grandfather, and told him that if he could organise for me to join your group, I would spy on you for him. It was the only way I could think to get out of being with Galien."

She huffed out a bitter laugh. "Self-interested as always. Why am I even surprised? What did you tell them about me?"

"Honestly?" A smile crossed his face. "I told them you liked needlework, and kept dreaming about some prince back home. I said you got bored in classes and kept making Finn do your homework for you. In short, I told them nothing of any value."

"Cario..." She hesitated, unsure of whether to believe him.

"You're right, my motives in going to my grandfather were selfish," he said earnestly. "But that doesn't mean I was ever willing to do what I told him I would. I pretended, Alyx. I swear to you."

She lifted her hands helplessly. "I have no reason to believe this.

After all the lies I've been told, mostly by the council... tell me how I can believe you, Cario?"

"Read my mind," he whispered. "Go on. I know you can. You'll see the truth in there."

His hands trembled in his lap and he'd turned pale as death. Alyx had never seen Cario so shaken, so utterly vulnerable. It was costing him to do this. With the secrets he kept from the world... and he was offering to let her into his head.

"No," she said, slowly, wondering if she was going to regret it, but making the choice anyway. "I believe you."

"You do?" Naked hope flared in his startling blue eyes.

"Yes." And she did. It wasn't in her to hurt him, and that's what she'd be doing if she read his thoughts. "Now tell me why you're really here?"

The mask settled back over Cario's face and he leaned languidly against the fountain. "The council thinks I'm here to report on you and Casovar both. I just wanted a holiday to Alistriem."

Alyx laughed.

Cario smiled in response, then sobered. "I came here to join you. I've made my choice, just like Tarrick. As long as working for the council allows me to remain with you, I'll continue to pretend."

She gave him a curious look. "You were a second-year apprentice like me. How have you passed your trials?"

"It's always been that the masters decide when an apprentice is ready to take the trials. Most of the time it takes about four years to learn and develop enough." Cario shrugged. "We both know I've been ready for some time."

"Why you and not Galien? They made him take the full four years."

"Being judged ready for the trials is not just about skill with magic. I suspect the council has been waiting and hoping for Galien to grow out of his psychopathic tendencies," Cario said dryly.

She nodded, pondering that. "You've heard that Casovar won't allow us to return to DarkSkull?"

"Yes. It factored in my decision to come here." His mouth quirked in a smile. "I figured Alistriem would be a nice long distance away from my family's fury."

"You're warming my heart with your devotion," she muttered.

He grinned. "Anyway, I was walking into Town Hall, all ready to tell my father that I was quitting the mage order, and I heard the news that the council had advertised a posting to Alistriem. Everyone was talking about it because the council hasn't had a formal representative in Alistriem in decades." He shrugged. "It was fairly easy after that to get my father and grandfather to pull strings and give me the assignment."

Alyx thought about that, curious as to what the council's true motives were. Cario's voice brought her back to the present.

"Anyway, I'm exhausted. Can you recommend a good inn?"

"Stay with me. Tarrick is staying at my house too, but he's out of town with the twins. It will be good to have the company," she said. "I'll have one of the Bluecoats escort you over there and write a note to our steward so he knows you're invited."

"Sounds great. Thanks, Alyx."

"Freshen up and have a nap. We can talk more later."

ALYX SAT BACK WITH A SIGH, pleasantly full after finishing every bit of the meal Safia had sent over with Cario. So far they'd discussed Cario's sea journey and the news that Galien and all members of First Patrol had passed their trials. It was a discomfiting thought to think those five now walked the world as fully trained warrior mages, but they weren't Alyx's problem to contend with. For now, anyway.

"So what are the council's views on Casovar?" she asked.

He glanced around. "Can we talk openly?"

"Casovar has a dinner engagement, and the Mage Guard have gone for the day too. It's just us in here." She shrugged. "Provided your mental shield is up, we should be fine. None of us have been able to establish yet whether Casovar has telepathic ability, but we're assuming he does."

"As you should," Cario agreed, then shifted forward. "Grandfather really didn't talk about Casovar much. His instructions to me didn't include anything about him, except to say that he was arrogant and unlikely to welcome my presence in Rionn."

"Why did Casovar quit working for the council?"

"That's easy. He's always been ambitious to a fault, yet there was no way he was getting a council seat anytime soon. They preferred to use him in the field because of his power. When your king offered him the post of lord-mage, I assume he jumped at it."

"So he grew up poor?"

"More middle-class, but yes. He wants what those above him have."

"I wonder how the king came across him?" Alyx mused. "Everyone knows he has limited contact with the council, so how did he learn about Casovar, let alone come to offer him the position as lord-mage?"

"Your previous lord-mage?"

"Astor? Yes, I suppose it must have been."

She wanted to follow that thought further, but a sharp knock on the door startled them both. It swung open to reveal Dashan, whose warm smile at the sight of her faded to rising anger when he saw Cario.

"What is he doing here?"

Alyx winced. "He's here as a formal representative of the Mage Council. It's a long story."

"Good to see you again, Lieutenant Caverlock," Cario said languidly.

"You want me to believe a mage apprentice is here as a formal representative of the council?"

"I passed my trials, Lieutenant. You'll notice I'm wearing black now."

Ignoring Cario, Dashan's furious gaze swung to Alyx, demanding answers. Cario glanced between them and rose to his feet. "I'll give you a moment."

Dashan waited until the door had closed behind him before demanding, "When did he get here?"

"Earlier this afternoon."

"And why haven't you sent him packing?"

"Because we had a long talk and he explained what happened."

"Oh, that's wonderful. And you didn't consider that maybe he's had months to come up with an excellent story?"

"No, because of course I don't have half a brain in my head." She rolled her eyes. "I believed him. You need to trust me."

Dashan's jaw clenched and he looked away from her for a long moment. "You can trust him if you like, but you can also let him know I'll be keeping a careful eye on him."

"I'm not going to tell him any such thing," she said tartly.

"Why is he here? What does the council want?" Dashan threw his hands in the air. "I'm not sure which of those two I trust less, and I don't want either of them near you."

"He was explaining his presence here when you so rudely interrupted. I thought you were on duty tonight?"

"I am. They assigned me to the palace so I wanted to come by and see you before my shift started."

Alyx sighed. "I don't find this over-protectiveness charming, you know. You need to get going before you're late to your shift and Cario starts to wonder what we're doing in here."

He grinned, the anger fading from his features as he stepped closer to her. "I know what I'd like to be doing."

"Ha. If you think I'm going to kiss you after that little tirade, you're—"

He cut her words off with his mouth and she melted instantly into him, allowing the kiss to last far longer than she should have before pushing him away. "Get out of here."

"Yes, my lady." He bowed extravagantly and grinned at her scowl. Opening the door, he gestured for Cario to come in. "Harm a hair on her head and I'll take you apart piece by piece. Slowly."

"Terrified, I'm sure," Cario drawled. "A pleasure as always, Lieutenant Caverlock."

Dashan slammed the door behind him so hard it rattled on its hinges.

"I am mystified as to why you keep him around," Cario said as he resumed his seat.

"Maybe one day you'll tell me your secrets and I'll tell you mine." She grinned at him. "Now, is there anything else I should know?"

"One more thing. The council has a spy here working on their behalf. Grandfather wouldn't tell me more—he said the spy won't be in contact with me as he has different tasking." Cario shrugged. "There's a good chance it's you the spy is here to watch. You should be careful."

Something inside Alyx relaxed. Despite the fact she truly believed Cario, Dashan's doubt had shaken that a little. But that snippet of information had gone a little way to prove his loyalty. Cario had no way of knowing she knew about Brynn already.

Her smile widened, and Cario raised his eyebrow at her. "What?"

"Much like you, Cario, the council spy in Alistriem also works for me."

The look of stunned surprise on his face kept her amused for hours afterward.

CHAPTER 16

Alyx balanced on the balls of her feet, loosening her shoulders. Then she focused her mind, taking several deep breaths. In and out. In and out. Her heartbeat steadied and her concentration sharpened. Slowly, she reached for her mage power, allowing it to spread through her.

Then, she opened her eyes and jumped.

Her body leapt into the air, and at the very last moment—when she was about to start falling back to earth—her magic kicked in.

Exhilaration flared when, instead of dropping to the ground, she hovered above it. Letting out a whoop of triumph, she drew upon more power and soared higher into the air.

Her magic reserves instantly began to drain. Reluctantly she let go, dropping back towards the ground and landing with a slight stumble. A wide grin spread over her face. Sweat slicked her skin, and her heart was pounding from exertion, but she'd done it! She had absorbed Mika's talent.

Still smiling, she rubbed a towel over her face and wandered out of the hot sun to a nearby table where a jug of water stood. Her first instinct was to hurry off and find Finn, tell him she'd absorbed another ability, and thinking of him took some of the shine off her triumph.

They still weren't back yet.

It had been over a month now, and Casovar refused to provide her with details of what her friends were doing, no matter how politely she asked, and she worried for them. Several attempts to reach Dawn telepathically had failed. Unsurprised—Alyx still had work to do to improve her telepathic skill and range—she was nonetheless disappointed not to have received contact from her friend. Perhaps the distance was even too great for Dawn.

Dropping into a nearby chair, she let out a sigh, resting the cool glass against the hot skin of her forehead. She hated knowing they might be in danger and she was powerless to help. And it didn't make things any easier that she was essentially cooling her heels in Alistriem. Her father continued to preach patience, promising the time would come when she would be of use, but as more time passed, her frustration grew. She'd promised Tarrick and the twins she'd have a better sense of Casovar by the time they returned, but she didn't.

She still didn't know if he could be trusted, not for certain, and Brynn hadn't brought anything definitive to her yet. He'd been hard to pin down recently, claiming increased tasking from the council. The burning knot of uselessness and frustration in her chest seemed to grow larger every day, and the only way to ease it was these practice sessions she forced herself through as often as she could. In the absence of formal training, she dragged up the memories of every lesson Howell and Rothai had given her. She pushed herself constantly, determined to increase her control and skill.

And not only with magic, either. Dashan had been there earlier, and they'd passed more than an hour in a sparring session before he'd had to report for duty. Her muscles were weary, but in a good way—the languid satisfaction she'd often felt at DarkSkull after a long, tiring day.

That satisfaction eased some of her pent-up emotion. At least by doing this she was preparing herself as best as possible for whatever was coming... whether it be Shivasa or whoever was behind the missing mages.

The determination surged again, and she put down the glass and rose, swinging her staff to loosen the tight muscles across her shoulders. She had more time for practice before she had to get ready for her evening plans.

After taking a few breaths to regain her focus, she swung her staff in her right hand and aimed the point at a wooden target a hundred paces away. She summoned her power again, and sent a controlled, low-energy concussion blast shooting from the end of her staff.

Far less bright and powerful than the strength of her mage power allowed, the modified concussion burst hit the target with a satisfying thump. It was a little off centre, but it gouged the wood nicely without exploding the thing into thousands of tiny pieces. Moving her aim slightly, she tried again.

It took a lot more effort, both in power and concentration, to control the strength, depth and flight of a concussion ball, than it did simply to let loose with everything she had. This one hit the centre of the target though, and a weary triumph flickered through her.

"Having fun?"

Alyx spun around in astonishment, heart leaping into her throat. Cayr stood by the small table in the shade, looking handsome and dapper despite the heat. It took a moment to process that he was actually standing there—she'd had no warning he would be back, and had assumed it would be a few more weeks. She was utterly unprepared to see him.

"You're back," she managed.

"I am." He smiled. "I'm not interrupting, am I?"

"Not at all." She walked over to join him by the table, busying herself with pouring another glass of water. "I had no idea you were supposed to be back today."

"I didn't want to make a fuss of it. Less chance of people crowding the streets to watch me ride in that way."

"Fair enough. How was the trip?" She gave him an apologetic look. "I'm sorry we made your father so angry he sent you away."

Cayr shrugged. "It's nothing. The trip was being planned anyway, Father just made it happen faster."

A whisper of thought touched her magic, too quick to catch, and she would never invade Cayr's privacy. "Is there something else?"

He poured himself a glass of water, clearly mulling over something.

Alyx waited for him to say what was on his mind, her own thoughts chaotic. She was going to have to talk to him, but now? Maybe it would be better to wait until he'd settled in back home, but that would only be delaying the inevitable.

"You're not as useless as Casovar thinks you are, are you?"

Taken aback—that wasn't the question she'd been expecting—Alyx affected casualness. "If I told you that, I'd have to kill you," she said lightly.

He raised an eyebrow. "You don't trust me?"

"I absolutely trust you. I just don't want to put you in a position where you have to lie to Lord-Mage Casovar, or your father," she said, becoming serious.

"I would never betray your confidence," he said earnestly. "Never, and you know that."

"I know, but I don't want to make you lie for me either." She smiled. "Let's just say, you're right. I'm not quite as useless as Casovar thinks."

Cayr sighed and nodded. Something flickered in his eyes, but it was so quick she couldn't quite read it. It was rare that she couldn't read him, and it startled her.

"Are you all right?" she asked softly.

"You're different since DarkSkull." He gave a little shake of his head. "I just came back from weeks away and I don't even get a hug?"

Inwardly, she winced, then reached out to take his hand. "I am pleased to see you, Cayr. And you're right, I have changed, but you're still my friend, and I still need you in my life."

"Not as much as you used to, though?"

She looked away, unable to lie. "I think that's part of growing up." Alyx wasn't going to give him false promises, but she kept her voice as gentle as she could. Inside her stomach was twisting up into knots so tight breathing had become difficult. She couldn't not tell him. She couldn't. It would have to be now.

"I came straight here because I missed you and wanted to see you." He visibly shook off his sadness and smiled a little, eagerness brightening them to a light blue. "But also because I have two important things I wanted to talk to you about. My father wrote to say that you're staying this time—Lord-Mage Casovar isn't sending you back to DarkSkull. It was the happiest news I think I've heard in a long time, and it only makes what I'm planning easier."

Alyx's heart sank. She could guess what was coming, and he had no idea, none at all. Guilt churned in her and she sucked in a breath—could she do this to him? She had to... but to cause him pain like that. It was unthinkable.

"You said two things. What exactly do you want to talk about?" she asked carefully.

He took her hands, blue eyes serious on hers. "Firstly, I love you, Alyx. These past weeks away, the whole time you were at DarkSkull, I thought about you every single day. I don't ever want anyone else."

Alyx shifted back slightly, unable to be so close to him. "We were apart for a long time, and I know we've always been best friends, but—"

"We were never just friends. I want to marry you, Alyx."

"I know," she whispered.

"I'm willing to take things slowly, to rebuild what we had. I'm not asking that we get married tomorrow, or even next month," he said gently. "But I would like to be able to put my arms around you, to kiss you, to tell everyone that we belong to each other. I want formal permission to court you."

She looked down at her feet. If only she'd known he was coming back today, she could have prepared for this, somehow made it easier... but that was foolish. No matter how prepared she was, it wouldn't change how badly her truth was going to hurt him. She took a deep breath, summoning her courage for what was going to be the hardest thing she'd ever done.

"Cayr... " She forced herself to look up at him. The words were there on her tongue, but she had to force them out, leaving her voice barely audible. "I can't give you what you want."

"What does that mean?" He frowned, puzzlement in his voice.

"I told you that when I was away this past year there was someone else?"

He stilled, the light in his blue eyes fading. "You said it was over."

"And I was telling the truth, at the time." She searched for the right words, struggling to find them. "But it meant more to me than I realised when we spoke. I was denying how I felt because I wanted us back and I didn't want to hurt you."

"Who?"

"I... " She hesitated, something inside her unable to land the final blow. The courage she'd had a moment earlier was gone, burned away by the hurt in his face and voice. "Cayr, if you asked me to marry you now, I would say no. It's not what I want."

For a long moment he was silent, utter shock creeping across his handsome face. He let go of her hands and stepped back, his head shaking a little. He truly hadn't ever considered this eventuality—she could see it in the depth of his growing despair, his difficulty in understanding what she was telling him. So instead he focused on the detail, blue eyes shooting up to meet hers again, dark and determined.

"Is it someone I know? It must be, if it happened at DarkSkull, and now it's come up again?" He ran an agitated hand through his hair. "He's here, isn't he? Is it Cario? I just saw him over at the palace. Casovar said he arrived a few weeks ago."

"Cayr... please." She forced the words out, trying to stop his rambling. But she couldn't say anymore, her resolve in tatters. All she could do was stand there while his heart broke into a thousand pieces. How could she do this to him?

"It's him, isn't it?" His eyes bored into hers. "Alyx, please, tell me the truth."

She bit her lip, tears welling in her eyes. His pleading tone cut right through her, burning a trail of grief and guilt through her heart. "Cayr, I'm so sorry. It's Dashan."

For a moment he looked utterly confused, as if she'd told him the sky was green. Then the realisation hit him—that this was real, and she wasn't messing with him. His face crumpled with hurt and despair, and when he spoke his voice sounded broken. "Dashan? You and... Dashan?"

She took a deep, shuddering breath. "Yes."

"Alyx, how could you... " The words burst out of him, raw and bitter. "How could he do this?"

"It wasn't something we did deliberately." She tried to explain, knew it was useless. The tears in her eyes spilled over, trickling down her cheeks. This was more torturous than any nightmare she'd had.

Cayr reached up to wipe fiercely at his eyes, his gaze darting everywhere as if looking for someone else to come along and tell him this wasn't happening. Eventually he looked back at her. "I don't understand." He sounded lost. "Tell me there's some explanation for all of this."

Her heart ached, and she wiped uselessly at her own tears. "There's an explanation, just not one you're going to like."

"What's that supposed to mean?" he burst out, hurt turning rapidly to anger. "You and Dashan don't even like each other that much. How did that change? What about us, Alyx?"

"I wanted us!" The words burst out of her, filled with her bitterness and pain. "I wanted us more than anything. You know that. I spent a year at DarkSkull thinking of nothing else but you and our future. But it changed me. Going back changed me more."

"It can't have changed what we are to each other." Anger darkened his blue eyes. "You can't just decide that's all gone!"

Alyx flinched at the raw hurt in his words, hating that she was the cause of it. This was so much worse than what he'd done with Jenna.

"I didn't decide anything," she managed, unable to hold the bitterness back. "Things happened to me that were completely out of my control, and they changed me. I'm not the same girl you asked to marry you two years ago. I lost her." Alyx's voice broke. "I lost all of it. My entire world before that day is gone, and it almost destroyed me."

He stared down at her for a long moment, but now she saw the hurt fading, instead to be replaced by a look of grim determination.

"Your love for me hasn't changed," he said. "I know it hasn't. Whatever this thing with Dash is, it can't compare to what we share."

Somehow, she cobbled together the courage for one final blow. Leaving him with any false hope would be cruel. "I'm not in love with you." The words came out in a whisper. "I'm so sorry."

Cayr shook his head and backed away. "He'll break your heart. Think about that, Alyx."

With those words, he turned and walked away. Alyx stared after him, forced to sit down as her entire body began trembling.

I'm so sorry, Cayr.

CHAPTER 17

I t was late afternoon by the time Alyx calmed enough to go back into the mansion. Once there, she went upstairs to wash the sweat from her skin with a cool, scented bath before sitting by the window to let the dark strands of her hair dry in the sun.

As dusk fell, she dressed in a light, sleeveless cotton tunic she'd had made since returning to Rionn. Loose pants made from similar cloth and a pair of intricately worked leather sandals finished off her attire. Her father was coming out of his study as Alyx came down the stairs. He stopped as he caught sight of her.

"Where are you going, Aly-girl?"

He sounded weary, and though she didn't want to add to his burdens, she loved him too much to lie to him. "Dashan's father is hosting a dinner for him. He was promoted to captain last week."

"It surprises me Tirian would bother, especially since he cast Dash off."

"Me too," she agreed. "But he's a ranking noble, after all. I suppose it wouldn't look good not to recognise your son's promotion in the Blue Guard. Even then, I think it's more because he thinks it might get Cayr to attend."

"Ah, yes." He matched her knowing look. "I heard he came back today."

"He was here earlier." Alyx tried to ignore the rush of guilt and grief she felt at hearing his name. "I don't think he's coming."

Garan rubbed at his forehead. "I heard Dashan's promotion was coming, and I'm glad for the lad. It's right his father acknowledges it. Goodness knows he's never done much else for his son."

"Thank you for saying that," she said softly.

"Enjoy your evening." He smiled tiredly. "We should talk soon, you and I."

"Is everything all right?"

"It will be." He smiled. "Go on. Don't let your too-serious father's worries drag you down. Congratulate Dashan for me."

"I will. And whenever you want to have that talk, I'll be here," she promised.

LORD-GENERAL TIRIAN CAVERLOCK lived in a palatial townhouse in the wealthiest district of Alistriem. It was an exclusive quarter at the base of the hill, along the banks of the waterfall and river. Torches lined the roads of these wide, paved streets. She hadn't been to the Caverlock mansion since late childhood—Dashan had been cast off at fourteen, and they hadn't been back since.

Two grooms were waiting in the cobblestoned courtyard as Alyx rode in, and one stepped forward to help her dismount and take Tingo's reins. She spent a few moments with the stallion, calming him and warning him to behave with the unfamiliar groom. He snorted his displeasure at her, but went off docilely enough. Another servant opened the front door at her knock, and she was ushered politely into the entrance foyer.

"Well, if it isn't Lady Egalion." A laughing voice greeted her.

Alyx fought a smile as Dashan bowed low, mockery in every line of his body, then straightened with a flourish. "If the lady would come with me?"

He took her hand and led her away from the entrance foyer, into a small coat room off the nearest hallway. As soon as the door closed behind them, he pulled her into his arms and kissed her. She kissed him back just as eagerly, her arms wrapping around his neck, her body moulding itself to his. He backed her up until she was pressing into the door, and proceeded to kiss his way down her jaw and neck. Her head fell back against the door, her body limp in his arms.

"Wasn't it only this morning we were doing this?" she murmured breathlessly.

He looked up from her neck with a grin. "I missed you since then."

"Me too." She laughed and kissed him again, unable to get enough of the way he made her feel, the way his touch made her heart race and her entire body feel alive.

In the days since Dashan's return, they'd spent any free time they'd had together. With Tarrick and the twins still away, and Cario busy with Casovar, Dashan and Alyx had been given a window of time where it could just be the two of them. They'd been amongst the most wonderful days of her life, hesitant as she was to admit that to herself.

"As much as I want to stay here forever." Dashan eventually pulled back. "My father is likely to notice I'm missing very soon."

"There's something you should know before we go out there."

"What is it?" he murmured, eyes darkening as he correctly read the emotion in her face. The emotional aftermath of her interaction with Cayr still resonated, and it would be a long time before the guilt faded.

"Cayr's back."

The light faded from Dashan's face and he stepped back. "I see."

"I had no idea he was returning today, but he came to see me. He was insistent on talking about us. He wanted to begin formally courting me." She hesitated. "Dashan, I had to tell him the truth."

His face cleared, and something inside her ached—he'd been expecting her to tell him she'd agreed to court Cayr. The surprise faded as he realised what she'd said, replaced by growing guilt. "You told him about us?"

"I couldn't lie to him, not after what happened with Jenna." She paused. "I'm sorry, but he knows you and I are... whatever we are."

Dashan sighed and took another step back, running a hand through his dark hair. "I wanted to talk to him myself, face-to-face."

"I know. But he was demanding to know who it was. I think he was moments away from challenging poor Cario to a duel."

A shadow crossed Dashan's face; he still didn't trust the mage, even after Alyx had explained everything to him. "I can't imagine how he must be feeling right now. I'll go and see him tonight, straight after this dinner."

"That's probably a good idea. I'm sorry."

"Don't apologise. I know you were trying to do the right thing." He reached for the door. "Come on, we'd best get to dinner."

"LADY EGALION." Dashan's father bowed politely. "We are honoured to have you here."

"Thank you for inviting me, Lord Caverlock," she said graciously.

He smiled. "Please come through."

Alyx glanced at Dashan as he offered his arm. "You didn't invite any of the Bluecoats from your unit? Surely Tijer and Casta at least would have come."

"This evening has nothing to do with my father wanting to celebrate my promotion," Dashan said. "I don't want any of my friends to see that."

"Yet you invited me?"

"You know me better than anyone," he said soberly. "You were always able to see the reality of my life, even when we argued constantly."

"I'm sorry things were so awful for you."

He paused for a moment to look down at her, letting her see some of the pain he kept wrapped up so tightly inside him. "The truth is, I needed you here with me tonight."

She squeezed his arm, wishing that they were somewhere private so that she could throw her arms around him. "Then I'm glad you asked."

There were an assortment of other lesser nobles gathered around the long dining table, along with a handful of Alistriem-based senior officers from the Blue Guard. Dashan's father took a seat at the head of the table, with Dashan on his left. Regan, Dashan's older—and legitimate—brother, and heir to the lordship, sat on their father's right.

Alyx, as the highest ranked noble there, was placed on Regan's other side.

Only two years in age separated them, but Dashan and Regan had never been close. Alyx suspected Regan had hated the sudden arrival of another child—albeit unwanted—to take his father's attention away from him. And as for Dashan, well, Regan was the legitimate son and he had everything Dashan didn't.

Regan promptly took the opportunity to be as charming as possible in a not so subtle attempt to gain her favour. Alyx responded as little as she could, but tried to be polite for Dashan's sake.

From the moment Dashan broke the news to his father that Cayr wouldn't be coming, he was essentially ignored. Tirian Caverlock and those seated at the top of the table spoke jovially about a myriad of things that did not include Dashan, who sat quietly and stared broodingly at his dinner. Alyx seethed on his behalf, her anger building, but she forced herself to keep quiet.

"Lady Egalion, you've known my brother for quite some time," Regan said amiably as empty plates were taken away in preparation for dessert.

"Since we were young children, yes."

"It always surprised me, little Dash managing to make friends with yourself and Prince Cayr."

"Did it?" she said flatly.

Undeterred by Alyx's clear lack of interest in the topic, Regan forged ahead. "I mean, he's never really amounted to much, has he? You'd think the king would have wanted his son to keep away from Dash. Your father too."

She looked up, trying to veil her irritation, and caught Dashan watching, listening to every word.

Lord Caverlock nodded at his eldest son's words and gave a chuckle. "I doubt he'd even have made captain if it weren't for the fact he was my son and the prince's friend."

Dashan's face had darkened to a thundercloud, and Alyx spoke before he could, not wanting Dashan's dinner ruined by another bitter argument between father and son. "Actually, sir, that's not true."

Alyx's voice had been mild but pointed, and the conversation around the table faded away as the guests pretended they weren't listening intently.

Caverlock sat back in his chair, clearly taken aback. "Lady Egalion, I'm sorry if I caused offence."

"I'm not offended, Lord Caverlock, just disappointed that you clearly haven't been told of the reasons for Dashan's promotion." Of course he had, and Alyx's tone indicated they both knew it. Conversation along the table had died completely now—even a servant carrying the first plates of dessert stood frozen by the door. A red flush was climbing up Caverlock's face, but he gestured politely for her to continue.

"For example, were you aware that the Mage Council sought Dashan's advice on the defence of DarkSkull Hall? That when they implemented his ideas, the number and severity of attacks on Dark-Skull diminished significantly?" She paused to stare at them all in turn. Most looked away from her glance. Some few didn't—they looked almost encouraging. It gave her fuel to continue.

"Commander Helson didn't write a glowing letter because he felt like it. Dashan and his unit made a significant difference to the security of DarkSkull Hall, not to mention the lives they saved when two Mage Council masters were attacked on a trip from Carhall. Dashan earned this promotion. He deserves to be a captain in your Blue Guard."

For the first time, Alyx looked at Dashan. He was staring at her in complete shock, his expressive brown eyes dark with emotion. She smiled at him before shifting her gaze to his father. "I hope that helps you understand better, Lord Caverlock."

Caverlock cleared his throat, tugged at his collar, then summoned a smile and sat forward again. "I appreciate your comments, Lady Egalion, and I am glad that my son made such an impact during his assignment as part of your protective detail."

"I'm happy to help." Alyx smiled, then picked up her glass of wine and took a sip, signalling an end to the conversation. After a few awkward moments, helped by the appearance of dessert, conversation resumed.

Soon after her speech, Dashan's leg reached out to touch hers under the table. The mood visibly lightened as it became clear Lord-General Caverlock was going to let Alyx's speech go without getting upset. Even more, he made a visible effort to include his younger son. She ignored the looks cast her way and focused on maintaining easy and polite conversation with those around her.

The evening finally wound up an hour later. Some of the guests left, while those remaining accepted Lord Caverlock's invitation to join him for a cigar and spirits in his private lounge.

"Will you come with us?" he asked Dashan, sounding sincere. "Regan and I would like the opportunity to share a celebratory cigar with the new captain in the family."

Dashan hesitated, surprise washing over his face. "I'd like to walk Alyx out first, but after, yes sir, I'd like that."

"We'll have a cigar waiting for you. Lady Egalion, thank you for coming this evening." Caverlock bowed politely to Alyx before leaving the room.

"Don't take too long." Regan clapped Dashan on the back before following his father out.

TOGETHER THEY STROLLED out of the house and down the pebbled path to the gates. Lord Caverlock had already sent to his grooms to have Tingo waiting for Alyx down at the gates, and they hovered there a moment, reluctant to part. Dashan dismissed the groom, and they waited until he was out of sight before continuing through the gates where they couldn't be seen by prying eyes.

"About what you said back there—" he began, but she cut him off.

"Don't even think about thanking me. I was only speaking the truth."

He glanced down at his shoes. "It's just that nobody has ever defended me like that before."

"I will." She leaned up, kissing him to reinforce the point. His arms settled around her and they kissed for a long time, content to be together. Eventually he pulled back a little, his arms around her waist loosening.

"I'll spend a short time with Father and Regan, but after that I need to go up to the palace and see Cayr." He sighed.

Guilt surged. "He was upset. He might not want to see you."

"I know, but I have to try."

"I hope it goes well." She tried to smile for him, knowing exactly how he was feeling. Dashan loved Cayr as much as she did, and the idea of deliberately hurting him was no doubt as awful for him as it was for her. "If I can get away, lunch in the city tomorrow?"

"Absolutely." He smiled. "Goodnight, Alyx."

"Before I go." She caught his hand, trying to stop the sudden nervous thumping of her heart. "I need to ask you something."

"You can ask me anything." His brown eyes were light as they regarded her.

"The conversation I had with Cayr today, it made something clear to me," she said carefully. "The king's ball is in a week's time. I need a partner."

He was silent a moment. "Are you asking me?"

The restrained hope in his voice almost made her cry. "Yes, Dash, I'm asking you."

"Are you sure?" he asked carefully. "I mean, if we go together, everyone will know."

"There's nobody else to hide it from but my father, and I don't want to do that any longer. He won't be happy, and he may not accept it, but that doesn't make hiding it from him right."

"You're allowing me to formally court you?" Uncertainty filled his voice.

She swallowed. "Yes."

"That means I will have the right to pick you up and take you to the ball, to have the first and last dance with you, and escort you home afterwards. It means we go to formal events together from now on."

"I'm aware of how courting works." The nervous tremor in her voice undercut her attempt at dry humour.

Dashan took a deep breath. "You have no idea how much you asking this means to me. But have you thought it through? The court won't react well. Your father could refuse permission. Nobody will accept a half-Shiven bastard courting Lady Egalion."

"I know all of that, and I won't pretend it doesn't scare me," she admitted. "But if both of us want this, then it's our only choice. As Lady Egalion, I can't have a secret relationship forever. Not if we want a future."

"And you want that for us?" He seemed unable to believe what she was telling him, both hope and delight warring in his eyes.

"Now that I'm staying, I think it's time to start building my future —a real one, not a fantasy built on hopes and unrealistic expectations," she said quietly. "And yes, I want you to be part of it. Do you? I know I haven't really asked what you—"

His hands came up to frame her face, the expression on his face causing the words to die on her tongue. "More than anything else in the world."

She hadn't realised how much those words would mean to her, and tears welled despite how hard she tried to hold them back. "Okay then."

"No tears," he whispered, wiping her cheek with a thumb. "I'm going to be here, at your side, forever."

His arms came around her, holding her tightly to him. Her head dropped forward into his chest, her eyes slipping closed. At that very moment, when she thought she was happier than she'd ever been, a shiver of foreboding ran down her spine. She'd brushed away his concerns, wrapped up in her own determination, but part of her knew courting Dashan Caverlock wasn't going to be easy.

CHAPTER 18

Alyx rode slowly back through the city. It was a warm
summer's night, and still early enough that the city streets
were thronged with people. Her emotions churned, lurching
from guilt and pain when she thought of her confrontation with Cayr,
to a bubbling giddiness at the thought of giving Dashan permission to
court her. Then she wondered how his conversation with Cayr was
going. Both men relied on their friendship so much, it was going to
hurt them badly to lose it, and over her, of all people. She wasn't worth
that. The guilt came flooding back.

In an effort to shake off her heavy thoughts, she focused more
intently on her surroundings, hoping that being out in the city she
loved would settle her. It was so surprising to see Casovar's tall figure
crossing the street a block ahead—heading into the party district—it
took a good long moment for Alyx to be certain it was him. He wasn't
wearing his customary mage attire, but the crisp strides and slight sag
to his shoulders were unmistakable.

Making a snap decision, she rode Tingo over to the nearest inn and
tied his reins to a post out front. A sharp gesture and a coin flicked to a
loitering groom ensured Tingo would be watched, and she headed on
foot into the party district.

These streets were even busier, and Alyx pushed through, catching sight of Casovar disappearing around a corner two blocks ahead. Speeding up, she cursed the light sandals she'd worn to dinner. She'd be able to move much faster in her boots.

Three blocks and two right turns later, Casovar paused outside a well-lit inn that had a sprawling garden area out the back. He looked around carefully. Instinct told her he was using not only his eyes but his magic too. She ducked into the alley she'd just passed, hurriedly reinforcing her telepathic shield. After a few long moments had gone by, she inched forward just far enough to see across the street where Casovar stood. Seemingly satisfied nobody was watching, he pushed through the door and disappeared inside.

Alyx counted under her breath. When she judged enough time had passed, she stepped out onto the street. Instantly a hand closed around her wrist, yanking her back into the dim light of the alley. Fear and magic flared together, and she was a second away from loosing a panicked concussive burst when she recognised Cario's face.

"Get off me!" she snapped, shoving him as hard as she could. "What are you doing?"

"Wait!" he hissed. "Look."

Heart still thumping, Alyx copied Cario as he pressed himself against the rough brick wall and peered around the corner. She opened her mouth to demand what it was she was supposed to be looking at when Dunnat's stocky form appeared walking down the street from the opposite direction. He, too, was dressed in civilian clothing, and paused outside the inn to look around before going inside.

"If I hadn't grabbed you, you'd have walked right into him." Cario sounded as irritated as she was.

"What are you even doing here?"

"I was enjoying a nice beverage at The Thorn up the street when I noticed you come skulking past. What possessed you to go following Lord-Mage Casovar?"

"He's not exactly the type to frequent the party district. And certainly not for friendly drinks with a captain in his Mage Guard."

"Hey! Do you think the both of you could stop looking both obvious and suspicious and get in here?"

Alyx spun, eyes widening at the sight of Brynn standing in one of the doorways leading off the alley.

"I'm serious," Brynn hissed. "Get in here."

With a glance back across the road at the inn, Alyx reluctantly conceded Brynn was right. She gestured for Cario to follow her and they pushed past Brynn into a dim hallway. Once he'd closed the door, leaving them almost entirely in the dark, his voice instructed, "Keep going straight down the hall. There are stairs at the end, go up two flights then go into the first door to your left."

Following his instructions brought them into a dusty, empty room that smelt faintly of mould. The only light came through a pair of dirt-streaked windows looking down over the main street. Alyx's mouth curled in distaste.

"Who is he?" Cario demanded.

"I take it this is Cario?" Brynn said as he closed the door behind him.

"Cario, meet Brynn. He's an old friend and he works for the council."

"I'm a spy," Brynn said flatly. "One who is very dubious about your intentions given what Alyx has told me about you."

"You have some intelligence then," Cario noted. "And you're the council spy in Alistriem. That fact alone makes me very dubious of you."

"Brynn is a trusted friend," Alyx said.

Cario gave a curt nod. "If you say so."

"Why did you bring us up here, Brynn?"

"To get you off the street before whoever it is Casovar and Dunnat are meeting with shows up." Brynn pointed to the window. "From there you'll get an excellent view of the garden behind the inn. I've spent my evenings for the past week and a half here. Casovar and Dunnat have showed up twice, and both times nobody came to meet them."

"Maybe they're just meeting each other?" Cario said.

"No," Alyx disagreed. "There's no reason for them to meet in the party district. They see each other every day at the palace."

"Indeed." Brynn moved to the window. "Maybe tonight will be the night."

"He's the lord-mage of Rionn, and narcissistic to boot," Cario pointed out. "You want us to believe he's willing to be repeatedly stood up by whoever he's meeting with?"

"It's a good point." Alyx agreed.

"The theory that he and Dunnat regularly go out for a night on the town together works for you, then?" Impatience threaded Brynn's voice.

Sharing a look acknowledging that point, Alyx and Cario joined Brynn at the window. Casovar and Dunnat sat at a table in the back corner, neither of them talking as they sat with full mugs of ale. The temptation to use her telepathic magic to read their thoughts was close to overwhelming, but she pushed it away in frustration. Too high a chance Casovar would detect her using magic.

A silence fell as they stood and stared out the window. After a short time, Alyx began fidgeting, bored and hoping something would happen soon. "This is what you've been doing instead of watching the Mage Guard?" she asked eventually.

"There are only a certain number of hours in the day." Impatience threaded Brynn's voice. "And I do have other tasks. If you want me to find out whether Casovar is trustworthy, I thought focusing on him would be smarter than following around his underlings."

"His underlings are dragging citizens out of their homes and beating them bloody for no good reason. If you could get proof of that to take to the king—"

Cario cut her off with a scornful gesture. "If your king doesn't already know what's going on in his city, Alyx, then he's not fit to sit on the throne."

The words resonated sharply with her. It was a thought that had been nagging at her for some time—if the Bluecoats and her father knew, then surely the king had to. But why hadn't he done anything about it?

"I'm sick of doing nothing," she said into the silence. "As soon as the twins and Tarrick are back, we're coming up with a plan. I don't care what my father says."

"It's not the worst idea, more reasonable than what you normally come up with," Cario drawled. "You've got the prince on your side too."

She caught Brynn's eyes flicking towards her at the mention of Cayr, one eyebrow raised. She gave a little shake of her head, and thankfully he changed the subject.

"They usually don't stay much longer than this if nobody shows," he said.

"Wait," Cario murmured. "A man just walked in. He's at least part Shiven, I'd swear to it."

"Where?" Alyx asked.

"He just went inside...wait a moment..." Cario pointed. "There. He's making straight for Casovar's table."

Alyx studied the man Cario was pointing to. He had the Shiven build and graceful manner of walk, but his ears were hidden by lengthy black hair and his skin wasn't as white-pale as Galien. His clothes were non-descript but well-tailored, and as he sat at the table with Casovar, he waved off the serving boy who approached with a sharp gesture that marked him as either self-important or noble.

"I would give anything to know what they're talking about," Brynn said.

"Could it be one of his spies?" Cario asked.

"That's the most likely answer. He doesn't look much like a spy though."

"Isn't that the point?" Cario sounded irritated.

The three men didn't talk long. The stranger rose from the table after only a few minutes of conversation. His graceful strides carried him out of the inn within moments.

"I'm going after him," Brynn said, turning for the door. "Don't either of you leave until Casovar and Dunnat are well away."

Alyx watched Brynn reach the alley and join the crowds along the main street. Casovar and Dunnat lingered only a few moments longer before also getting up to leave. They separated at the entrance and headed in opposite directions.

"I hope Brynn finds something," Alyx said as she and Cario went back down to the street.

Cario nodded. "I've had no luck winning Casovar over. He trusts me no more than he trusts you, despite my position."

"It's probably because of your position. I don't think Casovar is any more a friend of the council than he is of Garan Egalion's daughter," she said. "What does the council have to say about it?"

Cario gave a sharp laugh. "They won't even tell me what they're interested in here. Casovar has to be a part of it."

"Then why haven't they sent a spy to Rionn before now to watch him? No, there's something more."

"The something more is you, Alyx." Cario stopped walking. "There are now two mages of the higher order outside of the council's control. Wake up and realise what that means."

"They can't think I'm colluding with Casovar?"

"They don't know what to think. That's why they're worried, and that's why Brynn is here."

Alyx rolled her eyes. "I wish they'd worry about something important for a change. What a bunch of paranoid, scared old men."

Cario snorted in laughter. "I'd love to see you say that to their faces. Jokes aside, you don't want them seeing you as a threat."

"I know, I know. I'm staying clear of all Taliath not related to me, don't worry."

"You're taking this too lightly," he warned. "It's bad enough you have contact with two Taliath. If the council thought for a single second that you might have one as a lover—"

"I know the story!" she cut him off. "I know that was how Shakar became invincible, and I'm not an idiot."

He raised his hands in the air in surrender. "Fine."

Alyx stifled a yawn. "It's late. I'm going home. Did you ride down? I left Tingo stabled a couple of blocks away."

"I walked, so you go on ahead."

"It's fine, I'm in no rush. I could stand a walk back."

CARIO AND ALYX arrived home to find Safia still up. Glancing down the hall, Alyx saw the light under the door of her father's study.

"He's working late again?" she asked.

"I'm afraid so," Safia said. "I have a message for you, Lady. It was delivered by one of the Bluecoats a short time ago. I think his name was Josha."

"Thanks." Alyx took the note.

"Problem?" Cario asked, catching her frown as she read it.

"No."

"You sure?" He scrutinised her face, hopefully not seeing anything useful. "Where were you earlier tonight, anyway? I could have used company for dinner."

"I was invited to a formal dinner," she said vaguely. "And as much as I like you, I am not responsible for your entertainment here in Rionn."

"Yeah, yeah." He gave a mournful sigh. "See you in the morning."

"Night," she replied distantly, her focus returning to the parchment in her hands.

Dashan's unit was being sent on another patrol outside the city. His note was brief and polite, but she could read between the lines well enough. His talk with Cayr had not gone well, and she doubted anyone but Cayr had been behind the sudden orders for Dashan's unit. Sighing, she crumpled up the note and pushed it into a pocket. She would miss him.

Glancing down the hall, she warred briefly with the idea of going and talking to her father, telling him what she'd seen. Without knowing more about the stranger that Casovar had met with, however, it was unlikely her father would be willing to do anything. Resolving to talk to Brynn as soon as possible to find out what he'd learned, Alyx turned and followed Cario up the stairs.

CHAPTER 19

Alyx paused at the top of the spiral stairs leading down into the entrance foyer. It had taken her much of the afternoon to prepare for the ball, most of which time she'd spent trying to ignore the tightening knots of anxiousness in the pit of her stomach.

It wasn't the event itself that was the problem. She'd been to plenty of balls. It was more the fact that her father still didn't know about Dashan. Initially she'd not been sure it was worth the inevitable fight —there was no guarantee a relationship with Dashan would last. But it had, and now it was serious. While that fact made her both shocked and a little giddy at the same time, it meant she'd left it too long to tell her father. At least this way they'd be in public. Garan Egalion wouldn't risk a scene in front of his peers by losing his temper at the ball.

The situation with Cayr remained fraught. She'd tried talking to him on two different occasions since their confrontation, but each time one of his attendants had told her he was busy. It left her unsettled. Her best friend was hurting and there was nothing she could do about it because she was the cause—and now she was attending the ball with another man.

A man who stood waiting for her below.

The sight of him temporarily drowned all her doubts. For the first time since she'd known him, Dashan wore his formal Blue Guard dress uniform. A dark blue tail coat hugged his broad shoulders perfectly, sitting elegantly above a matching blue vest over a crisp white shirt. A silken blue wrap encircled his waist, and a black tie wrapped around the high, stiff white collar of his shirt, disappearing into the buttoned vest. Underneath he wore fitted black pants and flat, polished black shoes. To finish off the attire, a ceremonial sword hung from the blue sash at his waist.

He promptly spoiled the effect by reaching up to tug at his constricting collar in irritation. Alyx laughed, then walked down the stairs to greet him.

"I have to say, Captain, you certainly scrub up well."

He spun at the sound of her voice, the beginnings of a mocking response in his eyes fading away as he saw her.

"I take it from your speechlessness you approve of my choice in dress?" she asked, trying not to flush. She wore a long, calf-length violet gown that hung from her shoulders by thin straps, and fitted her body the entire way down. The material of the dress shimmered between many different shades of purple as she moved in the light. A pair of black, heeled sandals accentuated the length of her legs. Her hair she'd left loose in a shining wave down her back.

He strode towards her, stopping a proper distance away, but she could read in his body language how much he wanted to reach for her. "You look absolutely beautiful." He took her hand and kissed it.

"You look good yourself," she murmured, caught in his intense gaze.

"Is your father here?"

"No." She cleared her throat and took his proffered arm. "He left earlier. I told him I would take too long getting dressed and he should go without me. I thought that was best. I didn't want to start the night with an argument."

"You're absolutely sure?" Dashan asked, eyes searching her face. "We don't have to do this now."

It was a question she'd asked herself a thousand times, especially knowing Cayr would be there tonight. But there was so much uncertainty in her life, in the future, and the idea of facing all of that with Dashan at her side made her feel strong. So she gave him a firm nod.

"I'm sure. Let's go."

He led her outside and helped her into a waiting carriage. It rocked as he climbed in beside her and called for the driver to leave. The man called to the horses, and they jerked into motion.

"I've missed you this past week." Dashan pulled her close.

Not wanting to talk, she simply reached up to kiss him. He responded with an enthusiasm that made her breathless and dizzy.

"Have you spoken to Cayr?" he asked softly, pulling away.

"Not since the night you left. I've tried but he won't see me."

Dashan tugged at his collar again. "I wish so badly I hadn't had to do this to him."

"Me too." She sighed, resting her head against his chest.

"I really did miss you." He kissed her again, slowly, taking his time. Alyx pulled herself as close to him as she could get, realizing how terribly she'd missed being wrapped up in his arms. She became completely lost in the kiss, drowning herself in the sensation of Dashan's mouth and his body pressed against hers.

"Alyx!" He pushed her back gently.

The sharpness of his voice brought her back to reality; they were both breathing heavily and without knowing it, she had undone the buttons on his shirt and her hand was sliding over the skin of his chest.

"Sorry." Embarrassed, she pulled back.

"Don't be." He re-did his buttons, then took her hand to pull her close again. "But we're in a carriage on the way to the ball. It's not the best place to... you know."

"I didn't think that we would... " She stammered to a halt. This was new territory. Discomfort made her cheeks burn.

"One day I'm going to keep going until you don't even remember your own name." His breath was warm in her ear as he kissed her forehead. "But not now. We have time. I'll wait as long as you need me to."

She nodded against his chest, still trying to regain her composure.

After a long moment she leaned up to kiss his cheek. "I think it should be soon, Dash."

He smiled softly. "All right, mage-girl."

She kissed him lightly, then pulled away to sit on her side of the carriage. His hand remained tightly enclosed in hers.

IT WAS ONLY a short distance to the palace, and it wasn't long before the carriage pulled up at the base of the marble steps leading to the grand ballroom's entrance.

Doubt suddenly plagued her—maybe this hadn't been the best idea? But then Dashan's warm hand took hers once they'd alighted from the carriage. His touch relaxed her, and she tried to push her uneasiness to the back of her mind.

"Last chance to change your mind," he murmured, giving her a small smile as they reached the top of the stairs.

"I want to be here with you." And those words, at least, were true.

He dropped her hand and offered his arm instead. Alyx rested her fingers lightly on his forearm, and they stepped forward to join the short line of those being presented to the ball.

She took a deep breath as they came to the front of the line and the herald asked for their names and titles. Nerves fluttered like butterflies in her stomach, and she tried to keep the anxiety from showing on her face.

Then they were stepping through into the grand ballroom, and the herald was announcing them in his clear, penetrating voice.

"Lady Alyx Egalion and Captain Dashan Caverlock."

There was a noticeable beat of silence, during which many of the court looked up in surprise. She felt every single one of those eyes fixing on her, and as the moment dragged on she kept her head high, trying to ignore her heart thundering in her chest.

Then those behind them were announced, and the moment passed. Alyx sighed inwardly in relief and they walked down into the ballroom. Dashan leaned into her slightly in support. She smiled up at him, then as she looked away, her gaze caught on her father crossing the room to greet her. His face registered surprise, then confusion as he saw her on Dashan's arm.

For a moment she panicked. What have I done? But it was too late, Dashan was doing the proper thing and steering them over to greet her father.

"Good evening, Captain." Her father's greeting jerked her back to reality. His voice was tight and restrained, and Alyx read something almost like panic in his eyes. Her heartbeat, only just beginning to settle, began thudding again.

"Lord Egalion." Dashan bowed his head. "Good evening."

"Papa, we can talk if you like?" she said as genuinely as she could. "I know I should have told you before now, but Dashan and I are—"

"May I ask your indulgence for a short time, Captain?" Garan said, cutting off her words as if he hadn't even heard them. "There are some matters I need to discuss with my daughter."

"Of course, sir." Dashan frowned as he seemed to catch what Alyx had in her father's face, but he had no choice except to agree.

"Your father is providing me some assistance tonight, lad." Garan stepped closer, dropping the formality from his voice. "If you could help him with his efforts, I would very much appreciate it. Tell him I sent you over."

Dashan's shoulders straightened. "I'll do what I can, my lord."

"I'll come and find you soon." Alyx squeezed Dashan's hand. His eyes acknowledged her reassurance and he squeezed back.

"Lord Egalion." Dashan bowed his head again, and walked away. He glanced back at Alyx once he was a short distance off, offered her a smile, and then he was gone.

"Papa, what—"

"If you'll come with me, Aly-girl?" Garan interrupted. "And hold your questions for a few moments."

He led her through the crowded ballroom and out into a deserted hallway. After glancing around several times to make sure they were alone, he ushered her through a doorway and down another long corridor. It was an area of the palace she wasn't familiar with, and her puzzlement deepened as her father led her through a non-descript doorway.

Beyond was a small lounge. A fire crackled in the grate despite the warm summer evening, and the plush carpet was scattered with lounge chairs. Already in the room was Cayr, standing by the fireplace, and General Sparkish, sitting comfortably in one of the chairs. Both men seemed to have been deep in conversation, interrupted by the opening door. She'd never been so sorely tempted to use her telepathic magic.

"Casovar?" Sparky directed his question at Garan.

"Being thoroughly distracted by Lord Caverlock and his son. We've got some time before he notices us missing."

"Even so, we shouldn't spend too long in here," Cayr said, looking everywhere but at Alyx.

Alyx opened her mouth to ask what was going on, but was forestalled by her father turning to her with a puzzled expression. "Why would you bring Dashan to the ball?"

Alyx's glance flicked to Cayr, who shook his head and said coolly, "I didn't tell him, I felt that was your place. You should have told him earlier."

"Told me what?" There was an edge to her father's voice now.

Alyx determinedly didn't look at Cayr. "Dashan is here tonight because I gave him permission to court me."

"You gave him permission to... " Garan's voice trailed off, the confusion on his face deepening for a moment, quickly replaced by dawning realisation. "You mean, you and he—"

"I know that you should have given your approval too," she cut him off. "But, Papa, if you're going to say something about how he's not good enough for me because he's half-Shiven, I don't want to hear it."

"If only that was all it was." Garan rubbed his forehead, seemingly at a complete loss. His hand was shaking. Something was wrong. Badly wrong. Her fingers curled at her sides, and she suddenly missed the weight of her mage staff hanging down her back.

"Then what is it about?" She studied him closely, worry bubbling up in her. "I know I should have told you sooner, but... you look like something is terribly wrong. What is it?"

Dread struck at her when he simply shook his head. She'd never seen him look this shaken, and the fear in his eyes terrified her. "I hadn't realised about you and Dashan. I never even imagined that you would... "

"My lord, is everything all right?" Cayr frowned, glancing between Garan, Alyx and Sparky. The grizzled general looked equally at a loss. This wasn't anger at a daughter agreeing to court someone without permission. This was a lot more. Alyx's dread deepened.

"I'm fine, Your Highness." Garan waved away his concern.

"Someone tell me why I'm here," she said, fear making her voice sharp. "And why Lord Caverlock is distracting Casovar."

"We'd like to talk to you about Lord-Mage Casovar, and we'd prefer he didn't know we were meeting like this," Sparky replied, when Garan said nothing. "Take a seat, Lady Egalion, please."

Alyx obeyed, utterly confused. What had Lord-Mage Casovar to do with her bringing Dashan to the ball, and why was Sparky in the room? Above all, what had her father so unsettled?

"As you seem to have already gathered for yourself, Lord-Mage Casovar is not good for Rionn, Alyx," Garan began, seemingly gathering control of himself. "If things continue as they are, we estimate the Shiven will overrun us within the next two years."

"I didn't know things were that bad, but..." She stopped as his words sank in. "How do you know that?"

"He's mismanaging troops on the border, putting resources needed for the army into his ineffectual Mage Guard, and in short employing the wrong tactical strategies in the disputed area," Sparky said. "Casovar may be a powerful mage, but he is no military leader."

"If that's the case, surely the king has noticed?"

"Your father and I have tried several times to speak to him on the issue, but he has dismissed us each time," Sparky said. "Casovar's influence over the king is powerful."

"You knew about this?" Alyx demanded of Cayr.

"I did what I promised you I would," he said stiffly. "And when I looked further into the Mage Guard activities, I found a lot of things I didn't like. When my father brushed off my concerns, I went to your father for advice. He shared his concerns with me."

"Why wouldn't you tell me that?" Alyx spun to her father. The messages her father had been receiving from Cayr—and neither of them had told her what was going on. Anger was rising quickly inside her, but none of the dread had faded, making a potent mix. She could barely sit still. "I've repeatedly asked you to tell me what is bothering you."

"I haven't said anything for good reason. The lord-mage has telepathic magic. We have to be extremely careful about what he might read in our thoughts," Garan said. "As a Taliath, I'm invulnerable to his magic, but the rest of you aren't."

"Lord Egalion is careful about what he tells us and what he asks us to do," Cayr added. "Whenever I'm around the lord-mage, I fill my thoughts with silly things."

"And I focus on troop numbers and logistics," Sparky muttered.

Alyx was silent a moment as she processed what all this meant. "Papa, what exactly is it you're doing here, planning a coup?"

"Of course not," Garan said. "I've done nothing, just as General Sparkish has done nothing, while our power and influence at court have slowly been eroded. The truth is, we simply couldn't see what to do about it. The king is our oldest and dearest friend, Aly-girl. You have to understand that to even conceive of acting against him was abhorrent to us."

"Was?" she asked sharply.

"If something isn't done, Darien will lose his country." Garan sighed heavily. "That's what finally decided us."

"Decided you on what?" Impatience coiled with residual dread and anger, her foot tapping a rhythm against the floor. She wanted to know where this was going.

Sparkish looked at her. "We've come up with a plan to remove Casovar's influence and push him out of Rionn. If we can manage that, then Garan and I can re-establish our relationship with the king and hopefully rectify the situation with Shivasa before it's too late." He paused. "But we need your help."

"I've been asking what I can do for weeks, Papa," she said. Foreboding pressed down upon her like a lodestone. What was she missing? "What's different now?"

"Until Lord-Mage Casovar came along, Egalion was the most powerful house in Alistriem outside the royal family," Sparkish said.

"We are fortunate that the king's son has not been swayed as his father has. Prince Cayr sees Casovar as clearly as we all do."

There was a respect in Sparky's voice as he spoke about the prince that Alyx hadn't heard before. She glanced at Cayr's unreadable features, still not understanding where this was going. Her father came and sat in the chair beside hers, reaching out to take her hand in his.

"We propose to unite the Egalion and Llancarvan families through the marriage of you and Cayr. When Prince Cayr reaches his majority, he can begin to take on more responsibility and influence. With you as his wife, carrying the power and fortune of the Egalion house, you will share a power base that could remove Casovar's influence entirely."

And there it was.

"You want me to marry Cayr." She repeated his words, not sure she'd heard them correctly.

"Marry Cayr, and re-establish your influence amongst the court. Yes."

Such a simple word, but it hit her like a blow.

"What about the king? He wants Cayr to marry Jenna, because that's what Casovar wants."

"All amongst the most senior lords have agreed to throw their support behind a betrothal between you and Prince Cayr. The king will have no choice but to agree. As influential as Casovar is, nobody will support the prince of Rionn marrying a mage's adopted daughter. You are the most appropriate match for Prince Cayr, Alyx."

"Every powerful lord... " Alyx echoed. "You just got through telling me the threat Casovar's telepathic magic poses to your plans, yet you've been talking to all the lords!"

"I didn't tell them what I was planning." Impatience threaded Garan's voice. "I merely sought their views on a marriage between my daughter and the prince. From now on, we will all need to be very careful around Casovar."

"I will make my father agree to this," Cayr spoke for the first time, looking straight into Alyx's eyes.

"This was your idea, wasn't it?" she whispered.

"You are the one who pushed me, who wouldn't let it go." Fire filled his voice. "And you were right. I will be king of all of Rionn, not just the rich and powerful. What is happening to my people is wrong! I don't know why Casovar has so much influence over my father, but I will do what it takes to deal with him."

"You say we'll be overrun within two years, Papa." She tried to focus her thoughts, to think through what they were telling her. "Cayr won't reach his majority for two years, yet you think we can push Casovar out before then? And what about my magic, the twins—we're still half-trained, and without Casovar, we need to go back to Dark-Skull to finish training."

"Our marriage will solidify the connection of our two houses in the eyes of the other lords and increase your father's influence at court," Cayr answered for Garan. "You and I will solidify our influence with the youth of the court—the future lords that will be my power base. Casovar will find himself without allies. Together, your father and I, and Sparky, can begin taking on more of my father's decisions. Eventually we'll bring Astor back and formally replace Casovar."

"And at that point you can go back to DarkSkull, if it's still what you want," Garan added. "The twins too. Astor's job will be yours once you've passed your trials, and all three of you will be invaluable against the Shiven threat."

Alyx rose from her chair and went to the other side of the room, her mind frozen with shock. She was being offered everything she had ever wanted, and with that, she was being given a chance to save her country, to fight back against Casovar. The pull of that was undeniable, the attraction of what had once been her greatest desires. But that was just it, she wasn't that girl anymore. She was a young woman who loved Cayr, but only as her dear friend.

"Cayr, I've made things very clear to you," she said.

"You have." He couldn't entirely keep the pain from his voice, but there was something in him she'd never seen before. A resoluteness and steel that belied his usual cavalier attitude. This was Cayr growing into a man, and part of her couldn't help but be proud. "But this is what's best for Rionn. You should know your father and I discussed our marriage before I knew about... well, I thought I was doing what we both wanted. I'm not trying to trap you, but I am determined to do what is right for Rionn."

"I… " His words shook her. "A marriage of friendship, is that what you really want? Because I don't."

"The prince is right, Aly-girl, this isn't about either of you." Her father rose.

There had been no condescension in his voice, but even so the words triggered anger inside her. "I understand that, but will you really force me into a marriage I don't want? There has to be another way to deal with Casovar."

"You know that I love you too much to force you into marriage, but I also think it's time you grew up and realised you don't live in a bubble," he said firmly. "Life is not always fair."

The words hung in the air for a long moment, and she wasn't sure she'd heard them correctly. But the determined expression remained on his face, and her anger flared into a burning rage.

"Fair?" she whispered, her voice shaking with the force of the emotion she felt. "You think I won't face reality, Papa, that I don't know what life is really like?"

"Alyx—"

"I'll give you reality," she said coldly. "How about my first year at DarkSkull Hall? Did I tell you about the Shiven apprentice there that tried to kill me? He would have succeeded too, on more than one occasion, had it not been for the son you don't even know, my friends who you think aren't good enough for me, and sheer luck."

Garan blanched, as did Cayr. Both men reached for her.

She stepped back. "Did I tell you about the man who stood over Tarrick lying unconscious on the ground and tried to slit his throat? Did I tell you that I looked at that man, wanted him dead, and my magic killed him? Or how I watched his head explode into a mess of brain and blood right in front of me?"

She stopped briefly, chest heaving, unable to stop the torrent of words. "And then I chose, willingly chose, to go back to that hell because I thought I could help Rionn. This time I was beaten within an inch of my life on a sparring yard while all the students watched. The mage master was going to let my opponent kill me, and he would have, if I hadn't somehow managed to drag myself off the icy ground and fight back the way that Dashan taught me.

"And once I finally began to make some progress there, I was arbitrarily summoned back home and told to hold my tongue while being mocked and humiliated for weeks by a lord-mage who thinks I'm useless. I did all of that because you asked me to, and you stand there and accuse me of needing to grow up! You told me to trust you, yet you've betrayed me in the worst way imaginable."

There was a moment of stunned silence after she stopped, panting, emotion roping through her. Her forearms were alight with a silver-green glow. Through the blurred vision of the tears in her eyes, Alyx saw Cayr's horror, Sparky's grim acknowledgement of her words and her father, suddenly looking older than she'd ever seen him.

"Alyx, I'm sorry," Garan said eventually.

"You sent me there," she whispered. "You knew, you had to know, my mother went through the same thing. Yet you sent me there, and you refused to think about what that meant for me. So don't you dare tell me that I have no grasp on reality, or on what's fair!"

"You're right, that was wrong of me," Garan admitted. "You have clearly suffered already, and that breaks my heart, but it doesn't change anything. You say you want to protect Rionn, and this is how you can do it."

"I don't love Cayr." She looked at her childhood friend now. "I'm sorry, I don't. The last thing I want in the world is to cause you pain, but I won't lie to you either. If I did this, it would never be real."

Cayr opened his mouth to reply, but Garan cut him off. "Prince Cayr, Sparky, will you give me a moment alone with my daughter?"

"It's probably best if we both make a brief reappearance at the ball, to avoid Casovar becoming suspicious." Sparky went to the door and opened it to allow Cayr out before him. "We'll be back soon."

There was another moment's silence after the door closed, the only sound in the room coming from the crackling of the fire in the grate. Alyx's anger was fading, and with it the green glow of her magic. "Papa—"

"Alyx, no matter what happens between you and Cayr, Dashan can't be yours," Garan's voice cut her off.

"How could you know that?" she asked angrily. Her father met her eyes, and they were bleak with a terrible understanding.

"He's a Taliath."

The words cut through the room like a knife. Alyx stilled, the equal weight of despair and horror expanding and filling her chest until she couldn't breathe.

Then her heart broke.

CHAPTER 20

"N o," she whispered.

"You think I would be wrong about something like that?" Garan said softly. "I'm sorry, it's true. If you think about it, you know too."

Of course she knew.

The only shock was how she'd not realised it sooner. His agility and grace, his sublime skill with a weapon, with command. His instinctive tactical sense—he'd had those militia soldiers eating from his hand. How hadn't she seen it? Because she'd been conditioned not to—because they all had. Dashan was worthless, half-Shiven, a young man who preferred drinking, women and gambling over doing anything remotely serious. What a fool she'd been.

And how close to disaster they'd both come.

She nodded, dropping into a chair as her legs turned suddenly rubbery. Her mouth had gone dry and all the anger had drained from her. Now there was only an odd kind of numbness.

"There can be no future for you with Dashan, not with what you both are. You would be hunted and destroyed. The danger of what you might become—"

"You don't need to tell me of all people the consequences." She cut him off, unable to bear hearing it all again.

Garan moved to kneel before her, one tentative hand coming out to touch her hair. "I hadn't realised that you and Dashan were... or I would have told you about him sooner. I'm sorry, but you have no other choice. Rionn needs you to do as we ask."

Oh Dashan, I'm so terribly, terribly sorry.

Because she couldn't say no to this. Couldn't refuse to help save her country, the beautiful city she loved so much. But more than that, it was because in the past two years she'd become someone who couldn't even consider doing this to her friends... to put them in this position. Horror turned her stomach at the thought. All of them hunted mercilessly by the council. Tarrick's bright future ruined. They would stand by her, and they would die for it. And Dashan would too. Her heart lurched.

And underneath all that a trickle of fear—could she become another Shakar if she were invincible... surely not? But still that doubt wormed through her, insidious and potent.

Just like going to DarkSkull, there was no choice for her here. Only acceptance.

"I'll do it," she managed around the lump in her throat, unable to help the tear that trickled down her cheek.

"I am so sorry, Aly-girl." Her father's voice was thick with sadness.

Alyx looked up to meet his eyes. "I don't understand. You always treated him like he was nothing, like he was a waste of your time."

"I've known since he was about thirteen," Garan admitted. "By pretending he was nothing, by encouraging others to do the same, I was trying to protect him. Why do you think I allowed his close friendship with you and Cayr despite what I said about him? It kept him under my protection."

"That's why you've been so insistent I stay away from him, ever since I told you what I am. Did you truly think him not worthy of me, or was it all a pretence?"

"In all honesty, I'm not sure what I think of Dashan. I'm certainly aware of his reputation, but I also knew the boy and young lad he was. He was a good friend for you and Cayr. He grounded you both."

"More lies and secrets," she whispered, more tears spilling now. "You promised me no more."

"This was not my secret to tell."

"If you've known for so long... you could have trained him. You and the king were looking for Taliath potentials."

"Yes, we were, but you already know a part of me suspected that potentials were going missing along with mages. Besides, if it was known that not only was I a living Taliath, but was personally training one of them? It would have increased the danger surrounding all of us —especially you, and I wasn't willing to do that."

"I don't believe this," she whispered.

"You cannot breathe a word of this to anyone, not even Dashan," Garan said. "Ignorance protects him. He lives only as long as he escapes council notice. I know you're upset, but please, hear me on this!"

She shook her head, some of her fire returning. "I know what it's like to have part of your identity kept from you your whole life, and now you're asking me to do that to him?"

"I'm asking that you use your judgement. You know him better than I do. Will he accept that he has to hide, keep himself away from Casovar and the council? When you go back to DarkSkull in a couple of years, will he agree to stay here?"

No. Dashan wasn't afraid of the Mage Council, and he certainly wouldn't let fear of them stop him from doing anything, no matter how much danger he was in. And if he thought they posed a danger to her... he'd go right for them. A shiver racked her as she realised how perilously close to discovery they must have come in Tregaya, with Dashan's skill and command ability on such clear display to mages like Rothai.

"Aly-girl?" he asked gently.

A sudden thought occurred to her, a potential solution. "Send him to Ladan."

"What?" Her father looked startled.

"The two of them have a plan," she said quickly. "Part of Widow Falls' lands are close to the Tregayan border. If things come to war with Shivasa, they have a plan to move troops quickly and safely."

"Alyx—"

"Papa, this will hurt Dashan badly. Send him to Ladan, give him something productive to do. It will keep him far away, out of sight of Casovar and the council. Please!"

"All right." Garan nodded. "I'll talk to his father and have him issue the orders in the morning."

Her shoulders sagged. "Thank you."

"Alyx..." he hesitated. "I think it would also be best if we made it clear you only came with Dashan tonight because he is an old friend of yours and Cayr's. For the same reason Dashan can't know what he is, it can't be known that you and he were... "

"You're right," she said heavily. She was already about to cut ties with Dashan, she may as well repudiate everything they'd shared as well. The numbness was creeping back, holding off the terrible knowledge of what this was going to do to Dashan, of what it was going to do to her.

Garan sank back on his heels, looking utterly lost. "I never wanted you to have to go through what your mother and I did. How did we end up here?"

"You would have been better to send him away as a boy," she said bitterly. "Then I would never have known him."

"You don't mean that," he said quietly.

"No, I don't." She wiped furiously at her eyes.

A knock came at the door then, and she straightened, pulling away from her father's touch. "You'd better let them in."

She rose as her father opened the door to let the two men back in. Cayr's eyes went straight to her, and she nodded. "I'll do what you're asking."

He nodded soberly. "Thank you, Alyx."

Her father glanced between them. "We'll start putting it about quietly that the two of you are formally courting, close to becoming betrothed. As soon as we can get the king to agree, we'll announce the betrothal officially. I'd like to aim for a marriage within the year, that will give you a good period of time before Cayr reaches his majority to begin building your base of influence."

"Then it's done." Cayr nodded at her father, looking more authoritative than he ever had. He was hiding his hurt well, she thought, and hoped she could do the same. Maybe in time they could repair what had been fractured between them.

General Sparkish cleared his throat. "We'd best all leave separately. Lady Egalion, you and Prince Cayr first. Lord Egalion and I will linger here a while."

A sense of unreality settled over her as Cayr offered her his arm and they walked out of the room and back towards the ball room. The hubbub of conversation, laughter and music crashed over her, breaking her from her daze as she stepped into the room. Her gaze immediately found Dashan. He was on the other side of the room, smiling that laughing smile of his, talking with his father and Lord-Mage Casovar.

He looked up then, meeting her eyes clear across the space between them. The smile on his face widened, then his gaze shifted to her hand on Cayr's arm.

He knew.

The brightness in his brown eyes dimmed and all the laughter faded from his features. Then without a word to either Casovar or his father he turned and walked out of the room, not looking back once. Her chest tightened so thoroughly she struggled to breathe for a long moment.

"We should dance." Cayr's jaw was clenched, his blue eyes dull. He'd no doubt seen what she had. Nonetheless his voice was soft as he held out his hand to her. And she'd promised to do this, so she took his hand and allowed him to lead her onto the dance floor.

She resolutely refused to look in the direction Dashan had gone.

ALYX AND CAYR made a good show of it for the rest of the evening. They shared most of the formal dances together, and spent the time in between standing together talking, or making rounds of the room as a couple, speaking to the more important nobles.

Eventually, she pled exhaustion and Cayr walked her out to her father's carriage. They came to a hesitant halt before the open door.

"I had hoped this would be the perfect situation," he said, failing to keep the hurt from his voice. "Now we're both trapped, I suppose."

"I'm so sorry that I hurt you," she told him.

"You did," he said. "And tonight I've hurt you and Dashan both. But I meant what I said. I will do anything for my country, it's who I am. You made me realise that. I don't get any choice."

She looked away from him. "Neither do I. I don't want to talk about this anymore tonight."

"I understand." He helped her up into the carriage. "Good night, Alyx."

She couldn't find the words to reply.

As soon as the carriage dropped her at home, Alyx went upstairs and changed into an old tunic and breeches before slipping out her window and going straight to the stables. She took Tingo out a side gate so she wouldn't be seen, and rode down to the city. It was after midnight now and the streets were dark and quiet.

Her first instinct was right, and she found Dashan down at the docks. He was sitting on a wooden railing, staring down at his boat, which bobbed on the water below. He'd discarded his tailcoat and tie, and now just wore the vest and shirt, sleeves rolled up to his elbows. Alyx walked down the length of the dock and climbed up onto the rail to sit beside him. He glanced up at her arrival, but said nothing.

"I guess I have some explaining to do," she said, unsure where to begin.

His gaze remained firmly on the water below them. "It's over, isn't it?"

"Yes," she said simply, then took a breath and told him what her father and Cayr had asked of her.

After she'd stumbled to a halt he was quiet for a few moments, then, "Casovar is really that bad for us, huh?" He gave a bitter chuckle. "Well who didn't see that coming."

"It's not exactly a surprise, is it?"

Another beat of silence, then, "so you've agreed to marry Cayr?"

"Even since I came back, I've been so determined to throw off the constraints of being Lady Egalion," she said. "I figured deciding to go back to DarkSkull and be an apprentice mage meant I didn't have to conform anymore. I was wrong, and the worst part of it is that I've hurt you in the process. I am so sorry, Dashan." She took a deep breath, forcing out the words. "Yes, I'm going to marry Cayr."

Dashan let out a long breath, as if trying to contain his emotion. "He's always been the better match for you. You've been ignoring the constraints of who you are, but so have I. I'm never going to be anything more than what I am now."

The urge to tell him everything was close to overwhelming. Letting him think he wasn't good enough, that she didn't choose him, was agonising, a sharp physical pain in her chest. But her father had been right. Dashan would be safer this way. And she needed Dashan to be safe.

Clearing her throat, she changed the subject. "After what Papa told me about Casovar, I'm worried about Tarrick and the twins."

Dashan's face cleared as her words sunk in. "They don't know what they've walked into up there. You haven't heard from them at all, have you?"

"Not once." Worry surged. "Do you think you could get a message to them through the Bluecoats without Casovar knowing?"

"I can. You want me to include everything?" he asked carefully, eyes darkening again.

"Not specific details, in case it gets into the wrong hands, but enough they get a sense of what's going on." She looked away. "I won't mention anything to Cario for now given he spends so much time around Casovar, but I don't want Tarrick and the twins returning to the city blind. They might be able to help, too, once they know. Perhaps they can learn more about what's going on at the border."

"Consider it done, mage-girl."

He said nothing more, his gaze distant, out towards the ocean. She nodded to herself, making a useless effort to swallow back her tears as she swung down off the rail. It was time to go.

"Alyx?"

She looked up, questioning. The heartbreak in his eyes almost undid her, but his words held no censure. "I understand," he said softly. "I truly do. You're doing the right thing."

"I... " and suddenly she was back at DarkSkull on the night of the dance, when she'd sent him away the first time because it was the right thing to do. The pain of it now was even worse. "Good night, Dash."

"Goodbye, Alyx." He gave her his crooked smile. "You probably won't see me for a while."

"I know. Be happy, Dash."

The salty breeze was in her hair as she walked away, mounted Tingo, and rode back through the lonely city streets towards her home.

WHEN SHE REACHED THE MANSION, it was dark and silent, her father still at the palace. Alyx left Tingo in the stables and made her way slowly up the stairs to her room. Pausing on the landing, she stared down the hall towards Cario's guest room. The door was shut, and no light shone from underneath it.

Swallowing, she turned and walked down to her own room. After she had stepped inside and shut the door behind her, she slid down until she was on the floor, knees tucked close to her chest.

Dashan was a Taliath.

The numbness that had protected her all night so far began to crack now that she was alone. She started shaking, unable to control her reaction to the knowledge as she finally allowed it to sink into her mind. Dashan was a Taliath, and they'd been so close to...

Her breath shuddered as she let it out, and she hugged her knees tightly, trying to stop the uncontrollable trembling in her limbs. Everything she'd ever heard about the Taliath clamoured through her mind —Howell's warnings, Shakar, her own stupid, foolish promise that she would never take a Taliath as a lover.

Finally, she summoned the energy to rise and change into her nightgown, then climb under the covers of the bed. Despite the warmth of the night, she huddled under the thick blankets, still shaking, curled up in a ball.

Dashan's warm gaze floated into her mind, and she started to cry.

CHAPTER 21

Despite the late hour he must have gotten in, her father was already eating when Alyx came down to breakfast the next morning. Cario, of course, still slept. He rarely appeared at the mage offices before late morning.

She said nothing as she sat down and a servant brought her a steaming bowl of oatmeal. Sleep had been impossible and emotion had left her wrung out and exhausted.

"Can we talk?" he asked

She shrugged listlessly. "About what?"

"Alyx, stop it," he said in exasperation. "Be mad at me if you will, but please, talk to me."

"Fine." Her jaw clenched and she pushed her bowl away, giving up all pretence of eating. She wasn't hungry anyway. "Why didn't you tell me about Dash? You knew how much it upset me that you'd lied about Ladan my whole life, and now you've essentially done the same thing again."

"I did it to protect him." Garan leaned forward, earnest. "I worried that if you knew, Casovar could read it in your thoughts. I never for a second imagined you would ever... you had me completely convinced Cayr was the only man you would ever consider."

"You don't think I learned how to shield myself at DarkSkull?"

"Well enough to risk Dashan's life?" Garan countered. "I don't claim to be an expert, but I have seen firsthand how powerful Casovar is."

"There are always good answers for why you've lied to me or kept secrets," she said bitterly. "But that doesn't make it any better. I'm so sick of being kept in the dark."

"So you told Dashan what he is? You haven't kept it from him?"

Her mouth tightened as Garan's pointed comment hit home. Silence fell, and he sat back in his chair with a sigh.

"You conspired with Cayr, Papa. Do you have any idea how angry and hurt that makes me? You couldn't trust me, but you trusted him? You planned with him about the rest of my life." The bitterness made her words sharp and raw, so much so he flinched.

"Alyx—"

"Enough!" She gestured sharply. "I don't want to hear any more apologies. Tell me about Casovar. You said he was mismanaging troops because he's not a military tactician, but all mages learn basic strategy at DarkSkull. Not only that, but he had years of experience in the field working for the Mage Council—and why did the king even hire him if he couldn't prove his credentials? He shouldn't be doing such a bad job. Is he actively working against us?"

Garan let her questions wash over him, a glimmer of respect appearing in his eyes. She should have been relieved, but it only fed her anger. When was he going to accept she was more than a spoiled, naïve girl?

"Sparky and I have asked ourselves the same questions over and over, but I can't see any motivation for Casovar to be working against us. He was a respected council mage before he came here. He has a lot to lose by not doing a good job."

"Have you tried confronting him about his mismanagement?"

"Yes." Garan's face tightened. "He dismisses us and our concerns as if we were paranoid schoolboys."

Something about that rang oddly with her. "That's more than arrogance. He knows you're a Taliath, and therefore he knows your tactical experience." She paused. "How did he gain such influence over the king? Why isn't he listening to your advice? You're his best friend."

"That's easy. Casovar plays on Darien's fears of the Shiven and distrust of the mages. He started the moment he got here. He warns the king that unless Rionn manages the Shiven situation alone, the council will stick their noses in, take his power away. And then he spends every other second warning him that Shiven are everywhere."

She shook her head. Something wasn't making sense—she could almost hear Finn's voice in her ear whispering the questions. "So he's cunning enough to do that, but not smart enough to manage our troops properly?"

Garan sighed, the familiar weariness returning to his visage and aging him before her eyes. It was hurting him, what he was having to do to Darien, and it had obviously taken him many months of wrestling with his conscience to decide to do it. "Whatever the truth, we need Casovar out of Rionn. Darien isn't going to do it, so the lords will have to force the issue. That's where you come in."

She nodded. "The plan. I said I'd do it, and I meant it."

"The choices I made to protect you... " He reached over to take one of her hands. "You have to know I never intended for them to hurt you the way they have. Even more, I'm sorry that I failed to understand how it changed you."

She tugged her hand away, not willing to let him off the hook yet. She was still too angry and disappointed in him. "You can't keep me out of this anymore. I'll do what you ask, but in return you have to involve me," she spoke firmly, forcing him to meet her gaze. "No more 'protecting' me."

He nodded, speaking just as firmly. "Agreed, Aly-girl."

"Good. Then I'll see you later."

"I'm sorry things have to be this way," he said as she walked toward the door.

She paused in the doorway, shrugging slightly. "It's just real life, right?"

"I suppose it is."

His words, softly spoken and full of regret, followed her down the hall.

. . .

RETURNING TO HER ROOM, Alyx opened the doors to her massive closet and studied its contents with a critical eye. There were a couple of dresses she thought could stay, but the rest would be horribly out of fashion after two years.

Summoning a maid, she had the closet emptied of all but the two dresses, then dressed in her mage robes and went down to pen a quick note for Safia to send over to the palace. A short ride into the city brought her to the wealthy quarter and one of Alistriem's most exclusive tailors.

He was delighted to see her, spent several minutes bemoaning her absence from his store, then smothered her with fabrics and designs to choose from before summoning an army of assistants to take her measurements.

"You're taller," he muttered to himself once they'd finished. "Wider in the hips... but skinny." He looked up, spearing her with his gaze. "You need to eat more, My Lady!"

"Yes, Sorin." She couldn't help a smile at his clucking. "Can you have the first dress done by this afternoon?"

"For you, anything."

"You're my favourite for a reason." She chuckled. "Send the invoice to my father as usual."

IT WAS late morning by the time she made it to the mage offices. Cario gave her a curious glance as she walked in. "Where have you been?"

"Shopping." She glanced around. "No Casovar?"

"Not yet. I suppose he had a late night." His blue eyes narrowed. "How was the ball?"

"The same as every other ball." She shrugged. "Have any messages come for me?"

He nodded and passed her a folded piece of parchment with Cayr's seal on it. Opening it, she scanned the contents, nodding in satisfaction. "I'll have to be gone for a few hours this afternoon."

"May I ask what for?"

"There's an afternoon tea I've been invited to."

Confusion deepened on Cario's face. "Are you somehow thinking Casovar is going to be gone all day?"

"I don't care if he is or not. He'll need to start accommodating my social commitments now that I'm courting the prince of Rionn."

Silence filled the room for a long moment. Alyx turned her focus from Cario to the pile of reports she'd been given to review, ignoring him as he rose and went to close the door before returning to sit in the chair beside hers.

"I suppose I should offer my congratulations."

"You should."

"Will you kindly tell me what the hell is going on?"

Alyx closed her eyes for a moment, summoning the façade she would need from now on. Once she was confident it had settled over her face, she turned to Cario with a happy smile. "Cayr asked me last night, I said yes. My father has given permission. We're courting. Why are you so surprised?"

"I'm not, necessarily. You always said you and the prince were close. It seems sudden, that's all. Is something else going on?"

"Nothing." She laughed at his suspicion. "Be happy for me, Cario."

"All right." He shrugged, then grinned. "Imagine the look on Casovar's face when you tell him."

They both laughed.

DESPITE HER CAVALIER words to Cario, Alyx was hoping Casovar wouldn't make an appearance until after she'd gone. Unfortunately, he came through the door as she was rising to leave, Dunnat on his heels. Cario had gone in search of food for lunch, and so she was alone in the offices.

"Where are you going, Apprentice?" Casovar sounded distracted, long strides carrying him over to one of the maps hanging on the wall. Dunnat shrugged off his cloak, flicked a contempt-filled glance in Alyx's direction, then dropped a new pile of reports on her desk. Surprise flickered at the number of them—accounts of Shiven spies seemed to increase with every week.

"I've been invited to an afternoon tea."

Casovar turned away from the map, one eyebrow raised. "I thought I'd made my expectations clear. I require your presence Firstday through Sixthday during daylight hours. Your work for me is your priority. Social engagements can be arranged outside of that."

Alyx took a breath, kept her voice calm and polite. "Actually, Lord-Mage, while I appreciate that the work I do here is important for the safety of Rionn, I now have other duties. Prince Cayr and I have formally begun courting."

The tension in the room perceptibly thickened, though Casovar made no visible reaction to her announcement. "I am surprised. The king has not made mention of any plans for his son. After all, Prince Cayr is still two years away from his majority."

"We have been close since childhood. We did not feel it necessary to wait until his majority, and Cayr has secured the agreement of my father and the senior lords."

There was a faint tightening of his jaw at her carefully chosen words—he had not been consulted. Her peripheral vision caught Dunnat sitting across the room pretending to work, his gaze flicking in fascination between Alyx and Casovar.

"You understand that I cannot avoid social engagements now that I'm courting the heir to Rionn. It wouldn't be proper," she continued smoothly.

"I will speak to the king about your duties," Casovar said eventually, his voice cold. "I do not think an apprentice mage with no talent the most appropriate match for the future king of Rionn. Nor is it a sound strategic decision."

Alyx allowed a sickly-sweet smile to spread across her face, and kept her voice polite. "With all due respect, Lord-Mage, your role is to advise the king on Rionn's security, not his son's marriage. After all, I am the only daughter of Lord Garan Egalion, Rionn's most powerful lord. Having not grown up in Alistriem, nor spent much time around nobility, I can understand how you might not realise what a sound strategic match it is."

The tension thickened further, and Alyx subconsciously straightened her shoulders, refusing to be cowed by the menace he was projecting. Dunnat had given up all pretence of work, mouth opened slightly as he stared at them. In the end, Casovar must have decided he had no room to move, and gave a sharp nod.

"Go. We'll discuss my expectations of your work once I have spoken to the king."

"Thank you. I will see you tomorrow."

Unable to help herself, she flicked a cheerful wave at Dunnat on her way out. That toad of a man wasn't going to last a single day in the Mage Guard once she was Cayr's wife.

ONE OF SORIN'S assistants had just delivered her dress when she arrived home to change. Reluctantly leaving Tingo in the stables with Henri, Alyx asked Safia to order her father's carriage and went inside to change.

The dress was stunning, and despite herself a little trickle of delight shivered through her as she slipped it on and looked at herself in the mirror. The words she'd spoken to Dashan the previous night came back to her, and this time the shiver was less pleasant. It was clear now she'd never be able to escape this part of herself—the part that was a wealthy young noblewoman—but now she could use it to help her father and Rionn.

She just couldn't let it overtake her. Not ever again.

CAYR WAITED for her at the palace, all charm and politeness as he offered his arm to help her down from her carriage. For the first time in their lives a painful awkwardness sat between them, and instead of going straight in, Cayr pulled her aside.

"Despite everything I said last night, if you really don't want to do this, tell me now," he murmured. The new seriousness she'd seen in him the night before was still there, edged with sadness.

"Neither of us really has a choice." She offered him a genuine smile. He'd been right the night before, they were both trapped. Alyx by her combined mage and noble blood and Cayr by what she'd done with Dashan. "I realise how difficult this has to be for you too."

He nodded in acknowledgement of that. "After eighteen years of friendship, I don't want to let what happened ruin us. I'm angry and hurt, and I don't think that will go away anytime soon." He took a breath, eyes closing briefly. "But I also know—rationally—that you can't help how you feel... or don't feel."

The misery in his voice had her reaching out for his hand. "I don't want to lose you either. My feelings... you're still one of the most important people in my life, and I will give you whatever space you need. Outside this whole charade, of course."

His mouth quirked in an unexpected smile. "It will be just like the old days, you and me ruling the social scene of Rionn."

Her smile stretched to match his and for that brief golden moment some of her misery was gone. "Those days were fun."

THEY'D DELIBERATELY TIMED their arrival to be fashionably late, the sun warm on Alyx's bare shoulders as Cayr escorted her through to the garden where he was hosting the afternoon tea. The chattering conversation slowly died as they appeared together, although all eyes fixed on Alyx. She hadn't attended one of their social gatherings since before going back to DarkSkull.

"It's a beautiful day for a picnic," Cayr spoke easily into the silence. "I hope you all don't mind me moving the event outside?"

"An excellent call, my friend." Jaran was the first to speak. He'd grown out of his gangliness and was all courtly politeness as he smiled at Alyx before clapping Cayr's arm. "Good to see you, Alyx. Cayr, will you come over and settle something for us? Torn insists he can swim the distance from the wharves to the city beach, but we're in genuine fear for his life."

Cayr chuckled. "I would be too. Alyx, I'll be back soon."

"Take your time," she assured him.

Jenna Casovar sat at one of several small tables dotted around the grass, two young women with her. Both had been part of Alyx's coterie once, but neither could look her in the eye as she strolled over to join them.

"Lady Egalion, how nice of you to deign to attend one of our little events." Jenna's voice oozed false sweetness. Alyx almost laughed—oh, this she could do. This was more familiar to her than breathing.

"Hello, Jenna. Lissa, Mira. I do owe all of you the most tremendous apology." Alyx infused her voice with sincerity, taking a seat without being asked. "I've been so caught up with all this mage business and helping the lord-mage. I know I've neglected my friends terribly. Will you forgive me?"

A little silence, then Lissa spoke. "Your dress is stunning, Alyx. Where did you get it made?"

"At Fironu's, down on Welter Street. Sorin designed it himself," she said cheerfully. "But I wish I'd seen your dress first—the shade of lavender you're wearing is divine. You must tell me where you got the fabric."

"At Tessens, a block over." Lissa beamed, then added shyly, "It's nice to have you back."

"It really is. Of course we forgive you. It wasn't your fault the king made you go to that awful mage school," Mira added.

Their quick forgiveness took her aback. She'd expected to have to work harder, but both young women's eyes were warm and happy, and they'd leapt at the opportunity to welcome Alyx back.

"I..." she faltered, quickly summoning her cool façade at the calculating look on Jenna's face. "I have a lot of making up to do." A warm smile, more genuine than she'd intended. "Perhaps a trip to Fironu's together soon, my treat?"

"We would love that," Lissa gushed.

Mira shot a quick look at Jenna. "There's a brunch we have planned tomorrow, but since we haven't seen you in so long, perhaps we could cancel that and go shopping instead?"

Had she underestimated these girls in how completely she'd written them off as shallow and uncaring? Alyx bit her lip at the realisation that maybe she had. After all, they'd grown up together, and that obviously still meant something to them.

"I would really like that," she said softly.

"Wonderful." Mira reached out to squeeze her hand. "We want to hear all about you and Prince Cayr, too!"

"Not that we didn't see that coming." Lissa sighed mournfully.

Alyx settled her gaze on Jenna as a wide smile spread across her face. "Good, because I can't wait to tell you all the details. I really have missed you girls."

And just like that, she was back in.

CHAPTER 22

A few days later, Alyx used the excuse of another social event to escape the palace and ride out to visit Astor. Her godfather was nose-deep in writing a letter when she was shown in. He was so absorbed in his task it took him a few moments to realise she was there.

"Alyx!" He beamed at her. "Come in."

"Hello, Astor." She went over to sit by the open window where a cool breeze ruffled her hair. "You looked very involved in that letter."

He waved a hand. "Just writing to an old friend. What brings you by?"

"I wanted to talk to you, if you have the time."

He took off his glasses and sat back in his chair. "I'm sorry, I haven't any help for you with your nightmares yet. It's not for lack of trying though, and I promise you I'm not giving up."

"That's not why I'm here." She paused, eyes scanning his face. "I know my father has been careful about... information, but I assume he or Sparky have spoken to you about their thinking in regard to Lord-Mage Casovar?"

"They have," Astor said quietly. "They are both old friends."

If she'd been holding one of his books, she'd have thrown it at him.

"Damn it Astor, last time I was here you had me convinced Casovar was doing a fantastic job!"

He gave an impish smile. "You spend almost every day with a trained mage of the higher order who can read your thoughts whenever he wants. Really Aly-girl, I have asked you to stop treating me like a doddery old man."

She made a face. "I'm guessing it was you that gave Cayr and Sparky tips on hiding their thoughts from him."

He merely smiled.

She sighed, shaking her head. "Why did Casovar come to Rionn?"

"Why do you think? For the power and prestige of being Rionn's lord-mage. That's almost as good as having a seat on the council."

That corresponded with what Cario had told her. "How did you hear about him?"

"What makes you think—"

Alyx raised a hand to cut him off. "If you don't want me to treat you like a doddery old man, then don't behave like one. How else would the king have come across Casovar? He has nothing to do with the council, nor does my father, for obvious reasons."

"Young people think they're so smart." He huffed. "Fine, yes. I wanted to retire, and of course I still have contacts in the mage world. I assisted the king in finding a replacement."

She raised her eyebrows at him. "And you picked the least likable one of the lot?"

"I didn't much care how charming he was. I wanted someone with power."

"Not just power. You picked a mage of the higher order. So you knew the threat from Shivasa was coming before anyone else here did?"

For a moment he looked caught, as if he hadn't expected her to work it out. Then he shrugged. "We all knew it was coming. The king has been worried about the increasing frequency of skirmishes in the disputed area for a long time."

"And how much do you know about the council hunting Taliath potentials?"

The question took him completely off guard. It was the first time she'd seen genuine surprise on his face in years—Astor always presented a controlled front to the world. It wasn't surprise at her words, though. It was surprise that she knew. Familiar frustration curled her hands into fists. Was everyone lying about everything?

"Your response tells me all I need to know," she said sharply. "I don't suppose you ever thought to mention it to my father or the king, all those years they were looking for potentials?"

"I had suspicions only." He frowned. "What has gotten into you, Alyx?"

"Frankly, I'm sick of all the lying and the secret-keeping. You are one of a very small number of people in my life I trust, Astor, and I expect the complete truth from you. Understood?"

After a moment, he nodded. "All right. From now on nothing but honesty, although I'd appreciate a little less of that high and mighty tone of voice."

Ignoring that, she ploughed ahead. "Have my father and Sparky told you the detail of their plans?"

"I have an inkling," Astor said carefully. "But I am retired. I would prefer not to be involved."

"Rubbish! You know far more than you'll admit to and I don't believe for a second you want to stay out of it," she snapped. "And even if you did it doesn't matter. Rionn needs you."

"I have done plenty enough for Rionn."

"It doesn't matter what you have already done, it only matters what is necessary," she said, the words coming out more harshly than she intended.

"I suppose that's true," he said mildly. "I take it from your tone just now that your part in your father's plan was not chosen willingly."

"It doesn't matter," she said tersely. "Now, if we succeed in what we're doing, the king will need you again."

"He has you."

"I'm not fully trained. As soon as Casovar is out, I need to return to DarkSkull to complete my apprenticeship."

"I think you may find that the queen of Rionn has no time to be a mage, let alone the lord-mage. One of your young friends will need to fill that post, I think."

She waved a dismissive hand. "That's a long time in the future. In the meantime, I need to know that we have your support."

Astor stood, moving to his window. A speculative look crossed his face. "Be careful, Lady Egalion. You're heading into dangerous waters."

"You mean we are."

"I suppose I do." His gaze remained unfocussed, a long way away from her, and she wondered what he was thinking.

ALYX HADN'T SEEN Brynn since before the night of the ball—despite sending several messages asking to meet—so she was relieved to finally receive something from him the following day. As soon as she could, she responded to his offer of a time to meet at one of the more disreputable inns in the party district.

It was late, darkness having fallen hours earlier, and the inn was full to bursting. She'd been careful to use shielded bursts of telepathic magic on her way, and was confident she hadn't been followed. It took her a good while to push through towards the back of the inn where Brynn stood by a door leading to a back hallway. When he spotted her, he opened the door and slipped inside.

Alyx followed him through a few moments later, and walking down the hall, found herself in a small storage space lit only by a single lantern. Boxes sat stacked against the walls around them, leaving only a narrow passage between.

"I'm sorry I've been gone so long," he spoke as she closed the door. "I had to travel back to Tregaya to speak with the council, and it took me longer than... Alyx, is something wrong?"

"What do you mean?" she asked in surprise.

He moved closer to her. "You look terrible."

She laughed. "Thanks, Brynn! I do not look terrible."

"Yes you do. You're pale, and there are shadows under your eyes," he said, then, "Where's Dashan?"

Her heart clenched at the mention of his name, and it took almost everything she had to keep her voice casual when she replied. "He's out of the city on assignment. I'm tired because Casovar has been working me longer hours than usual, and I'm trying to juggle that with the number of social events that are now part of my life." She shrugged. "What took you to Tregaya? I've been burning to know what happened when you followed that man who met Casovar and Dunnat."

He opened his mouth as if to question her further, but shook his head at the fierce look she fixed on him. "The council have officially ordered me to investigate Casovar."

"Really?" Surprise filled her voice. "Why? What about the man you followed from the inn that night?"

Brynn let out a breath. "He's the reason I went straight to the council rather than come back here to report to you. I followed him a week north towards the disputed area. On the second night out of Rionn I managed to get right up to his campsite, where I watched him use magic to start a fire."

Alyx's eyebrows shot upwards, but Brynn held out a hand to forestall anything she might say. "In Gosper I followed him to an army camp. He was allowed in, and marched out—heading north—with a unit of the army the next day."

"A mage with fire ability met with Casovar and Dunnat in Rionn before joining an army unit heading to the disputed area?" Alyx clarified.

"Yes. And when I spoke with Romas, he told me there are currently no active council mages who are male, Shiven and possess fire magic."

"A Shiven mage is in communication with Casovar," she murmured. The potential implications of that were astonishing. Had a Shiven mage been implanted in the Rionnan army? She should be surprised, but she wasn't. The lord-mage was up to a lot more than being bad at managing Rionn's army. "I wish you'd told me this before leaving."

"I wanted to take my suspicions straight to the council in the hope they would do what they did, which is authorise me to conduct an official investigation." Brynn was animated.

Alyx half-listened, still thinking over what he'd told her. After a moment she looked up. "I have something to tell you, but this is for your ears only. It does not go to the council. Am I clear?"

"I'm your friend before being their spy," he said quietly.

She nodded. "My father and Lord-General Sparkish spoke to me just over a week ago, which is why I've been trying to reach you. They believe Casovar is mismanaging the Rionnan response to the Shiven incursions, to the degree they feel we could be invaded within two years."

"What?" Brynn's eyes widened.

"But what you're telling me indicates there's much more to it," she said, thumping a hand against the nearest box in frustration. "We need to find out what he's up to."

"I know. I'm doing my best," Brynn said. "What is your father doing about it?"

"He, Cayr and General Sparkish have come up with a plan to get Casovar out of Rionn," she said carefully. "I am to marry Cayr. By marrying, we'll form a power base that rivals Casovar's influence, and my father has won the support of the other lords."

Brynn looked confused. "What?"

She smiled. "I'm surprised you haven't heard, the news is all over the city."

"I don't understand. You and Dashan—"

"Are over." Alyx stood. "I can't stay. Do you have anything else for me?"

"No," he said, frowning. "Alyx—"

"Please let me know as soon as you do. I'll be waiting for your message." Alyx paused as she placed her hand on the door handle, debating with herself. The question had been eating at her ever since the ball, and she couldn't bring herself to leave without asking him. "Did you know?"

It was a vague question, but the silence in room turned thick, and Alyx had her answer. Eyes closing, she leaned forward to rest her head against the door. Not Brynn too. The taste of more betrayal was bitter in her mouth, feeding the anger and frustration that still burned inside.

"It was my job to find and track them," he said eventually, all the life drained from his voice. "Yes, I knew what he was."

"Why didn't you tell me?"

"Because I don't care." She turned, surprised by the vehemence in his voice. "I don't care that he's a Taliath and you're a mage of the higher order. It means nothing to me. It shouldn't to you either."

"How can it not?" She stared at him. "We can never be together, and you knew that. You should have told me. If you were truly my friend, you would have."

"Alyx..."

"I don't want to talk about this anymore." She turned the handle, pushing the door open.

"Alyx, wait!"

"What?"

"You can't forget that Casovar is a mage of the higher order with telepathic magic. All this planning... he's going to find out eventually. You have to be careful."

"We are." She walked out, slamming the door behind her and pushing her way through the crowded inn without looking back.

It had been well over a month since her last nightmare, but once again he slid into her mind without a deliberate attempt to cause her pain. Despite this, her terror was instinctive, borne of his total control and how helpless it made her. Not wanting to let on how afraid she was, she remained silent, curling her mind into a tiny ball.

"*There's no need to be afraid.*" He sounded amused—probably at her attempt to hide her fear from him. "*We want the same things, you and I.*"

His amusement sparked her pride. "*You've been terrorising me for over a year. I have good reason to be afraid.*"

"*I was... over-enthusiastic.*"

Was he serious?

She tried not to let her incredulity leak, instead asking tentatively, "*What do you want with me?*"

"*You have power that could be of use to me. Our goals align.*"

Alyx didn't respond. Something told her that getting drawn into conversation with this mage wasn't a smart idea.

He gave the equivalent of a mental sigh. "*You can protect those you love by standing with me, Alyx Egalion. I want the council gone, and I will do anything to make that happen. There's no good reason for you to stand in the way.*"

Again, she refused to reply. His hold on her mind tightened fractionally, as if annoyance or anger were tempting him to cause pain, but it didn't come.

"*I do not seek the death of the Taliath.*" His voice oozed sincerity. "*They don't deserve to die. They should be protected and trained, and allied with the new mage order that I will create.*"

She didn't want to listen to this, didn't want to acknowledge the part of her that wanted to listen. "*You showed me images of destruction, people dying.*"

"*Not the Taliath, not your father or brother,*" he whispered. "*Not Dashan...*"

Her eyes squeezed shut, as if that would make any difference to the voice invading her dream.

"*Only the council.*"

And then he was gone, his last words echoing through her sleep.

CHAPTER 23

Bright sunlight shone through the arched windows of the atrium, falling across the wooden floors and luxurious sofas scattered around the room. Alyx and Cayr sat together on a particularly plush sofa by the window, momentarily left alone.

"How was your morning?" she asked idly.

"I spent it reviewing the newly-signed Tregayan-Zandian trade agreement," he said. "Not exactly fascinating stuff, but parts of it will be useful for us."

"I agree."

"How are you going with the lord-mage?" He lowered his voice. "Has he given you any problems since my father's announcement of our betrothal?"

Alyx winced. Several weeks had passed since she and Cayr had begun courting, and the king had agreed to a formal betrothal two days earlier. The work her father had done with the lords had made it impossible for him not too agree "Nothing overt, but he's furious. Even after all the lords lined up to express their support, I'm astonished he didn't talk your father out of it."

"He tried," Cayr said soberly. "But despite Casovar's influence over him, your father did a superb job corralling the lords to put pressure on him. They don't like Casovar any more than we do."

"That's one mistake he's made," she mused softly. "Behaving with such arrogance he's put the entire court offside."

Cayr's mouth quirked suddenly. "And believing that you're useless, when I can tell you're far from it."

She couldn't help returning his smile, but then shook her head. "We shouldn't be discussing—or thinking—about any of this while we're inside the palace."

"You're right." He frowned.

Sadness filled her as the levity left his face—Casovar wasn't the only thing that had dimmed some of the light in Cayr's blue eyes these days. "How are you?" she asked, squeezing his hand.

"This is hard," he admitted. "Being here with you like this, it feels right and natural, but I know it isn't. It's all a façade. I wish so badly we could go back to how things used to be."

"Me too," she whispered.

"I feel so alone."

Alyx leaned into him. "Despite everything, I'm still your friend. I'm still in your corner, no matter what. You're not alone."

"But I am," he said, giving her a crooked smile. "I don't mean to sound petulant, but seeing you all the time makes the hurting worse. I feel more alone when I'm around you."

"I'm so sorry," she whispered, understanding exactly what he meant.

"The safety of Rionn is more important than both of us." He reached out to sling his arm around her shoulders, voice firming. "We'll work it out."

Pride seared through her at the man Cayr was becoming, and the smile she gave him must have showed how she felt, because his eyes lightened and his smile turned genuine.

He pulled her closer—both of them spotting the approach of some of their friends at the same time—and Alyx pulled away with a light laugh, doing her best to give Cayr a moony look as she did. Lissa and Mira dropped into chairs nearby.

"Alyx, you simply must tell us where you got those shoes!" Lissa exclaimed.

"I think that's my cue," Cayr said dryly. He leaned over to kiss Alyx on the cheek before rising to his feet, bowing to the ladies, and walking off towards Jaran.

"You are so lucky," Mira swooned. "He's so handsome."

"He certainly is." Alyx allowed smugness to fill her voice. "What about a shoe shopping trip tomorrow? I'll take you to the store I got these from."

She looked up as one of the palace servants appeared, bowing low. "Lady Egalion, there's someone here asking for you."

Frowning, Alyx glanced over to see Cario hovering by the door. He was wearing his serious expression, which immediately worried her. Cario never looked serious if he could help it.

"I'm sorry, ladies. It seems as if the lord-mage needs to see me."

"WHAT IS IT?" she asked under her breath as they walked through the halls towards the mage offices.

"Your friends are back," he said.

"Back, as in here at the palace?" She spun towards him, shock flooding her.

"As in, with Casovar right now," he said. "They were less than thrilled to see me, as you can imagine, so I took the opportunity to leave. I figured you'd want to know."

"He didn't tell me they were coming back. They didn't tell me." She frowned. Why hadn't Dawn contacted her telepathically?

Cario hesitated, catching her arm as they approached the door. "I don't know them like you do, but there's something... "

Worry surged, and she pushed Cario's arm off to start walking again. "Tighten that mental shield of yours."

Alyx opened the door, halting two steps into the room. Tarrick sat on a chair directly across from her, one leg stretched out before him. His pants were ripped and a white bandage was visible underneath. The twins hovered behind him, both pale. Finn's eyes took in her dress and hair, his face tightening fractionally.

218

"Lady Egalion." Casovar's voice caught her attention. He was seated in a chair near Tarrick. "You're interrupting."

"What happened?" The words spilled out. "Tarrick, are you all right?"

"I'm fine." His jaw was clenched in visible anger, eyes firmly fixed on Cario where he'd come in behind Alyx. Casovar glanced between them, curiosity beginning to creep across his face. Instinctively, Alyx sought to draw his attention away. "Lord-Mage, I apologise for interrupting. May I sit in? I assume you're debriefing the apprentices and I'd like to hear what they have to say—it may assist in my review of reporting."

His gaze swung back to hers and she relaxed slightly. "You may. Mage Duneskal, you may also join. The council will be interested in what we discuss."

"Tell me you're all okay." Alyx sent the thought as tightly shielded as she knew how, but couldn't go any longer without being sure. Across the room, Dawn gave a very faint nod. The worry in her chest faded a little.

"As I was saying, Lord-Mage, we were attempting to scout the main Shiven camp north of the disputed area, as per your order," Tarrick said. "We were ambushed, but not before gaining a solid idea of their numbers."

"There was no discernible increase in troop size since the last count," Dawn spoke, taking over from Tarrick. Alyx frowned as Tarrick's shoulders relaxed fractionally. "No substantive change in the cache of supplies as far as we could tell either."

"That accords with the information I've received." Casovar sat back. "It seems we don't need to worry about an imminent attempt to annex the disputed area. And that's why I've brought you home. I'd like to spend a few weeks on your training."

"Yes, sir," Finn said. "Tarrick should be off that leg for a couple more days at least."

Casovar nodded, his interest seeming to fade rapidly as he rose to his feet. "Go home and get some rest. I'll expect you back here the day after tomorrow."

"I'll have my carriage brought around," Alyx offered as soon as

Casovar was out the door. "Cario, will you help him down? The twins look like they're about to keel over."

"I don't need help," Tarrick snarled.

Cario lifted both hands in the air. "Fine. Walk by yourself. Alyx, how about I go and organise your carriage?"

"Thanks."

"What is he doing here?" Finn demanded once he was gone.

Alyx lifted a hand. "Not here. Let's get Tarrick home."

"I'd rather go to the twins' house." Tarrick winced as he lifted himself out of the chair. "Further away."

"Fine." Her worry came flooding back, and she reached out for his arm. "Are you really okay?"

"It's just a little gash." His face softened. "Finn fixed me up, I'll be fine."

"It's true," Dawn reassured her.

Her gaze flicked between all three of them. While Dawn seemed to be telling the truth, something else was hovering between them. All looked tense.

Something had happened.

AN HOUR later they were settled in the A'ndreas' warm living room. Both parents were out working. While Finn cleaned and re-bandaged Tarrick's leg, Alyx sent Cario straight to the kitchen to make a pot of tea. When he returned, the tenseness in the room thickened perceptibly.

"It's not what we thought," Alyx said, forestalling their questions. As succinctly as she could, she told them Cario's side of the story, finishing with, "I believe him."

"I'm here because I have no respect for the council or what they do," Cario spoke into the silence that followed. "I came because Alyx —and you—are my friends, and I respect your values and your friend-ship. That is the truth."

Tarrick and the twins stared at him, faces slack with astonishment. They'd never seen Cario without his mask of amiable arrogance before, and his honesty clearly moved them as it had her.

220

The twins shared a glance, after a moment nodding slightly at each other. Tarrick stared at Cario for another moment before giving a stiff nod. "If Alyx trusts you, then you can stay."

"Not the warmest welcome I've ever received, but I'll take it." Cario placed the tray of tea down and took a seat, pulling the chair back so he could stretch his long legs out. Nobody made a move for the steaming pot.

"He's wearing mage robes." Tarrick looked at Alyx. "If he's really here to join us, what's his official reason for being in Alistriem?"

Cario sighed. "I'm here as a representative of the council. The position came up after I passed my trials, and I organised to have it assigned to me."

"You passed your trials?" Tarrick's eyes widened comically.

"I did." Cario shrugged.

"Now that's sorted, I want to know what's going on." Alyx looked at each of them in turn. "Did you get my message from Dash? Why didn't you tell me you were coming back? And why was Tarrick afraid that Casovar was going to read his thoughts back there?"

"We got your message." Dawn spoke first. "Congratulations on your betrothal, by the way."

Alyx waved a dismissive hand. "That's not important right now. Quit stalling."

"Your message made us pay closer attention to what was going on up in the disputed area," Dawn said. "And we were lying to Casovar back there, hence me jumping in to take over from Tarrick. I have a better mental shield."

"You were lying about being ambushed?"

"No, that part was true. We were lying about the troop numbers we saw. On the surface, the numbers were similar to what we'd seen before," Finn explained. "But Dawn picked up more minds—they were hidden in deep bushland a short distance off. At least double the number of soldiers."

Fear struck at her. "So invasion could be imminent?"

"We think so."

Alyx glanced between them. Something was off. Finn's gaze was darting all over the place and Tarrick looked grim, even more so than his usual sober expression. Dawn was fidgeting, her left foot tapping against the floor.

"What else?" she asked, unable to stop the dread seeping into her voice.

The twins shared another look. Alyx tried to quell the urge to knock their heads together.

"Today would be nice." Impatience threaded Cario's voice when they hesitated further.

Tarrick nodded. "We think Lord-Mage Casovar is involved with the new military commander the Shiven have. That's why we lied to him—he's actively working against Rionn."

A tense silence fell over the room. Finn sagged back into his seat while Tarrick stood, seemingly unable to stay seated.

"Alyx, your father's plan to oust Casovar seems sound... " Tarrick began, then hesitated. "But we fear that by the time your plan is realised, it will likely be too late."

"Too late for what? The drama is killing me. Spit it out, will you," Cario drawled.

"Fine. We think the new Shiven commander is Shakar," Tarrick snapped.

A deep silence filled the room. Alyx looked at Cario, checking to see whether he'd heard the same thing. He looked as bewildered as she felt.

"Shakar is dead."

The words didn't come from Alyx or Cario, and all eyes snapped to the newcomer in the doorway. The hood of his mage cloak was pulled back, revealing Brynn's boyishly handsome features.

CHAPTER 24

It took a long moment for Tarrick and the twins to process who stood there. Alyx stared between them, wondering if she should say something, wondering what she could say. Nothing came.

"Brynn?" Tarrick took a tentative step forward, astonishment written all over his face.

"It's me." He smiled. "I'm alive."

"I don't believe this," Dawn said in wonderment.

"Oh, mate!" Finn leapt up from his chair and crossed the room to pump Brynn's hand enthusiastically. "You have no idea how good it is to see you."

"We missed you so much!" Dawn threw her arms around him tearfully. "I can't believe it!"

"I missed you too," Brynn told them, looking teary himself. "A lot."

Tarrick's gaze shifted to Alyx with a frown. "Why don't you look surprised?"

Alyx winced in anticipation of the reaction she was about to receive and shot Brynn a glare—surely he could have warned her! "Because I'm not. Brynn has been working for me ever since we arrived in Alistriem," she said.

"How long have you known he was alive?" Tarrick demanded.

She hesitated, tried to hold Tarrick's gaze. "Since not long after we went back to DarkSkull."

"You knew he was alive and didn't tell us?" Finn didn't seem able to believe it. His green eyes had darkened with a mixture of hurt and anger.

"That was my fault," Brynn spoke. "I insisted she not tell you. It was too dangerous with Romas's telepathic ability."

"I don't care," Finn said flatly, looking straight at Alyx. "You knew how much we were hurting over Brynn's death. You knew. How could you not say anything?"

"It was a deliberate choice, and for that I am sorry," Alyx said. "But I would do it again if I had to, and I would do the same thing if it were any of you in that position."

"You keep behaving as if the Mage Council is some evil monster out to destroy everything," Tarrick said coldly, glancing in disgust between Alyx and Brynn. "You have reason to question them, I understand, but you act and speak as if you're better than them, above them. And yet here you are keeping secrets just like they do."

"I agree. You deliberately allowed us to believe something that wasn't true," Finn said. "Something that caused us pain. That's something the council would do, Alyx."

That stung more than she would like to admit. Alyx glanced at Brynn. He'd turned white, but despite herself she felt little sympathy for him. He had a habit of keeping things to himself that hurt other people.

"I don't know what to think," Dawn said quietly as Alyx turned to her. And that hurt most of all.

"As much as I can understand why you'd be upset," Cario's voice broke the silence. "There are more important things to discuss right now, particularly if what you said about Shakar is true. Recriminations can wait."

"What are you even doing here?" Alyx asked Brynn pointedly.

"I followed you from the palace," he admitted.

Tarrick's jaw clenched and he looked away for a moment before giving an angry shake of his head and looking at Brynn. "You're the council spy?"

"I am." Brynn said. "And if you wouldn't mind continuing to tell us what you've learned, I'll tell you if I have anything to add at the end."

"He can be trusted," Alyx said quietly, when Tarrick hesitated. "Despite what the council have done to him... there's time for that story later, but for now you just need to know that he's still the Brynn we knew."

Tarrick took a deep breath, reaching up to pinch the bridge of his nose. "Fine. We think Shakar is alive and working for the Shiven leader."

"It was Dawn that picked it up," Finn said. "She heard his name in the thoughts of Shiven prisoners; prisoners that later killed themselves rather than give up any information about their new commander."

"I am certain of what I heard." Dawn added, "I think Shakar is alive, and he's in Shivasa."

"There must be another explanation. The council killed him," Alyx said. "The war wouldn't have ended if they hadn't. And even if somehow he was still alive, he'd be too old to be a threat."

"The council never recovered a body," Cario spoke into the silence.

"What?" She turned to him.

"My grandfather told me the story once," he said softly. "The final battle against Shakar went on for days. The council had mustered every single mage it had, and they cornered Shakar in a small town called Serrin. By the end, over a hundred mages were dead, including all living mages of the higher order. There was a magical explosion right where Shakar was, and it destroyed everything around it, including the buildings. Every living thing in the area was killed. The blast was so intense that it pulverized everything in its path. There were no bodies."

"And you're suggesting Shakar survived that somehow?" Alyx asked.

"I don't see how, but nobody ever recovered his body. It was assumed there was nothing left of it after the blast." He shrugged. "The council truly believes Shakar is dead."

Alyx rubbed her forehead, the beginnings of a headache throbbing at her temples. Casovar was a problem, but one that had become almost manageable, or at least one they had a plan to deal with. But Shakar...

"Suffice to say, we have to take Casovar out cleanly and quickly." Tarrick leaned forward. "If he's in league with Shakar—"

"No," Cario said decisively. "Casovar is the lesser threat, and there's a plan in place to deal with him already. If Shakar is truly alive and at the head of this renewed Shiven effort, we are in a world of trouble, and when I say we, I mean everyone from Rionn to Zandia."

"Hold up, this doesn't make a lot of sense." Alyx shook her head. "Even if we assume Shakar didn't die, the battle in Serrin took place what... fifty-two years ago? How is it he's not a doddery old man by now, and why has he waited this long to re-appear?"

"We talked about this a lot. Your first question could be explained by magic," Tarrick guessed. "It might be he's absorbed a power that allows him to extend his life."

"If that's the case, maybe that partially explains why he hasn't reappeared until now," Finn said. "Maybe he only discovered the magic recently, sometime in the last few years."

"That logic is thin," Cario said flatly. "I've never heard of a mage with the ability to extend his or her life."

"That doesn't mean he didn't find one. And what if he's been using all this time to plan?" Dawn spoke into the ensuing silence. "The situation with Shivasa has been building for several years now, same with the threats against the mages. Last time he fought the council he did it openly and they threw everything they had at him. Maybe this time he's trying to conceal what he's doing until it's too late."

"By using Shivasa as a tool to achieve his end game?" Finn said. "Which is what exactly?"

"Last time it was to supplant the Mage Council," Tarrick said. "He wanted absolute rule over mages."

Destroying the council. Those words rang a bell in Alyx's mind, but Finn spoke before she could chase the thought down.

"As I keep saying, we need to tell the council about our suspicions," he said. "If Shakar's alive, the council is the only entity with the resources to deal with it."

"You take this to the council and they'll laugh you out of the room," Cario said. "You need proof. If you're right about Casovar working with Shakar, then he's the proof you need."

"Okay." Tarrick thought for a moment. "The first thing we need to do is re-form Third Patrol. We may not be at DarkSkull any longer, but we have a battle to fight."

"You're all going to have to be so careful around Casovar," Alyx said pointedly. "Tarrick, that means no lazy shielding. Do your best to avoid being around him."

He gave a short nod, clearly still angry with her.

Finn rose. "Brynn, will you join us for dinner? I have a million questions for you, and I'm sure Dawn and Tarrick do too."

He seemed wary. "I know I've upset you, so don't feel like you have to—"

"We missed you terribly," Dawn said. "Please stay."

"I'd love to," he replied.

"Cario and I should stay close to home in case Casovar has his Mage Guard watching us." Alyx stood too. "It's time we start behaving like he's a genuine threat."

"What about Shakar?" Tarrick said. "We need to come up with a plan."

"The three of you are exhausted," Cario said. "And Alyx is right—we shouldn't linger here too long."

"Fortunately he gave you tomorrow off, so we can meet again first thing," Alyx added.

Neither Tarrick or the twins protested Alyx and Cario not staying for dinner, and even Dawn seemed cool when saying her farewells.

"They've clearly had an awful time up north, and the Shakar thing has probably been eating at them," Cario said as they headed home together. "They'll be in better moods tomorrow."

"I hurt them," she said. "And they're angry with me. It's fair enough. I'd be furious in their position." In fact she had been in their position constantly the past two years, and the anger that caused had never gone away. Instead it continued to simmer inside her. And now she was doing the same thing to others. A rush of bitterness joined the anger and she had to take a deep breath to force it all down.

"Life doesn't let you do everything right all the time," Cario said. "Finn knows that better than the rest of you. They'll be fine."

"I hope so."

. . .

"You've been distracted all evening, Aly-girl," her father said as they settled in his study. "Is everything all right?"

"The twins and Tarrick came back today," she said. "We managed to meet this afternoon."

"They had news?"

She nodded distractedly. "Papa, it's—"

A soft knock at the door cut off Alyx's words and they both turned as Safia pushed it open. "Lord Egalion, I wasn't aware you were expecting visitors, but another lord is approaching the house. He has a retinue with him, but they're not Bluecoats."

Garan frowned. "I'm not expecting any visitors. You'd best show him in. I'll be right there."

"Not Bluecoats," Alyx murmured to herself as Safia left.

"Odd," Garan said. "Presumably the Bluecoats on the gates recognised him though. It's late for a visit. Maybe he's one of Sparky's—"

"Oh!" Alyx leapt to her feet in realisation and ran for the door, ignoring her father's startled shout.

The lord was being shown in by Safia when Alyx came out into the entrance foyer. A step behind him came a muscular warrior with a shaved head and fierce expression.

"Ladan!" She broke into a run towards him, reading the surprise flashing on his hard face the moment before throwing her arms around him in delight.

"Aly-girl." His strong arms closed around her, holding her tightly to him. She buried her face in his neck, embarrassed by the tears threatening. "Are you all right?"

"I am now." She swallowed and stepped back, hurriedly wiping at her eyes. "You came."

"Lord Egalion, Lord Ladan Mirren of Widow Falls to see you."

Safia's voice echoed across the cavernous foyer. Alyx spun to see her father had reached the hall and stopped dead, staring at Ladan as if he couldn't believe his eyes. Emotion worked on his face, and his hands clenched and unclenched at his sides.

"Lord Egalion." Ladan stepped away from Alyx, shoulders rigid. "I apologise for arriving unannounced at such a late hour."

They looked more alike than Alyx had realised, seeing them standing close like this. They were of the same height and colouring, and the strength in Ladan's features were an echo of his father's.

"I am very glad to see you, Ladan." Garan offered his hand.

Ladan stared at it for a very long time, before slowly, very slowly, reaching out to take it. "Thank you, sir."

And with that, the tension eased slightly.

"What brings you here?" Alyx broke the silence.

"I had been considering visiting, as you asked." His green eyes shifted to her. "And when Dashan arrived on orders from you, Lord Egalion, he told me about Alyx's courting of Prince Cayr."

"I see." She ignored the despair that surged at the reference to Dashan, and instead focused on the little bit of happiness that came at the realisation Ladan, protective as always, had come to assess her future husband.

"You'll stay here, of course." Garan injected just enough authority into his voice that he gave Ladan no choice. "Your men can be accommodated in the barracks with my Bluecoat detail and your second is of course welcome to stay in the house with us. Safia, please organise the rooms at once."

Safia bowed silently and left. Ladan gestured to Romney. "Romney, Lord Garan Egalion. Lord Egalion, this is Romney, my second."

"Well met." Garan nodded acknowledgement.

"Sir." Romney bowed his head.

"We can't stay long," Ladan said. "A few days only. Widow Falls remains vulnerable while I'm gone."

Yet he'd risked it to come and see her. Warmth filled Alyx, dispelling some of the misery that had been building up in her for days.

"I'd like to meet Prince Cayr," he continued now. "And speak with the king, if possible."

"I can arrange it," Garan said.

"Good. Romney and I will see my men settled in the barracks and then we'll take our leave for the evening. We've ridden a long way today."

Garan looked thoroughly bemused as Ladan and his second strode back out the front door. Alyx smiled again.

"He's your son."

"He's a grown man," Garan said, a dazed expression on his face. "I remember a boy."

CHAPTER 25

Alyx arrived at the A'ndreas house the next morning to find Dawn sitting out on the front porch, a little smile on her face as she watched a group of children across the street playing. The smile faded at Alyx's appearance. "Where's Cario?"

Alyx shrugged. "He wasn't up when I left. Maybe Tarrick's scowls yesterday scared him off."

"He was well within his rights to behave like that, you know." Dawn looked away. "All of us were."

"You're still angry with me." Alyx sighed and took a seat beside her friend.

"We talked a lot with Brynn last night. He tried to explain why he hadn't told us, and I do understand, but at the same time... "

"Knowing there are good reasons for being lied to doesn't help much does it?" Alyx said as Dawn trailed off. "I'm sorry."

"I thought that we trusted each other above everything else." Dawn's voice was sad, and it cut through Alyx like a knife. "But you prioritised Brynn."

"Dawn, I—"

"I'm not angry anymore, truly." Dawn turned to her with a smile that seemed genuine. "Come on, let's go inside."

Alyx hesitated, wanting to continue the conversation, to fix what she suddenly felt had been broken somehow. But the words weren't there, and Dawn was already getting to her feet.

"Where's the traitor?" Tarrick asked when Dawn and Alyx joined the young men in the front room.

"Still asleep, I think," Alyx said, rubbing at tired eyes. "But someone else is coming to join us. Ladan arrived in the city last night."

Almost as soon as the words were out of her mouth, a knock sounded at the front door. Dawn left them to get it, and moments later Ladan's tall frame filled the doorway.

"Sorry I'm late," he said, serious as always.

"Come in, Lord Mirren." Finn gestured for him to enter. "Can we get you anything?"

"No thank you, we're fine."

We?

Alyx's gaze went straight to the man that came through the doorway behind Ladan, her heart thudding against her chest at the unexpected sight of Dashan. She took a step towards him before she'd even realised it, wanting to throw her arms around him and feel his settle around her. He didn't notice, gaze firmly directed away from her.

"Team." He grinned at them all. "I heard we're back to secret meetings and plotting. Did my invitation get lost in the mail?"

"Dashan! Where have you been?" Tarrick rose to shake his hand. "We asked at the barracks for you yesterday but Nario said you were off on some secret assignment."

"I'd tell you but then I'd have to kill you," Dashan said easily, clapping Finn on the back and flashing his smile at Dawn and Brynn. He continued not looking at Alyx, and it stung. Her heart ached—with him away she'd been able to ignore how badly she missed him, but to see him alive and well and so close... it hurt more than she'd imagined it would.

"What is it that you have to tell us?" Ladan asked impatiently.

The attention of the room swung to the lord of Widow Falls. Alyx hid a smile, glad for something else to focus on. Dashan settled back in a chair and put his boots up on the table. She fought not to roll her eyes, gesturing for Tarrick to fill them in. The Zandian spoke quickly and concisely. As he did, Ladan's expression turned grim, while Dashan's eyebrows shot skyward and he gave a low whistle.

"Why are we having this conversation without my father, the king or the prince in the room?" Ladan demanded as soon as Tarrick finished.

"Because we haven't had time to plan our next step yet, and I think we need to consider it very carefully," Tarrick answered. "The fact that so many people in close contact with Casovar already know is bad enough. We shouldn't widen that circle unless we really have to."

Ladan nodded sharply, seeming to accept that. "The Mage Council needs to be told at once."

"You think they'll believe us without any evidence? Half-trained apprentice mages who have been out of their control for several months?" Alyx asked her brother.

His jaw tightened. "Then what are you planning to do about it?"

"Our priority is to get proof," Tarrick said.

Dashan lifted an eyebrow. "And where exactly do you think you're going to find that convenient proof lying around?"

"Casovar's house," Finn said, unravelling a folded piece of paper onto the table. "Dawn and I drew this up last night. Casovar's home is in the rich quarter right on the riverbank. Luckily for us, it's built higher than the homes around it. You can see his upper level from a row of warehouses across the other side of the river. Three of them are currently empty." He pointed to the hand-drawn map.

It was the first time Alyx had heard the plan, and it sounded pretty thin. "You think there is proof of Shakar's existence in Casovar's house?"

Dashan shifted forward to look at the map, eyes narrowing as he studied it. Ladan joined him, pushing Finn out of the way. The scholar sighed and ceded the space. "If Casovar is working for Shakar, then they must be communicating somehow. I doubt Casovar is keeping records of that in his offices at the palace. Too much chance someone might stumble over it."

That was true enough, and Dashan's little nod indicated he agreed.

She couldn't help looking at him, trying to see how he was. His hair was longer than regulation length, curling over his ears, and he hadn't shaved in a couple of days, but he seemed well. In fact, he looked good —her attraction to him hadn't faded at all, her mind conjuring up the memories of the last time he'd kissed her. Roughly, she pushed them out of her mind, burying the pain that went with them.

"They could be communicating telepathically," Dawn added. "But it's not the easiest method for complex planning, so we have to hope there are some physical records."

Alyx tore her eyes from Dashan and rubbed at the growing ache in her temples. "So if not at the offices, then there's a chance he keeps them at his house. We'll have to break in."

"Given his house is right on the river, it would be best to swim in. No more than two people or the risk of being spotted is too high." Dashan was still looking at the map. "Dawn, you and someone else can sit in a warehouse and keep watch. If the alarm is raised, you'll know and can contact those inside the house instantly."

"Then I have to go in," Alyx said. "Dawn can speak to me clearly and quickly."

Dashan nodded, still not looking at her. Even so, his next words set her heart thumping. "I agree. I'll be the one to go with you."

"I think I would be better to go," Tarrick disagreed.

"Council spy sitting right here," Brynn spoke up. "I've sort of been trained for this type of thing."

"No," Tarrick said. "I want you focusing all your efforts on finding alternative avenues of proof of Shakar's existence. We can't rely only on Casovar. I'll go in with Alyx."

"Alyx and I grew up here. We know the area, and probably Casovar's household, much better than you do," Dashan pointed out. "In the event we get spotted, we may be able to talk our way out of it. If a Zandian mage is caught inside Casovar's house, how do you propose to explain yourself?"

Tarrick looked at Dashan, clearly weighing the sense of what he'd said. Dashan smiled to break the tension. "How about you and Cario loiter in the streets around Casovar's home? If we're spotted and the alarm is raised, you can create a diversion for the Mage Guard until Alyx and I get clear."

"Fine," Tarrick said decisively. "If Cario ever makes an appearance. Dawn and Finn will take up an observation post in the warehouse. Alyx, we'll need to run this by your father first. And Prince Cayr."

"No." She shook her head decisively. "Cayr can't afford even a whisper to get out that he was involved in breaking into one of his lord's homes. Neither can my father. It would destroy their credibility with the lords, not to mention ruin our plan."

"You're betrothed to the prince. It's not like you could afford to get caught either," Ladan pointed out.

Across the room, Dashan stiffened. Alyx glanced at him, then immediately looked away at the hard expression on his face. "I won't get caught. We do this on our own."

Dawn added, "besides, all of this falls apart the instant Casovar reads something of our plans in your thoughts, so the fewer people who know, the safer."

"We'll be fine," Finn said, glancing at his sister. "I've still got an almost constant headache from all the practicing you've been making us do."

"And Casovar has no reason to be within a mile of me, so we're fine," Dashan added dryly.

Now it was Alyx's turn to freeze, guilty knowledge instantly making her afraid everyone would guess Dashan was a Taliath. Instead, all eyes shifted to Ladan, who they already knew as a Taliath.

"If Casovar is working for Shakar, would he report Lord Mirren to the council?" Finn asked.

"I am standing here," Ladan spoke tersely. "Casovar doesn't scare me, but there's no sense in being foolish. I have no need to go anywhere near him."

"I think we should do this tonight. We really can't afford to put it off any longer," Tarrick said.

Alyx's breath caught—so quickly. But Ladan had been right. If Shakar was alive... the sooner the council acted the better.

"All right," Dashan said.

"I should go." Alyx stood. The walls of the room were beginning to press in, and she needed to get out, breathe some fresh air.

"I'll come with you," Ladan said.

Tarrick nodded. "We'll stay and plan in more detail for tonight. If anything changes, we'll find a way to get you a message at the palace. Alyx, if you find Cario, fill him in?"

"I will. See you later."

Finn followed them out. Sighing inwardly, but not surprised, Alyx gestured to Ladan to go ahead and waited for Finn to catch up. They lingered on the front step awkwardly for a moment. Eventually Finn took a breath, looking like he was searching for the right words. "This is not me trying to pry into your personal life, but I wanted to ask... are you happy? About marrying Cayr, I mean."

"It's... complicated," she admitted. "Marrying him is the best way to force Casovar out of Rionn, especially if we can't find proof of his connection to Shakar. And you know I love Cayr."

His mouth quirked. "A friendly warning, then. You and Dashan just spent that entire discussion pretending like the other didn't exist. I'm astonished Dawn didn't pick up on the wall of tension between the two of you. If she wasn't so upset over Brynn and Shakar, she would have."

The last thing she wanted was Finn trying to work out why she'd decided to marry Cayr. She needed him to believe it was for the reasons she stated. So she forced a laugh. "Come on, you know Dashan and I are regularly angry at each other. That's all it is."

"I'm not an idiot," he said. "You don't have to talk about it if you don't want to, but don't lie to me."

"Ok, fine. I don't want to talk about it," she snapped, pushed to anger by his questions and her own fear.

Finn stiffened. "I won't mention it again."

She immediately felt bad, and an apology was on the tip of her tongue, but he'd already turned and walked back inside.

"Dammit!" She lashed out with her foot, kicking the wall by the door hard. The throbbing at her temples had evolved into a full headache by the time she joined Ladan, waiting with the horses out in the street.

"Are you all right?" he asked.

She sighed. "I'm frustrated. Dealing with Casovar every day is not easy. And now with Shakar of all people... how do we deal with that?"

He moved closer. "Is that all that's bothering you?"

She huffed out another sigh. "No."

"What do big brothers do, Aly-girl?"

She looked up at him, so tall and formidable. "Look after their baby sisters."

A smile curled at the corners of his mouth. "We don't really have to talk about you and courting, though, do we?"

Alyx chuckled. "Nobody is allowed to court me, then? Just so we're clear."

"That's absolutely right. You're too young."

Now she laughed. "I'm eighteen, big brother. Besides, good luck trying to beat up the prince of Rionn."

"Right." He frowned.

"Cayr is my oldest friend. He's good to me," she said honestly. "Don't blame him for any of this."

"I don't care how good or decent anybody else is, Aly-girl, I just want to make sure you're happy and safe."

"Cayr wants the same things for me."

"You're still too young for a betrothal." He scowled. "What does our father say about it?"

"Our father has expected Cayr and I to marry since we were children. He's approved it." She smiled. "What about you?"

Ladan's eyebrows shot up. "What do you mean?"

"You're twenty-two. You should be courting some young noblewoman by now, subject to my approval, of course."

"I don't have time for that."

"You don't have time, or you don't have the faintest clue how to talk to women?" Alyx burst out laughing as the scowl on her brother's face deepened. "You know you can't court anyone when you're throwing every single person who sets foot on your land out on their ear. Or when you're scowling horribly at them like you are at me right now."

"I'm too busy for courting," he snapped. "And I don't want some pampered, perfectly coiffed, gossipy court girl either."

"I understand that." Alyx's smile faded. "I have to go."

"I know," he said. "If you want to... you know, talk... uh... I'm here."

"Thanks, big brother." She leaned up and kissed him on the cheek. "I'm really glad you're here."

ALYX ARRIVED home to find Cario sitting on the top step, bulging saddlebags at his side. His horse was lazily cropping grass by the driveway and he held a bulky package in his hands. As she grew closer, she realised it was a letter. He wasn't wearing his black mage robes and dread began uncurling inside her stomach. Part of her already knew what was coming.

Dismounting, she walked over to the base of the steps, looking up at him. "Where were you this morning?"

"Writing this." He held up the letter. "It's for my family, telling them I'm officially resigning from the mage order."

The words were like a blow, but she tried to keep her voice even. "You're leaving."

Her gave her a wry smile. "You're a smart one, Egalion."

"I'm not. I just know what running away looks like," she said coldly, anger covering up the hurt that was rising like a tide. "I thought you came here to join me."

"That was before Shakar was alive." Cario rose gracefully to his feet and walked down to stand in front of her. The sun lit the golden tints in his curls, making it difficult to look straight at him. "I have no desire to be part of a war, and that's exactly where you're heading."

She gaped at him. "You think I want to be part of a war? Cario, you know as well as anyone that none of this is what I wanted. I wanted Cayr and marriage and a quiet life amongst the court of Alistriem. Not being a mage. Not Shakar. None of it."

"That's where we're the same," he said intensely. "I came here to be part of that life—to be at your side when you were queen. I enjoy politics, and I like and respect you, and I knew we could be a good team."

"We don't always get what we want," she said savagely. "And be careful, because sometimes when you get what you thought you wanted, it's far from perfect."

He let out a mirthless laugh. "So I'm guessing your betrothal to the prince isn't as wonderful and perfect as you've been making it out to be. I figured. The difference between you and me is that I'm willing to walk away from who I am. I don't need the rich family or the power, and I don't have to be a mage. I'm done."

"How can you walk away when you know Shakar is alive? After everything we learned at DarkSkull about what happened last time."

"You should be asking yourself the opposite question," he countered. "What difference will I make against a mage like Shakar? None. Everything is a choice, Alyx. You don't have to make it your responsibility to fight him."

"I'm not. It's the council's responsibility. It's mine to help them."

"Help the murderers of children and innocents?" Cario's mouth curled. "Really? Help the men who have manipulated you and lied to you because they covet your power?" He paused, his voice turning pointed. "Help the council that would murder the man you're in love with because of what he is?"

Alyx blanched, taking almost a full step back. The terror rose up unbidden, and Cario must have seen something of it in her face, because he shifted closer, voice lowering.

"I will never tell another living soul, you have my word," he murmured. "But if I figured it out, others will."

She felt sick. "How did you... "

"You forget I'm an outsider with intimate knowledge of the council. I've seen Taliath potentials before, and I had not known Dashan before we met. I had no pre-conceptions of the man. Fortunately, none of the DarkSkull masters had as much exposure to him as I did last year, but you cannot allow him to go back there with you. You understand?"

"Why didn't you tell me?"

Genuine surprise flashed over his face, and then he frowned. "I assumed you knew. I admit I was surprised you'd brought him to Dark-Skull with you, but then I supposed you hadn't had any control over who was in your protective detail. Your father, surely, must have known?"

"He didn't tell me until very recently," she said, bitterness filling her voice.

Cario nodded in realisation. "And so you agreed to marry the prince. That explains so much. I should have seen it."

"This isn't the point." She shook her head, changing the subject back. "You know how much I hate the council, what they've done. I don't trust them for a second. But it's not about the council. It's about protecting my home, the people I love. My magic allows me to do that."

"I have neither a home, nor a family I care to protect." He stepped back. "So I'm choosing to walk away."

The anger and hurt and fear were swirling in her chest, and it was impossible to tell which emotion was the strongest. In the end, she was simply left feeling weary, the headache back to throbbing at her temples.

"Fine," she said. "Good luck, Cario. It was nice knowing you."

Without giving him a chance to respond, she turned and walked up the steps and inside the house.

She didn't look back.

CHAPTER 26

Alyx only had to work in the mage offices for an hour or so before the excuse of afternoon tea allowed her to escape mid-afternoon. Cayr joined Alyx, Ladan and her father at the Egalion home, the invitation a result of Ladan's request to meet the prince. Cayr was fascinated to meet Alyx's older brother, and Ladan was civil, although she was amused to note he did not make it easy for Cayr to converse with him.

Conversation stayed purely casual. Unless they had something specific to discuss, they never brought up or referenced their planning when together. Not only did Casovar have telepathic magic, but Alyx's father was unconvinced the lord-mage wasn't using other methods of spying.

"That Mage Guard are a disreputable lot," he'd told Alyx. "And I wouldn't bank on Casovar not having his own spies."

Personally, she thought Brynn would have found out by now if Casovar had spies of his own. The man was so arrogant with his power, he probably didn't think he needed anything more than his own abilities. But it was always wise to be cautious.

"Did Tarrick and the twins bring any interesting news back with them?" Cayr asked carefully as dinner wound up.

"There is news, but it's not certain. I'd rather wait until we're more confident before I talk to you both."

"It's bad, though." Her father correctly read the grimness in her tone.

"It could be," she said carefully, sharing a look with her brother. "But we need confirmation. As soon as there is something to tell, I'll fill you both in. I promise."

"All right, Aly-girl."

As the sun began lowering in the sky, Ladan and Garan made their excuses, and Cayr asked her to take a walk in the gardens with him.

"Could we eat breakfast together tomorrow instead?" she asked. "I'm feeling really tired. I might have an early night."

He frowned in concern. "Are you all right?"

"I'm fine, it's probably the heat." She touched his hand. "Come for breakfast?"

A smile curled at his mouth. "I will."

IN HER BEDROOM, Alyx changed quickly before slipping out the window. She wore simple clothing, not wanting to be marked as either mage or noble. After a fierce internal debate, she left her staff behind —it was always a reassuring weight between her shoulders but it was also distinctive. Something people might remember later. Her mage knife sat in its usual place in her right boot. Her long hair was braided tightly at the base of her neck.

Instead of riding Tingo down to the city, which would have been far too conspicuous, Alyx cut through the palace gardens and used the faint trail she, Cayr and Dashan had marked out as children. It took her all the way down the forested hillside to the docks.

The evening was still warm, despite the fading light of day, and by the time Alyx reached the docks almost an hour later she was sweating lightly. The area was alive with people taking advantage of the balmy weather. Small boats dotted the bay, visible by the little lanterns hanging from their sterns. Unbidden, the memory of a night-time sailing trip with Dashan broke into her thoughts—curled up with him on the deck, watching the stars as he taught her their names. The slide of his body along hers as they kissed. His soft laughter in her ear.

Enough! She deliberately erased the memory from her thoughts and focused on what was ahead. The last thing she could afford was distraction. That was over and done with, no matter how much it hurt.

From the docks, Alyx cut through the back streets of the wharf district and headed straight for richer quarter along the river. Tarrick and Dashan lingered on the pavement outside one of the busier inns, looking to any passers-by like good friends out for the evening.

"Cario?" Tarrick lifted his eyebrows when she appeared alone.

"Not coming," she said shortly, then summoned her magic and reached out for Dawn. "We're here and ready to go."

"Finn and I are in the warehouse. We've got a good view over the river to Casovar's home."

"The twins are in position." Alyx opened her eyes. "Let's go."

Affecting laughter and ease, the three of them strolled towards the river before splitting up. Alyx and Dashan made their way through the rich quarter towards the most palatial homes along the riverbank. Like her, Dashan was out of uniform. He wore a simple knife at his waist, and his sword wrapped up in oilskin and concealed under a cloak.

Neither of them spoke.

They circled Casovar's home from a block away, standing in the shadows of a street corner and studying the place for a while. Lights lit up some of the windows, but the majority were dark. The gates were shut, two of the red-cloaked Mage Guard standing out front. Alyx hoped that Casovar would still be at the palace, but his servants would likely be awake and preparing for his return. Jenna, too, would be home.

"*Dash and I are ready to go in. What can you tell us?*" Alyx sent to Dawn.

"*I don't think Casovar is home yet. The top floor is dark. Jenna is home—I can pick up the thoughts of one of the servants helping her with a bath, and there are others awake on the ground floor, in the kitchen, I think. Finn can't see anything unusual in the grounds. It seems like a regular night in the house.*"

"Good. We'll go in now."

"*Good luck.*"

"Dawn says it's all clear," Alyx murmured, speaking for the first time.

Dashan nodded, his dark eyes scanning the home. "Good."

He led the way as they headed down the street and ducked into a narrow alley between two high-walled estates. The dark space led down to the banks of the river, with the walls of each property running all the way into the water. The night was humid and still, and dark water lapped gently against the shore.

"You know how to swim, right?" Dashan raised his eyebrows as he shrugged off his cloak and left it lying in a dark corner.

Grabbing onto his attempt at normality, Alyx shot him a mock scowl before wading out into the cool water, diving underneath as soon as it was deep enough.

Swimming under the dock of the nearest estate, they stuck close to the bank and eventually came up underneath the wooden dock of the Casovar home. A single boat was moored there, empty and dark. When nothing loomed out of the night, they swam under the dock to the shore and came out of the water in its shadow. The house loomed over them—only a back garden separated them from its stone walls.

"There will be guards patrolling the garden," Dashan murmured, crouching beside her. "Can you tell where they are?"

His close presence was distracting, and she had to concentrate hard to summon her magic to reach out and pick up the thoughts of anyone nearby. Seconds later, she heard two distinctive thought patterns. One man was thinking longingly of the end of his shift, while the other was focused on memories of a brothel he'd visited the night before. Ugh!

"Straight through there." She opened her eyes and pointed. "Two of them walking backwards and forwards in a straight line."

Dashan snorted. "Far from Blue Guard material. Let's go."

They ran forward at a crouch, ducking into the garden well away from where the guards were. They used the shadows cast by a line of trees to sneak past and reach the house.

"Casovar's quarters are all on the top floor, even his office," Dashan murmured as the two of them slipped inside a side door, finding themselves in a dim, empty corridor. Water dripped from their soaked clothing, and Alyx could only hope the wet patch on the floor wouldn't be noticed in the darkness. It someone came along here with a lamp, they were sunk.

"How do you know?"

"I might have been chatting to one of the servant girls earlier today."

Alyx fought not to roll her eyes. "I don't suppose this servant girl told you where the servant stairs are, did she?"

"Follow me." His grin flashed at her as he moved off, eventually stopping by a small door and turning to raise his eyebrows at Alyx. A touch of magic assured her nobody was on the stairs, so she nodded and they slipped through into the narrow stairwell.

Plush carpet lining the hall on the top floor forced them to walk carefully along the edges, hoping the water dripping off them wouldn't be immediately noticeable to anyone coming upstairs. No lamps had been lit, but moonlight shone through a couple of open doorways where curtains inside hadn't been drawn closed.

"Dawn, we're on the top floor. Anything to worry about?"

"We can't see any lights on up there," Dawn responded instantly. *"I can't sense any minds either."*

"The twins don't think anyone is up here," Alyx said softly.

"According to the servant I spoke to, Casovar's study is down the end of this main hall. How about you take that and I'll go through his bedroom?" Dashan asked.

"Sure. Be quick as you can. I want to get out of here before he returns."

Alyx used another touch of telepathic magic as she opened the door to Casovar's study and slipped inside. She didn't pick up any thoughts and relaxed slightly, allowing her eyes to adjust to the dim interior.

A large desk sat over by the window, covered in papers and books. A tall bookcase covered most of the wall to her right, and a fireplace the wall to her left. Moonlight shone through the arched windows, pooling on the desk and giving just enough light to see by. A glance out the window showed all was quiet along the riverbank, so Alyx sat and began going through the papers.

It was a tedious job. She scanned through summaries of mining agreements, farming in the south and personnel reports on Casovar's staff. She got through to the bottom of the first pile without finding anything of relevance to Shakar.

The second and third piles were more interesting, dealing with Rionn's military deployment along the border and into the disputed area. She read these more carefully, but there was nothing untoward about them that she could tell. Most of the reports were written by army commanders detailing their unit's activities. A few had been written by Dashan's father, protesting the number of Bluecoats Casovar wanted sent north.

The more time that passed, the more the kernel of anxiousness in her chest—there since they'd entered the house—began to grow. By the time she'd finished searching through everything on the desk, it was beating at her like a drum. They'd been inside too long, and Casovar would surely be back soon. He never stayed much later than this at the palace.

From the desk she moved to the bookcase, scanning the shelves for anything out of place. Nothing jumped out at her, and she concluded that there was nothing to be found in Casovar's office.

"Alyx, his carriage is coming down the street. He'll be there in minutes."

Dawn's calm voice was a sharp counterpoint to the panic that leaped through Alyx. Opening the study door, she glanced about to make sure the hall was empty, then left in search of Dashan.

"Two Mage Guard heading for the stairs!" Dawn was far less calm now.

At the same moment, the door down the end of the hall clicked, and Dashan appeared. He mimed to Alyx that he was coming, and started moving towards her.

"Hey! Who are you?"

Alyx froze. Two red-cloaked soldiers appeared at the top of the main stairs at the end of the hall. At the sight of the two strangers in the dim hallway they reached instantly for their swords.

Dashan—much closer than Alyx—spun to face them, drawing his sword at the same time. Moonlight falling through a nearby window danced on the blade as the guards rushed him without further challenge.

By the time Alyx reached him, Dashan had killed both soldiers. She skidded to a halt, wincing as more shouts sounded below and the alarm spread through the house—someone had heard the dead guard's challenge.

A moment later, the tell-tale whine of a crossbow bolt sounded from the shadows at the top of the stairs.

There was no time to think. No time to wonder whether she could do it.

Shouting incoherently, she slammed the end of her staff into the ground and summoned a flood of magic. A green-edged mage shield sprung into existence around her and Dashan. Less than a second later, two crossbow bolts slammed into the shield with a static hiss and dropped to the ground. More bolts followed, all crashing harmlessly into the shield.

Jayn's magic. She had it. Her heart thudded in belated relief. They'd almost both died standing there in the hallway.

"He's seen our faces." Dashan spoke before she could think, running forward and straight through her shield. She stared at him— the first evidence she'd ever seen of Taliath invulnerability shocking her into stillness. She barely processed as he reached the top of the stairs before the crossbowmen could reload, sword slashing down quickly.

"Alyx!" he snapped.

He was running back towards her, heedless of what he'd done, sword dripping blood. Shaking herself in an attempt to regain focus, she urged Dashan back towards Casovar's office.

"There's no way out this way," he shouted, glancing back. The sounds of bootsteps on the stairs were growing louder.

Ignoring him, she pulled Dashan into Casovar's office and slammed the door behind them.

"What now?" Dashan demanded.

Alyx swung her staff and sent a tightly controlled ball of energy at the study windows. It smashed the lock and sent the windows swinging outwards.

"Come on!" She grabbed his hand and dragged him towards the window.

"Alyx, we're four floors up!" he protested.

"Trust me!"

He hesitated, met her eyes, then nodded. She continued their momentum and they leaped up into the window ledge, and then out into the night.

Alyx summoned every inch of Mika's ability she could muster and used it to halt their fall. The effort required almost beat her; Dashan was heavy, and she was barely able to stop them both plummeting to their deaths. Right at the end, her strength ran out and they dropped the last few metres into the river.

River water ran into her mouth and nose as she plunged deep. Kicking upwards, she broke the surface, spluttering and rubbing water from her eyes. Weariness pulled at her, making her limbs lethargic and slow. She pushed through, forced her will on her body to keep moving. Her magic had faded to a dull flicker. The shield and subsequent use of flying magic had utterly drained her.

"We have to swim across to the other side," Dashan called. "They'll be after us any minute."

She nodded, trying to regain her breath. He swam over, wrapping a solid arm around her and helping her swim. They managed to make it to the shore as shouts and footsteps sounded on the Casovar dock, along with several bobbing lanterns. Alyx staggered out of the water, still supported by Dashan's arm.

"The Mage Guard will be searching the streets any moment, not to mention Casovar," Dashan said. "We need to hole up somewhere. My father's house is only a couple of streets away."

"Won't he protest if we show up there?" Her teeth chattered, the drain of her magic use leaving her defenceless against the cold water soaking her clothes, even though it was a warm night. "Not to mention ask a lot of questions."

"As far as I know, my room is still empty." Dashan gave her a quick smile. "And we both know I'm a master of sneaking in and out of my room without him knowing."

Alyx chuckled wearily. "Fair enough, let's go."

"Can you let Dawn know what's happening? It would be good to know where Tarrick is. And she and Finn should get clear of that warehouse as quickly as they can."

She shook her head. "Need a minute before I can use magic again."

His arm around her shoulders tightened, and she ignored the worry that flickered over his face. Instead she focused on forcing her legs to stay upright as they moved away.

They made it the short distance through the streets without encountering any of the Mage Guard. Dashan led her along the back wall of his father's home, and in through a tiny side gate. Fortunately, his room was on the ground floor, and the spare key he'd always kept hidden in a bush beneath the window was still there. He opened the window and helped her into the dark room.

"Safe," she said in relief, closing the window behind him and sagging against the wall.

"And soaking wet," he noted. "I'll go find us some towels."

He ducked out the door, and Alyx slumped into one of the chairs by the window, her mind going back over the events of the evening. They'd been caught, but the only two guards who'd clearly seen Dashan's face were dead. Unfortunately, she'd found nothing at all to prove Shakar's existence.

Dashan eventually reappeared with one arm full of towels, the other carrying two mugs of steaming liquid. "Found some soup heating in the kitchen," he explained. "It should help restore your energy."

"Thanks." She took the mug and sipped at the soup. It was delicious, filling her body with warmth. As she drank, Dashan wrapped a towel around her to soak up some of the river water, then busied himself lighting the lamp sitting by his bed. The soup restored enough energy that she could coax the tiny reserves of her power into life.

"Dawn?"

"Alyx, are you all right?" Relief and worry mixed in her friend's mental voice. *"Casovar's home is lit up like a beacon and the streets are crawling with Mage Guard and City Guard officers."*

Alyx closed her eyes, fighting through her weariness. *"We were seen inside the house, but got away. Dashan got us to his father's house and we're holed up there. Let Tarrick know we're safe, and all of you need to get out of the area."*

"Will do. Did you find anything?"

"No, I'm sorry."

"It's all right. Is there anything else we can do?"

"Go home and keep safe for now. We'll talk tomorrow."

"Dawn?" Dashan asked when she opened her eyes. He'd taken the other chair, his soup already finished.

"Yes. You were right—the streets are crawling with soldiers. Good idea to come here."

"Did you find anything back there?" he asked.

"Nothing at all, and I had a pretty good look through everything in his study."

"Me neither. There was nothing in his room but closets full of expensive clothing." Dashan stood again, running a hand through his hair in frustration. "Damn, we obviously looked in the wrong place!"

"I have no idea what we're going to do next." Alyx sighed, bitter disappointment filling her.

"We'll think of something," he said, then paused, looking at her. "Or maybe Brynn will find something. If Shakar really is out there, then there is evidence of it. There has to be."

"I suppose."

Silence fell for a while as Alyx finished her soup then placed it on a small table nearby. By then her headache was throbbing again and she sank further into the chair, one hand lifting to rub uselessly at her temples.

"I want you to tell me what's wrong." Dashan's voice had that determined quality that she hated. Frowning, she met his dark gaze.

"Isn't it obvious? We got caught breaking into Casovar's home, and killed two of his guards, all for nothing."

"No, there's something else. You forget how well I know you." His eyes searched her face. "I've been away weeks, and the change in you is obvious."

"I'm fine. I'm just tired."

"Dammit, Alyx!" He shot to his feet, eyes snapping with anger. "I let you go because I thought he would make you happy, I thought it was what you wanted. I can't sit here and see your misery and not try and help."

"It is what I wanted."

"Then what's wrong?" he demanded.

250

"I can't... " She took a breath. "I can't talk to you about this."

The anger faded from his face, to be replaced by hurt. "As much as I try, I can't regret what happened between us, but sometimes I wish I hadn't been so stupid."

"What do you mean?"

"You're far out of my reach. You always have been and always will be. I should never have allowed myself to love you, I should have known better. I could never compare to what you have with Cayr," he said wretchedly. "And now you won't even talk to me anymore."

"Love me?" Her voice came out strangled, her chest flooded with emotion.

He cocked his head, gaze softer than she'd ever seen it. "Oh, Alyx, wasn't it obvious?"

She couldn't say anything. She wanted to tell him everything, that he was the only one she wanted to talk to, that hiding everything inside was killing her, that she missed him and wanted him.

But she held back. She couldn't tell him any of those things.

He nodded sadly when she didn't respond. "I think we should stay here for the night. Take the bed, I'm going to go and find another spare room."

She nodded, her throat still too full to speak. She wanted him to stay, was confused and dismayed at how much she wanted him to share the bed with her, but all the words stayed clogged inside her, unable to be expressed.

"I'll come wake you before dawn," he said, then left.

The tears came once the door was closed, silent and streaming down her face until she thought they'd never stop.

CHAPTER 27

Alyx crept home in the half hour before dawn, stripped off her clothing and fell into her soft bed. By the time she woke again, morning sunlight was streaming through her window. Her magic reserves were back, not quite at full strength, but enough to use. The headache had gone too, though weariness still tugged at her.

Her father and Cayr were both in the dining room when she walked in, finishing up their breakfast. Ladan was nowhere to be seen. Belatedly, she remembered that she'd promised to have breakfast with Cayr. Guilt joined the tangle of emotions bottled up inside her chest.

"It's unlike you to be up so long after dawn these days, Alyx." Her father greeted her with a smile.

"I must have been tired." She smiled and leaned down to kiss his cheek. "Good morning, both of you."

"Ladan is up and out already." Garan answered her unasked question. "I have no idea where. The same applies to your friend Cario—Safia told me he packed his things and left yesterday."

"He's gone from Alistriem. It's a long story." After serving herself some porridge from the side table, Alyx took the seat beside Cayr. She was ravenous after the previous night's activities, and dived straight into her breakfast.

"Orange juice?" Cayr passed her a glass.

"Thanks."

"Do you feel better this morning?" he asked. "You still look pale."

"I'm fine." She found a smile for him. "I'm sorry I was late for breakfast."

Their comfortable silence was interrupted soon after by the front bell ringing through the house. Shortly after, Safia appeared with Lord-Mage Casovar in tow. Alyx tensed. Cayr glanced at her, then discreetly reached out to touch her hand.

Garan rose to his feet. "Lord-Mage, this is a surprise."

"I apologise for calling on you so early, Lord Egalion," Casovar said, bowing his head when he caught sight of Cayr. "Your Highness."

"Lord-Mage," Cayr said pleasantly.

"No need to apologise." Garan resumed his seat. "Prince Cayr was just sharing breakfast with my daughter and me. Can I have the servants get you anything?"

"I'm fine, thank you." Casovar glanced at Alyx, grey eyes as cold as always. She stared back as calmly as she could, inwardly shoring up her mental shield.

"What can I do for you this morning?" her father asked, drawing Casovar's gaze away. Her shoulders relaxed a little. Cayr's hand on hers tightened momentarily, and she squeezed back.

"I have some disturbing news." Casovar's gaze flickered between all three of them. "My home was broken into last night. Two Mage Guard soldiers were killed in the process, and as you can imagine, I'm quite upset about the whole affair."

Garan looked genuinely startled. "Do you know who was behind it?"

"Not yet," Casovar said. "But there were two intruders; one was a Taliath, the other a mage."

A cold fist of dread closed around Alyx's heart, and she was more grateful than she could say for Cayr's quick and casual response.

"A mage and a Taliath?" The prince allowed a touch of incredulity to fill his voice. "Are you sure?"

"Yes, Your Highness."

Alyx fought to maintain a calm expression. Where had Casovar gotten the impression that one of the intruders was Taliath? He hadn't been there. Only the two dead guards had seen Dashan.

"Surely you must be mistaken." Garan frowned. "I know you're aware of my past, Lord-Mage, but I can assure you I didn't break into your house last night. There are few, if any, other Taliath living—certainly none in Rionn."

Alyx was impressed by her father's ability to lie so well, although she supposed it gave him confidence knowing Casovar couldn't read his thoughts.

"I am certain, Lord Egalion," Casovar said. "More, I believe the Taliath is Shiven."

Garan cocked his head, giving a perfect impression of genuine puzzlement. "Why do you think that?"

"I'm a mage of the higher order. That gives me many... specialist abilities."

It wasn't an answer, but Garan let it go with a little shrug. Alyx tried to keep her expression interested and slightly puzzled. She didn't dare say anything, terrified the guilty knowledge would be written all over her face.

Cayr smoothly changed the subject. "What's being done to find them?"

"The Mage Guard is investigating the matter as a priority. Witnesses report that the mage had the ability to fly. It is a unique talent amongst mages, and it shouldn't take long to identify them if they trained at DarkSkull Hall. Once I have the mage, it won't be long until we have the Taliath in hand also."

"If the Taliath was Shiven, then the mage probably was too," Garan said dismissively. "Which means it is unlikely they trained at DarkSkull."

"Perhaps," Casovar acknowledged.

"I will speak to my father about this," Cayr said. "I'm sure he will devote whatever resources you need to find the intruders."

"Thank you, Your Highness."

"I share your concern over the affair, of course, but is there a reason you've come here this morning, Lord-Mage Casovar?" Garan asked.

Casovar's cold grey eyes glanced at Alyx for a moment before he turned back to her father, a cool smile on his face.

"I thought you should know. Whatever prompted the break in may lead these intruders to invade other wealthy residences. You might wish to consider increasing your guard."

"Was anything taken from your residence?"

"Nothing at all."

Garan stood. "It sounds to me like the invasion of your home may have been a more personal attack. Perhaps the intruders expected you to be home. I think you're the one who should increase his guard."

Casovar's mouth thinned. "I have no need of guards with my magic."

"Indeed." Garan smiled. "And as a Taliath, I could say the same. Good day, Lord-Mage."

It was a dismissal, albeit a polite one, and Casovar stiffened. Alyx had rarely been more impressed by her father.

"Good day." Casovar turned to go, then paused. "I ask that you keep the details of what I've told you confidential. It will assist in verifying witness or other reports if it is not widely known that the intruders were mage and Taliath. My servants have already been given strict instructions on the subject."

"Nobody will hear anything from us," Garan said smoothly.

"I'll walk you out," Cayr offered, rising from his chair.

The room remained silent until the sound of Casovar's and Cayr's footsteps had faded from hearing.

"Tired, was it, Alyx?" Garan said, an edge to his voice. "What were you doing last night?"

She winced. "It's probably better you don't know."

His faced hardened. "You and Dashan broke into Casovar's home, didn't you?"

Normally she found her father's anger intimidating, but no longer. Weariness flooded her at the thought of another argument. "Yes."

Garan said nothing for a moment. He lowered himself into his chair, gaze fixed on her the whole time. When he did speak, his voice was low and scathing.

"What were you thinking to expose Dashan so carelessly? You

heard Casovar—now he knows there is a Taliath alive and in the city. How long do you think it will take him to work out who it is?"

"We didn't expect to get caught," she said, warding off the panic rising in her. Dashan would be fine. "He wanted to go with me because we both knew the area better than the others. It made sense at the time."

"It was foolish in the extreme," Garan snapped.

The door swung open, admitting Cayr. He took one look at both their faces and heaved a sigh. "So it was you last night, then? Who was the... Alyx, you've gone white! What's wrong?"

"It's nothing."

"It's not nothing," he disagreed. "If you'd been caught last night, all our plans would be ruined."

"Two guards were killed!" her father added. He was looking at her like he didn't know her any more, but that only made her angry at him again.

"We had good reason for what we did," she said, trying to defend herself.

Garan's mouth thinned, and he stared at her for a long moment before snapping, "Safia!"

The steward appeared a moment later, serene expression on his face despite the obvious tension in the room. "Yes, sir?"

"I don't want any servants near this room until I say otherwise."

"Yes, sir." Safia bowed and disappeared.

"Talk. Now," Garan said firmly. "And no more blathering about wanting to find out more before filling us in."

Alyx nodded, lowering her voice. "While Tarrick and the twins were in the disputed area, they identified the new leader of the Shiven forces. Worse, they think Casovar is actively working with this leader."

"Who is it?" Cayr demanded.

Alyx looked away from him, meeting her father's steely gaze. "Shakar."

"Shakar?" Garan went rigid in his chair. "That's not possible."

"It's hard to accept," she acknowledged. "But the information suggesting Casovar is working against us is close to certain—Dawn is a powerful telepath mage. And if it is Shakar that he's working with, we need to get proof, or at least some actual evidence, to take to the Mage Council."

"And you thought to find that proof in Casovar's home?"

"Yes." She sighed, sinking back in her chair. "But we found nothing."

"Who or what is Shakar?" Cayr spoke into the silence.

Glancing at her father, who nodded slightly, Alyx gave Cayr a succinct rundown of what she'd learned about Shakar at DarkSkull. By the time she'd finished, he looked worried, but it was clear he didn't understand the implications as well as her father did.

"Alyx, you're a noblewoman who will one day be queen," he said. "No matter what the reason, you can't go around breaking into lord's homes. You know as well as I do the consequences if anyone at court found out."

"But I'm not just a noblewoman, not anymore." Alyx looked at them, her voice taking on a pleading quality. "I've been trying so hard to make you both understand that. I've killed. I'm what DarkSkull made of me—a mage warrior."

"Alyx—"

"You've killed people?" Cayr spoke with the same horror in his voice that was clearly written on her father's face. "I know you said you killed a man who was trying to kill your friend, but... there's more?"

Alyx nodded. "Tarrick, the twins, Cario and myself, we were Dark-Skull Hall's Third Patrol. We worked alongside Dashan and his Blue-coats. Our role was to protect DarkSkull. We fought and killed more than once."

"Carhall... " Garan's voice trailed off. "That's why you were there. I can't believe I didn't see it. You were riding escort duty. I thought it was ceremonial, but it wasn't, was it?"

"No. In fact, we were ambushed on the way back. Many died."

"And what Lord-Mage Casovar said, about the mage being able to fly?" Cayr asked.

"I'm a mage of the higher order, like he is," she replied. "I have many skills, one of which is flying."

Garan sat back in his chair, something like the weariness she was feeling settling over his face. "When I sent you there, I never thought... "

"You should have." The words came out more sharply than she'd intended. "But maybe you'll believe me now. Casovar is a threat to Rionn, and I'm not going to sit idly by and attend social picnics while that continues. And if Shakar truly is back... I'll be helping the council destroy him."

Cayr and her father looked at each other, but neither of them challenged her. Instead, Cayr changed the subject. "What about the Taliath Casovar mentioned? Who is he?"

Alyx didn't want to keep the truth from him anymore. Cayr was one of the people she trusted most in the world, but he was no mage that could protect himself with a mental shield.

"It's safer for him if you don't know," she said gently. "You know why."

Cayr's face twisted. "I'm starting to realise why my father distrusts the mage order so much. I'm the prince of Rionn, yet I can't trust my father's lord-mage not to invade the privacy of my mind. Worse, I'm kept from information I need to know because of it."

"Cayr—"

He waved a hand and stood up. "I hate how all this has changed everything. You've become part of a world that I don't understand and couldn't even if I wanted to. Lord Egalion, I should go. Thank you for breakfast."

"Cayr, wait." Alyx rose from her chair and caught up to him at the door. "I can't help any of this, but I hope you know that no matter who I am or what I do, you're always going to be one of the most important people in my life."

"We spoke about mages of the higher order only a few days ago, and you didn't tell me what you were. Why?" he asked, anger and hurt warring on his face.

"For the same reasons I can't tell you who the Taliath is." She sighed. "It's dangerous, what I am, more than you realise."

"Will you tell me what you mean by that?"

"I will, but not now. When we have some time."

His face softened a little, though he still looked sad. "All right. I'll see you later."

She nodded, leaned up to kiss him on the cheek. "Bye, Cayr."

Her father was staring out the window when she returned to the table, and she wondered what he was thinking about.

"You still angry at me?"

"Furious," he said dryly. "And don't even try to tell me you didn't say anything because of Casovar's telepathic ability. I'm immune."

"I needed to do something, Papa, and I knew you'd tell us not to."

"You were reckless," he said shortly. "And not only in risking Dashan. You put our plan at risk. If the court finds out you were involved, the lords' support for your betrothal will vanish in a puff of smoke."

"I'd like to know how Casovar knows anything," Alyx murmured, almost to herself. "Only two guards saw us last night, and they're both dead."

All at once her father sat up straight in his chair, startling her. "Aly-girl, your mother!"

"My..." Her words faded as she realised what he just had. "I have to go!"

He reached out—quicker than thought—to take her arm, his eyes serious as he forced her to meet them. "Do what you need to do, but promise me you'll be careful and discreet," he urged. "If Casovar is truly working against us, then he's an adversary, a much more immediate one than Shakar."

"I have some experience at dealing with adversaries, Papa."

"Not one as dangerous as this, Aly-girl." His words followed her out the door.

SHE STEPPED outside to find the driveway and green lawn filled with horses and soldiers—Ladan's men. Romney hovered at the periphery, barking the occasional order to hurry up.

"Romney!" Alyx strode over to him. "Where's Ladan?"

"In the stables, My Lady," Romney's scowl faded as he addressed her. "He wants to leave this morning."

She managed a smile for him. "I hope we'll see you back here again soon."

His lips twitched, the closest to a smile she'd ever seen on the veteran warrior. "I hope so too, Lady Egalion."

LADAN HOVERED over a table in the tack room of the stables, Dashan at his side. A map lay unrolled on the table before them. Her brother was dressed for riding, heavily armed. Dashan wore his Bluecoat uniform, his hat holding down one corner of the map.

"You planning to say goodbye before riding off?" Her sharp words caught both men's attention, and they looked up.

"Of course I was," Ladan said in irritation, then seemed to notice her agitated state. "What's wrong?"

"I need to talk to you. Papa and I just realised something."

Dashan reached for his hat. "I should go."

"No, please stay."

Their gazes met and held for a moment, and he capitulated with a small smile. Something inside her relaxed.

"The first thing is that Casovar somehow knows... " Alyx hesitated —she'd been about to say Taliath, and cursed herself. Tiredness was making her careless. "He knows a mage broke into his home last night."

"How?" Dashan demanded. "Only the two guards saw us, and they're both dead."

"I honestly have no idea."

Ladan glanced at Dashan, then her. "You'll have to be careful. More than careful given you don't know exactly what he knows."

"I will." She brushed off his concern. "More importantly, Papa insisted I tell him the reason we broke in. It made him realise something."

"What?" Impatience threaded his tone.

"The information our mother discovered. Why she left you and went racing off. We thought she learned something about the missing mages—we were right, but it was more than that. Ladan, what if she found out about Shakar being alive!"

Her brother's eyes widened, and he absently reached up to run a hand over his short hair. Then, he sat abruptly. "He killed her."

"Don't go racing too far ahead," Dashan warned. "We don't know for absolute certain yet that he's alive. Besides, Romas said your mother was travelling to meet him. It sounds like she was going to warn the council, not confront Shakar."

Alyx met her brother's eyes. Dashan's words were logical, but they weren't true. Garan knew their mother better than anyone, and he'd guessed instantly what she would do—confront Shakar.

"She's the proof we need for the council. If we find out what happened to her, we find the proof," she urged.

"The letter." Ladan shot back to his feet. "After your visit last year I sent some men searching for the mage named Terin. They didn't find out much, and then we were so busy with the Shiven on our borders I didn't do anything further."

"What did they find out?"

"He was a mage, like we guessed, but he retired from the council years ago. Romney heard word of a place he might have gone to, but that was all."

"You have to track him down. If you can find Terin, maybe you can learn what he told our mother."

"That's assuming he told her anything." Dashan weighed in again. "It could have been pure coincidence that he was in the area when your mother learned whatever it was that made her leave."

"What other options do we have? There was nothing in Casovar's home, and he's so suspicious of us now, we can't do much more here."

Ladan began pacing. "I need to get home. Widow Falls is vulnerable as long as I'm away."

"This is more important, and I can't go. Casovar would never give permission for me to leave Alistriem for an extended time without good reason, and I'm still technically under his command," she said.

"Romney is capable, Lord Mirren," Dashan said. "Send him back to Widow Falls to manage things until you get back."

Ladan stayed silent, staring grimly at the floor, and Dashan glanced between them. "I should get going. My shift starts soon."

"You've been assigned back to Alistriem?" she asked.

He nodded. "Lord Mirren and I surveyed the border area to the north of Widow Falls and put together a plan for the king. Those plans have been passed to Prince Cayr. It is now for the king to decide what to do."

"Be safe, Dash," she said softly. "You don't need me to tell you to keep your head down after last night. Casovar is already searching the city for those responsible."

"You too. Lord Mirren, best of luck."

Once he'd gone, Alyx spoke into the ensuing silence. "I know it's a longshot, but we need to do something, Ladan."

"I agree. I'll do as you ask." Ladan nodded.

Alyx hesitated. "You spoke to Cayr about your plans?"

"I did." Ladan rolled up the map and turned to stuff it into one of his saddlebags. "He is a good man. I sense that he will do everything he can to make you happy."

She shook her head, dismissing those words as something she didn't want to deal with. "He mentioned the other day that he wanted to send more resources to Widow Falls?"

Ladan's jaw clenched. "He gave me little choice in the matter. In fact, I need to make sure I get back in time for the arrival of new soldiers."

"Tell me as soon as you find out anything about Terin."

"If I can find the blasted man. I can't spend too long searching," he warned, then hesitated. "I offered Dashan the position of Romney's second. Romney is getting older, and his job is a dangerous one. After Romney's retirement, Dashan would head my forces."

Tears filled her eyes and she turned away to hide them, leaning her palms on the table for support. "Ladan, he's a Taliath."

For a moment there was silence, then a warm arm wrapped around her shoulders. "I know."

"Tell me you didn't hide it from me too," she whispered.

His arm around her tightened. "No. I suspected, and so I spoke to Papa about it. It's part of why I came here—he told me you knew already."

Nodding, she turned into his chest, taking the comfort he was offering. Ladan's gruff voice spoke over her shoulder. "The Bluecoats will never make full use of Dashan's skills, and if he stays in Alistriem he will always have the taint of his half-Shiven blood hanging over him. I hope he takes me up on my offer. He's become a... friend."

"Look at you, making friends." She smiled through her tears, then wiped them away and stood back. "Thanks, big brother."

He nodded, hesitating. "If he chooses to join me, I'm going to tell him. I won't hide things from someone I expect to trust me implicitly."

"I think you should," she said. "If he wasn't in so much danger here in the city, I would have told him already. I hate keeping it from him. But with you he'll be as safe as he can be."

His hard face softened. "Be careful, Aly-girl. I hate leaving you here alone with that snake of a lord-mage."

"I'm not alone, and I'll be fine. I look forward to hearing from you."

He hugged her once more, and then he was gone.

CHAPTER 28

The following week passed uneventfully. While the Mage Guard investigation continued, no arrests were made, and Casovar's attitude towards Alyx and her friends didn't change in any meaningful way.

While the lack of results should have made them relieved, it left them the opposite. They didn't dare meet privately too often, and when they did, they kept their discussions short. All were anxious, restless with the need to do something—anything—to deal with the fact Shakar might be out there.

"What more can we do?" Tarrick reminded them one night over dinner at the A'ndreas home. "Brynn is out there searching for evidence and Ladan is tracking down Terin. We can't risk going near Casovar again in the short term."

"Maybe one of us should go to the council anyway," Dawn suggested. "We might be assuming incorrectly that they won't believe us. Aren't we being irresponsible by not doing more?"

"Irresponsible is walking away from the whole mess," Tarrick muttered. He hadn't taken news of Cario's departure well. Of all of them, Tarrick's sense of honour was most deeply offended by Cario's decision.

"Maybe you're right, sis," Finn said. "Tarrick, you could go. You're a Tylender. Maybe they'd listen to you?"

"Casovar would question why Tarrick has suddenly left," Alyx pointed out. "But Dawn is right. Why don't we give Brynn a few more days to find something, and if he has no luck, we ask him to go? His word might carry more weight than ours."

"Two days," Tarrick said firmly. "I don't want to wait any longer."

So they continued working under Casovar's scrutiny—always in the back of their minds the knowledge that if their mental shields failed at the wrong moment, even a single lapse in concentration, he could know everything.

Casovar kept to his initial promise that he would keep Tarrick and the twins in Alistriem to spend time on their training—the single positive amongst all the anxiousness. It was impossible to know what his real motivation was, equally impossible to tell how much, if at all, he suspected them of being involved in the break in at his home. Dawn claimed his thoughts were locked up tight, and neither she nor Alyx had enough confidence in their telepathic skill to try and read his thoughts without detection.

"The only mage I've come across with such an impenetrable shield is Romas, and now you, Alyx," her friend confided one night as they sat in one of the palace gardens together. Finn and Tarrick had gone to get some sparring training in with Dashan and his Bluecoats. Alyx had begged off, claiming that she didn't dare risk word getting to Casovar that she was capable with a staff, and Dawn was exhausted after a particularly intense session with Casovar earlier in the day.

"Me?" Alyx asked, startled.

"Yes." She chuckled in amusement. "It's like you're hiding the secret code to open a chest full of gold or something the way you clamp down on your thoughts."

Her friend was joking, but it was impossible to share her amusement. She was hiding so many secrets—it was exhausting, both the effort it took to maintain the shield and the guilt that swamped her along with it.

"The training sessions with him are dangerous," Dawn continued, oblivious to Alyx's turmoil. "He works us to exhaustion, which makes it difficult to maintain a shield."

"At least if nothing else we'll all be experts at shielding by the time we get back to DarkSkull," Alyx said dryly. "Howell will be impressed."

Dawn looked startled at her words. "You want to go back to DarkSkull?"

"Do we have a choice?" Alyx lifted her eyebrows. "Once Casovar is out of Rionn and Astor is back to being lord-mage, we have to finish our training. Unless like Cario you want to stay out of the fight against Shakar?"

"I do, actually." Dawn's face turned bleak. "When I think about what we've learned from the time when Shakar was fighting the council... so many mages died. That could be us. It will be people we know and love."

"Maybe we can prevent a war," Alyx said, trying not to shiver. "If we neutralise Casovar, and the council can act to remove Shakar before he does any damage."

"Maybe," Dawn said, but she didn't sound any more convinced than Alyx was.

A comfortable silence fell as they settled back and watched a cloud of fireflies zooming through the night sky around them. It was relaxing, and some of the knot of tension inside her begin to uncoil.

"I was surprised when we got your letter," Dawn spoke eventually.

Alyx knew instantly what she meant. "Agreeing to marry Cayr was the right thing in the circumstances. I just wish it had come up two years ago, when I actually wanted it."

"I have to admit it's rather surreal to be having this conversation with you." Dawn gave a little smile. "You pined over Cayr for so long. But you wouldn't have necessarily had much choice in marrying, right? At least you and Cayr are good friends."

"All that is true," Alyx agreed. "And I think I would have been fine with it, happy even, if I hadn't already..." She stopped herself, shaking her head when Dawn looked puzzled. "I'm being self-pitying and maudlin, and I'm sorry. You're absolutely right, I'm luckier than I could have expected to be."

Dawn's arm crept around her. "As long as you know I'll be here if ever you're willing to admit you're not fine."

TWO WEEKS after the break-in at Casovar's home, Alyx, Cayr and her father attended a formal dinner with the king and several other senior lords. Now that they were officially betrothed, Alyx sat with Cayr rather than her father, although he was still directly across the table from her.

Casovar sat beside him, and Sparky and Dashan's father were there too, along with Jenna and Dashan's older brother. The lower half of the table was similarly filled with lords and their wives all familiar to Alyx.

Conversation flowed easily. Though there were faint shadows under his eyes, the king was in a good mood, and the wine and food flowed freely. Earlier discussion had centred around Cayr's betrothal—still considered big news amongst the court—and Alyx had done her best to smile and blush and appear like a young woman thrilled with marrying the prince.

Fortunately, the conversation had eventually moved on, freeing her from their attention. Her glance fell on Casovar, considering. Brynn had left a few days earlier for Tregaya after having no luck in Alistriem finding proof of Casovar's connection to Shakar.

None of them held out much hope that the council would believe them without proof, but all agreed they couldn't wait any longer without doing something.

As if summoned by her thoughts, Dashan's brother spoke into a lull in the conversation, asking Casovar if he'd made any progress on finding out who had broken into his home.

"None at all, I'm afraid." Casovar put down his napkin. "I have no doubt that I will eventually find the perpetrators, but it is proving more difficult than I expected."

"An unfortunate affair." The king frowned. "And unprecedented. The City Guard does an excellent job keeping the crime level in the city down, and I can't remember the last time a lord's home was broken into."

"Lord Egalion suggested that the motive may have been personal," Casovar said smoothly. "He could be right."

"Indeed. There haven't been any other break-ins since," Garan said.

"When you catch them, they'll experience the full weight of my justice," Darien promised.

Cayr shifted at Alyx's side, and she reached out to discreetly touch his hand. He gave a slight nod and settled.

"It shouldn't be too much longer, Your Highness." Casovar settled his pale grey eyes on Alyx. "Not much longer at all."

He knew.

The words screamed through her mind, the ice-cold certainty of them settling in her chest like a stone. It took everything she had to smile lightly at him, then pick up her wine glass and take a casual sip.

"Lord-Mage, has Lord Dunkeld received any further information on the unrest in Shivasa?" Tirian Caverlock asked, unknowingly saving Alyx by breaking Casovar's gaze. The lord-mage turned away and replied, but she didn't hear what he'd said over the sound of her thundering heart.

He knew.

HER STOMACH WAS STILL TWISTED in knots by the time dinner was over, and she'd had to force herself to keep eating, not wanting to betray to Casovar that anything was amiss.

Afterwards, she and Cayr took a walk in the moonlit gardens. It was a warm evening, the moon bright and full above them, but it was impossible to enjoy the beauty surrounding her.

It didn't take Cayr long to pick up on her mood. "What's wrong?"

She glanced around, ensuring they were alone. "I think he knows it was me who broke into his house."

"What makes you think that? You said nobody saw you that survived."

"Just now at dinner... the way he looked at me." A chill went through her just thinking about it. "He knows, Cayr. I'm not sure how much he knows, or whether he has any proof, but he knows."

"All right, take a breath," he soothed, running his hands along her arms. "You're tense and on edge. All of us are. If Casovar knew, he would have acted by now."

"Maybe," she muttered. "Or maybe he just doesn't have proof."

"Even if you're right, then without proof he can't do anything," Cayr said.

Alyx stepped away, unable to stand still. "We can't keep this up much longer. Eventually he'll sense something in one of our thoughts, and if he knows it was me, he can find—or manufacture—the proof he needs. It's a matter of time."

"You're not to worry about me," Cayr said, the force in his voice taking her by surprise. He stood straight shouldered before her, the determination of his features making him look older than his nineteen years. This was the future king of Rionn talking to her. "I will make Casovar see me as nothing more than a silly prince too in love to think straight. I won't give him a reason to suspect me. I promise you."

Her shoulders relaxed slightly. "Thank you. Cayr, I... "

"What is it?"

"You are going to make a fine king. A better one than your father, I think."

He seemed stunned by her words, how confidently she'd spoken them. After a moment he cleared his throat. "I hope so."

"I know so." She smiled sadly. "You should go before someone comes looking for us. Technically we should have a chaperone."

"All right." He hugged her briefly. "I'll see you tomorrow."

"Good night."

Worry clawed at her as she watched him walking away. Resolutely, she pushed it away, refusing to allow herself to have doubts. Everything was going to be fine.

CHAPTER 29

Once again, he wasn't trying to hurt her. She fought, as always, more from stubbornness now than anything else, but it was to no avail.

"*We want the same things, Alyx Egalion.*"

She closed her mind off, refusing to acknowledge him.

A light chuckle. "*Your determination is impressive, but we both know I can see through you. The council is twisted and corrupt. You know that as well as I do. I just want to see them gone. Don't you?*"

Her sleeping body curled in on itself, hands clutching at the bedsheets. She didn't want to listen to this, fought to keep herself apart from him.

"*We're the same, you and I. We want the same things. The Mage Council should be destroyed.*"

"*We are not the same!*" The response was instinctive, out before she could stop herself. But even before the words had left her mouth, her heart started thudding. Destroying the Mage Council. She'd heard that recently—talking with Tarrick and the others after they'd come back, after they'd gotten through telling her that they thought Shakar was alive...

Shakar.

The darkmage who'd burned for the destruction of the council in the same way this man haunting her nightmares did. Shakar—the extraordinarily powerful mage of the higher order who had possessed the ability to create nightmares. Howell had been so close to realising. Her stomach heaved and her shock and horror were so powerful they were almost enough to send her flying out of the nightmare. His magic caught her though, inexorably dragging her back—and she barely noticed. Even in a dream it was a struggle to catch her breath, to process what she now knew to be true. No, no, no. Fear flooded her, dark and overwhelming.

"*Shakar...* " the word leaked from her mind unbidden.

It had to be. Who else could have the power she felt every time she was dragged into his dream? He was alive, and he'd been the one haunting her nightmares, talking to her. His delight curled through the dream at her realisation.

"*I was starting to wonder when you'd figure it out.*"

She was wrenched away then, the vision of a battlefield flashing before her eyes. It was blurry, unclear, but Tarrick was there, along with Cario and the twins. A blast of magic exploded right where they were standing, and Alyx watched in slow-motion as they were destroyed in front of her.

"*That doesn't have to be their fate,*" A crooning whisper, almost pleading. "*You don't have to stand against me. We could take the council down together.*"

She twisted away from him, fighting, clawing, to no avail. All rationality had left her. This was animal fear making her desperate to get away, to escape him. But while he was no longer trying to hurt her, his magic gripped hers with insulting ease.

"*With me, you would be allowed your Taliath lover,*" he whispered, triumph infusing his thoughts. "*If the council was gone, he would be safe. You could have him.*"

"*No.*"

"*It's what you want.*"

"No!" she screamed, coming awake and sitting bolt upright. Her breath came in shuddering gasps as she tried to re-orient herself to the waking world. The moon above was bright, illuminating the plains surrounding the small town Casovar had sent them to. The cluster of roofs and fields were just visible in the distance, and Tarrick's sleeping form lay a short distance off. A soft night breeze played with tendrils of her hair.

She tossed off her blanket and stood, the adrenalin flooding her body leaving her unable to sit still. The tall grass of the plains brushed by her legs as she walked up a small hill, stopping at the summit. At the top she began pacing, her body alternately chilled and too warm. Her hands trembled. She tried focusing on the view as a distraction—she could see out over the west coast of Rionn, and south and east to the grassed plains surrounding her—but it didn't work for long.

Finally, after all this time, she knew the source of her nightmares.

Shakar.

And he wanted her to join with him.

She shivered again as the sweat began drying on her skin. The nights were cooler, and they would only grow colder as they settled deeper into autumn. She and Tarrick were not far from the large village town of Reside. Casovar had sent them there, claiming reports from the Mage Guard that the Shiven had a safe house for their spies in the town. He wanted Tarrick and Alyx to investigate.

After two days of following up on the scant details contained in the Mage Guard report, they'd found no evidence of Shiven spies or a safe house, and were now on their way back to Alistriem.

The whole thing had increased Alyx's anxiousness to extreme levels. Had there truly been reports of a safe house, or had Casovar wanted them out of the city for some reason? Tarrick, who often trusted Alyx's instincts even more than she did, was equally worried. Neither of them had wanted to leave the city, but there had been no way to avoid it.

Shakar.

Alyx shuddered. Her thoughts were going around and around, trying to avoid the mere reference to what she'd realised.

"Alyx?"

She stopped her incessant pacing—Tarrick was climbing the rise towards her. "Sorry, did I wake you?"

"I noticed you weren't sleeping and wanted to make sure you were okay." He stopped a short distance away. "Something is wrong. Another nightmare?"

"He wanted to talk to me again." She swallowed. "There's something else."

Tarrick's eyes went wide with shock as she told him. "That's... I don't even have words for it. And he wants you to join him?"

"He says the council is corrupt and needs destroying, and he can see enough in my head to know that I'm not a big fan of the council either."

"Anything else?"

Alyx looked away and shook her head, hating lying to him. But if she mentioned what Shakar had promised her, that destroying the council would keep Taliath safe... she dreaded Tarrick looking at her like she was the enemy, like she might be tempted by that offer. And she wasn't. Would never be. Alyx slammed shut the tiny part of herself that tried to reason that maybe... No.

She expected fiery words and a promise to protect her always, so she was surprised when he walked over and pulled her gently into a hug. "Can I do anything to help right now?"

"I'm fine. Go back to sleep. It's not long till dawn, and I won't be able to go to sleep, so I think I might just keep watch."

He squeezed her arm reassuringly before heading back down the hill. Alyx remained where she was, staring out into the night and trying not to think of anything.

A short distance away, one of the horses snorted, possibly irritated by one of the night insects. She glanced down at them, but they quieted soon after. A moment later, a familiar mind brushed across her thoughts—a sense of urgency—then it was gone.

The only telepath that was close enough to be familiar to her was Dawn, and Alyx immediately closed her eyes and focused, drawing upon her magic. When the faint tendril of thought tickled her mind again, Alyx grabbed hold of it with her magic and used more power to bolster the link. Her reserve started to drain quickly; she wasn't as powerful a telepath as Dawn.

"*Alyx?*" The voice was faint with distance.

"*Dawn, what is it? Hurry, I'm about to lose hold of you.*"

"*Dashan...*" The voice broke off, then came back. "*He's been arrested... Casovar's men.*"

"*What?*"

Alyx's surge of panicked emotion snapped her tenuous hold on the link, and abruptly Dawn was gone. Frantically, she tried again, using up the reserve of power she had to cast out her mind again and again.

Nothing.

Cursing under her breath, Alyx jumped to her feet and ran down the hill towards where Tarrick slept. She shook him roughly, then continued past to start rapidly rolling up her bedding.

"What?" Tarrick mumbled, coming awake. "Another nightmare?"

"Get up. We have go," she snapped. "We were right to be suspicious—he did want us out of the city. There was no damned safe house." She swore, mostly at herself. Why had she allowed herself to be sent away, and Tarrick too? The two strongest warrior mages... if Casovar knew what she was. Now she was certain of it.

"Casovar?" Tarrick blinked. "Why? What's going on?"

"Dawn just contacted me. Dashan's been arrested by the Mage Guard." Alyx hefted her rolled blankets and strode over to stuff them into Tingo's saddlebags.

"Why?" Tarrick asked, rolling his own blankets.

"I don't know."

"Then get back in touch with Dawn and tell her to go to Prince Cayr," Tarrick said. "He can do something much faster than we can."

"The distance is too far. I tried reaching her again but failed," Alyx said shortly, tightening the girth strap with far more force than was necessary. Tingo protested, dancing away with a snort. "Hurry up, Tarrick!"

They were gone within minutes of Alyx getting Dawn's message.

THE GRASSES SPED past them along with the remainder of the night. By dawn, they'd slowed the horses to a walk to rest them, then let them stop at the first stream they passed to drink.

After that, they were galloping again. By mid-morning, the hazy outline of Alistriem grew visible on the horizon. The golden palace was the first thing to come into full focus, the sun surrounding it in a halo-like glow.

They swept in along the northern road at full gallop, forcing those ahead of them to make room. The citizens on their way into the city took one look at the galloping war horses and mage-clad riders, and scurried aside with alacrity. Alyx felt a twinge of guilt at the clouds of dust they left in their wake, but it didn't come close to registering against the fear for Dashan that was beating at her like a drum.

As they raced through the city gates, she reached out to try and contact Dawn again. This time she found her quickly and easily.

"*We're at home,*" Dawn said, before cutting off.

Alyx sent a picture of the A'ndreas house to Tarrick's mind, and he nodded, leading them off the main streets. Both horses were breathing hard and lathered in sweat as they rode into the small garden off the street. The twins' father hovered anxiously by the gate.

"Finn asked me to see to your horses. They're waiting for you inside."

"Thank you, sir." Alyx gratefully passed him Tingo's reins.

"You're welcome." He hesitated. "I'm worried. Are they going to be okay?"

"I'll do everything I can to protect them," she promised.

She and Tarrick strode quickly into the house, Alyx already speaking as they entered the front room. "What's going on?"

Finn glanced at his sister. "Dashan was arrested by the Mage Guard early yesterday evening. He was at one of the local inns when it happened. Casovar claims he is a Taliath—the one that broke into his home and murdered two of his Mage Guard."

The blood drained from her cheeks, and she dropped into the nearest chair, trying not to let fear overwhelm her. "Damn it. This was all deliberate... getting us out of the city." Shakar coming to me, promising Dashan would be safe if I joined him. All of it planned perfectly.

Tarrick looked down at Alyx, then over at Finn, frowning. "What makes Casovar think Dashan is a Taliath?"

275

"Think about it," Finn said carefully. "What we've seen Dashan do, how well he fights. I think Casovar might be right about him. In fact I think we've been fools not to see it ourselves."

"I still have trouble reaching his thoughts," Dawn added softly.

Rubbing at her temples, Alyx let out a sigh. "Casovar is right."

At once the attention of the room was on her, and she could sense the mingled shock and fear in their thoughts and on their faces.

"You're not surprised... you knew he was a Taliath?" Dawn asked in confusion.

"Not for long." Alyx explained what her father had told her. From the corner of her eye, she saw Finn turn white and sink into a chair. She refused to look at him.

"Be that as it may, Dashan's involvement in the break-in has to be more of an educated guess on Casovar's part. Nobody saw his face, or Alyx's," Tarrick said calmly.

"I think you're wrong," Alyx said quietly. "I think Casovar has known all along it was Dashan and me in his house that night."

"How could he know?" Tarrick objected. "You said only the two dead Mage Guards saw your faces."

"What if he was in their thoughts before they died?" she said, and shocked silence flooded the room. "It's the only thing that makes sense. There was no reason for them to be on the top floor that night —it was empty. We never considered that Casovar might use his telepathic magic to undertake periodic checks on his house when he's not there."

Tarrick sat heavily. "And if he truly is working with Shakar... Shakar knows what you are, Alyx, from your nightmares. Casovar could have known all this time."

"And we thought we were being so clever in fooling him." She laughed bitterly at her arrogance—she'd thought Casovar the arrogant one, and the whole time he'd been playing them.

Dawn's eyes widened in shock. "Shakar is the one giving you nightmares?"

Alyx nodded, explaining quickly and concisely.

"Even if everything you say is true, Casovar still needs proof before he can act against Lord Egalion's only daughter," Dawn echoed Cayr's words.

"He can get proof if he makes Dash talk," Finn said.

"Dash would never talk!" Alyx rounded on him angrily.

"Casovar is a mage of the higher order, Alyx, be sensible!" Tarrick countered. "He can do things we've never even thought about. Dash will talk, sooner or later."

"He's a Taliath," she snapped. "That night, he walked right out of my mage shield. If anyone else tried that, they'd have been knocked out or worse. Casovar can't touch him."

"Taliath invulnerability only lasts as long as the person's physical strength does," Finn pointed out. "And I'm sure Casovar isn't above more mundane methods of torture."

"Then we have to get him out." She shot to her feet, urgency thrumming through her. The thought of Dashan being hurt... tortured... because of her. No.

"You're going to march over there right now and break him out of jail?" Tarrick took a step towards her. "You do that and Casovar will have us all arrested."

"I'm an Egalion," she snapped. "He can't arrest me."

"Even if that were true, and I don't necessarily think it is anymore, he can certainly arrest your friends," Finn argued.

Her fists clenched with the mingled anger and frustration building in her chest, her nails digging painfully into her palms. She took a deep breath. "Dashan is our friend. I'm not leaving him to be tortured by Casovar into giving us all up."

"This is about more than rescuing Dash," Finn said, his face pale and set. "He's a Taliath."

Alyx entire body stilled. "I see."

He continued, unflinching in the face of the fury that had to be snapping in her eyes. "The council will view him as a threat. He is a threat."

"Finn!" Dawn protested, glaring at her brother. "What are you talking about?"

"I'm not saying we should tell the council, but let's not forget the danger here. Shakar is alive—the prime example of what can happen if a mage of the higher order gets too close to a Taliath," he replied.

"You're talking about our friend," Dawn said quietly, her entire focus on her twin, her eyes pleading with him. Finn lifted his hands in the air, eyes miserable but determined.

"Being our friend doesn't change what he could do," Tarrick said heavily. "If a mage of the higher order like Galien were to absorb his power somehow..."

"Then we keep him away from Galien," Dawn said flatly.

"What about Alyx?" Finn's words rang starkly through the small room and one by one they all turned to her. It hadn't even crossed their minds that Alyx might become a threat because of Dashan's Taliath power. She met his gaze, unable to speak.

"Now Alyx is a threat too?" Dawn's voice had an ugly edge Alyx had never heard before.

"I'm stating facts, Dawn, not trying to demonise anyone," Finn said, exasperated. "She's a mage of the higher order with the potential to be invulnerable if she absorbs Taliath ability."

"You're being deliberately literal," Dawn snapped. "Shakar is the single example of a mage absorbing Taliath ability. There's no record of it ever happening before, even though mages worked alongside Taliath for decades. He was the lover of a Taliath, that's the single difference. And Alyx is marrying Cayr."

"Is she?" Finn looked directly at Alyx, meeting her gaze without fear.

Alyx fought to appear calm and unaffected despite the sudden panic racing through her. She had not thought through the implications of Finn knowing about her and Dashan. Would he tell them?

"Why do think I'm marrying him!" She pounded the words into his head, unable to control the force of the sending. Dawn frowned, picking up something but not knowing what. Finn rubbed at his head, shaking it a little before dropping his gaze to the floor.

"What are you talking about?" Tarrick sounded impatient.

"I am marrying Cayr." Alyx's voice was icy as she called upon every inch of noble hauteur she could. "I will not allow Dashan to be harmed and I will not allow any of you to go to the council about him. If you do, I will stop you."

"How exactly?" Finn's eyes flashed with anger.

Deflated at his implication, Alyx could only stare at him. "I would never hurt any of you. You know that."

"No, but you've been lying to us."

"About Dashan?" she said. "My father only told me a few months ago. He pointed out, and I agreed, that the fewer who knew, the safer Dash would be. I haven't even told him."

"You've lied about more than that," Finn insisted.

"Brynn asked her to keep his secret, and while I don't necessarily agree with her decision, Alyx wasn't trying to hurt us," Dawn said, misunderstanding Finn's words.

Finn looked at Alyx, then sighed heavily. "We've all spent a lot of time with Dashan this past year, including Alyx. I'm worried she may have absorbed his power. And even if she hasn't, the perception... if the council had any idea about Dashan they would come for her and him. Likely us too. She's already in enough danger. We can't hide from Shakar and all the resources of the Mage Council."

Alyx was in such a state of fear and anger it felt as if the emotion might burst out of her at any moment, and she had no patience left. "Dashan being a Taliath makes no difference in this situation. He is our friend. Have you all forgotten that? What would we do if it were Finn in this situation, or Tarrick?"

Tarrick nodded slowly. "So we finally come to this, when you take command of Third Patrol from me."

Alyx rounded on him in frustration, feeling beset from all sides. "That's not what this is about."

"Yes it is," he said. "If I order you now to do nothing about Dash, because it only puts the rest of us in danger, will you obey me? If I order Dawn to contact Romas and inform him that we have found a Taliath potential, would you obey me?"

Alyx stared at him, then looked around at the others. "No, I wouldn't. I couldn't, Tarrick."

"Then I can't enforce my orders on you." Tarrick took a seat, matter-of-factly. "You're in charge now. What do you propose we do?"

She sank back in the chair. This was insanity. "You all agree with him?"

"It's been coming a long time," Dawn said in her calm way. "You are the mage of the higher order amongst us."

"I'm willing to follow you," Finn said reluctantly.

This wasn't what she wanted—she needed her friends to trust her, to support Dashan when he was in trouble. But instead they'd hesitated. And when it came down to it, she wasn't going to let anyone hurt Dashan. If that meant taking charge and making them follow her lead, then so be it.

"Fine. Then we are going to help Dash. I'll speak to my father and Cayr, get a better idea of his situation. In the meantime, you should all lay low. I'll send a message through Dawn when it's time to meet again. Agreed?"

"If you go and see Dashan openly, Casovar will know and it will only add to the evidence against us," Tarrick said.

"You need to stay away from him anyway," Finn added. "Just to be safe."

"I'm not a complete fool." Alyx strode for the door. "I'll see you all later."

CHAPTER 30

By the time Alyx stepped through the front doors of her home, she was weary and gritty from the road, and emotionally exhausted from the nightmare, the argument with her friends and fear for Dashan. Her shoulders literally sagged with the weight of it all.

"Aly-girl! I wasn't expecting you for another day." Her father came down the stairs to her right. His drawn features indicated he was as tired as she was.

"You've heard about Dash?"

He nodded. "I take it that's why you're home early. How did you find out?"

"Dawn contacted me. Tarrick and I rode all night."

"Come with me." Garan gestured towards his study, following her in and closing the door.

"What do you know?" Alyx asked.

"Probably not much more than you do. Dashan was picked up by the Mage Guard last night and has been charged with murder. It's a hanging offence, if Casovar can find proof."

"I knew he knew," she muttered, beginning to pace. "But why wait until now to move? Has he given any indication we're under suspicion?"

Her father smiled slightly. "There are Mage Guard watching the house right now. From what my contacts tell me, they're sitting just outside the walls. Does that answer your question?"

Alyx scowled and closed her eyes. Pushing aside her weariness, she reached out with her telepathic powers. Skipping over the estate's servants and guards—those she knew—she searched until she found two unknown minds. They were sitting on horses outside the Egalion estate, their focus on the mansion. Inwardly, she cursed herself for missing that. She must really be tired.

"Damn." She opened her eyes. "That means Casovar knows Tarrick and I are back."

"Which means he'll expect you at the palace first thing tomorrow, and he'll likely have questions. He'll also be watching you very carefully."

Alyx slumped into a chair. "I can't let Dash be hanged, Papa. Casovar will either find or fabricate enough evidence against him eventually."

Garan looked at her carefully. "Does he know Dashan is the Taliath? Or is that something else Casovar made up, and just happened to guess rightly?"

"He knows. Shakar has been in my mind for months," she said bitterly, explaining about her realisation. "Those nightmares were him."

Her father sighed and wrapped an arm around her shoulders, offering what comfort he could.

"I'm scared, Papa," she mumbled into his chest.

"I know," he murmured soothingly. "No matter what happens, I'll be here to protect you. Now, you're exhausted. Why don't you go upstairs and wash, and I'll have cook make something for you to eat? Food and clean clothes will make everything better."

"I don't have time." She shook her head. "The longer Dashan sits in that cell—"

He raised a stern hand to cut her off. "Washing and food are nonnegotiable, but once you're cleaned up I promise we can talk about what to do next while you eat."

She smiled. "All right."

A QUICK SCRUB IN WARM, soapy water did make Alyx feel much fresher, though weariness still tugged at her every movement. She came downstairs to find Cayr being ushered in the front door by Safia.

"Alyx, you look exhausted." He reached out to touch her arm in concern.

"I'm okay." She briefly covered his hand with hers, reassured by his presence. "You've heard about Dash, I take it?"

"I've just come from speaking with him," Cayr said.

"You did?" Alyx's head came up in astonishment. "Is he all right? Is there anything you can do?"

"He's fine—they haven't touched him yet." Cayr's voice lowered. "Are we alone here?"

Alyx closed her eyes, briefly sweeping the house with her telepathic magic. None of the servants were within earshot. "We're alone."

"Is it true—he's the Taliath that broke into Casovar's home with you?"

"It's true," she said softly.

Pain flashed over his face and he backed away from her. "That's why you agreed to marry me. I thought maybe there was a chance, that we could... that you still loved me."

Alyx took a breath, found the courage for honesty—he deserved at least that from her. "Yes. I tried to tell you how I felt. You refused to listen."

"I suppose I did," he said bitterly. "More fool me."

"I—"

He made a sharp gesture, cutting her off. "I can't force Casovar to drop the charges against Dashan. Legally, he's allowed to pursue an investigation. I can insist that Dash be released until Casovar has enough proof to formally arrest him and have my father sentence him."

"Cayr, thank you," she breathed.

"It's not a permanent solution, and it won't give you much time.

Casovar is determined, and I expect he'll go straight to my father and convince him to reverse my orders. Eventually, his questioning of Dashan will bring your involvement and that of the other mages to light. Then he'll have what he needs to arrest all of you. Our plan will be over before it even began."

"I know that."

"So does Dashan," Cayr said. "Once I've organised his release, he plans to disappear from the city before my order can be overturned. He thinks—and I agree—that an escape and the ensuing search will confirm his guilt in everyone's eyes and remove the need for Casovar to investigate further. That will buy us more time."

"Where will he go?"

"Dashan thinks it best neither of us know the details. He's figured out Casovar knows it was him in his house that night, but is uncertain how much he knows because Casovar's accusation that he's a Taliath confuses him. Either way, what we don't know we can't tell—and Casovar can't read in our thoughts." Cayr paused, searching her face. "Dashan is doing the right thing. His absence will allow us to continue our plan to remove Casovar."

"I don't think we can wait that long," she said reluctantly. "Proof or not, I'm certain he knows it was me in his house. That means he'll suspect Tarrick and the twins, and even you, no matter how good an act you put on. Worse, I learned last night that Shakar is definitely alive, and he's working with Casovar."

Cayr ran a hand through his hair distractedly, and she sympathized with the stress building in his face. "If you're right... "

"We still have some time." She tried to reassure him. "Convincing your father to act against Dashan will be far easier than convincing him to act against my father, or you."

He nodded. "I can have the orders issued to release him as soon as you think best."

"Let me talk to my father and Tarrick and let you know." She hesitated. "Cayr, the way I feel about Dash, if the wrong people knew it would get us both killed. I have to protect him, and that means staying away. Him leaving is the best thing."

Tears shone in Cayr's eyes. "As much as this hurts, I love you both. Be sure I will do what I can to protect you and Dashan."

"You're a good man. A better person than I am."

"Maybe." He shrugged. "But as you've said to me over and over, none of us has had much choice in this. I'll wait for your word. Be safe."

"What did Prince Cayr want?" Garan asked as she entered his study.

She took the proffered mug of spiced cider and plate of sandwiches and sat in a chair near the window, telling him of Cayr and Dashan's plan between bites. "How close do you think Casovar is to moving on us? I don't mean for breaking into his home, I—"

"I know what you mean," Garan said. "I'm impressed you saw that coming."

"It's inevitable. Casovar's goal is surely total rule in Rionn, especially if he's working for Shakar. To do that, he has to get rid of you, Sparky and the king's other closest supporters."

"Dashan's right in that his escape will be taken as confirmation of guilt, but if your instinct is right in that Casovar already knows you were the mage... " Garan considered. "He'll have to come for me and Sparky first, as the most powerful and trusted lords. That will take more than suspicion of you. I judge we've got weeks, maybe months. No longer."

"Cayr and I can't marry that fast, and even if we did, it won't hold Casovar for long. Cayr has no true power until he reaches his majority, and once he does he'll be in true danger if he doesn't appear malleable." Alyx fretted. "And I can't protect him properly until I'm fully trained."

"Our plans need changing," Garan agreed. "I'll speak to Sparky as soon as I can."

"We're in some serious trouble, Papa," she said soberly. "Not just Rionn, the entire continent; Tregaya, Zandia, everywhere."

"Shakar." He sighed.

"The way Finn tells it, it took the entire mage order to confront him and win last time, and that was after Shakar had almost destroyed the continent."

Garan leaned back in his chair. "I believe you. What do you intend to do?"

Alyx rose. "I don't know yet. First we need to get Dashan safely out of the city. Do you have a way to get a discreet message to Cayr? Unless you disagree, I think it's best he release Dashan as soon as possible, tomorrow if he can."

Garan nodded. "There's a way. I'll get it to him tonight."

"Good. Brynn has been gone a few weeks, so hopefully he'll be back soon with word from the council, and we can plan better what to do next."

Garan nodded slowly and put down his glass, crossing the room to stand before her. "I've been thinking about what you said to me, and I want you to know that I love you. Warrior mage or young noble-woman, I love you more than anything else. You're beautiful, strong and brave, and I'm so proud that you're my daughter."

Alyx went into his embrace easily. "I love you too, Papa."

UPSTAIRS, Alyx changed out of her mage attire, dressing in darker, non-descript clothing. As she changed, she contacted Dawn. *"Cayr can issue orders to have Dashan temporarily released until Casovar finds enough proof to formally charge him with treason,"* she explained. *"Dashan plans to leave the city and disappear. He thinks that will confirm Casovar's suspicions and take some of the heat off the rest of us. Papa agrees it should give us time to plan what to do next."*

"I hope it works, I'll let Finn and Tarrick know," Dawn sent, then, *"And I'm glad Cayr can get him out."*

"So am I." Alyx hesitated. *"I'll see you tomorrow."*

Alyx slipped quietly down the stairs, opening the front door just as a familiar Bluecoat was raising his hand to ring the front bell.

"Casta!" She smiled a greeting, hoping he wouldn't ask questions about her odd attire. "What brings you by?"

He didn't return her smile. "I was hoping to speak with you, Lady Egalion. I realise it's improper, me coming to you like this, but I—"

"Casta, stop." She raised her hand. "You can always come to me. I hope you know that."

A little smile. "Thank you, my Lady. I'll only take a moment of your time, I promise."

"Come in." She stood back from the entrance.

He hesitated. "Outside might be better. If you're heading out, perhaps I can walk you to the stables?"

Frowning, Alyx stepped out and closed the door behind her. Casta fell into step as they walked towards the stables.

"Is something the matter?" she asked him.

"I wanted to ask about Dashan, Lady Egalion," he said diffidently. "The lads and I have been worried about him. Do you think he did what Lord-Mage Casovar says he did?"

"I don't think that matters to Casovar," Alyx said carefully. "I'll be honest with you—Dash is in serious trouble."

Casta processed that as they came to a halt by the stable door. "If there's anything we could help with... anything you could think of, you'll let us know?"

She frowned at the odd note in his voice. "What exactly are you saying, Lieutenant?"

"Tijer and me were there when he bought that." Casta gestured at the bracelet on her wrist. "So I know you're someone we can trust. I'm saying we'll do whatever we can to help him, Lady Egalion. You understand me, I hope?"

Alyx flushed hotly, hoping the darkness hid it from him. How had he even seen the damn thing? And why am I still wearing it? As discreetly as she could, she pulled her sleeve down over her wrist.

"I understand, and you have my genuine appreciation, Casta." She paused, choosing her words carefully. "A temporary release order will go out tomorrow. No doubt Lord-Mage Casovar will have his Mage Guard watching Dashan carefully until such time as he can re-arrest him."

"No doubt," Casta agreed easily.

"If Dashan could get out of the city, leave and not come back, he would likely be safe."

Casta was quiet for a moment, then, softly, "I think I understand you perfectly, Lady Egalion. I should let you go, I've taken up too much of your time already."

She nodded, cleared her throat. "About the bracelet... whatever you might assume about—"

"Dashan is a brother, my lady." Casta cut her off politely. "There's nothing for us to tell or know without his say so."

She nodded. "Good night, Lieutenant."

"And to you too, Lady Egalion." He tipped his hat and strode away.

ALYX LEFT Tingo at the empty warehouse they'd used to watch Casovar's house and headed on foot into the city. Climbing up a roof access ladder to reach the city jail without being seen was easy enough. Once there, she crouched down and closed her eyes, using telepathic magic to scan the minds of everyone inside to learn where Dashan was being held. By the time she'd established that, then the best way to get there from the roof without being spotted, her head was aching and exhaustion made her limbs tremble. She had just enough telepathic strength left to distract the guards outside the door to the wing of cells holding Dashan and slip through.

Dashan lay sprawled on a small cot in a cell at the far end of a long hallway of cells, arms folded behind his head, brown eyes hooded and watchful. He groaned when he spotted her. "The reason I sent Cayr to talk to you was so that you didn't risk yourself coming here."

She raised an eyebrow. "I hear you've gotten yourself into a bit of trouble?"

"Oh, you know, this kind of thing happens to me all the time. The rats and I have a great escape plan though." He gave her a lazy smile, and she couldn't help but smile back.

He rose and strolled towards the bars. "What brings a high-born lady such as yourself down to visit the riff-raff?"

"You thought I'd let you leave Alistriem without saying goodbye?"

"Yes," he said pointedly. "Because I'd rather end this without anyone else getting into trouble. It's bad enough that Casovar has gotten it into his head that I'm a Taliath. I didn't realise the man was insane as well as evil."

Her hands reached up to curl around the bars, her eyes searching for his so that he would understand what she was about to tell him. There was no need to hide it anymore. Casovar knew, and Dashan couldn't be in any greater danger.

"Alyx," he murmured, as always catching her mood. "What is it?"

"You are a Taliath."

Once spoken, the words lifted an enormous weight that she hadn't even realised she'd been carrying. Hiding this from him had been beyond painful—he deserved to know what he was, deserved to know that he wasn't worthless, that he was special.

He huffed a laugh, then sobered as he realised she was serious. "What are you talking about?"

Tears welled in her eyes, a result of the relief flooding through her, but she smiled through the tears, smiled for him so he would know she meant it. "I told you there was more to you than just a soldier. It took me too long to see it, but you're a Taliath."

He cocked his head, uncertain. "Are you sure?"

"I'm certain," she told him firmly. "There is no doubt."

"Huh." He shook his head, clearly still having trouble believing it. "Fighting has always been the one thing I was good at, but I had no idea."

"And now that you know you must be careful, especially once you're out of here," she insisted, keeping her voice low. "You know what the council will do to you if they find out."

There was a beat of silence as he processed that, and then dawning realisation began spreading over his face and his dark eyes shot to hers. "When did you realise I was a Taliath?"

"I didn't. My father told me. He's apparently known for years."

"When?" Dashan's voice was suddenly intense.

"Dash..."

"Tell me when."

She looked down at the floor. "The night of the ball."

Silence fell between them. More weight lifted—the truth leaving her spirits momentarily light as a feather. When Dashan spoke again, his words were whisper quiet. "That's why you agreed to marry Cayr."

She swallowed, looked up to meet his warm brown eyes and gave a little nod. "Yes."

He moved as quick as lighting and took her hand, prying it away from the bars and holding it with aching gentleness. "That's why you've been so miserable. You feel trapped."

Her tears welled again when he so neatly understood what she was feeling. He always understood. It made her joyously happy and desperately sad at the same time. His next words washed over her, confirming how well he understood.

"Then I definitely have to go, no matter what I... " he cleared his throat. "It will keep the others safe from the council. Even more importantly it will keep you safe. They'll never know, I promise you. I'll disappear."

"I wish you didn't have to," she whispered, her heart feeling like it was being crushed in a vice. Why did this have to hurt so much?

"It's what's best," he murmured, gently rubbing her knuckles with his thumb. "And not just for your safety, and the others. It wouldn't be fair to Cayr."

"I know." She tried for a smile but failed dismally.

"I want you to be happy. Cayr can make you happy, he always has."

"You be happy too," she said fiercely. "And safe. I need to know that you'll be happy and safe."

"You promise me the same and we have a deal." He gave her his soft half-smile, and it lit up his face.

Alyx closed her eyes and leant her forehead against the cool iron bar, raising his hand to her mouth to kiss it softly. His other hand came up to cradle her head, gently stroking her hair.

"I love you," she whispered. The words were so easy to say in the end. After all the confusion and misery, it was a relief to be honest with herself and with him. His hand stilled. She raised her head to look at him with a sad smile. He was regarding her with tears in his dark eyes, an expression of unbelieving wonder on his face.

"I do," she whispered again. "I love you."

"Me too," he whispered back, his voice taut with emotion.

With a deep breath, she removed her hand from his and then stepped away from the bars.

"Good bye, Dash."

"I'll be seeing you, mage-girl." He saluted her.

ALYX PULLED herself up through the air vent and carefully replaced the grate, pausing a moment to take a shaky breath and regain her composure. Standing, she froze at the sight of Finn across the roof from her, his staff drawn.

"Finn, I... " Her voice trailed off and the words hung between them.

"Give me a good reason I shouldn't report both of you to the council right now." The determination on his face chilled her. This was a side of Finn she'd only ever seen brief glimpses of, where his cold rationality and logic took over.

"He's going away," she said. "As soon as Cayr gives the order to release him, he's leaving and I'm going to stay here and marry Cayr. I only came to say goodbye. Isn't that enough for you?"

"Have you slept with him?"

"That's none of your business," she snapped.

"It's all our business, Alyx. If you absorbed his invulnerability you'd be a danger to us all."

His blithe assumption floored her, and then sparked her temper. "You're suggesting I could be like Shakar?" she demanded. "How could you even think that? We are friends, Finn."

"I'm saying this because you're my friend." His grip on his staff shifted, tightened. "I don't think you'd ever be intentionally evil, but look what you've done already. You took control of us earlier because you could, because you decided that freeing Dashan was the most important thing to you. You've been keeping secrets from us for months because you thought it was best."

"Tarrick gave me control."

"You took it from him!" Finn shouted, his green eyes dark against a face that had turned pale. "I trusted you to do that. And then I find you've run straight to Dashan. If you were invulnerable too, what couldn't you do, to protect the people you loved? None of us could stop you."

Her anger boiled at his accusations, his lack of trust in her. She thought they'd had more faith in each other than this. It hurt, and that hurt fuelled her anger. She was so sick and tired of the people she cared most about underestimating or distrusting her. "I took control because you and Tarrick were too afraid of the fact he's a Taliath to help a friend," she snapped. "Look at you, standing there with your staff. Are you going to attack me? After everything we've been to each other?"

"Are you going to make me attack you?" he demanded, and his eyes glistened with tears now. "I'm trying to save both of us."

Her magic rose with her anger, thundering to be let out, to explode, and her arms lit up in a green glow. Finn shifted, something like despair flashing over his face, and it hit her... this was Finn, one of her dearest friends, and she was thinking of using her magic against him?

Standing on that rooftop, for the first time ever Alyx was afraid of her magic. Of what she could do with it.

Her anger shattered into a million pieces and she took a deep, sobbing breath. The light of her magic winked out of existence. When she spoke, her voice was full of the tears welling in her eyes. "You've always been there for me, all three of you. You've saved my life and you've supported me through all the awful things that have happened to us. I ended my relationship with Dashan the moment I found out, Finn, and I did it because I could never betray the three of you that way. I'll do whatever you want me to. Just tell me what that is."

His hands trembled where they held his staff. "Stay away from Dashan. Give Third Patrol back to Tarrick and trust him enough to do the right thing for all of us."

"I'll do it." She spoke without hesitation.

Slowly, he lowered his staff, then sheathed it down his back. He scrubbed at his face and looked away. "I'm sorry that it turned out this way."

"I'm sorry that you didn't have more faith in me." She swallowed, tried not to sway on her feet. "Now please, leave me alone."

He nodded and left. As soon as he was gone, Alyx sank to the ground, sobbing until she had no tears left to give.

CHAPTER 31

"Dashan Caverlock is a traitor and a criminal," Casovar said. "You will not make any effort to see or help the Shiven half-blood. Am I clear, Apprentice?"

Alyx's nails dug so tightly into her palms they drew blood, but her voice remained polite. "Yes, sir."

"That goes for the rest of you," Casovar's gaze travelled over Tarrick and the twins. "I—"

The door slammed open, and Casovar cast an annoyed glance at the Mage Guard soldier that walked in. "What is it, Tordren?"

"Lord-Mage." He bowed hastily. "There's a fire in one of the markets. A unit of Bluecoats has cordoned off the area and isn't allowing anyone in or out until the blaze has been contained."

"The Bluecoats are over-stepping their mark as usual, but why do I care about a fire in the markets?"

The young soldier flushed at the contempt in Casovar's voice. "Part of the area they've cordoned off includes the eastern city gates." His flush deepened at Casovar's withering stare, but he gamely persevered. "They won't let anyone in or out, sir. Not even Mage Guard."

"Very well. I will speak to Lord-General Caverlock to clear the matter up," Casovar said icily.

"Yes, sir."

Casovar turned to Alyx and her friends. "Get back to work! I'll return to check on your progress later."

As soon as he and Tordren were gone, all eyes turned to Dawn. She raised a hand, bidding them wait, before giving a firm nod. "They're out of hearing range. Nobody else is around."

"You think that was Casta and the others?" Tarrick asked Alyx.

"Probably." She nodded. "They'll be keeping the gate clear for Dashan to get out once Cayr issues the release order."

Finn winced. "I hope we're not around when Casovar finds out Dashan is gone."

Alyx couldn't look at him. Dawn glanced between the two of them —she had to know something of what had happened, the twins were too close for her not to, but it didn't seem as if he'd told her everything.

"What's going on?" the telepath demanded.

"I—"

"No." Dawn cut her brother off. "If I didn't value you both so much I would have read your minds by now. Something is going on between the two of you, and I'm sick of the secrets. Whatever it is, Tarrick and I deserve to know."

Finn gave a little shrug and turned to Alyx, lifting his eyebrows. Tarrick seemed puzzled, but he nodded in support of Dawn.

"I don't know if this is the best place to... " Alyx instinctively tried to stall, but then shook her head. Dashan would be gone soon, and then it didn't matter what Casovar might read in their minds about him. "No. Dawn, you're right. You deserve to know."

"Well?" Tarrick said impatiently.

Alyx sighed, fixing her gaze firmly on the opposite wall. *This is harder than I could have ever imagined.* She dreaded their reaction more than anything.

"Dashan and I had a relationship." She paused, sucked in a breath. "Finn seems to think that makes me a threat to everybody, even though I ended it as soon as I found out what he is."

The ensuing silence was so thick Alyx could feel it pressing down on her. Several long moments passed before she was able to summon the courage to look at them.

"You had a romantic relationship with Dash?" Tarrick clarified, the look on his face indicating he was caught between disbelief and confusion.

"Yes."

"How serious?"

Alyx opened her mouth, hesitated, then made the deliberate decision to lie. Finn's accusations had undermined her faith and trust in their friendship, and she had to protect Dashan, and herself. "It wasn't serious, just a casual thing. You know me and Dash, we couldn't go half a day without arguing." She flashed them a smile. "Even if I hadn't learned he was a Taliath, it wouldn't have lasted long."

Dawn was frowning. "Then why didn't you tell us?'

"Because you were away in the disputed area. By the time you came back it was over. There was nothing to tell."

"You still should have told us," Finn said flatly.

"Why?" she snapped. "So you could report him to the council like you threatened to do last night?"

"Enough!" Dawn cried, and Finn closed his mouth abruptly. "Both of you have done the wrong thing, and yelling at each other about it will only make things worse."

Tarrick spoke into the ensuing silence. "Dawn is right. It's good that Dashan's leaving, for more reasons than the obvious. Alyx, if the council knew you'd had a relationship with a Taliath, no matter how casual, you'd be in as much danger as he is."

Alyx reached up to rub at her aching temples. "We all know that. Besides, I'm not invulnerable."

"I don't think they'd care," Finn mumbled.

"He's right. We don't talk about this ever again, and none of us breathes a word of it to anyone," Tarrick insisted. "Am I clear? Finn, that means you too. And if you really have got some idea in your head of reporting Dashan to the council, then you get rid of it right now. I won't allow it."

Tears welled in Alyx's eyes. Always Tarrick's first instinct was to protect her, even when she'd hidden something so important from him. Even when she was still lying. But telling the truth meant telling Finn too, and she didn't trust him with that knowledge anymore. Her heart ached in physical pain at that thought.

Finn's eyes were on Alyx when he spoke. "I'll do as you say, Tarrick."

"For what it's worth, I'm sorry," Alyx said. "I'm sorry for not telling you, and I'm sorry for taking control of Third Patrol. Tarrick, the job is yours. Whatever you decide to do next, I'll do it. I trust you."

He bowed his head slightly. "Thank you."

"Are you happy now?" She forced Finn to meet her gaze, challenging him to say different.

"I'm sorry, I—"

"I don't want to hear it," she cut him off, still furious at his lack of faith in her, even though part of her knew he had good reason for it. "Let's just move on."

He stiffened and gave a short nod.

Dawn glanced between Finn and Alyx, concern written in her blue eyes. Taking a breath, she focused on Tarrick. "What comes next? I'd like to know why Shakar is haunting Alyx's dreams. Could it be he sees her as a threat?"

"If that's the case, Alyx should be dead already. He's taken out all the other powerful mages one by one—assuming he's behind the missing mages," Finn said bluntly.

"He doesn't want to destroy me, he wants me to join him," she said.

"He couldn't expect you to do that willingly, not unless he's offered you something in return," Finn said, piercing her with his gaze.

She stiffened, but didn't back down from him. "He promised me the Taliath would be safe once the council was destroyed."

"I suppose he means all the Taliath that aren't killed trying to stop him from destroying the world," Dawn said dryly.

Alyx smiled, relaxing slightly. "I suppose."

"It's disturbing that he knows you so well," Finn said, clearly choosing not to challenge her further.

"You know what doesn't make sense to me?" Tarrick said. "He was presumed killed fifty years ago—where has he been this whole time?

And if he's planning to try and destroy the council again, why hasn't he tried yet?"

"I've been thinking on that," Finn said. "Last time Shakar made no attempt to hide what he was doing, and he ended up with the entire mage and Taliath orders hunting him down. They cornered him in Serrin and almost killed him. If I were him, I'd do things differently the second time. I'd plan."

"Fifty years of planning?" Dawn raised an eyebrow. "That thought gives me chills."

"The disappearing mages? Unrest in Shivasa? Increasing tensions with Rionn? Attacks on DarkSkull?" Finn ticked off each statement with his fingers. "I wonder who first suggested to the council that it would be a good idea to get rid of the Taliath?"

"He's trying to destroy the world first, before stepping in to take it over," Tarrick muttered.

"And what have we got to stop him?" Finn asked.

All eyes turned to Alyx, and she instantly began shaking her head. "Don't look at me. Being a half-trained mage of the higher order doesn't make me the solution to Shakar. As much as I hate to say it, we need the council and all its resources. Brynn should be back any day, and by then Dashan will be safely out of the city. We'll have a little bit of time to plan what to do about Casovar, and then Shakar."

"Do you think Dashan is safely away yet?" Dawn wandered over to the window.

Alyx stood, unable to sit still any longer. "I'll go and see Cayr. He can tell me if the orders have been issued."

"Good idea," Tarrick said. "The rest of us will get started on those reports, give Casovar no reason to believe we've been doing anything but working hard while Dashan escapes."

ALYX HEADED towards the royal wing, figuring she would be most likely to find Cayr with his father at this time of day. She walked slowly and pasted a smile on her face, greeting those she recognised in the halls cheerfully.

When Jenna appeared, gliding down a thickly-carpeted hallway and looking as stunning as ever, Alyx groaned inwardly.

"Lady Egalion, how nice to see you."

She almost laughed at how insincere the words were. "Jenna. How are you?"

"I'm looking for my father, actually. Have you seen him?"

"Earlier. He went to speak with Lord-General Caverlock and I haven't seen him since," she said. "If you'll excuse me, I'm going to visit Cayr."

Alyx had been unable to help needling Jenna, and felt quick satisfaction at the flash of anger in the young woman's eyes.

"I'll come with you." Jenna hid her reaction quickly, her voice polite as always. "Perhaps my father will be with him. They spend a lot of time together, you know? My father has a lot of respect for Prince Cayr."

"Does he?" Alyx spoke dryly. She wondered if Jenna knew anything of her father's plans or ambitions. The girl had never seemed stupid to Alyx—she'd always gotten the sense there was a cool intelligence underneath the beauty. Not for the first time, she wondered at Jenna's origins. "How old were you when he adopted you?"

"Five. My real parents died in a fire." She frowned a little. "I don't really remember much about that time."

Curiosity—mixed with a touch of sympathy she'd never admit to—temporarily overrode Alyx's distaste for any sort of conversation with Jenna. "Why would Lord-Mage Casovar adopt an orphan girl?"

Jenna seemed unbothered by the question, and gave a little shrug. "Father and I have been useful to each other."

Alyx laughed dryly. "I see. He gives you dresses, wealth and status, and you give him the appearance of a loving family man who performed the selfless act of taking on an orphan girl to raise. The king must have loved that quality when it came time to choose a replacement for Astor."

"I concede that you've won, Alyx." Jenna stopped walking suddenly, dropping the polite tone and speaking with cool honesty. "And I have no intention of demeaning myself by fighting with you over Cayr."

Taken-aback, Alyx said nothing, and Jenna continued into the silence. "Nor am I foolish enough to suggest that we should be friends. I hope we can agree to a truce, however. After all, we both inhabit the same world."

"I'm not interested in a truce with you, Jenna Casovar, because we're not at war," Alyx said eventually. "There was no fight over Cayr. He was never going to choose anyone but me. You stay out of my way from now on, and we'll get along just fine."

Not waiting for Jenna to respond, Alyx continued walking. A moment later Jenna caught up to her and they walked in silence for a moment before, "I'm not your enemy, Lady Egalion."

"You could have fooled me."

The Bluecoats on guard outside the king's audience suite acknowledged Alyx's appearance by standing aside, the younger of the two blushing when Jenna favoured him with a bright smile.

The reception room was empty. Jenna wasn't far behind as Alyx continued through, pushing open one of the tall arched doors leading into the formal audience chamber.

Two steps in, she stopped dead at the sight before her, her mind not quite understanding what her eyes were telling her.

The king sat in his chair, head lolled back, his familiar blue eyes glazed over. Casovar was leaning over him, intense concentration turning his features more gaunt than usual. One long-fingered hand hovered over the king's blond hair. The prickle of magic was live in the air, carrying straight to Alyx. The lord-mage's concentration was so intense he hadn't registered her entrance. But Jenna's shocked gasp echoed loudly in the utter silence.

Casovar's head snapped up, grey eyes locking straight onto Alyx's. A snarl flashed over his face. Her lunge forward was borne of instinct screaming at her to help the king, but Casovar made a sharp gesture, eyes darkening as he summoned his offensive magic.

Desperately she reached for her own magic, already knowing she was a step too slow. Her boots pounded on the marble, silver-green light beginning to coalesce around her arms, but then his magic descended around her like a cage.

Thinking quickly, she did the only thing she had time to do—send a burst of magic out in a frantic distress call before succumbing to the clamps of his power closing over her mind.

Just like Shakar, he had her.

The last thing she saw was the look of complete and utter shock spreading across Jenna Casovar's beautiful face.

Then there was only blackness.

CHAPTER 32

When Alyx drifted awake, memory was slow to reassert itself. When it did, panic set in and she tried to move. Pain flared white-hot as her wrists slammed up against iron manacles. Her breath escaped in a gasp, and wincing, she looked around.

Her back was pressed flat against a wall, arms spread out to either side, and she was in a small, dim room. Her feet barely touched the floor and were tightly enclosed in manacles even thicker than those holding her wrists.

Fear surged as she realised how securely she was being held and she struggled desperately for a few chaotic moments, but it was no use. Eventually she stopped, panting from the effort. The skin of her wrists was chafed raw, stinging and painful. A moment later she cursed herself for a fool—she was a mage!—and reached inside for her magic.

Nothing happened.

Alarmed, she tried again.

Nothing. She couldn't access her magic. Panic slammed through her in a wave so profound she found herself gasping for air. Several moments passed before she calmed enough to think straight. Her heart raced and her skin was clammy with sweat.

She had to calm down.

One deep, shuddering breath, then another. One more. Slowly, her heartbeat returned to something approaching normal, and she fought to hold on to that calm. One way to do that was to focus on her surroundings. She was in a room, but where?

The walls were wood, the dirt floor dry and uneven. A closed door stood opposite her, the knob rusted over. There was a window to her right, but it was grimy and cracked. Through it, Alyx could make out the green of tree branches. In the corner by the door was a small table that held a carafe of dark red wine and a single glass.

She had no idea where she was, didn't even know how long she'd been unconscious. Casovar could have taken her anywhere. The panic threatened to surge through her again, and she held it back with an effort. Focus!

She was in the middle of trying to work out whether there were any weaknesses in her manacles when a door sounded in the distance and footsteps approached. Alyx tensed, steeling herself for whatever was coming.

The door opened with a click and Casovar walked in, his face an expressionless mask as his cool grey eyes ran over her. "You're awake."

"What do you think you're doing, Lord-Mage Casovar?" Alyx summoned every inch of hauteur she possessed and hurled it at him. "Let me go at once!"

"I think not." He crossed to the table and poured himself a glass of the wine. Her eyes fixed on him as he took an appreciative sip. "I would suggest that you don't try to escape, either. I'll kill you if you do."

So they weren't pretending anymore. That was fine. She was sick of pretending with this roach of a man who had done his best to make her life miserable for months.

"I don't know why you haven't killed me already," she said, voice thick with loathing.

"Oh, I'll have to," he said. "Now that you've seen the true extent of my... influence over the king."

Fear surged but she fought it back with bravado. "My father will hunt you down like the dog you are."

Casovar chuckled. "He doesn't even know I have you. He might suspect, but without proof, or knowing where you are, there's nothing he can do."

"Jenna saw what happened."

"She's my daughter. She'll do as I tell her. Besides, you're an obstacle to her ambitions, aren't you?"

Alyx turned cold, all her bravado fleeing despite her desperate attempts to hold onto it. Casovar saw it in her face and his smile turned triumphant.

"That's right. And even if your father wanted to do something, he couldn't. You forced my hand. He's under arrest and being held in the palace cells. General Sparkish and Astor too. Nobody is coming for you, Lady Egalion."

"The king would never allow that." Alyx refused to believe him. He was trying to get inside her head.

"Oh, but he would, once I suggested it to him." Casovar moved closer to her. "It was so hard, telling him yesterday that his closest friends had been planning to betray him, but when I showed him proof... well, he had no choice but to sign their execution orders."

Alyx pulled uselessly against iron. "I don't believe you."

"I don't care whether you do or not." He shrugged and took another sip of the wine. "It's only a matter of time before I have your friends in custody as well. I know exactly where they are."

Alyx said nothing, merely stared at him. If he was telling the truth, then they were lost. If he wasn't... then talking wasn't going to help her situation. Her mind fixated on his words—yesterday he'd met with the king. So he couldn't have taken her too far, not in a day. She was still close to the city, possibly somewhere in the hills around the palace if the trees she glimpsed outside were anything to go by.

Casovar looked at her with open amusement. "All I need to do before I kill you all is find out exactly how much you know, and who else knows it."

"It sounds like you know everything already."

He moved even closer, raising one fingertip to trace her cheek and jaw. She refused to give him the satisfaction of reacting, even though his touch made her skin crawl. "So pretty. But I need to be sure who knows about Shakar, of course."

"Never heard of him."

He chuckled. "I almost believed you then, Alyx."

He moved his hand to her jaw, then clamped it around her throat. She choked, struggling for air. His hold only tightened.

"I'm fairly confident you haven't gone to the council yet." He chuckled. "Smart—they'd never believe you without proof. I was concerned you'd sent that pureblood council mage with a message, but I took care of that problem. Who else knows?"

She tried to swallow, choked, shook her head. Her heartbeat thudded in her eardrums. Worry for Cario temporarily replaced her fear. What had Casovar done to him?

"I suppose you'll never tell me willingly," he murmured in her ear. "It's just as well I'm a mage of the higher order."

His magic invaded her mind without warning, his pleasure in the pain he caused evident. Alyx screamed soundlessly at the agonising pain that shot through her skull. He ravaged through her thoughts and memories, ripping and tearing, looking for what he wanted. It was so sudden and so violent she almost couldn't react in time. But she did. Heedless of the pain and violation, she took her knowledge about Shakar, about Brynn's message to the council, and the core of her magic, and retreated, shrinking away from Casovar into the tiniest amount of awareness that she could manage.

Once that was hidden away, she simply endured as he tortured her, sensing first his pleasure at what he was doing, then his frustration when he couldn't find what he was looking for. Soundless tears streaked down her cheeks.

After what seemed like an eternity, he withdrew, letting go of her throat and stepping away.

Alyx sagged against the manacles holding her wrists. It took her a moment to realise the whimpering sound she could hear was coming from her. Her throat was bruised and sore and a pounding headache tore through her skull.

"I can keep at this for some time," Casovar said conversationally. "How long can you last before you go mad, I wonder?"

"I don't know anything," she whispered. "You saw that."

He reached up and backhanded her across the face. Her head slammed back into the wall, and she couldn't stop the cry of pain that burst out of her. Warm blood trickled down her cheek from the gash he'd opened up, mixing with her tears.

"I know what you are!" he raged at her, momentarily losing his calm. "You think you've been so clever, hiding it from me, but he knew."

"I'm a second-year apprentice with barely any training," she whispered through the pain. Shakar knew she was a mage of the higher order, but he hadn't done what Casovar was doing now—he didn't know her deepest thoughts, the depth of her training or knowledge. Maybe she could convince him she was no threat.

Casovar studied her, his cool expression slowly rebuilding—piece by piece—over his face, covering the rage within. "Then you know you can't stop me learning what I want to know."

His words sounded fuzzy, and she blinked, trying to keep her groggy thoughts in order.

"Maybe I should talk to your father?" he continued. "How long do you think he would last watching you in agony?"

"Leave him alone!"

He hit her again, and Alyx tasted blood inside her mouth. Consciousness faded, the world turning blurry. This time when he tore into her mind it was harder to hide. Her strength was fading rapidly, but she held desperately to that tiny core of knowledge, protecting it, forced to let him tear through the rest of her mind unhindered.

Her heart broke when he reached the memories of Dashan and their time together, and she felt his scorn and amusement.

"He will die too," Casovar whispered into her mind. "Slowly, I think. Maybe I will even let you watch."

Even if Alyx had wanted to fight back now, she no longer had the strength for it. He was slowly destroying her mind. Any residual strength she had left was needed to keep from him the depth of what she was and what she knew.

"It's a shame the council brainwashed you with their fear of the Taliath," he chuckled, and it was like razor blades in her skull. "He could have made you invulnerable to me. I've yet to have success absorbing that particular ability. I'd thought the loving bond of father and daughter might... but Jenna proved a spectacular failure there as well."

Eventually he released her again. Alyx's eyes slid closed, and she wished desperately for the pain to go away, almost wishing he would kill her and be done with it. Nausea flooded her, and it was an effort not to be sick all over the floor. His violation had been complete.

"I'll be back later," he told her, before walking out the door.

ALYX SPENT the remainder of the night and most of the following morning hanging from the wall. Nobody brought food or water. By the time midday sunlight shone through the single window, she was feverish and sick. Her head ached, the muscles in her arms burned from the painful position they were in, and her old shoulder injury throbbed unceasingly.

She drifted in and out of consciousness for hours, and each time she woke, she was less and less sure that she was going to survive. Casovar was going to kill her, and likely her father and Sparky too. She'd been an idiot to ever think they could best him.

In one of her more lucid moments, she tried once again to work out where she was, but it was useless. She didn't recognise the building she was in, and had no way of knowing how far Casovar had brought her while she was unconscious. Tarrick and the twins would search for her, but Casovar would be expecting that. He wouldn't have taken her anywhere they could find. Besides, they were more than likely on the run themselves, trying to keep from being caught.

When the lord-mage finally returned that afternoon, he was positively gleeful.

"Not much of a Taliath, your Shiven half-blood." Casovar moved in close, breath warm against her face. She shuddered, physically ill at the sensation. "He tried to escape, of course, but it took less than six hours for the Mage Guard I sent to find him."

Alyx stared ahead, glassy-eyed, refusing to react to Casovar's words.

"My men say he barely put up a fight," Casovar murmured in her ear. "Perhaps he knew he would soon die."

If she had any strength left, the grief and fear she felt at those words would have sparked her magic then. But it lay there trapped inside her, unable to be used. Even if she could, her head was too foggy, her body too sore, his domination over her too complete.

Oh, Dashan, I'm so sorry.

"Ah, you've noticed I see?" His eyes flickered to the manacles. "I have been so looking forward to trying them out. The metal has been infused with the power of a mage who can block all magic. Isn't that an ironic creature?"

Alyx swallowed.

"My only dilemma now is who I should kill first," Casovar continued. "Your father, your lover, or your friends?"

"I will never bow to you," Alyx managed to whisper through her tortured throat.

He moved quickly, backhanding her across the face and then invading her mind.

"Please, no," she whimpered, but her revulsion only added to his pleasure.

This time he wasn't looking for anything—he was only interested in causing her as much agony as he could without killing her. When he was finished, Alyx was barely conscious and inwardly screaming with pain. She sagged against the wall, wondering if she was dying. Part of her hoped she was.

He stepped back. "You will bow to me, Lady Egalion. When I take you to watch them die, when I force you to choose who dies first, then you will bow to me. You will plead and beg for their lives, and you will tell me everything you know."

Alyx looked away. "No."

"Yes." He opened the door. "I'll be back for you soon. Then we'll see which one of us is right."

This time when he left, three Mage Guard entered the room. One of them was Dunnat.

He smiled at her.

Alyx barely processed his appearance through the pain still burning in her head, the soreness of her body. Footsteps sounded as he left the room, then returned. Then he was suddenly right in front of her, putting a cup of water to her mouth. Alyx managed to swallow a couple of mouthfuls before Dunnat smirked and tossed the remaining water in her face.

A scraping sounded as he drew his knife from his sheath, then her entire body convulsed as a white-hot line of fire opened up along her left forearm. She screamed.

"You should tell the lord-mage what he wants to know," Dunnat murmured in her ear, twisting the knife in her flesh before withdrawing it.

Alyx said nothing, her breath sobbing in mingled pain and fear. After a long moment Dunnat stepped away and wiped his knife on her robe before sheathing it.

"Think on what I said, Lady Egalion."

CHAPTER 33

When Alyx drifted back to consciousness, it was to the sounds of running feet and shouting outside. Pain swamped her, both mental and physical. Someone had torn a strip off her tunic to bind the wound on her arm, but it had been carelessly done, and blood dripped slowly to the floor. She tried to stop a groan, and as a distraction, looked over at the window. The darkness outside told her it was still night, though she had no way of knowing how long it would be until dawn.

Dunnat and the two men inside the room with her drew their swords, but made no move to leave. Clearly their orders were to stay with her. That meant there were probably more Mage Guard outside. Casovar hadn't been careless with her security.

The door to the room shuddered and splintered as someone kicked it. A second kick and the whole thing came flying inwards, sending one of the waiting soldiers crashing to the floor.

Then there was a Taliath inside the room. His usual too-serious face was calm with a perfect focus she'd never seen as his sword rang through the air, the speed and grace of his movements belying his silvering hair. He moved so quickly that he was literally a blur to her groggy vision. Dunnat died first, his head almost severed from his neck. The other two men died seconds later, before they'd even had time to register what was happening.

"Alyx?"

"Papa?" she whispered, staring at him in disbelief. He stood in a classic swordsman's stance, tall and proud and so much more than she'd ever seen him. The sword he held... it was a match for the one at Dark-Skull, the one whose beauty had so riveted her. He ran to her, sheathing the magnificent sword at his hip in one smooth movement.

"Are you all right?"

"Hurts..." she managed.

"It's going to be all right, Aly-girl." Garan tugged at the manacles binding her wrists. "Tarrick!"

Her father's bellow did nothing to prevent Alyx drifting back towards unconsciousness. She fought it, knowing there was something she had to ask, had to know, but not quite able to grasp it.

"I've got it." Tarrick's calm, measured voice sounded nearby.

"Quickly. She's bleeding badly."

Alyx, fading, was dragged back by her father's sharp voice. Her eyes flickered open.

"I can't touch them." Tarrick sounded confused. "My magic just... it won't touch the manacles."

"Allow me."

Alyx was sure she must be hallucinating Cario's familiar acerbic voice, the sight of him raising a hand and calling the keys tucked in Dunnat's tunic straight to his hand. He tossed them to Tarrick, who quickly stepped forward to unlock the manacles.

She fell, but was caught in her father's arms before hitting the ground. He cradled her gently to his chest. The blackness closed in, and she fought for a moment's clarity.

"Papa..." It took such an effort to speak. Dashan? But the words wouldn't come.

"Shush, Aly-girl, it's all going to be all right."

She allowed her head to slump into his chest as he carried her out of the room. Dead Mage Guard bodies littered the larger room outside and Cayr stood where the front door had once been, his sword drawn and bloodied.

310

"Is she all right?" he demanded.

"She's badly hurt, but it's hard to tell the extent of it here," Garan replied. "We need to get her out."

"Follow me," Tarrick said, moving off at a run down the hall.

Unable to hold on to consciousness any longer, Alyx allowed the blackness to claim her.

SHE AWOKE COCOONED in warm blankets on a soft bed. Her body was sore and tired—the gash in her forearm throbbing in time with her heartbeat—but her thoughts were clearer and the pain in her head had receded to a dull ache. It took another moment to remember what had happened. The flood of memory and emotion that triggered had her curling up in the bed, mouth opening in a silent scream.

"Aly-girl?"

Her father's voice. He'd come for her. She was safe. Taking a deep breath, she opened her eyes. He was sitting in a chair by the bed, eyes dark with concern.

"How are you feeling?"

"Better." Her eyes fell on the sword sheathed at his waist. "You came for me."

"I will always come for you." He leaned over to kiss her forehead. "I love you."

"You were amazing."

"Not as much as others." He smiled.

She hesitated. "Papa, is Dashan... Casovar said he'd..."

His hand reached out to take hers. "He's fine, I promise you."

Relief swamped her. She sagged back against the pillows, wanting to ask more, but forestalled by the door opening.

"Alyx!" Finn appeared at the door. His shoulders were slumped and his face was drawn, but there was a light in his eyes at the sight of her awake. All the anger that had raged between them recently was gone in the concern that spilled out of him and her relief at seeing him standing there.

"I'm alive." She pushed herself up on the pillows, wincing as she forgot the wound in her forearm and tried to put weight on it. "And I'm guessing that's due to you, once again. Thank you."

His gaze furrowed. "You were in a bad way."

"Yeah." When she glanced down, it was to find her hands were trembling. Remembered terror swept over her and it took a moment for her to get her emotions under control. "Where are we?"

"A safe house in the city, far from the palace." Tarrick entered the room. "Dawn and Cario are on watch outside. Nobody's looking for us in this part of the city yet."

"Cario?" Alyx asked. "I didn't imagine him?"

"No, you didn't," Finn said. "But that's a story for another time. You need rest."

"Wait... how did you find me?"

"Brynn. He spent a lot of time following Casovar around these past months—he knew that isolated hut was a place Casovar liked to keep prisoners."

She swallowed. The questions were piling up now, all desperate to come out. "Brynn's back? What about Cayr? Is he all right?"

"He's fine," Garan soothed. "Casovar knows of his role in your escape, so he's keeping clear of the palace for now. None of us really thinks the king is that far gone he'd order his son's death, but I'm sure Casovar isn't above organizing an 'accident'."

"Papa, no you don't understand." She lurched upwards. "Casovar is using magic on him, to force the king to his will. I walked in on him doing it, Jenna too, that's why he took me."

Garan's face turned grim at her words, but he soothed her nonetheless. "If that's true we'll keep Cayr safe here. Stop worrying, and rest."

"I owe you all my life," she said softly. "Thank you."

"It's dangerous to stay here too long. We've maybe got another day or two at most before Casovar's men discover us here." Garan stood. "We'll leave you to get some sleep."

There was a knock at the door down the hall. Tarrick and Finn disappeared out the door, Finn with a small wave in Alyx's direction.

"Rest." Her father touched her shoulder, and followed the others out.

She slid back down under the covers once they were gone, pulling the quilt up and over her head so that she was in darkness.

Dashan was all right. Clinging to that as a talisman against the memories that threatened to floor her once again, Alyx closed her eyes and tried to sleep.

Instead, all she could see was the pleasure written on Casovar's face as he tore through her mind.

WHEN ALYX WOKE from a restless doze and pushed back the quilt, the quality of the light coming through the window told her it was late afternoon. Cario sat in a chair in the opposite corner of the room, long legs stretched out before him. He looked like he was asleep, but when Alyx stirred, his blue eyes opened instantly.

"Do you need anything?"

"No, I feel better than I did." And she did. The few hours' sleep had done her a world of good. "You came back."

He shifted in his chair. Glanced down. Looked back up to meet her eyes. "Casovar sent his goons after me. It must have taken them a while to track me down because I was two weeks on the road before it happened. I killed them all." He flicked at a piece of lint on his breeches, the casual gesture belying how he must have felt about that. "I knew if he was willing to come after me—a formal representative of the council and grandson to a councillor—it wouldn't be long before he moved against you."

"Where were you going?" Alyx lifted herself on the pillows, this time being more careful of her arm.

"The south coast. I had some idea of setting up as a tutor in one of the larger cities."

"Teress would be nice. They have lovely beaches, and the fish caught in the bay there are supposed to be the best in Rionn."

"I'd heard that."

"You could have kept going," she said neutrally.

A faint smile flickered across his face. "Do you remember the conversation we had back at DarkSkull—you said that you considered

313

me a friend, and that one day, I'd have to tell you what I was hiding behind my indifference?"

"I remember."

"The answer is nothing. Or at least, that was the case then."

She frowned. "You truly care about nothing at all?"

Cario was silent for a moment, then he stood and picked up his chair, bringing it close to the side of her bed. Once he'd put it down, he sat, resting his arms on the top of the chair.

"When I was fourteen, I befriended a kitten that had been born in my grandfather's stables. He was orange, with four little white socks, and he was prettier and stronger than the rest of the litter, so he appealed to me. My father caught me playing with him one day. I can still remember the smell of the straw nearby and the warmth of the sun through the barn windows, the sharp staccato of my father's boots. He didn't approve, he thought I should have a puppy instead, one of the big, vicious hunting dogs his kennel-master bred. The following morning when I went to the stables, my kitten was gone, as was the entire litter. There were more litters after that, of course, but I made sure never to befriend a particular kitten ever again."

Cario's eyes had been trained on the quilt covering Alyx while he spoke, his gaze distant with memory. After a moment's silence, he gave himself a little shake.

"It's no traumatic story, I grant you. Just a parent doing what he thought best for his child."

"There's more," Alyx said softly.

"They all knew I would be a mage very early on. It was inevitable given my lineage," Cario said. "When I was eight, my father decided I should learn to fight. I hated every second of it. The tutor he found for me was harsh and strict and I ended each lesson with cuts and bruises. My mother found me crying in the stables after one particularly brutal lesson. I told her that I didn't want to learn to fight, that I hated it. I'll never forget the disappointment in her eyes, and later in her voice, when she told my father about it.

I never wanted to see that disappointment in my parents' eyes again, and so I returned to my lessons with a renewed resolve. I accepted the bruises and the cuts and I applied myself to learning. It worked, and for the first time I realised that if I became what my parents, what my grandfather, wanted me to be, things would go easier. My life could be good."

When he lapsed into silence again, Alyx spoke. "You don't have to—"

"I became the model son. I learned everything they wanted me to, both in sparring and my lessons, and I learned it well. They approved of me, and because I was what they wanted, they loved me. But inside I was empty, because I knew they didn't love who I truly was.

The things that I wanted, I couldn't have. And if I gained them for myself, like that kitten, they were taken away from me. So I learned not to want things, and to pretend to be the perfect mage scion they wanted, and I learned that was easier than pain. Even feeling empty was better than yearning, or grieving."

"I can understand that," Alyx murmured.

"What I couldn't stop was the anger, and the hate. The fact that I was their son, yet they wouldn't accept me for who I was... none of them wanted who I am. I didn't want anything to do with the mages, or the mage order. I hid the breakout of my magic from them for four years before it became impossible to keep hiding it. I figured I would go to DarkSkull, do this one last thing to be the perfect son, the perfect grandson, and then I would leave and never, ever go back. After DarkSkull, I could be free."

"Why are you telling me this now?"

"An attempt to explain why I left, and why I came back." He hesitated. "After I was attacked... I hated having to kill those men, but I realised in that moment that in my desperate attempts not to feel, not to care, I'd let my anger and bitterness turn me into someone I didn't want to be. I am different to my family yes, but I want to be better than they are, not just a different type of awful."

"You helped save my life," she said. "And you did it because I'm your friend, not because I'm a mage of the higher order, or a tool that you can use in the future. You already are a better person than your family, Cario."

"Not yet, but I will be," he said. "I'm going to stay. I don't want to, and I hate the thought of war, but I'm going to stay and help you."

She smiled, tears welling in her eyes. "You have no idea how glad I am to hear you say that."

"All right, then." He nodded to himself. "I should let you get some rest."

"Cario?" Alyx stopped him at the doorway.

"Yes?"

"You know that I accept you, right? I don't have any preconceptions about who I want you to be. You're my friend, all the bits of you, even that annoying smirk you get sometimes, or your superior tone of voice when you think I'm being an idiot."

He gave her both the smirk and the tone of voice. "Well, you do some stupid things sometimes, Lady Egalion. Like getting yourself captured by Lord-Mage Casovar, for instance."

She threw her pillow at him.

CHAPTER 34

Trying to rest proved fruitless. Whenever she managed to push away memories of her torture, her thoughts would go straight to Dashan. Her father had assured her that he was okay, but she needed to hear it again, or at least know where he was.

Deciding to find her father and ask—hoping it would give her some peace of mind—she pushed off her blankets and clambered slowly out of bed. Every muscle in her body seemed like it was clamouring for primacy as the most painful, and it took some time to get upright.

Her mage attire sat neatly folded on a nearby stool. Determinedly ignoring the trembling of her body, she pulled the clothing on, then limped down a narrow hall, pausing to listen to the voices filtering through the partially open door at the end.

"Casovar has control of the palace and the king." Her father's voice. "The city is a different matter. At least a third of the Blue Guard is in open rebellion against the Mage Guard. The remainder of the Blue-coats are under Tirian Caverlock's control for now, but his grip is loosening as he fruitlessly tries to get Casovar to let them back into the palace."

"He's expelled all the Bluecoats from the palace?" Tarrick sounded shocked.

"Only Mage Guard are in there now. Casovar is claiming the king is in danger from his rogue lords—that's us—and that the Bluecoats can't be trusted to protect him," Garan said. "As long as he has the king, he'll maintain control of the army."

"You should let me go to my father," Cayr said, voice ringing with determination. "Who knows what Casovar is doing to him? He's not only my father, Lord Egalion, but your king!"

"Casovar can't afford to hurt him, Your Highness," Garan said calmly. "He controls the city—and effectively the country—through your father."

"The Bluecoats and Mage Guard are fighting in the streets. That's not control. I want this situation resolved as quickly as possible before innocent people are harmed. My father would never hurt me."

"Cayr, no." Alyx pushed open the door and limped in, her gaze sweeping over Cario and the twins as well as Cayr, Tarrick and her father. "You don't understand. Casovar controls your father with magic. You can't combat that."

"Alyx!" Relief filled the prince's face and he came straight over, wrapping her in a gentle hug.

"I'm all right," Alyx reassured him, stepping away. "But you need to listen to me about Casovar."

Stubbornness flashed in his blue eyes. "You're the one who told me I'm responsible for more than just the court. People are going to start getting hurt. The fighting will turn into looting sooner rather than later. I won't have that happen."

"I understand, but you can't fight Casovar's magic alone. Trust me."

He hesitated, then gave her a sharp nod. "For now."

Dawn came over to take Alyx's arm and lead her to a seat. "How are you feeling?"

"Better than I was, thanks to Finn." Alyx tried not to wince as sore muscles protested her movement. "Where's Brynn? Did I imagine hearing he was back?"

"He's back, but only for a short time. Right now he's out collecting supplies and a fresh horse with the help of some Bluecoats," Tarrick said, glancing at Cayr.

"I'm sending him to Carhall tonight," Cayr said. "Over the past months I've grown a greater appreciation for why my father dislikes and distrusts the Mage Council so much, but burying our head in the sand is no solution. Brynn is to request formal assistance from the Mage Council on my order. It's time to get proper help."

Alyx didn't miss the looks of respect shot Cayr's way, and the same feeling was likely reflected on her face. But it wasn't time for niceties. "Good. Now, what are we doing here?"

"Casovar is combing the city looking for us, using any spare Mage Guard that aren't locking down the palace or fighting Bluecoats. I think he's managed to get the king to authorise using City Guard too," Dawn said. "I can sense their thoughts."

"I don't know how much you overheard, but Casovar has publicly announced we were behind an attempt on the king's life, one which he foiled," Finn added.

"And there's nobody there to counter his claims," Cario said.

Alyx looked at her father. "What's being done about it?"

"Our priority is getting out of the city before we're found—we've been waiting on you to be well enough to move," Garan said. "A diversion has been planned to take place on the opposite side of the city. When it happens, we'll leave via the east gate. Horses and supplies are waiting for us, and we'll ride straight for Widow Falls. Ladan will be able to shelter us for a short time until we come up with a longer-term plan."

Alyx frowned. "Your plan is to run away? What about Casovar?"

"What other choice to we have?" Garan said. "While he controls the king, our ability to make a stand against him is non-existent."

She shook her head. "If we run now, it will take months to re-establish ourselves into a position of strength, even if the council agrees to Cayr's request. Then potentially months more to move against Casovar. We don't have that time, not when Shakar is out there. Who knows when he plans to move against the council?"

"What are you suggesting?" Cario drawled. Something in his eyes told her he knew what she was about to suggest. His little nod bolstered her.

"That we confront Casovar now, separate him from the king and re-establish control of Rionn." The idea of going anywhere near the lord-mage was terrifying, but rationally it was their only choice. Even so, she couldn't stop the trembling of her hands at the thought of it.

"Alyx, no," Finn said. "Casovar already got you once, and he knows what you are. You're injured, no match for him. None of us are."

She forced a strength into her voice that she didn't feel. "Casovar got me because I was alone and unprepared. Together, we're much stronger. Thanks to Finn, I'm just a bit stiff and sore. Besides, Casovar may know what I am, but he thinks I'm a barely trained apprentice. He doesn't know what abilities I have, or how strong I am."

Silence fell.

"How can that be?" Cario asked.

"He used his magic against me, including attacking my thoughts." Alyx fought to keep her voice steady. "But I kept that from him. That and our knowledge of Shakar. It was all I could hold back... but I managed it."

"You resisted him?" Tarrick stared at her. "Damn, Alyx, you must be powerful."

"Not really. He still... " She swallowed. "The point is, nothing has changed. He'll be expecting us to run, so we have to do the opposite."

What she didn't tell them was that if they ran, she wasn't sure she'd ever be able to summon the strength to face Casovar again. She had to do this now, or she might never be able to.

"I won't allow it," Garan said flatly. "You're in no shape to face down a mage of his power, and even if you were healthy, you're only half trained."

"Your father is right," Tarrick said.

"I'm with Alyx," Cayr said unexpectedly. "My father is in danger and I'm not going to run away and leave him to his fate. I am Rionn's prince and I refuse to hide."

"How would you do it?" Finn countered, looking at Alyx. "Stroll up to the palace and confront Casovar in a mage duel? How do you plan to get through all the Mage Guard surrounding the place? What if Casovar uses the king as a hostage? What if you get the heir to the throne killed in the process of trying to rescue his father?"

Alyx rose to her feet, turning to Tarrick. "I gave you back control of Third Patrol, and I meant it. Now I ask you to trust me with this. If we run now, we lose whatever advantage we have. The decision is yours."

His dark eyes met hers, jaw clenching. It was a gamble, but she had promised Finn, and now she had to bank on Tarrick's willingness to trust her instincts.

Eventually he gave a sharp nod, and her shoulders sagged in relief. "Alyx is right. It's risky, but we don't have time to take Casovar down the slow way."

"Tarrick—"

Alyx cut Finn off with a sharp gesture. "It's your job to find solutions for all the problems you just raised, Finn. Dawn, how long do you think we have until someone finds this safe house?"

"It depends on whether Casovar starts searching himself. For now, I think we're safe for another day, but no more."

"Then we go tonight."

"I won't allow this, Aly-girl," Garan said quietly, a thread of steel in his voice.

The refusal sparked her anger—always there simmering, and now it flared hot, momentarily dispelling her fear and the pain of her injuries. Alyx forced herself to stand straight and tall, giving the appearance of strength and hiding the weakness she felt. "You don't get to say that to me anymore, Papa. I'm done with your refusal to see what I am, and your unceasing overprotectiveness. I am doing this, and you can't stop me."

His face tightened, his anger leaping just as hotly as hers as she threw the words at him. She didn't care. She adored her father, but she wasn't going to let him rule her any longer. Before Garan could say anything, however, Cayr rose to his feet.

"Actually, in the absence of my father, I am the one who has final say here." He spoke mildly, but with enough firmness in his face and voice that none considered gainsaying him. "We will do as Alyx suggests. Lord Egalion, you will do whatever is needed to assist them. Am I clear?"

For a long while silence filled the room.

It was Dawn who broke the silence, rising to her feet. "I'll start regular telepathic sweeps, that should give us some forewarning if Casovar or any Mage Guard get near enough to find us."

"Prince Cayr, you can't come," Finn spoke then, eyes flicking to Alyx before settling on the prince. "That's the first solution. It is critical that you remain safe in case it all goes wrong."

"He's right," Alyx said calmly, swinging to Cayr as he opened his mouth to protest. "We will do our best for your father, but your responsibility is greater than him. You said it yourself—you are Rionn's prince."

He gave a slow nod, and in that moment, seemed to shed all remnants of youth. "I accept that."

"And Papa, it will be your job to protect him."

He lifted an eyebrow. "So you're planning on sidelining me while you and a handful of half-trained mages take on Casovar? You're smarter than that."

"If we fail, Cayr is the only chance of regaining power in Alistriem, and he won't be able to do it alone," she said evenly, meeting her father's eyes. "So yes, I'm sidelining you. For now." His mouth thinned, but she gave him a tired smile. "Don't underestimate this handful of half-trained mages, Papa. We might surprise you."

ALYX SAT by the fire in the front room, sipping a glass of warm mead and revelling in the momentary peace. She'd managed another hour or so of sleep, but after that she couldn't lie still any longer. She hadn't managed to get her father alone after their meeting, and worry for Dashan nagged at her. The murmuring sounds of conversation drifted from the larger room at the back of the house—no doubt Finn and the others planning furiously. She briefly considered going to ask them, but was afraid of letting on how much she cared.

The front door clicked open and her father appeared, startling her —her magic hadn't warned her of the approach of a Taliath. He shrugged off his cloak and hung it by the door. Her gaze fixed on him as he moved—it was different than she'd ever seen, powerful but with such grace. She'd never imagined she would ever see a fully trained Taliath in action, but the previous night... it had been a wondrous

322

sight. How could the council have ever wanted to remove the Taliath from the world?

"All these years, you've been hiding yourself. Making yourself lesser," she said. "Just for me."

"And for Ladan too."

"Thank you, Papa."

"If you have children one day, you'll understand that a parent would do anything—gladly—to protect their child."

She nodded, taking another sip of the mead, her eyes falling on the magnificent sword at his hip. "May I see?"

He drew the blade out, its soft ring like music drifting through the room. It lay heavy in her open palms when he passed it to her, a long glimmering blade of sharpened steel. The hilt had been crafted from ivory and dyed a deep midnight blue. Garnets set into the hilt glittered in the firelight, artistically placed to look like leaping flame.

"Your mother named it Heartfire," her father murmured. "She thought the name suited me, but I often thought it described her much better."

Alyx's fingers traced reverently over the blade and hilt wishing once again she could remember Temari Egalion. Eventually she handed the sword back, clearing her throat. "I don't want to fight with you, Papa, but I have to do this. I wish you could trust me."

He let out a sigh, re-sheathing his sword before sitting. "I do trust you, but at the same time I'm frantic with worry."

"I know exactly how that feels." She gave him a half-smile. "Casovar told me that he'd arrested you, Astor and Sparky, and that he'd caught Dashan. He told me he was going to make me watch him kill you all," she said. "He must have been lying, but it was effective. I don't think I've ever been so scared, not even when Galien was trying to kill me at DarkSkull."

"He wasn't lying, not entirely." Garan stretched out his hands to warm them by the fire. "He never got Astor, the wily old bastard was gone when they showed up at his house."

She stared at him, heart thudding in sudden fear. "What do you mean? You said Dashan was okay. Tell me you weren't lying!"

"It's all right. I wasn't lying," he soothed, his hand resting on her arm. She nodded, trying to calm her racing heart. It was too much. The past couple of days had left her emotions fragile and strung out.

"Tell me, please."

He gave her arm another squeeze, brow furrowed in concern, before sitting in a chair beside hers. "Casovar came to the mansion with a unit of Mage Guard within an hour of you disappearing. Dawn was at the house—she'd come straight to me after receiving your telepathic distress call. I told her to run and warn your friends and Cayr. The arrest order was signed by the king. I was put in a cell with Sparkish and told we'd die as soon as Casovar got the king to sign an execution order." Garan gave her a wry smile. "I was so frantic about you by that stage I barely heard what they were telling me."

"Oh." Alyx processed that, then cold fear gripped her again. "What about Dashan? Are you sure he's all right?"

"I'm sure." Garan frowned. "He was here earlier."

Her heart clenched. "He was?"

"Yes." Garan looked at her in growing realisation. "Of course, you wouldn't know. I don't suppose anyone bothered to mention it."

"Mention what?"

"Cayr must have issued Dashan's release order before Casovar got you. He was released before Casovar could stop it, and somehow some of his Bluecoat friends learned about it. Several of them closed down the area around the east gate after setting a fire in one of the markets."

"Then why is he still here?" Worry surged again.

Garan sighed. "The Bluecoats helping Dashan heard about the arrest orders for Sparky and me and told him about it. Instead of fleeing the city, he went straight to Tarrick, who presumably told him you were missing and I was in the palace jail. The next thing I knew Dashan was giving himself up to the Mage Guard at the palace."

She shot up in her chair, heedless of aching muscles. "He what?"

"They took him straight to the palace dungeons, which is exactly what he wanted, of course," Garan said dryly, then paused, as if debating with himself over whether to say anything further.

"Tell me," she demanded.

"When they brought him down... I've never seen Dashan like that before. The rage shone from his eyes, but it was cold, contained. He had a purpose, and nothing was going to stop him from achieving it. He scared even me," Garan said. "He waited until the guards were about to open the cell beside mine and then he went berserk. He killed them all, the first with his bare hands. It was over in seconds, and then he calmly took the dead guard's keys and let Sparky and me out." He shook his head. "We fought our way out of the palace and came straight to this safehouse."

Alyx found herself perilously close to weeping. Dashan had gone straight for her father. Of course he had, he knew how much Garan meant to her. "How did you find me?"

"Luck, in the end." A dark shadow flashed over her father's face, an echo of the terror he must have felt for her. "Brynn returned. He knew about the hut where you were being held. He'd followed Casovar there once before and thought that might be where he was holding you."

"And Dashan?"

Garan sighed. "You heard me talk about the Bluecoat rebellion before? He's leading it. They're furious they're being kept away from the palace and they know Casovar tortured you. Dashan and those loyal to him are telling every Bluecoat that will listen that Casovar is using magic on the king. They're hampering the Mage Guard search for us and forcing Casovar to keep most of them at the palace." He shook his head. "I had no idea Dashan had so much support in the Blue Guard."

"I did," she whispered.

"While you were sleeping earlier, he dropped by to see how you were and ensure we were still safe. I told him of your plan to face Casovar now, and he said he would help. I don't know exactly what he's planning, but Sparky is in on it too—he's in the back room now talking with Finn and Tarrick."

She couldn't hide the tears welling in her eyes and trickling down her cheeks, and Garan reached out to her, tortured sadness on his face. "I never wanted you to know how this feels. I am so sorry."

"Not your fault." She leaned into him, allowing herself to take the comfort he offered. "I'm glad you're here."

. . .

BRYNN APPEARED in the late afternoon laden down with bulging saddlebags. Despite the deep shadows under his eyes, he had a bright smile for Alyx when he saw she was up and about, and happily accepted her hug of gratitude. "I just wish I'd been quicker in returning from Tregaya."

"Any luck with the council?" she asked.

"I actually think I managed to convince Rothai there's a possibility Shakar is alive," Brynn said. "He promised to talk to Romas. I didn't linger to see what happened, I wanted to get back here as soon as possible."

The door swung open. "I thought I heard voices," Tarrick said, followed by Cario and the twins. "Did you get everything you need?"

"I'm ready to go." Brynn shrugged. "Why do you all look so grim?"

At a raised eyebrow from Tarrick, Alyx filled him in on her plan. Thankfully, he merely nodded. "Dangerous, but smart. The last thing he'll expect is you coming at him now, and if he still doesn't know the extent of your magic... well, you can definitely use that to your advantage."

"Sparky just left." Finn eased into a chair. "I think we've managed to come up with a workable plan."

She waved a hand. "Let's hear it."

Once he'd finished, the room dissolved into silence. A small smile tugged at Alyx's face. "If Sparky holds up his end, I think it could work."

"He wouldn't say how, but he says he can take care of it," Tarrick said.

Brynn gave them a mournful look. "I can't believe I'm going to miss out on all the fun."

Alyx didn't laugh at his attempted joke. "No, you get the excitement of another trip to Tregaya alone and without any protection. Stay safe, Brynn."

"You too, Alyx."

CHAPTER 35

T he wind gusted, playing with the tendrils of hair that had escaped her braid and filling her cloak so that it whipped around her ankles. They ran in single file up the hill, Alyx unerringly following the trail she'd marked out with Dashan and Cayr as children. Dawn was immediately behind, her magic soaring around them to detect threats. Tarrick, Finn and Cario brought up the rear.

Alyx tried to focus on managing her breathing as they ran, but found it impossible to relax enough to find a rhythm. With each step closer to the palace, her chest tightened further with dread. How could she think to face Casovar and win, especially after what he'd done to her? Even thinking about what had happened in that room left her shaky and nauseated.

At the top of the hill waited two shadowy figures, one tall and lean, the other stocky, his usual smile flashing despite the seriousness of the night. Their familiar faces calmed her for a brief, blessed moment.

Tarrick pointed at the two bodies lying still on the ground. "Any problems?"

"They found the wrong end of my sword." Roland dug his boot into the Mage Guard soldier at his feet.

"Keep your voice down," Tijer warned, looking to Alyx. "The gate is clear. Nothing in the garden besides these two as far as we could tell."

As expected. Casovar didn't know about Cayr's secret exit from the palace. Alyx nonetheless glanced at Dawn, who confirmed Tijer's words with a nod. She pushed open the gate and they quickly slipped through. Inside the wind was calmer, the garden protected by the palace walls, and she pointed Dawn towards a particularly tall tree near the gate.

"It's easy to climb and you'll be well hidden in the foliage."

"Good luck." Dawn reached out to squeeze her hand.

Alyx squeezed back, holding Dawn's gaze. "Together."

A smile ghosted over Dawn's face, then she let go and headed for the tree.

"Tijer, Roland, you're with me," Alyx spoke softly. "The rest of you, are you sure you know where to go?"

"Your instructions were clear, we'll be fine," Tarrick said patiently. "See you soon."

Cario gave her a faint nod of reassurance, and Finn even smiled. Then they were gone, disappearing in three different directions into the darkness. She buried her fear for them and turned to the Bluecoats.

"As I understand it, we're going for the king?" Tijer asked in an undertone.

"Yes. He's the priority, is that clear? You're to keep him safe above everything else."

"Not to worry, My Lady, we've had that particular instruction drilled into us since enlistment day." Roland's smile flashed again in the darkness.

"We'll need your magic to get us past the Mage Guard crawling all over the place, though," Tijer added.

"Follow me."

Alyx summoned enough magic to probe ahead with her telepathy, but not too far, unwilling to risk the possibility of Casovar sensing her near. In this manner, she led the Bluecoats through the dark gardens. Twice they had to stop, freezing into stillness, as patrolling soldiers passed by. Both times the Mage Guard were in groups of four—

Casovar wasn't taking any chances. Eventually they made it to Cayr's bedroom window, Alyx swinging it open and climbing inside.

"The prince's bedroom?" Tijer asked as he slipped through after her.

"Yes." Alyx concentrated while Roland came in and quietly slid the window closed. Beyond Cayr's front door the corridor was full of the thoughts of Mage Guard—at least six. More than she'd hoped for.

"Do you think we could fight through?" she asked, relaying the news.

"No need." Roland moved quietly to edge open the bedroom door. A moment later, he opened it fully and went through. Tijer gestured for Alyx to follow. Instead of going to Cayr's front door, though, Roland headed for a narrow corridor connecting Cayr's lounge to another smaller room he used as a study. Halfway down the corridor, an exit led into a small private garden.

"The prince's garden shares a wall with that of his parents," Tijer murmured. "Only those assigned to guard the royal family are told about it."

Not even Alyx had known that, and she felt a flash of relief that Dashan had sent these Bluecoats to help.

Nothing disturbed the darkness as the three of them slid open the door into the garden and ran straight for a low wall to the left. Once they were over that, Alyx followed the Bluecoats to a window she assumed led into the king's bedroom—their target. She and Tijer sank into the shadows on either side while Roland worked on the catch and inched it upwards slowly enough that it didn't make a noise.

He went in first, Alyx's heart thudding into the silence that followed. She jumped when he reappeared suddenly, waving them in. Tijer gave her a leg up and she climbed in, cursing under her breath when her boot knocked against the window frame. Inside, it took a moment for her eyes to adjust to the dim light cast by the open window.

"He's here," Roland breathed. "But there's at least two Mage Guard on the other side of the bedroom door. I heard them talking."

Alyx pointed both Roland and Tijer to the bed, gesturing that she would guard the door. The two Bluecoats gently pulled back the bedcovers, and at the expressions that crossed their faces, her heart began pounding.

Eyes on the door, she tip-toed over to Tijer, the closest, making a questioning gesture.

"He doesn't look good," Tijer murmured in her ear. "And he's unconscious."

She glanced down at the bed—it was hard to tell in the dim light, but the king's skin was deathly pale. His chest rose and fell sluggishly. A flash of regret went through her for not bringing Finn.

"Get him awake as quietly as you can," she murmured before returning to her post at the door. Tijer leaned in to murmur to the sleeping king.

Darien awoke with a start, and even though Roland's hand immediately closed over his mouth, the king jerked backwards in fright, head banging against the backboard. A moment of tense silence followed in which the king's eyes widened at the sight of Alyx, and he realised the man holding him down was a Bluecoat. Then shouting broke out from the other side of the door.

"Get him out!" Alyx screamed as the door flew inwards. "Go!"

The first soldier through the door came straight at her. She barely had time to duck before his blade swung through the air where her head had been. Drawing magic, she yanked the sword from his hand, lunged with her knife and drove it into his side. Yanking it out, she turned on the second guard, divesting him of his sword before embedding her knife in his chest.

It was over in seconds. Breathing hard, adrenalin flooding her, Alyx stared through the door, but no one else was coming. Two dead men lay at her feet, their blood pooling on the floor. Sickened, she tore her gaze away.

The king!

She spun around, but Darien was gone along with both Bluecoats, curtains billowing inwards from the open window. Her shoulders relaxed fractionally.

"*Alyx!*"

"*Dawn? What is it?*"

"*Casovar has Tarrick.*" Panic beat through Dawn's mental voice, despite her attempt at calm. *"They're in the ballroom. Casovar caught him trying to get the doors open."*

Alyx sheathed her knife and started running. *"The others?"*

"Cario successfully unbarred the front gates before he was spotted—he's in a fight, but all right for now. Finn too, he managed to get the kitchen entrances unlocked. Bluecoats and army soldiers are pouring in at both locations, but the palace is full of Mage Guard and they're swarming to intercept." Dawn paused. *"I can't see Tarrick properly because Casovar is using his magic. Do you want me to come?"*

"No, stay where you are. I'll get to Tarrick."

She'd hoped they'd be able to do this—get the king out and the Mage Guard smothered—without encountering Casovar. A slim hope, but one she'd clutched hold of fiercely.

It wasn't to be.

Alyx stretched her legs out into a sprint, racing through the back corridors of the residential wing of the palace. She got almost all the way to her destination without being seen, but eventually rounded a corner to see six red-cloaked soldiers running down the hall in her direction.

Ducking back the way she'd come, she raced up a set of stairs to the first floor. Her breath was burning in her chest by the time she reached the gallery above the ballroom, but she barely noticed that or the sweat trickling down her face—her eyes were frantically searching the open space below. The ballroom seemed oddly lonely in its empty state, lit only by a few wall torches.

There.

Alyx skidded to a halt, her gaze catching on Casovar standing in the middle of the floor, Tarrick gasping at his feet. The lord-mage had one hand raised as Tarrick writhed, clutching at his throat.

"Where is she?" Casovar shouted.

Tarrick's forearms lit up with his magic, a bright pearlescent glimmer that dispelled the shadows, but Casovar was merciless, tightening his hold until the glow flickered and died.

With a ruthless determination, she turned her terror for Tarrick into strength feeding her magic. Then, she backed up as far as she could before breaking into a run, her momentum taking her up to the gallery railing in one leap and then she was launching herself out into open air, arms spread wide, knees drawn up to her chest. Using just enough flying magic to control her fall, she slammed into Casovar, her boots in his back, sending him crashing hard to the floor.

His head bounced against the marble with a loud crack and Alyx rolled smoothly away. Tarrick gasped, rolled over. She scrambled over to him, but he was already staggering to his feet, one hand at his throat.

"Go!" she yelled at him. "The Bluecoats need help. I'll take Casovar."

"Alyx... " He hesitated, glancing towards where the lord-mage's prone form was already beginning to move.

"Go, Tarrick, please! I can't fight Casovar if the Mage Guard come flooding in here."

"Be smart, Alyx," he said, before turning and running.

Casovar's mocking laughter cut through the room and Alyx spun back to face him. Blood trickled down his neck, but none of his agility seemed to have been affected as he rose to his feet. "What exactly is it you think you're going to do?"

Alyx forced herself to meet his eyes. This was it. Nausea surged so strongly she whimpered, unconsciously taking a step backwards.

I have to be strong. She willed herself to live up to those words, trying to ignore her visceral fear and drawing upon more and more of her magic.

I can be strong.

"I'm going to kill you," she said.

The two concussive bursts almost appeared to move in slow motion as they sailed towards the lord-mage, lighting up the room with their silver-green glow. Shock rippled over Casovar's face and he barely raised a shield in time to deflect them.

She was already running as the successive booms went off, allowing the concussive force to wash over her before leaping high, bringing her staff slamming down towards his head. He ducked aside at the last moment, gesturing desperately with telekinetic magic to yank the staff from her hand.

Alyx landed lightly, reaching out and tugging the staff back from his loose grip. The shock on his face deepened as they regarded each other, both breathing heavily.

"I'm no second-year apprentice," she panted. "And I'm just as powerful you."

"You're stronger than I thought, to keep that hidden." His jaw tightened, and his eyes turned dark. "But you can boast all you like. We both know you pose little threat to me."

Alyx swallowed, straightened her shoulders. "You tried hard to break me, but you failed."

Casovar threw back his head and laughed again, cold eyes coming back to rest on hers. "We both know I broke you, girl. I tore you apart."

She shuddered in memory, her grip on her staff suddenly slicked with sweat. Her heart was pounding too hard in her chest, and she couldn't tear her eyes away from that implacable gaze. His magic slid into her mind, just like before, and she froze.

"You're pathetic," he hissed. "And I own you."

Her knees hit the floor with a thud and she let out a low moan, hands reaching for her head. Her staff clattered to the floor. She tried to fight but he was too strong—he'd dominated her before and he was doing it again.

"*No.*" It was only one word, one single word, but spoken with such a tightly controlled fury it broke right through Casovar's mental hold. Dawn attacked without hesitation, ripping Casovar's thoughts out of Alyx's head with an icy confidence that shook the lord-mage so utterly he was slow to respond.

"Dawn..." Alyx gasped, one hand scrabbling against the marble floor as she desperately tried to regain coherency.

"*I've got you, Alyx.*"

And she did. Casovar reeled back, one hand clutching at his head, mouth snarling as he battled her. Alyx closed her eyes, taking a single deep breath to centre herself. I have to do this. She was still alive. He hadn't beaten her. Not yet.

And she wasn't alone.

Forcing herself back to her feet she drew on her magic, summoning a concussive burst and flinging it at Casovar. He gave a massive roar of effort, managing to fight Dawn off in time to leap aside from Alyx's magic.

After the bright flash faded, she blinked rapidly, one hand reaching out to call her staff back to her hand. Casovar was running, heading for one of the doors leading out to the gardens.

She stumbled into a run after him, shaky legs still not fully under her. He spun around before disappearing outside, sending a roaring wind at her. Not quick enough to erect her shield in time, Alyx was caught up in his wind-magic and hurled back into the ballroom. Her flying ability kicked in, controlling the free fall and allowing her to land lightly on her feet.

She stood there for a moment, trying to catch her breath and regain her focus. The terror was still there, and it took everything she had to fight it back, to immerse herself in the magic that burned bright and hot inside.

"You okay?" Dawn's voice was a balm to her anxiety, and she almost smiled.

"I'm good. Thank you. You saved my life."

"He knows from our thoughts about the Bluecoats storming the palace." Exhaustion made Dawn's mental voice faint, but she persevered. *"He's going to flee with the Mage Guard. Go... get him."*

The link snapped out, but Dawn's determination had given Alyx the strength she needed.

She would show no less courage than Dawn had.

RUNNING AFTER CASOVAR, Alyx burst through the door and into the chaos of battle. A full cohort of Mage Guard filled the opposite end of the garden, engaged in a bitter fight against a rapidly shrinking number of Bluecoats trying to prevent them from leaving.

Casovar was halfway between her and the fight, making straight for his soldiers. They were clearly trying to fight through to the gate that was part of the secret route the king had used to flee during the Shiven attack on the palace. It seemed Casovar had had an escape plan in place.

Raising her hand in the air, Alyx sent a bright concussive burst flying at Casovar's back. The flash of light warned him and he stopped mid-run, calling upon his own magic to raise a shield.

"Why are you running?" she taunted. "Afraid of us, are you?"

"Foolish girl," he sneered in contempt. "You're all going to die. If not today, then soon."

He sent fire at her, bright orange balls reminiscent of Fengel. Alyx spun her staff, slammed it into the ground and pushed out as much power as she could. Jayn's shield shimmered into the air around her. The fireballs hit the ward and flared out of existence.

At the same moment, she dropped the shield and summoned her offensive magic. Concussion bursts thundered through the air towards Casovar. As they crashed against his shield, blue lightning forked across the sky above. Bright light flashed, and then came the sonic boom as her concussive magic spread out across the field.

Not letting up, Alyx sent more concussion bursts flying at Casovar, simultaneously using her telekinetic power to try and yank the mage staff from his grip. Satisfaction flared briefly as she sensed how much power he had to draw upon to fend off her attack, but a moment later he seemed to find his balance. The last of her concussion bursts crashed against his shield, and a brief silence hung between them before shouting, screams and the ring of steel quickly filled it.

Her gaze flickered behind Casovar, where too-few Bluecoats were trying to hold their own against what had become a wall of red-cloaked soldiers trying to drive through them towards the exit. More Mage Guard were arriving, clearly being pushed out of other areas of the palace. Or maybe Casovar had summoned them. She wavered, uncertain whether to go after Casovar or help the Bluecoats.

"Cover us, Alyx!" Tarrick's voice called from behind her, and then he was running past, Finn and Cario with him, Bluecoats streaming behind them, heading straight for the fight at the other end of the garden.

Frantically she summoned more magic, throwing everything she had at Casovar before he could attack them. Hope surged at their appearance. If the Bluecoats could deal with the Mage Guard, and she could hold Casovar here, they could end him. End all of it now.

But he was powerful, and he wasn't backing down without a fight.

He retaliated quickly, and for several long moments her focus narrowed entirely to feeding energy into her shield as his fire and concussive power rained down on her.

As she hunkered down under the shield, the cries from the battle raging in the garden took on a different note, and her eyes widened. The number of Bluecoats had doubled—and she recognised some of them, Josha and Nario, and then... there, Casta too! Not only were there more, but they were rapidly re-forming into solid units, closing ranks and taking on the Mage Guard as a disciplined group. A new fighter led them, not wearing blue or red, but wielding a sword that caught the light of every flash of magic and sent it spinning out around him.

"On me, Bluecoats!" he roared over the fighting. "Form up on me!"

Dashan cut through the Mage Guard lines with Tijer and Roland at his back, forcing the red cloaks around them to break and scatter. The Blue Guard responded quickly to his shouted commands and his energy, and now suddenly it was the Mage Guard looking scattered, breaking away in smaller groups.

Then Dawn's voice was in her head. *"Alyx—Tarrick, Cario and Finn are coming back to help you now the Bluecoats have the upper hand. I'm on my way too."*

It was a tightly shielded sending, but Casovar's magic must have sensed something, because his magical attack on her faded and his gaze flickered away from the battle, narrowing on Finn and Cario as they re-appeared, edging around him warily. Her magic told her Tarrick was there too, staying in the shadows.

She clutched her staff, using every shred of determination she possessed to ignore the weakness trembling through her muscles. She'd used too much magic with the shield and now she dropped it to conserve strength. She had to hold on... just a little longer.

"You think you're going to make a difference?" Casovar laughed at them, looking genuinely amused. "A healer and a council traitor."

"I am no traitor, Lord-Mage Casovar." Cario moved as casually as if he were taking an afternoon walk, deliberately drawing Casovar's attention away from Finn as he came up beside her and laid a hand on her arm. The balm of his healing magic swept through her, restoring some of her energy. "I am a representative of the Mage Council. They want you dead as much as Alyx here does."

That shocked Casovar, the emotion rippling across his face. "Lies."

"I am the grandson of Councillor Duneskal and a full-blooded mage warrior. Do you really think I'd be here if the council hadn't sanctioned it?" Cario raised an eyebrow.

Casovar smiled then. "The council's support is of little matter. They'll be destroyed too, soon enough."

"You're talking about Shakar, I suppose?" Cario asked.

A twisted sort of hate crumpled Casovar's face. "You all think you're so clever. So sanguine in the face of your certain destruction."

Casovar spun and flicked his hand, and fireballs shot from the end of his staff towards Alyx and Finn.

Alyx shouted a warning, thrusting out her right hand and using her magic to pull the fireballs off course. Casovar fought her, and for a moment they pitted their strength against each other. He was the more experienced mage, and Alyx only barely managed to pull the fireballs off line. They shot past Finn's head as he ducked, frantically scrambling away from Alyx.

"You should give up now," Casovar hissed. "Do that, and I might not kill you."

Tarrick stepped out of the darkness to Casovar's left, forearms lighting up in a pearly glow. "We don't give up, Lord-Mage Casovar."

"Then you'll die."

Casovar spun his staff, sending a whirlwind spiralling outward from his body. It was a magic Alyx had never seen before, and it gained strength as it spread outwards. Her shield was useless as the air spun right through it, picking up each of them and sending them flying in all directions.

Angry, Alyx drew on every bit of strength she had and sent her flying ability outwards, grabbing onto Tarrick, Cario and Finn and controlling their flight. Once again, her strength was pitted against Casovar's, and she fought bitterly to hold onto them.

Casovar let go suddenly and they dropped to the ground. Alyx fell hard as her magic failed, and she sat up, wincing, pain stabbing through her bad shoulder. Casovar watched them a moment before striding towards Alyx, the expression he wore murderous.

"I'm afraid." She whispered the thought, almost to herself.

"*Me too, but I'm here.*" Dawn sounded stronger than she had, but still weary. "*Let's finish this.*"

"Alyx!" Tarrick shouted a warning.

She staggered to her feet and faced the oncoming threat squarely. Cario had fallen some distance away, and was scrambling around behind Casovar, whose focus was entirely on Alyx. The sight of Dawn, standing close to her twin, bolstered her.

Her grip on her staff tightened. She could do this. She was going to do this. And she didn't need to do it alone.

"*Cario, this will go better if he doesn't have his staff.*"

His blue eyes shifted to hers, and she read his acknowledgement in them. A small smile flickered at her mouth. A glance at Tarrick, then each of the twins in turn. The connection between them—the one they'd forged in adversity at DarkSkull and used to beat Galien—surged with magic.

Alyx swung her staff and sent concussion ball after concussion ball directly at Casovar. Tarrick stepped up beside her and followed suit. Finn came to stand behind them, a hand on each shoulder, flooding them with every bit of his healing strength. Dawn unleashed her magic on Casovar's mind, battering his mental shield with everything she had left.

The lord-mage summoned his shield to deflect the concussion bursts, then raised his staff, gathering his magic to fight back. At that same moment, Cario threw his head back and let out a roar. He extended his right arm, body rigid with effort, mouth curling in a snarl as he pitted his strength against Casovar.

The lord-mage fought to keep hold of his staff, but it was a losing battle. Mage of the higher order he might be, but there was no mage alive who could match Cario's telekinetic skill. A moment longer and the staff flew from Casovar's hand across the garden and into Cario's. The blonde mage slumped, gasping for air, sweat streaming down his face.

Before Casovar could turn his power on Cario, Alyx resumed her attack, forcing blast after blast to burst from her staff. Finn's energy replaced some of her draining magic, but it took everything she had to employ the utter focus and effort required to do what she was doing. Casovar was close to overwhelmed, but he wasn't beaten yet. His sheer power charged a shield that was becoming almost annihilated by a continuous blast of concussion energy while his mental shield was battered without respite.

She stood firm, refusing to back down until his shield broke. It weakened slightly at her onslaught. Beside her, Tarrick slumped and faltered, at his utmost limit. Alyx gritted her teeth, willing herself to continue. Her concussion bursts lost some of their power, but she kept going.

Casovar's shield flickered before strengthening.

Her legs trembled and sweat poured down her back, but she forced herself to keep sending her magic soaring through the night. Casovar couldn't hold on indefinitely, not when he was being attacked from all sides, and he knew it. He let out a furious roar and Alyx felt him gather up every bit of strength he had left.

It was terrifying to behold, the sheer power he had, and the skill with which he used it. Desperate, he attacked their minds. Tarrick was already out, and now the twins faltered, both driven back by Casovar's mental attack. Cario swayed on his feet, nothing left in him.

Alyx alone remained standing.

Casovar strode across the grass towards her. He battered at her mind, a smile of triumph spreading over his face. She cried out, fighting back, pushing him away, refusing to let him beat her. The memory of him tearing through her mind distracted her, weakening her for a moment. It was all he needed, and he was inside her mind again.

No.

This time she didn't have to hide.

Alyx didn't know how she did it, or where that final reserve of strength came from, but it was there. She screamed aloud as she tore him from her thoughts. Casovar stopped mid-stride, shock written all over his face.

Then his shield failed spectacularly, winking out of existence.

Without thought, Alyx released two more concussion bursts. They sailed straight at Casovar, hitting the mage in his chest and face. A concussion ring swept outwards as they exploded, and Alyx clasped both hands over her ears, her chest squeezing so tight she couldn't breathe.

Then, the light faded and Casovar was no longer standing there. The two blasts had disintegrated him completely.

She dropped to the ground, gasping for air and suddenly feeling as if she were going to vomit up the entire contents of her stomach. Too much. Far too much magic. Blackness darkened the edge of her vision.

"Alyx!"

Dashan's voice, she'd recognise it anywhere. She tried to look up, vision blurry, body not properly responding. He was moving towards her, but then Tarrick stepped into his way, holding him back.

She slumped to the ground, unconsciousness claiming her.

CHAPTER 36

For the second time in a week, Alyx awoke battered and exhausted in the soft bed at the safe house. Rain pattered against the window to her right. It took only a moment before memory assaulted her. She sat up, glancing down at her trembling hands. Concentrating on them only made the shaking worse. Her head ached, and her body was sore all over.

"You're awake." Cayr appeared at the door, saving her from the panic that had begun creeping into the back of her mind. Relief replaced it—he was okay. "How are you feeling?"

"I'm fine," she lied. "I... is everything under control? The king?"

He sat beside her, taking her hand in his warm one. She clung tightly to it. "Father is weak but all right. Finn thinks that whatever Casovar was doing to him, it was draining his body's strength. He's thinking clearly now, though. The Bluecoats are firmly back under Lord-General Caverlock's command and on duty at the palace."

"The Mage Guard?"

"Those we've caught are under arrest. Dawn is helping us track down the others."

"Good," she said, swallowing. "How did your father react to everything that happened?"

"We've had a long talk," he assured her. "He's upset, and furious we went behind his back, but your father, Sparky and Astor have been his dearest friends his whole life. He trusts them, and me."

She relaxed a little, leaning back into the pillows, but Cayr hadn't missed how tightly she was gripping his hand. "Your father is okay, Alyx. He's terribly worried about you, but I convinced him my father needs him more than you right now, and Finn assured him you were going to be fine. Even so, I'm sure it won't be long until he visits."

"Thanks. Are the others all right too?"

"Tarrick and Cario are back at your home, sacked out in the spare rooms. They'll probably sleep for hours." He smiled faintly. "Finn is helping with the wounded and Dawn with tracking down the remnants of the Mage Guard."

"Then why am I here?"

"Your father was worried about you after the battle," he said. "There were still some Mage Guard soldiers on the loose. He thought this was the safest place for you until you woke up. It's surrounded by Bluecoats."

Relief at that news brought back her weariness. "I know you must have a lot to do as well. Thank you for coming to ease my mind."

Cayr hesitated. "I haven't spoken to Dash, but I know he survived the battle. One of the Bluecoats told me he's left the city like he originally planned to do."

She closed her eyes, stifling the pain that thought brought her. "Do Tarrick and Finn know that he's gone?"

"Yes. The Bluecoat, your friend Casta, told me he'd spoken to them already. Casta wanted to see you too, but you were still sleeping at the time."

"Thanks." She tried to keep the grief from her voice, but Cayr knew her too well.

"Alyx, I'm sorry. I can see how..." he faltered, then took a breath and let go of her hand. "I know you too well not to be able to see how you feel about him."

His withdrawal made her sad, and for a moment she stared at their hands resting near each other on the covers. "I'm sorry too. You will never know how sorry I am."

"I know." He sighed. "That doesn't make it hurt any less."

"I understand. I still...." It was her turn to falter. "I care about you so much, and I'll do whatever you need."

"I don't think we should marry," he said. "It's not right, for either of us. Rionn will manage, especially now your father has returned to being a Taliath and Casovar is dead."

"I think you're right." She swallowed. Even though it wasn't what she wanted anymore, there was still a sting to the knowledge that the thing she once so desperately dreamed about was gone forever. "There is a greater threat out there, and I think I'm one of the few people who can help stop it. That's why I can't stay here in Rionn. The threat Shakar poses is bigger than all of this."

He nodded sadly. "I wish you didn't have to leave."

"Me too." She smiled faintly. "One day I'll be back to stay."

"I'll leave you to sleep." He leaned over to kiss her forehead, lingering for a long sweet moment, and then he rose and left.

As soon as she was alone, it was impossible to rest. She couldn't rid her mind of the memories of Casovar torturing her, raging through her mind unchecked. She'd hoped killing him would make all the horror go away, but it was still there, lurking in the back of her thoughts. He had broken her, if only for a short time, and she somehow had to live with that.

Eventually she managed a fitful sleep. Not long after, the nightmare claimed her. She was still weak and exhausted, and had no strength to fight Shakar's power as he dragged her relentlessly down the familiar dark tunnel. He was angry about Casovar's death, and his anger tore away the veneer of civility he'd maintained in his more recent contact.

But he was smug too. She might have defeated Casovar with the help of her friends, but she'd almost killed herself doing it. Casovar's power was nothing compared to Shakar's; she had no hope of destroying him. He was cruel, twisting his hooks deep into her mind, bringing back the remembered terror and pain of Casovar ransacking her thoughts and memories.

"*No more pretences, girl,*" he hissed. "*You've chosen the wrong side. My Hunters are coming for you. Best start sleeping with one eye open.*"

Alyx awoke gasping, the screams lodged in her throat and unable to escape. Sweat soaked through the nightshirt she slept in and ran in rivulets down her face. Terrified, alone, and still not fully awake, she reached for her magic, seeking Dawn, or someone who could hear her. But there wasn't enough inside her, only a tiny spark, nowhere near strong enough to reach her friend.

Pulling the blankets back over her, she huddled against the headboard, shivers racking her frame. Time passed, she wasn't sure how much. The darkness closed around her so completely she was forced to get up and light the candle on the table by the bed so that she could breathe.

The sound of the window sliding open almost made her scream in terror, her body instinctively scrabbling backwards against the headboard, her magic too weak to summon. A tall figure swung through the window, landing lightly enough not to make a noise.

"Alyx?"

"Dashan!" She was out of the bed in an instant, hurling herself across the room and into his arms. They wrapped fiercely around her and she shuddered, gripping his shirt and pulling herself as close to him as she could get.

"What are you doing here?" she mumbled, so much relief flooding through her she could barely stand.

"I came for you." He gently tugged her back so he could look down at her; he was wearing his determined expression. "I know what he did to you, and then I saw you after the battle. I was frantic, but they wouldn't let me see you, so I found a way."

Alyx swallowed. "I'm not okay, Dash. They don't know... I couldn't tell them, but what he did... I can't..." she gasped, unable to get the words out, the panic creeping back.

"Hey." His hand cradled her cheek, his arm steadying her, calming her. "Shush, it's all right. It's going to be all right."

"I don't know if it will." She dropped her head into his chest, fighting back tears.

344

"Let it out, sweetheart." He rubbed her back gently. "Let it out. It's me, I'm here."

So she did. She cried, long, heart-wrenching sobs, and Dashan soothed her with his voice and his arms and his hands, telling her over and over that he loved her and that it was all going to be all right.

When the sobs finally subsided, he leaned back and used the cuff of his shirt to gently wipe the tears from her face. "Better?"

She nodded. "A little. I thought you were leaving?"

"I am, but I'm taking you with me."

"I can't—"

"My intention was only to come here and say goodbye before I left, to make sure you're okay." He framed her face with his hands. "But you're not okay, and I'm not leaving you like this. I'm getting you out of this city tonight and nothing is going to stop me. Will you trust me?"

Already she felt better, the warmth of his hands and presence soaking through the ice that Casovar had left in her. She met his warm brown eyes. "I'm in love with you, Dashan."

He stilled, the soft smile she loved so much lighting his face up. "You mentioned that."

"You ask me to trust you, and I do. I trust you with everything I am. But I also have responsibilities that I can't walk away from, no matter how deeply I love you."

"I'm not asking you to walk away from anything." He reached out, tucking a strand of hair behind her ear. "I know that you can't come away with me forever. But before you can do anything, you need to heal. I can help you do that."

She hesitated only a moment longer before giving him a silent nod. He smiled and stepped back, turning away while she dressed and collected her mage staff. She tried her magic again, relief flooding her when she found enough to use telepathic power.

"Dawn?" Alyx winced at the realisation she was waking her friend from deep sleep, but it couldn't be helped. *"I'm so sorry to wake you."*

"Is there something wrong, is someone hurt?"

"No, everything is fine."

"Are you all right? You sound strange... did you have another nightmare?"

"I'm physically fine." She paused. *"But I'm going away for a little while. A few days."*

"What? Where? Alyx, you're not making any sense." Dawn was trying to collect her sleepy thoughts.

"There's something I need to do, and I'll be back soon, I promise you. Tell the others for me?"

"Tarrick will be furious. You can't just disappear. Shakar is out there."

"I have to," Alyx whispered. *"I'll be back as soon as I can. Take care of them for me, Dawn."*

Alyx cut off her magic before Dawn could protest, and erected her mental shield. Even that small effort caused the beginnings of a headache throbbing at her temples. Guilt warred with resolve inside her. They would never understand this, and they wouldn't forgive her for it either.

"Ready?" Dashan asked.

"You want me to climb out a window?" She raised an eyebrow.

He sighed. "I thought you were a warrior mage."

She smiled genuinely for the first time in weeks, lifting her arms to wrap them around his neck before leaning in to kiss him. He pulled away instinctively, concern and adoration flickering in his eyes. "We can't. The council... "

She took a breath, finding the resolve inside herself and reaching down to take hold of his hand. "They will want to kill us whether we're together or not. I'm not their puppet, and I make my own choices."

"If you choose this... " He hesitated. "We won't be able to be together, not fully, I mean."

"Unless we can find some way to stop me absorbing your abilities?" She met his eyes. "I know. And we'll have to keep it secret from everyone to prevent putting the others in danger. It will be difficult and frustrating, I'm under no illusions."

"You're sure?" His gaze searched hers, looking for any sign of doubt. She gave him none.

"Yes," she said simply. "And to be clear, I won't be marrying Cayr."

Before he could say anything more, she pulled him down to her and kissed him, tugging him as close as she possibly could. He returned the kiss, sending every nerve ending in her body screaming to full aware-

346

ness. Oh, how she'd missed this, the way he made her feel! His touch and love flooded through her, already soothing away the sharpest edges of the memory of her torture at Casovar's hands.

Eventually they parted, Dashan's forehead resting against hers as their fingers entwined. "I love you, Egalion."

"Good," she said, stepping back. "Then give me a leg up to that windowsill."

CHAPTER 37

Alyx leaned back against the prow of the boat as it bobbed gently on the water, gazing up at the night sky above. The stars were so much brighter out on the open ocean—an immense carpet of sparkling diamonds. Did Shakar ever look at such beauty? And what did it make him feel when he did? The sudden rocking of the boat shifted her attention to Dashan as he heaved himself up out of the water and onto the deck.

"Much better," he said, shaking water all over the place.

Alyx said nothing, content to simply lie there and watch him. He wore only a pair of shorts, revealing every inch of his muscular upper body and fair Shiven skin tanned by the summer sun. His chocolate hair was slicked against his skull, and water droplets trickled down his skin. Another smile crossed her face. How scandalized everyone back home would be if they knew she was alone on a boat with a half-naked man!

"What are you grinning about?" Dashan finished wiping himself dry and came to sprawl out beside her, one arm lazily reaching out to wrap around her shoulders.

She shifted closer to him. "Oh, nothing important. You planning on telling me where we're going?"

"While you were away with Tarrick I got a message from Ladan—he sent it to me on the assumption Casovar was watching you and the others closely. The message said he'd found a location for Terin."

Alyx scrambled up. "Where?"

"All the message said was that it was in south Rionn. I wrote back straight away, told him I'd meet him in Ester in three weeks, but I wanted to let you know before I left, and you were away with Tarrick. Getting arrested ruined that plan."

"So we're going to meet Ladan," Alyx realised, then raised an amused eyebrow. "You told him to meet you in Ester?'

"Well, if this guy really is Terin, he's more likely to talk to the child of his old friend than a stranger," Dashan said. "This way it's even better, the both of you can go."

"But not you," she said quietly.

He took her hand, entangling their fingers. "When I first got the message, I figured I would meet Ladan in Ester and take him up on his job offer. I thought it would be best for everyone if I left Alistriem. Now... well, I have to go to ShadowFall Island, don't I? See if anyone's still there. See if I can be trained."

She nodded, accepting that, and they fell into a comfortable silence. Alyx revelled in the feel of him so close, his arm around her shoulders, his warmth at her side.

"Not that I want to bring the mood down, but... " Dashan hesitated. "You spoke with Cayr?"

"Yes." She sighed. "He initiated the conversation. He knows me well enough to realise my feelings, as much as it breaks his heart. I don't know if I can ever forgive myself for that."

"I know exactly how you feel." Genuine pain flashed across his face. "After everything he's done for me, and I repay him like this."

Alyx turned towards him. "Despite everything, it feels right to be here. I'm so sick of denying how I feel, to myself, to everyone else."

He kissed her, capturing her lips gently with his own. She returned it happily, one hand splayed on his chest, another ruffling the hair at the base of his neck.

"Can I ask what changed?" he said tentatively. "I never imagined in a thousand years you would ever feel like this about me."

She sat up, considering how to answer. "I never imagined it either, not for a second, and I'm not sure exactly when that changed. But when Cayr told me in Carhall that he hadn't sent you with me to Dark-Skull, that you'd volunteered to come..." Her voice trailed off. "It was like a lamp had been turned on in a dark room, and I was so confused. Even though I knew how I was beginning to feel, I denied it."

He reached out for her hand again. "When I heard you were going back to DarkSkull, I couldn't bear for you to be on your own again. I thought at least having a familiar face with you would help."

"Why did you care so much?" she asked. "You didn't even like me back then."

"It's true, you were stubborn and proud and so damned caught up in your own little dream world," he said, a teasing smile tugging at his mouth.

"Thanks." She scowled.

He sobered. "Do you remember my tenth birthday?"

"Should I?"

"My father beat me that morning. I think I had accidentally spilled wine in his study the night before."

Of course! Alyx nodded as the memories came back. "I remember. Cayr and I came over to help prepare for your birthday picnic. You were limping and you had a massive bruise on your cheek. You said you fell over, but I knew you were lying."

"Your father was there too, he'd brought you in his carriage." Dashan chuckled. "In front of all of us, you demanded that he 'repri-mand Dash's father at once' because he'd hurt me."

"Did I? I don't remember that."

"You practically threw a tantrum. You were furious, especially when your father told you to behave and be quiet. That only made you angrier."

"I remember being angry," she mused. "I didn't remember why until now."

"That was my best birthday ever, until this year."

She looked at him in surprise. "Why? You were hurt."

"You were only seven years old, but on that day you made me believe that there was someone in the world that cared about me, really cared, enough to get so angry I was hurt that she even yelled at her adored father." Dashan's eyes were dark.

"I didn't realise... " she trailed off at the implication of his words.

"How could you?" he said. "But I loved you from that moment. I knew that I never had a chance, but I loved you. Alyx, I've loved you since I was ten years old."

Alyx stared at him, unable to speak for a long moment because her heart was so full.

"I was a fool," she said. "A stupid fool."

"A beautiful fool." He smiled at her, then sighed. "This whole Taliath thing is the absolute worst rotten luck."

She grinned. "I don't know. I am a wealthy noblewoman. If you weren't all muscular and handsome and such a skilled fighter, I probably wouldn't have looked twice at you."

His laughter rang warmly through the night air. "In that case, I am suddenly very glad that I'm a Taliath." He paused, sobering. "How sure are you that only us sleeping together could result in you becoming invulnerable?"

She winced. "Pretty sure. It's a risk, us being in close proximity, but Shakar is the only one that ever managed it, so it's impossible to know for certain."

His eyes fixed on hers. "And how certain are you that becoming invulnerable is really that terrible? And don't even try to tell me it would automatically turn you into an evil monster."

Her own thoughts on that had become increasingly complicated, and he waited patiently while she tried to find the words to explain. "Nobody starts out as an evil monster, Dash. They become that way because of circumstances and the choices they make." She hesitated. "I almost attacked Finn with my magic."

"Alyx," he murmured. "The key word there being almost. Have some faith in yourself."

"It's not just that. The council would kill us in a heartbeat if they found out. They wouldn't hesitate for a second. And Tarrick and the twins, even Cario, they would try to protect us. Cayr too. I won't put their lives in danger like that."

He nodded thoughtfully. "I do understand that. And while the others are my friends, you are my entire world, mage-girl. If hiding our relationship and being apart keeps you safe, then I'll do both willingly."

"We're going to be apart anyway," she said sadly. "I have to go back to the council, and you need to learn to be a Taliath."

Dashan slid down until he was lying flat out on the deck, pulling her down beside him. She curled up around his body, sighing in contentment as his warm arms came around her.

"It won't be forever," he murmured, kissing her on the forehead. "It's been a long day. Sleep, Alyx."

"Wait a second," she mumbled as she relaxed against him. "If you've loved me since you were ten, why did you keep pulling my hair until you were fifteen?"

He laughed, his chest vibrating pleasantly against her ear. "Because it was fun."

ALYX BLINKED bright sunlight from her eyes as Dashan woke her with a gentle touch. She'd slept a lot in the four days they'd been sailing, her mind and body recovering from Casovar's torture and her overuse of magic in the battle against him. At first she hadn't been able to sleep without waking screaming from nightmares, nor had she been able to stop the trembling in her hands whenever she thought about what had happened. At least the nightmares had been normal ones, and not instigated by Shakar.

"You were muttering in your sleep." He squatted beside her on the deck, worry in his dark eyes.

"I was dreaming about Casovar," she replied, sitting up and stretching. "Thanks for waking me. Is it time to eat?"

"We're only a few hours' sail from our destination, but it's not long till sunset, so I'd prefer to anchor here for the night."

"Okay." Alyx rose to her feet and looked around them. She could just make out the hazy outline of the western Rionnan coast in the distance, but otherwise they were surrounded by the blue of the ocean.

As the sun set over the horizon, they ate their dinner of freshly grilled fish and the stale remains of the bread Dashan had brought with him.

"How are you?" he asked.

"Better than I was," she said, and it was true.

Over the previous four days, she'd told him bits and pieces of what had happened to her—the way Casovar had ravaged her mind and tainted her memories of everything good, how she couldn't think of that night they'd danced together at DarkSkull without feeling Casovar's scorn as he'd rifled through that memory.

The first time she'd spoken of it, Dashan had tensed in anger, his body literally vibrating with the desire to do something, anything, to Casovar. But the lord-mage was dead, and Dashan quickly learned that all Alyx really needed was his hand in hers, and the warmth of his love.

But it wasn't all about Casovar. Throughout the sunny days and into the nights they talked about everything, conversations ranging from the most inconsequential and light-hearted things, to their deepest fears and concerns.

Dashan told Alyx of his fear that he would never be good enough, that he would fail when it mattered most. She told him of her fear that she'd never be strong enough to face down Shakar.

The long hours of sleep and rest, combined with warm sunshine, good, simple food and Dashan's unwavering reassurance had worked wonders. The trembling of her hands faded, and the memories caused her less pain when she thought of them. Parting from him she dreaded, but this time they'd had together she would hold onto always.

"If you need more time—"

"No." She shook her head. "We have too little time as it is. I need to get back to Alistriem as soon as possible."

He sighed, settling back against the prow. "And I need to get to ShadowFall Island."

She heard the words he didn't say. "You're not running away," she said firmly. "You can better protect yourself against the council if you're trained. Besides, you're the one who told me there might be things you can learn about Shakar on the island. He spent a year training there, after all."

"I know all that," he said. "I hate the idea of leaving you alone, that's all."

"I hate it too," she said quietly.

353

• • •

THE SMALL BOAT approached the town as the morning sun turned the ocean a bright turquoise, a stiff breeze filling the sails and increasing their speed. With a few deft turns of the sail, Dashan aimed them towards the smaller of two jetties jutting out from the coastline.

Buildings clustered on the hillside leading down to the shore, and other fishing boats bobbed at anchor close to the jetties. People walked through the streets, others down by the beach. A group of children were swimming under the watchful eye of two adults not far from the larger jetty.

"Welcome to the town of Ester." Dashan appeared beside her at the prow. "Is he there?"

She nodded, pointing towards the tall figure standing on the road running along the shore, only a few paces away from the beginning of the jetty.

"Good." But he sounded sad, echoing the melancholy she felt at their imminent parting. He squeezed her shoulder, then returned to the sails.

In a short time, Dashan had them bumping gently up against the jetty. He jumped gracefully from the boat and onto the deck, looking around watchfully before turning back to Alyx.

"Pass me the mooring rope."

Alyx picked up the heavy coil of rope, and was working out the best way of tossing it to him when she heard him sigh.

"It's rope, not a snake. Stop worrying about breaking a nail and throw it up here."

"I am not worried about breaking a nail." She scowled.

He grinned, deepening her irritation. "I know you. Look at you there in your perfectly tailored mage uniform. Of course you're worried about breaking a nail."

Alyx threw the rope at him with more force than was necessary, but he only laughed as he caught it and wrapped it around the mooring iron.

"Let's go, mage-girl." He leaned over to give her a hand off the boat, but she ignored it with a sniff and jumped by herself. Her mage powers were still a little unsteady so she didn't try flying.

"You are a very irritating man."

"But you love me anyway." He caught her hand.

"I was clearly experiencing a moment of madness when I told you that." She tugged her hand from his and crossed her arms over her chest.

"You're cute when you're angry with me."

"You're not cute in any sense of the word."

Dashan threw his head back and laughed, before swinging his arm around her shoulders and pulling her into his side. "I adore you, Alyx Egalion."

Unable to hold on to her irritation, Alyx smiled and pressed closer to him for a moment before stepping away. "You're staying?"

"No. I've got enough supplies to get me to ShadowFall."

She took a deep breath. "I suppose this is it, then."

Eyes dark, he kissed her. For a long time, there was only the feel of him, and the joy of them both together. Eventually he pulled back, his hands framing her face.

"You go and do what you need to do. Remember always that I love you and I'm thinking about you." He kissed her again. "As soon as I can, I'll come to you. I promise."

"I'll be waiting," she whispered.

"Stay safe," he said. "For me."

Alyx smiled through her tears. "If you promise me the same, we have a deal, Dashan Caverlock."

CHAPTER 38

L adan was watching the departing boat as Alyx reached the end of the small jetty and joined him. He was silent for a moment, then, "I was expecting Dashan."

She hid her amusement in a sniff. "He brought me instead. Sorry to disappoint you."

He considered that for a moment. "Not marrying Prince Cayr, then?"

"No." She shook her head.

"Good."

She fought a smile. "I'm glad you think so."

"Not that that situation is any better." He glanced meaningfully at the departing boat. "How do you always manage to get yourself in so much trouble when I'm not around?"

"Maybe you should be around more." She shrugged. "I take it you got Dashan's message?"

"He's lucky I did." Ladan was irritated. "High-handedly ordering me to leave Widow Falls while it's under constant attack to travel to this tiny village and instead of showing up himself he leaves you here."

"He knew I needed you," Alyx said simply. "What do big brothers do?"

His entire face softened. "All right, Aly-girl. Let's go."

She scrambled to keep up with his long stride as he headed towards the town. It wasn't long before they reached an inn. Two high quality horses stood tied up out front, bulging saddlebags on their backs. "We can rest here tonight, if you like. Start out tomorrow."

She shook her head. "Let's start out today. Which one's mine?"

He pointed to the chestnut on the left before crossing to the other horse and mounting in one smooth movement.

"We need to work on your conversation skills," she grumbled. "Where are we going?"

"A small town called Apara. That's as far as I could track him. It's about

two days' ride from here." He turned his horse and urged him into a canter down the street. Smiling to herself, Alyx mounted and spurred her horse after him.

"ARE you going to tell me what happened?" he asked that night as they camped by the ocean. The firelight flickered over his features, accentuating the hard lines of his face. Nodding, she settled back into her blankets and told him everything, succinctly and without emotion.

"Casovar kidnapped you," he repeated into the silence that followed the end of her tale.

"Yes."

"He's dead?"

"Yes."

A beat of silence, then, "You're okay?"

"Not really. But I will be."

He made a gesture towards the ocean. "He helped you?"

"More than I can ever say."

Another silence. "This trip we're on. It's really that important?"

"I have no evidence for it, but instinct tells me that learning the circumstances of our mother's death could be crucial. At the very least, if we can confirm she did learn that Shakar is still alive, it will help us convince the council."

"And how is the council going to defeat Shakar when they couldn't the first time, and this time they've hunted down and killed their strongest allies—the Taliath?"

"If you've got a better idea, I'd like to hear it."

"I do have a better idea." A stubborn look filled his face. "I say forget the council. Their motivations are dubious at best, and they're corrupt and impotent. In my book, they're not a huge step above Shakar in terms of morality. Leave them. Do this yourself."

"Defeat Shakar myself?" Incredulity filled her voice. "Me and what army of mages?"

"What army of mages do you have with the council? Ones you can't trust? Ones who would kill you if they knew who you loved." Bitterness filled his voice. For the first time Alyx realised how deep her brother's antagonism towards the council ran.

"I will never forgive the council for what they've done," she said gently. "But this is greater than me. Shakar won't only kill mages. He'll kill innocents too. The council can bring all the mage warriors and expertise together in a way that I can't. We have no choice but to work with them."

"I understand your logic, but one day I think you're going to find I'm right." He stood. "Get some sleep. I'll take first watch."

THEY REACHED Apara the next day, and inquiries in town led them to the farm of the local named Terin. Alyx and Ladan left the horses at the farmhouse and walked through the fields. The property was characteristic for southern Rionn, set amidst rolling emerald plains under a clear sky. In the far distance, the ocean sparkled in the afternoon sun.

A man worked alone in one of the fields, the trickle of his magic clear as day to Alyx as he hunched over a row of failing wheat. He wore scuffed breeches and shirt, his boots careworn leather. A shock of grey hair spilled out from under a green cap, and as they drew closer, she could make out a grizzled beard and large, tanned hands.

"Are you Terin?" Ladan called out.

He started violently, so focused on his work that their arrival was a complete surprise. A suspicious frown deepened wrinkles on a leathery face as he brushed soil from his hands and rose to his feet.

"Who's asking?"

"My name is Alyx. This is my brother, Ladan."

It was impossible to miss the flare of recognition that flashed across the man's face and she relaxed slightly—this was who they were looking for. He wasn't tall, his back stooped from years of farming, and he didn't wear a mage robe. There was no staff in sight, either.

"What do you want?"

"You know who we are, don't you?" Ladan stepped forward, one hand resting on the hilt of his sword.

"You look like her." This was directed at Alyx, then, as he looked at Ladan, an already grumpy tone turned downright terse. "And you look like him."

Ladan and Alyx shared a quick look—he didn't like their father?

"We have some questions for you. Will you talk to us?" Alyx asked. "It's important."

Terin turned around to pick up his shovel. "I'll talk to you."

THE HOUSE WAS as careworn as its owner, but neat and tidy. Terin waved them to chairs in the sitting room, but didn't offer food or drink. Alyx and Ladan stayed silent as he settled into a chair opposite them, giving him time to collect his thoughts.

"I knew your mother at DarkSkull," he said eventually, his gaze distant, lost in memories. "It's not much fun being a lesser mage there. Plant magic is far from lesser, in my opinion. But I always wanted to be a farmer, and that means nothing in the mage world. So lesser I was."

"Our mother wasn't," Ladan said.

"No." Terin's expression cleared. "She was everything the order idolised. Not that she cared about that."

"You knew my stepfather, too? Hodin?"

"I did. Those two were close. They were second year apprentices when I started, but their master—Astor, I think?—I never met him... anyway, he'd just left DarkSkull to take up a different post, and their new master was the same as mine and he sometimes combined our classes. My magic didn't break out until the end of that first year, even though I was one of the oldest initiates ever to go to DarkSkull.

Temari and Hodin had time for me, even though everyone else shunned me."

"You know that she died?" Alyx asked.

Abruptly Terin's face closed over, and he gave a casual shrug. "I heard when everyone else did. I was a council mage until I retired a couple of years ago."

"She met with you right before she disappeared. What did you tell her?" Ladan asked.

"I don't know what you're talking about."

Ladan's face darkened. Alyx reached out to touch his arm, speaking before he could. "Terin, Shakar is alive."

His reaction was barely noticeable this time, but it was there. "That's insanity. He's long dead."

Ladan shook off Alyx's hand and rose to his feet, hand returning to his sword. "He's not, and you know it. I have no time to mess around, old man. What did you tell our mother all those years ago?"

"Are you threatening me?"

"You're damn right I am." Ladan stepped forward and hauled Terin to his feet. "Start talking. Now!"

Alyx considered protesting, but doubted she would have any effect on Ladan when he was in one of these moods. Besides, they needed to know what Terin knew.

"I usually let your mother know when I was in the region on council business. She wrote to me soon after arriving at Widow Falls so I knew she was there. The last time I wrote to her I never heard back. A couple of months later I heard she'd died," Terin said. "That's all I know."

"He's lying because he's afraid," Alyx said flatly, allowing her magic to seep out through her hands. A bright green glow lit them up, and Terin's gaze was drawn inexorably to it. "I'm just like my mother, Terin, so you know I can take the truth from your mind if I wanted to. I'd prefer not to go that route, but I will if you don't start telling us the truth."

His eyes challenged her. "We all learn to shield at DarkSkull."

"You want to test me?" She raised an eyebrow. "Because I am confident I can break through your shield in seconds. It will hurt." She gentled her voice. "You have good reason to be scared, we understand. But you know as well as we do that Shakar being alive means people are going to die. Mages have already died. I want to stop that and I need your help to do it."

He let out a breath and dropped back into his chair, shoulders slumped in defeat. "My parents were both mages who fought in the war against Shakar. While they were away fighting, they left me in the care of friends in a temporary camp near Serrin. Shakar found the place and attacked. I was three years old. They hid me in a wine cask. I heard everything that happened. I felt the magic that was unleashed. I felt his magic. I never forgot that night. I was barely three years old, but being so utterly terrified? So completely sure you're about to die? That's not something you ever forget."

Alyx glanced at her brother, putting the pieces quickly together. 'You felt his magic again, didn't you? It was you who told our mother Shakar was still alive."

Terin nodded. "I was sent into northern Shivasa by the council, ostensibly to work on a failing farm for a few months, but they also wanted me to collect information on the activities of the Shiven army in the region. I made it a habit to drink of an evening in the local inn frequented by soldiers. One night I walked in the door and I felt it, the trickle of his magic. The shock was so profound it was like ice freezing over my veins. I wanted to run and never look back, but figured he would notice that. So I walked inside, ordered my drink and sat at a table in a corner of the room, pretending like I wasn't more terrified than I'd ever been in my life." He shuddered, eyes bleak with remembered terror. "He didn't stay long, but they were the longest minutes I've ever experienced."

"And he never knew you were there?" Alyx murmured.

"No. I had my shield up the whole damn time and I sat as far from him as I possibly could."

"Then what did you do?"

"When my assignment was over I went to Widow Falls. By then, I'd begun to wonder if maybe I'd imagined the whole thing. I knew for sure the council would laugh me out of the room if I tried to tell them about it. But your mother... when I told her, the look on her face."

Terin shook his head slowly. "It was as if suddenly everything made complete and utter sense to her. She believed me. I tried to argue with her, point out all the reasons it couldn't be true, but she was adamant. Temari was the most stubborn person I've ever met, and once she got an idea into her head..."

"What did she do?" Ladan asked when Terin's voice trailed off.

"She said that Shakar must be behind the disappearing mages." Terin took a breath. "Foolish woman. She thought that by facing him, by killing him, she could go back to her family. I tried so hard to reason with her. She listened to me at first, even wrote a letter to the new head of DarkSkull."

"What changed her mind?" The grim anger in Ladan's voice had momentarily been replaced by a note of yearning, a need to know what had happened to his beloved mother.

"She argued that Shakar was old and the fact she knew him would make it easier to get him alone. Then she would have the upper hand. Plus the advantage of surprise." Terin shook his head. "Even then I wasn't convinced—he'd outwitted the council and stayed alive all these years, surely that made him even more dangerous. But she was desperate to go home, she missed Garan so much... she missed you, Alyx."

Tears filled her eyes as emotion hit her like a punch in the gut. Beside her, Ladan had gone still.

"She... " Alyx cleared her throat. "He killed her, then."

"I assume so." Terin's eyes closed. "The last time I saw her, she was heading off to face him."

"Why didn't you ever tell anyone? The council?" Ladan demanded. "If you've known all this time he was alive, how could you keep that to yourself? Mages have been dying!"

"I was terrified. If he killed Temari, and he knew I knew? He would come for me too."

"You're a coward."

"Ladan, be kind," Alyx said sharply. "You think the council would have listened to him if he went to them with a story of feeling Shakar's magic? When he was three when it first happened?"

"They would have listened if he told them our mother went after him and ended up dead," Ladan said. "Who else could kill a mage of the higher order?"

He was right, but it was too late now to assign blame. They needed to focus on how this information helped them. Alyx sat back in her chair, thinking. "What made my mother think she could track down Shakar? How did she know where to look?"

Terin's gaze darted between them, the fear in it unmistakable.

"Tell us." Ladan's voice was granite.

"She made me show her the memories of what I'd seen and heard in Shivasa." Terin let out a long breath, as if letting go of something he'd been holding in a long time. "She recognised something about the man I'd seen. Not his face, I never saw that, but a mannerism, I think."

Alyx sucked in a breath. "Are you telling us she recognised him?"

A sharp nod. "She wouldn't tell me who. Didn't want to put me in more danger. But she said it was someone she knew, someone from the mage world. She said he must have been hiding himself, changed his appearance, maybe even used magic to do it."

Alyx and her brother looked at each other. Now they had something. A real lead. Shakar wasn't a man who'd been hiding for decades, no, he'd walked amongst the mage council. People would know him.

"We have to go." Ladan stood. "Thank you for answering our questions."

"We all know I should have come forward earlier." Terin was looking at his feet. "Good luck with what you have to do next."

Alyx paused at the doorway, looking back. Terin had sagged into his chair, looking old and beaten. "Terin?"

"Yes?"

"She really wanted to go home?"

Terin gave them a sad smile. "More than anything else in the world. Being apart from Garan was killing her."

"Did you know the reason she left us, why she went to Widow Falls?"

Something flickered in his eyes, a spark of bitterness that brought life back to his features. "The damned Mage Council and their terror of the Taliath. Yeah, I knew."

"Killing Shakar wouldn't have solved her problem with the council."

"She thought it would. She figured if she could destroy Shakar for good this time, save all those lives, the council would have to leave her and Garan alone."

"Is that why you don't like him? Because he could have made her invulnerable and put her at risk?"

Terin barked out a laugh, genuine mirth in it. "He did make her invulnerable. She had Taliath ability from the first moment they became lovers, only the council was too stupid to figure out she was hiding it from them."

Alyx froze, shock spearing through her. "What?"

"That's the real reason she left you," he sobered. "She knew they'd figure it out eventually, and then they'd come for her and Garan both. Running and hiding was the only chance she had to keep you all alive."

She swallowed back tears as Ladan's hand landed reassuringly on her shoulder. "So the council was right about how Shakar became invulnerable?"

"Temari thought they were. She absorbed nothing from your father before they became lovers." Terin's gaze turned distant. "Garan Egalion was everything I wasn't. Tall, handsome, confident. The finest Taliath of his generation. The last Taliath, now."

"Not the last." Ladan said quietly.

CHAPTER 39

Ladan left reluctantly, a day's travel from Alistriem, to return to Widow Falls. They fought about it, a fight Alyx won after she pointed out that first, she could look after herself, and second, nobody knew where she was and therefore the chances of being attacked were low. She didn't tell him about Shakar's threat of sending his Hunters after her.

"You need to make sure Widow Falls is secure," she added. "The border crossing near Tregaya could become critical."

He left in a huff after extracting a promise that she would send a message as soon as she returned safely home. She went to an inn for the night, almost enjoying being alone as she sat at the bar eating dinner. The separation from Dashan was already painful, but she pushed that away. He would come back to her in time, and until then she needed to concentrate on Shakar, and learning how to defeat him.

ALYX APPROACHED Alistriem just after midday the following day, turning Ladan's horse away from the city and up the road towards the palace. The Bluecoats on the front gates of her home were clearly taken-aback at the sight of her, and she smiled a greeting but didn't linger to chat.

Safia was nowhere to be seen as Alyx stepped into the empty foyer. There she paused—the house was silent, indicating nobody was home, and she debated whether to go straight to the palace and see if her father was there or wash and change first.

Just as she'd decided to go and get Tingo to ride over to the palace, a door slammed down the hall and moments later her father appeared, moving with quick strides into the foyer. He was so deep in thought he didn't notice her until he was halfway to the door.

"Hello, Papa." She smiled at the surprise on his face. "Did you miss me?"

"Aly-girl," he said in astonishment, jogging towards her. "You're back."

"I am." She threw her arms around him with a laugh, and he hugged her back tightly.

"Where have you been? How have you been? What on earth possessed you to disappear like that?"

"I've been travelling, looking for information." She answered his questions one by one. "But I wasn't well when I left and I needed the time away to heal."

A shadow flickered across his face. "And now?"

"Now I'm on the mend," she assured him.

He hugged her again, the fierceness of it betraying the depth of his worry. "I'm glad."

When he finally let her go, she stepped back and arched an eyebrow, trying to lighten the mood. "Even though I must have caused a huge scandal before I left? Surely I've totally humiliated the family name?"

"Yes, well, your killing of Lord-Mage Casovar did cause some mutterings, though the people on the streets are singing our praises for getting rid of the Mage Guard."

"That's not what I'm talking about."

Garan eyed her, then let out a resigned breath. "Right. You mean the fact that you broke your betrothal to Cayr and vanished from the city? Well, for a start, we haven't made any official announcements, so nobody is sure what happened. Including your dear father."

"Are you asking me what happened?"

"I think I can probably guess. The happiness shining out of your eyes is unmistakable to a father, and I'm supposing I can attribute that to a certain young Taliath?"

"I know you don't approve," she said. "I am sorry for that. What if I just say that I haven't done anything irresponsible, and that I was also with Ladan, and leave it at that?"

He turned grave. "The truth is, I like Dashan. He has more than proven himself a capable, honourable young man, and I would like him only for that look of happiness he's put on your face. But I've been through the same thing with your mother, and I know the danger you're putting yourself in. I fear for you both. Still, I trust you to do the right thing."

"I knew I loved you for a reason," she said cheekily. "How have things been here?"

"Slowly improving. Sparky and Caverlock have regained full control of the army and Blue Guard and the king has formally disbanded the Mage Guard. Only just in time, too, because the disputed area has essentially turned into a battleground. Shakar is a formidable commander, and Shivasa isn't even pretending to respect the old rules anymore. I fear our northern border will soon be under real threat."

Alyx hesitated. "And Tarrick and the others?"

"You'll probably find them at the A'ndreas home," Garan said. "They've been assisting Sparky and the king. That Tarrick of yours has a sharp military mind, and Cario is quite the diplomat."

"I'd best go and speak to them," she said. "But first, are you heading over to the palace?"

"I was."

"There's something we should talk about before you go. Casovar inadvertently told me something interesting while he was..." Garan's face darkened, and she hurried on before he could start dwelling on her capture. His pain would only re-awaken hers. "Anyway, I have an idea of how to use the information, but I'll need your help."

"I'm intrigued." He smiled. "Let's get you something to eat in the kitchens and you can tell me all about it."

TINGO WAS EXCITED to see Alyx and almost wrenched her arms out of their sockets trying to run away with her down the road. It took several minutes and the firmest tone she could manage to calm him so that he stopped fighting the reins.

The twins' mother answered the door, smiling at Alyx's question as to whether the twins were home. "They are, Lady Egalion. Please come in and I'll show you through."

All the way down the hall, Alyx wrestled with her anxiousness. This wasn't going to be pleasant. At a gesture from the twins' mother, Alyx stepped through into the large front room, projecting calm confidence. Tarrick and Finn sat on the single sofa, their attention on papers lying on the table before them. Dawn sat opposite them, looking equally focused on whatever was being discussed. Cario was absent.

"Hello," she spoke into the room.

"Alyx!" Finn was the first to speak, his expression mingling surprise and something else she couldn't name. He glanced over at his sister.

Dawn looked weary, and there was an inflection of sadness in her words when she spoke. "We've been worried about you. I'm glad to see you well."

Tarrick rose to his feet, features settled firmly in a scowl. "What were you thinking to walk away like that? Where have you been?"

"I was with Ladan. He found Terin, and we went to talk to him."

Eager interest flashed over Finn's face, but Tarrick spoke first, anger filling his voice. "You've been gone for over a week, leaving the rest of us here to worry about you without even knowing when you'd be back. Did you consider us at all?"

"I had to go." She couldn't keep the edge from her voice as some of her recently buried pain trickled out. "I promised Dawn I'd be back soon and I meant it. And I didn't leave on a jaunt. Ladan and I talked to Terin, and what he told us is enough to convince the council about Shakar."

This time Finn got in first. "What did you find?"

She gave them a full run down. "We have to assume my mother found Shakar and he killed her."

Tarrick sighed. "You should have spoken to us before leaving, allowed me at least to come with you."

"You cut me off," Dawn added, fire flashing in her blue eyes. "You could have reached out at any time to let us know you were okay and you didn't. That's not how friends treat each other."

Alyx winced as the words hit home. Her only excuse—that Dawn would have known she was with Dashan if she'd reached out—certainly wouldn't help the situation.

"I know," she said as gracefully as she could manage. "What I did was poor behaviour, and I apologise."

A moment's silence, then Dawn's searching gaze. "Are you all right?"

"I wasn't." The most honest words she'd spoken to them yet. "What he did to me... I needed to go, just for a short time, and I needed my brother."

A short silence, then Dawn spoke, her voice aching with resignation. "There was a time we could have helped you. And I know that finding out about the council murdering Taliath has come between us, and the revelation that Dash is a Taliath made things even worse. But if we don't find a way to work past this, how can we hope to defeat Shakar?"

"It's not up to us to defeat Shakar," Tarrick said bluntly. "That's the council's job."

"He's right," Alyx agreed. "And we need to help them do that, so first we have to finish our training."

"Back to DarkSkull?" Finn asked.

Tarrick gave a short nod. "Warning the council and finishing our training are our first priorities. We can work on the other stuff later."

"Agreed," Finn said, relief evident in his voice.

Alyx glanced at Dawn, reaching out with her magic "I know you're right, but I don't know what to do about it. We just have to take it one step at a time."

Dawn gave a little nod, then forced a smile to her face. "When do we leave? I'm hankering for dawn breakfasts already."

Alyx matched her smile. "Give me a day to reassure myself things are steady here, and then we leave."

They would be fine. In time.

CARIO FOUND Alyx later that night as she sat in her father's study. A warm fire crackled in the grate, and she sipped at a glass of his finest spirits.

"I just came from the twins' home. They told me you were back." His voice came from the doorway. "Mind if I join you?"

"Please. We should talk."

Cario nodded and poured himself a glass before crossing to lean idly against the stone fireplace. He turned the glass over in his hand, gaze far away as he studied its contents.

"We're going back to DarkSkull," she said. "Leaving tomorrow. What will you do?"

He smiled faintly. "Come with you. Once Romas learns what happened, how you defeated Casovar, none of you will be apprentices anymore. Whatever happens next, I'll follow."

She relaxed. She'd been more worried than she'd realised that Cario would want to leave again.

"They were terribly worried for you," he said after a moment.

"I know."

"The thought crossed my mind that you might have run off with Dashan." Cario's expression gave away nothing of what he felt about that.

She frowned, injecting confusion into her voice. "Why would you think I would do that?"

"Because you're in love with him."

For a moment she debated denying it, pretending she had no idea what he was talking about. Instead, she raised her eyebrows, challenging him. "And if I had run off with Dashan?"

He shrugged slightly. "You told me that you accepted me for who I am, even the bits you don't like."

"I meant it."

"In that case, I can accept you for who you are, including the bit where you are a mage of the higher order in a relationship with a Taliath."

Alyx stilled, meeting his intense blue gaze, wanting so badly to believe him. "Cario, I'm going to need someone to trust, someone who knows everything and can accept it. Someone who can trust me in return."

He pushed away from the fireplace and sat down in the chair beside hers. Carefully, he reached out to place his glass down on the table nearby. Then, he met her eyes.

"Tell me everything, Alyx. You do that, and I am your man."

ALYX SIGHED in resignation when Cario left for bed only to have her father appear in the doorway.

"I saw the light on and hoped you were still up," he said, coming in. "I did what we talked about earlier, including speaking discreetly with Casta and Tijer. The guards are waiting on your word now."

Alyx gave a little smile. "I think I might leave it until tomorrow."

Garan gave her a knowing look, but didn't say anything. She stifled a yawn. Her conversation with Cario hadn't done anything to lessen her weariness. "Have a seat, Papa. There's something you need to know."

He took a seat in the chair Cario had vacated, stretching his long legs out towards the fire. Her eyes travelled the handsome planes of his face, the wrinkles around his eyes and mouth, the grey in his temples. Then she thought about spending twenty years without Dashan, thinking he didn't love her as much as she did him, and her heart broke a little.

"I'm going back to DarkSkull tomorrow."

He said nothing for a moment, then gave a little nod. "I'd hoped it wouldn't be so soon, but I accept that you're going back. I want you to know that I understand now who and what you've become, and I'm prouder of you than I can ever say. I'm sorry it took me so long."

She reached out to squeeze his hand, another weight falling from her shoulders. "There's something else I have to tell you, Papa. My mother left us and went to Lord Hodin Mirren because he was her best friend. They were together at DarkSkull, an odd pair that didn't quite fit in. DarkSkull, it forges friendships like that," she said. "That's what I have with Tarrick and the twins. Cario too."

"I see that now," he said, eyes intent on her face. "And I'm sorry I didn't before."

She shook her head. "You don't understand... my mother went to Hodin because he was the one person in the world she trusted apart from you. And he took her in and protected her at Widow Falls for the same reason. But they weren't in love. They were friends."

"Aly-girl, I—"

"Let me finish." She raised a hand. "She wanted to come home to us, to you. That's what I learned while I was away. She had another friend, Terin. He learned that Shakar might still be alive, and when he told her... she knew instantly. She knew he was behind the mages disappearing, knew he was the threat to us."

"She went to face him." Garan's voice was hoarse, emotion darkening his eyes.

"Terin said he tried to stop her, tried to tell her she was being foolish. But she wouldn't listen. He said it was killing her being apart from you, that she was desperate to come home. She wanted her family back so badly it clouded her judgement."

Tears streamed down Alyx's face as she spoke. She wished so badly she could remember her mother, a mother who'd loved her, who'd died because she loved her so much.

Her father lifted a hand to cover his face, his shoulders beginning to shake. "Could you give me a moment alone, Aly-girl?"

"Of course." She leaned over to kiss him on the top of his head. "I love you, Papa. She did too."

As Alyx walked out of the room and down the hall, her father's whispered words followed her.

"Oh Temari, I should never have let you go."

CHAPTER 40

Alyx awoke suddenly, the murmur of her father's voice in her ear. Her eyes flashed open to see him hovering in the dimness by her bed.

"Several unidentified armed men coming over the south wall," he murmured.

Instantly she reached out with telepathic magic, scanning the surroundings of her home but finding only familiar minds. "How do you—"

"Taliath ability, no time to explain," he cut her off. "Can you warn your friends?"

Alyx rolled out of bed, pulled on boots and robe and called her staff to her hand. It glimmered faintly in the darkness as some of her power leaked into it. *"Dawn, I think we're under attack. I can't sense anyone but my father is certain."*

Her friend had been asleep, but it didn't take her groggy mind long to assimilate Alyx's words. *"I'm waking Finn now. Tarrick's sleeping here tonight. We'll be there as soon as we can."*

"No, stay where you are, but pack your things. If this is what I think it is, we need to leave the city tonight. I'll come for you soon."

To her credit, Dawn merely acknowledged her instructions and broke away.

"Cario!" Alyx prodded his sleeping mind next. "My room. Now!"

"You reached them?" Garan asked as Alyx's eyes flew open.

"Yes. Cario's coming to us. How many of them are there? I can't sense anything with my magic."

"Hard to tell, the sense I get isn't precise." Garan spun, sword flashing, as Alyx's door opened, but it was only Cario, fully dressed and holding his staff.

"What's going on?"

"An attack," Alyx said tersely. "I can't sense them but Papa can."

"We're sitting targets here, let's go," Garan said, making for the door.

They'd just about made it to the door when the glass of all three bedroom windows exploded inwards simultaneously. Alyx reacted instinctively. Swinging her body around in front of her father, she held out her staff and erected her mage shield just in time. Deadly shards of flying glass hit the shield and dissolved into dust.

A cold night breeze blew into the room, bringing with it several warriors swinging through the broken windows. Moonlight glinted from their naked blades.

"Papa, run!" Alyx shoved him away, her first instinct to protect her father.

By the time she swung back around, the first attacker was on her, his blade swinging at her head. Alyx brought her staff up, countered the blow, and sent the sword swinging from the man's hand. Before the next one could come at her, she raised her hand and summoned the power to send a blast of concussive energy at them.

Nothing happened.

Cursing, she tried again. Nothing. Her mind flew back to the hut where Casovar had held her, the sinking panic of not being able to reach her magic. By then her moment of reprieve was over and the closest warrior lunged. She backed up rapidly, studying her opponents. They were dressed head to toe in black, with a single silver medallion hanging from their necks. One of them swung right by her face as she ducked desperately to avoid another swiping blade.

Alyx swore again. She was competent with her staff, but not enough to take down a room of clearly-skilled swordsman. That realisation ran through her head in the seconds it took for another one to come at her. She lifted her staff to block but was beaten to it as her father's sword slid into the space. He stepped up beside her, flicked his wrist, and the enemy's blade went flying.

"I am a Taliath, remember?"

"Right." She smiled, despite the circumstances. "Back to back?"

"Sounds good."

"Alyx?" Cario hovered by the door. "My magic isn't working!"

"I know. Go and see if the servants' stairwell and side exit down to the stables is clear," she called back as she ducked under a flashing blade and came up swinging.

Never in her life had Alyx been so glad of Master Howell and Dark-Skull's insistence that each student learn how to fight with a staff and no magic. It was disconcerting, being in a fight without access to her mage power. The warriors attacking them were extremely good. She weaved, ducked and twisted, lashing out with her staff when she had an opportunity, but finding it hard against so many opponents at once. During one brief flash of respite, Alyx looked up and noticed more coming through the windows.

"It's clear!" Cario's voice cut over the sound of clashing steel.

"Good—get down to the stables and ready the horses! We'll fight our way clear and meet you there."

Several moments of desperate fighting followed, weariness beginning to tug at her in the burning muscles of her arms and breath rasping in her chest. Then Garan managed to briefly clear a path to the door.

"You first," he said, stepping forward to take the brunt of the attack. "I'll be right behind you!"

Alyx swept her staff outwards, lunging forward at the nearest warrior and giving herself space to run for the door. A glance backwards showed her father swiftly dispatching the two swordsmen nearest him before following her into the hall.

They sprinted through an open door at the opposite end of the floor, and Alyx paused on the other side, gaze searching the dimness around them. This far from the warriors, she could access her magic, and used it to slam the door shut behind them before dragging a nearby wooden chest over to block it. Just as it fell into place, her magic vanished. Loud thumping came from the other side of the door.

"Come on," she panted. "We have to get to the stables."

"Any reason you didn't use magic back there?" Garan asked, breathing fast but still easy.

"Something is blocking it. I think it's the medallions they're all wearing," Alyx panted. "The range on them isn't far, but close enough, they completely stifled my magic."

"That's reassuring," Garan said mildly.

They pounded down the servants' stairwell and burst out into the cold night air. Pebbles from the drive crunched under their boots as they ran for the stables, Garan's long strides quickly outdistancing Alyx.

The stable door flew open, almost collecting Garan, and Cario appeared leading Tingo. The stallion was yanking hard on the reins, clearly picking up on Cario's urgency.

"I've got him!" Alyx shouted, grabbing Tingo's bridle and leading him away from the door. The stallion snorted unhappily, but stopped fighting her hold. By the time she'd swung into the saddle, Cario had led Garan's horse out and was heading back in for his own.

The moment Cario reappeared she turned Tingo's head and urged him into a gallop for the gates. Black-clad warriors came spilling out of the front doors, but the three horses were already disappearing through the gates.

DAWN, Finn and Tarrick were mounted and waiting in the street outside the twins' home when Alyx, Garan and Cario came racing up. The street was otherwise empty, most of the houses dark as their occupants slept.

"What the hell happened?" Tarrick demanded.

"An attack," Alyx explained as quickly as she could, then added what Shakar had threatened in her last nightmare. "I'm pretty sure they were sent by Shakar to assassinate me."

"That explains it!" Cario suddenly sat up straighter in the saddle.

"What?" They all turned to him.

"The secret behind all the mage disappearances. Nobody could ever figure out how so many mages were caught unawares, or unable to fight off whoever came for them. Shakar found himself the perfect attackers, skilled Shiven warriors with the ability to block mage power by the medallions they wear. Those poor mages wouldn't have even known they were coming."

"That makes a certain awful sense," Tarrick said.

"But that begs the question of how Alyx knew?" Dawn turned to her.

"I knew about the metal because Casovar used manacles made of it when he was holding me captive. He told me how it worked."

"Better question, how were you able to warn us tonight?" Cario asked.

"My father," she said, giving them all a pointed look. "The Taliath."

"It's a Taliath ability," Garan said into the ensuing silence. "We can sense approaching danger."

"If Shakar is hunting you, you can't go home," Dawn said. "Neither can you, Lord Egalion."

"If I leave, Papa can stay in the palace," Alyx said. "He'll be better protected, and if I'm gone, they won't go after him."

"I don't think so." Garan shook his head, glancing at his sword. "I'm not afraid, but Shakar will know that I'm a Taliath once again, as will the Mage Council. I won't be safe here much longer."

"We were planning to go back to DarkSkull anyway." Finn turned to Alyx.

"Exactly, and leaving tonight will make no difference." She regarded her father thoughtfully for a moment. "You'll come with us. I know somewhere you can go where you'll be safe and where you can do some good."

"Widow Falls?" Dawn picked up what she was thinking. "Riding fast, it won't take too long to travel via Lord Mirren's home."

"I agree." Tarrick picked up his reins, turning his horse. "Let's get moving. We should put as much distance between us and the city as we can before dawn. Who knows if the Hunters will follow us?"

"Papa, will you take Tingo for me?" Alyx swung down from the saddle. "There's something I need to do before I leave. I'll catch up to you all soon."

Tarrick scowled. "If you have some foolish idea in your head to go back and face those medallion-wearing—"

"Nothing like that." She laughed at how vehement he was. "I want to say goodbye to Cayr."

"Oh." An almost visible fission of relief went through all of them. "Don't be long."

"I won't."

ALYX ALIGHTED outside Cayr's bedroom window without a sound. Never in all her years climbing in to see Cayr had she ever thought that one day she would simply be able to fly in.

How things had changed.

He was sitting on his bed, fully clothed and studying a piece of parchment by lamplight. A rush of gladness went through her at seeing him—he would always be her dear friend, the one who used to know her best, and she was going to miss him terribly.

Surprise, and a touch of pain, flashed over his face at the sight of her, but his smile was warm and welcoming. "Alyx!"

She met him halfway across the room, going easily into his hug. "Hi."

"I've been worried about you. You're okay?"

"Getting there," she said. "How about you?"

"I've been busy," he said. "If you're asking beyond that, well, you broke my heart."

"I'm sorry."

"I know you are." He offered a sad smile and sat on the bed. Alyx joined him, searching for the right thing to say. She would never, ever regret giving herself to Dashan, but she deeply regretted hurting Cayr the way she had.

"I love you." She took his hand. "I truly do."

"Me too, Alyx. I'm going to miss having you around." His mouth quirked in a smile. "The late hour and look on your face tells me you're here to say goodbye again."

"It's necessary, I'm afraid. I was attacked earlier," she said, and then explained everything to him. "Shakar knows I'm here, so it's not safe to stay. I need to go back to DarkSkull Hall and help gather the mages to fight back."

Cayr processed that for a moment. "Where's Dash in all of this? Is he with you?"

"He's gone to ShadowFall Island in the hopes there might still be teachers there to train him as a Taliath. You and I are the only two people alive who know that," she said. "If the council finds him... "

"I'm aware," he said quietly. "And you know I'll protect him as best I can."

"We'll all protect each other." She squeezed his hand. "That's what we do."

Cayr took a breath. "My father... he's well again, but I think he lost something with what Casovar did to him. He's not the same. And we're in such danger from the Shiven, let alone Shakar."

Alyx gave him a contemplative look. He had that serious air about him again, the one she'd feared he would never have. "It was you, wasn't it, that used the City Guard to stop the Mage Guard raids?"

"I promised you I would take a serious look at their activities, and when I found the truth... " His blue eyes darkened, and she felt a sliver of sympathy—knowing all too well what it was like to have long-held illusions shattered. "But then my father sent me away so abruptly. I didn't have time to do much more than assign a trusted unit of City Guard to intercept any raids as discreetly as they could."

"You chose well," she told him. "They did a remarkable job."

"You were right to challenge me," he said, quiet dignity ringing through his words. "I won't ever forget what you said. I will be king of all Rionn."

Alyx reached up, turning his face to hers and forcing him to meet her eyes. "You don't need me or Dashan to be a great leader for Rionn. Cayr, this is your time to shine. Keep Rionn safe for me. I want a home to come back to."

His back straightened at her words, and acceptance turned his face into a sober reflection of what innocent light had once shone there

"I will."

She hugged him tightly. "Goodbye, Cayr."

"Goodbye, Alyx."

FROM CAYR'S room she made her way through the palace to a far less ornate corridor and a plainer doorway. A single Bluecoat stood outside the door.

"Lady Egalion." Tijer's narrow face creased into a relieved smile "It's good to see you."

"And you, Tijer. My father says he spoke with you and Casta?"

"He did. We'll do our best, My Lady."

Alyx paused, her hand on the doorknob. "I'm leaving tonight, and I don't know when I'll be back. Thank you, Tijer, for your protection and your friendship. I won't ever forget it."

He gave her a low, graceful bow before straightening, his hand on his heart.

"We'll miss you, Lady Egalion."

JENNA SAT BY THE FIRE, attention on the book in her lap. At Alyx's entrance, she looked up, fear flashing over her beautiful face.

"Lady Egalion."

Alyx pulled a chair over to sit opposite, then settled herself in it "Here's my first piece of advice, Jenna. Never show your fear."

Jenna frowned slightly, and she put down the book. "Why are you here? To gloat?"

"No. I'm actually here for a favour."

"You expect me to believe that?" Jenna showed a flash of her old hauteur, huffing out a laugh.

"Your adopted father became quite chatty when he was holding me prisoner," Alyx said. "Amidst all the torture, he told me something very interesting."

"Whatever it is you want, I'm not interested." Jenna shook her head. "Arrest me, kill me, do whatever you like. I'm not stupid, I know my life here is over."

Alyx waited a beat after Jenna had finished talking, then looked her straight in her stunning blue eyes. "I think one or both your parents were Taliath, Jenna, and I think Casovar murdered them on the orders of the Mage Council."

The young woman swallowed, a bright sheen of tears glistening in her eyes, but instead of letting them fall, she held her chin high. "If that's true, why did he keep me? Why not kill me too?"

"He kept you in the hopes that if he raised you, one day you'd form a close enough bond that he could absorb your invulnerability," Alyx said bluntly. "He wanted power, and he wanted to be invincible. Shakar played on those ambitions quite successfully."

"Did it work?" Her voice was raspy, as if speaking around a lump in her throat.

Alyx shook her head. "No. So far, only one way has proven to allow a mage to absorb Taliath ability, and that's through being lovers."

There was a long silence. Apart from the tears that still glistened in Jenna's eyes, it was hard to tell what she was thinking or feeling. Eventually she spoke again. "Why are you telling me this?"

"Casovar wouldn't have kept you unless he thought you were a Taliath potential too."

A spark of interest flashed on her face, quickly hidden. "What do you think?"

"I'm trying to read your thoughts right now and I can't. We could try proving it by me throwing a concussion ball at you and seeing if you were invulnerable." Alyx gave a little smile. "It's tempting."

Jenna huffed out a laugh of genuine amusement.

"My friend Dawn was able to read your jealousy of me once, but then she's a particularly powerful telepath with the ability to pick up on emotion, not only thought." Alyx paused. "I have little doubt you're a Taliath potential."

"So what's this favour you want, Lady Egalion?"

Alyx rose to her feet. "I'm leaving Alistriem tonight, but I'm loathe to leave Cayr unprotected. The Bluecoats are good, but a trained

Taliath is better. My father has given orders for you to be released on my say so. You'll be given a stipend to remain at court."

Confusion swam in her eyes. "You want me to protect Prince Cayr?"

"Two Bluecoats named Tijer and Casta have agreed to teach you to fight in secret. Tijer is on guard outside the door now. You can trust them with your life, but outside that, only you and I can know about this. If the council ever learns what you are, they'll kill you." Alyx paused. "My father will return to court eventually, and then he can explain what I don't have time to about the Taliath. Until then, you'll have to trust me."

Jenna shook her head, gesturing to her fine dress and silken slippers. "You think I can become a fighter?"

"Better than a fighter, Jenna Casovar. A Taliath." Alyx cocked her head. "He murdered your parents and used you for years, hiding your real worth from you and turning you into a perfect little lady. Are you going to continue to allow him to do that to you?"

Jenna thought about that for a moment, and then she stood up. "Actually, it's Jenna Aridlen. That was my parents' name."

Alyx stepped closer, allowing her magic to fill the air around them. "You betray me, Jenna Aridlen, and I'll kill you before the council can."

Jenna smiled, eyes turning sharp as diamonds. "First lesson understood, Alyx Egalion. Never show your fear."

CHAPTER 41

Crossing the border into the disputed area undetected was easy enough with both Alyx and Dawn able to steer them clear of any Shiven patrols. In a small group, they made quick time, stopping only for brief periods to rest and water the horses. In a week they reached Widow Falls, escorted over the final distance by Romney and his warriors.

Ladan was waiting for them, a small smile crossing his face when he saw Alyx. She went straight into his arms. "Hello, big brother."

"Little sister. I am glad to see you well."

"We actually can't stay, we're on our way to DarkSkull," Alyx said. "But Papa and I need to talk to you."

He nodded. "Come through. Tarrick, Finn, Dawn—Romney will take you to the kitchens. We've a meal prepared for you."

It wasn't long before Alyx and Garan were settled by the fire in Ladan's study. A servant appeared with a tray of food and drink, but disappeared quickly at a sharp gesture from Ladan.

"What did you want to discuss?" he asked once the door had closed.

Alyx gave him a quick rundown of what had happened in Alistriem, including explaining about Shakar's medal-wearing Hunters. "Ladan…" She paused, meeting his eyes. "I want you to go to ShadowFall Island." He frowned. "I can't do that. I'm needed here." "Even so, you are a Taliath and you should be trained. Rionn is going to need you. I'm going to need you," she said. "That is why I bought Papa here. It's isolated enough that he should be safe, from the council and Shakar, but he can also protect Widow Falls while you are gone."

"What makes you think anyone is even on the island anymore?"

"There is no guarantee of course," Garan spoke. "But there were always non-Taliath teachers there, part of the community that formed the school. Some of them may still be alive. At the very least there may be records of training, maybe even something specific to Shakar."

"This is my home, I am responsible for it," Ladan insisted, rising to his feet in agitation. "I can't leave."

"Son." The word rippled through the room, and Ladan stilled. Garan rose to his feet. "Trust me with your home. I can see how much you love it, and I will protect it with everything I have. Allow me to do this for you."

Ladan turned slowly, his expressionless mask gone as he looked at his father. Alyx held her breath, expelling it in a rush when Ladan gave a slow nod. Garan's shoulders relaxed fractionally. "Thank you, Ladan."

"I wasn't just asking for me," Alyx spoke into the silence. "Dashan is on ShadowFall Island. If there is anyone left… he faces a long time of training there, and he doesn't always do well when he is alone. It would be good for him to have a friend. Rionn needs both of you as fully trained Taliath."

Ladan stepped towards her and reached out to touch her arm. "I will do as you ask."

"Thank you." She hugged him.

"When will you leave?"

"First thing in the morning," she said. "Come on, let's go join the others and spend some time together before we have to part again."

THREE WEEKS AFTER LEAVING ALISTRIEM, it was almost like old times

s they found themselves travelling along the road from Weeping Stead
o DarkSkull Hall.

"Do you think they'll be pleased to see us?" Finn broke the silence
hat had been lying heavy over them all morning.

"They'll be pleased to see Alyx," Cario noted. "She's their coveted
nage of the higher order. They'll be less pleased with the news we're
iringing."

"What do you think would be the best way to handle it?"
inn asked.

Tarrick shrugged. "We ask to speak to Master Romas, and Alyx
ells him everything."

"And if he doesn't believe her?" Dawn wondered.

"Brynn has already spoken to them," Alyx said grimly. "In fact, he
hould be here waiting for us. And if Romas won't listen... well, then
'll let him into my mind to prove it. Whatever it takes, we have to
onvince the council."

Tarrick looked back at them. "We're just about at the gates to the
iridge."

A cold wind whipped up, blowing Alyx's cloak back from her shoul-
lers. The cloak had become necessary as they set out that morning—
he air was icy cold, and the scudding clouds overhead warned of
now later.

"A roaring fire would be nice right about now." Finn sighed. "I miss
Rionn's warm weather already."

"And the sunshine," Alyx said softly. "I miss the sunshine."

At the sight of the bridge, they glanced at each other and spurred
heir horses forward in tacit agreement. The wind whipped up again as
he horses moved into a canter. Leaves and other debris scattered
inder their hooves, the sound echoing loudly down into the gorge.

Foremost in Alyx's mind was a hot fire and hearty meal. They'd
ieen riding almost non-stop for three weeks dodging Shiven patrols,
ind the trip hadn't been big on creature comforts.

The gate opened with a loud screeching at their arrival. Urging
heir horses back into a canter, Tarrick was the first to reach the end of
he narrow gorge and emerge onto the valley floor. He reined in so
iuddenly that Finn's horse ran into him before he could pull up. Imme-

diately behind, Alyx desperately yanked Tingo to the right and he jumped sideways, barely missing them.

"Tarrick, what are you doing?" she snapped, focused on getting Tingo back under control.

He didn't reply. He was staring, ashen-faced, down into the valley. She'd never seen that look on Tarrick's face before, and dread began creeping through her veins even before she turned to look in the same direction. An instant later her mind was deluged with Tarrick's and Finn's unshielded thoughts as both their shields crumpled under the weight of emotion, so potent she almost fell from the saddle.

"Stop!" Dawn screamed, her hand flying to cradle her head. "Shield! Please, stop!"

The flow of distressed thoughts slowed a little, enough to allow Alyx to think. But she didn't want to think... didn't want to see what was before her.

DarkSkull Hall was a charred mess.

Two huge chunks had been gouged in the thick stone walls of the female dormitory, and smoke curled out from inside, ribbons of it torn apart by the wind as it drifted higher. The fields had been reduced to ashes. The stone block holding the majority of classrooms was gone completely, leaving only a few foundation stones where it used to stand. One half of the stables was a charred ruin. The main hall and male dormitory building looked to be the only ones untouched by destruction.

Their friends. Howell. Grief leapt in her chest, bright and hot, and without thought Alyx kicked Tingo into a gallop towards the hall. There had to be something she could do. Help in some way... something. Surely they couldn't be...

The first body came into sight before the steps leading up into the main hall. Tingo caught the scent and reared spectacularly. Alyx half slid, half fell out of the saddle, leaving Tingo to back away, snorting in distress.

Her stomach heaved as she dropped by the body. It was one of the masters, Dirrion, she thought, though it was hard to tell. The lower half of his body was charred black, and the look of the rest indicated he'd been dead at least a couple of days. Her stomach heaved again and she vomited onto the grass beside him. The wind kicked up, carrying with it the scent of ashes and death. Alyx struggled to her feet and drew her staff.

Any hope she had dying inside her, smothered by the rising tide of grief, she ran up the steps and through the shattered front doors. Lingering smoke clogged her nostrils, and she coughed. Over and over she scanned the area with her telepathic magic, but found nothing. No thoughts. Just deafening silence.

More bodies lay across the hall entrance, most charred beyond recognition. Alyx heard boot steps behind her. Cario, his staff raised helplessly, the same grief on his face.

"Tarrick?" she managed.

"He's gone to check around the other buildings. Finn's searching the bodies for any survivors."

"I can't hear any thoughts," Dawn appeared, half-sobbing with distress. "There's nobody alive, I can't hear anything."

Bracing herself, Alyx stepped into the hall. The last time she'd been in there, the hall had been alive with lights and music for the dance. She'd danced with Dashan, then kissed him out in the garden.

Oh Dash, I need you.

The hall was full of bodies, the intermingled scent of burning and decay sickly sweet. It looked as if the attackers had dragged most of the dead inside and left them to rot. Alyx gagged again, the contents of her stomach threatening to come up.

Ruthlessly she pushed away the nausea and continued walking through, magic attuned for anyone that might still be alive. At the sight of Mika's lifeless blue eyes, his young body impossibly small at her feet, she broke into a run out of the hall. No.

Her boots pounded on the stone steps, breath rasping in her chest. The scent of smoke told her what she would find, but she kept going anyway, stumbling through the burnt doors of DarkSkull's library.

Howell lay in the middle of the floor. A sword thrust had killed him, not magic—blood had pooled and dried around the wound in his chest. Behind him, the books he'd loved had been destroyed, most burned to ashes. She could taste the ash on her tongue, breathed in the particles with each tortured gasp.

She knelt by his body, ignoring the blood, and reached out to close his clouded brown eyes. They were cold to the touch and she shuddered, trying desperately not to fall apart.

"I'm sorry, sir," she whispered. "I'm so sorry."

A wave of Dawn's thoughts hit her then, both their minds unshielded with grief and horror. She'd found Rickin's body. Alyx swayed with the force of her friend's emotion, and scrambled away from Howell's body, unable to look at it anymore.

In a daze, she went back downstairs, almost falling twice from not paying attention to where she was going. Tarrick and Cario stood at the entrance to the hall, Finn not far off, cradling his sister to his chest.

"This is it," Tarrick whispered. "The future of the mage order, it's lying dead in this room."

"Did anyone see Brynn?" Cario asked. "Or Jayn?"

Silence met his question.

"We need to get out of here," Alyx muttered. "I need to get out."

A blast of cold air hit her as she emerged outside, cooling the sweat on her skin. She continued down the steps and over to Tingo, where she rested her head against his warm neck and tried to get herself under control. He snorted, but stayed still. Breathing was difficult around the lump in her throat, and silent tears streamed down her cheeks. She wanted Dashan's arms around her so badly it hurt.

"Someone's coming." Cario's voice, sharp enough to break her daze.

Alyx spun around. Dawn was pointing towards the eastern valley wall, where one of the paths led through the tree-covered slope to the south-eastern watchtower.

"Best we go meet them." Scrubbing at her wet cheeks, Alyx hefted her staff and took a step away from Tingo.

"Wait!" Tarrick's voice stopped her. "Do you think that's smart? What if it's whoever did all this?"

"Then I'll kill them all." Her voice came out caught between a snarl and a sob, but she'd never meant anything more in her life.

Halfway across the burnt fields, Alyx stopped and waited for the distant group of people to approach. As they came closer, she sent magic flowing through her staff. It lit up with a pearly green shimmer.

Tarrick came to a stop at her right shoulder, Cario at her left. The twins hovered behind.

"Approach slowly," she called out. "Any quick moves, and I'll kill you where you stand."

They did as she asked, slowing their pace and holding their empty hands out to show they were unarmed. Alyx recognised the lead figure as soon as he came into view, despite his sooty, haggard appearance.

"Rothai!"

He stopped before her, utter relief filling his face at the sight of her. "You're alive. We saw you coming... I hoped it was you."

She swallowed, found the strength to talk at the sight of Jayn amongst the mages hovering behind Rothai. Jayn lived! "What happened?"

"DarkSkull was attacked two days ago." He paused. "By Shakar."

"Are you sure?" Tarrick spoke.

"Certain." Rothai's eyes were terrible as they met hers. "Those of us that survived have been hiding up on the valley wall in case he came back."

"Dawn?" Alyx asked.

"He's telling the truth," she replied.

Alyx allowed her magic to fade from her staff. "They're all dead."

Rothai's shoulders sagged. "I know."

"What now?" Finn wondered aloud.

"Come with us," Rothai said. "We have food and shelter up at the watchtower, and can talk more there."

As DUSK SETTLED over the valley that evening, Alyx stood looking down at the horror and destruction that had once been a thriving mage school. She didn't know what to do, how to comprehend the sheer magnitude of it all.

"He did that by himself."

She started as Rothai came up beside her. He still had the same grave face, sharp blue eyes and black hair. Before, she'd disliked him intensely. Now it seemed he'd barely survived as he fought for Dark-

Skull Hall. Jayn had told her earlier that without him, nobody would have survived.

"Which part?" she asked.

"See those gouges in the wall the size of a field?" Rothai pointed. "They weren't done by siege engines, they were caused by a single blast of Shakar's magic. I watched him do it."

A shiver ran down her spine at the thought of such power. Those walls had been several feet thick, and Shakar had crushed them with a single blast?

"What about the Mage Council? And Galien?"

"Galien is alive as far as I know. Romas is dead, but the rest of the council is still alive."

"We came to warn the council, to help them defeat Shakar. But they couldn't stop this." Alyx stumbled to a halt. Ladan had been right. Those old men who'd sat around an ornate table in Carhall talking about how far they'd go to hold onto their power, they weren't going to stop Shakar.

"You can."

She spun to look at Rothai, shocked. "I don't have anything that approaches that sort of power."

"On the contrary. We all felt it, when you first came here. Your entire aura leaks powerful magic." A strange intensity flickered in Rothai's pale eyes, a stark brightness against the encroaching darkness. "You have more potential than all of us put together, Magor-lier."

Magor-lier. She'd heard the word before—something Tarrick had said in their first year at DarkSkull. The oddness of the word had stuck with her. It was an old mage title, used by the most powerful warrior mage that led the mage order in battle.

Alyx shook her head. "Why did you call me that?"

"Magor-lier?" He looked at her with a grim smile. "Because you are the most powerful mage alive, and you are now our only hope."

"You're asking me to lead you?"

He gave a little shrug. "I'm not asking, Magor-lier. There is nobody else."

Rothai turned to walk away, but Alyx stopped him with a touch. "You almost let me die, that day on the practice yard."

"You needed to be tested." He paused. "Needless to say you passed even more spectacularly than expected. Rest, you're going to need it."

Alyx remained where she was after he'd walked away, studying her hand as it glimmered with a pearly sheen. The magic was easy to summon now, and for the first time since her confrontation with Finn, the beginnings of fear trickled through her.

What will I become?

~

To be continued in The Mage Chronicles book four - *Heartfire*

~

Want to delve further into the world of *The Mage Chronicles?* By signing up to Lisa's monthly newsletter, *The Dock City Chronicle,* you'll get exclusive access to advance cover reveals, book updates, and special content just for subscribers, including:

- A short ebook with a collection of short stories from *The Mage Chronicles* universe;
- A pronunciation guide;
- Exclusive content from Lisa's other fantasy series;

Head to Lisa's website to sign up!
lisacassidyauthor.com

~

Consider a review?

'Your words are as important to an author as an author's words are to you'

Hello,
I'm really hoping you enjoyed this story. If you did (or even if not), I would be humbled if you would consider taking the time to leave an honest review on GoodReads and Amazon (it doesn't have to be long - a few words or a single sentence is absolutely fine). Reviews are the lifeblood of any book, especially for indie authors like me. Not to mention a review can absolutely make my day!
Thank you so much for reading this book,
Lisa

ALSO BY LISA CASSIDY

The Mage Chronicles

DarkSkull Hall

Taliath

Darkmage

Heartfire

Heir to the Darkmage

Heir to the Darkmage

Mark of the Huntress

A Tale of Stars and Shadow

A Tale of Stars and Shadow

A Prince of Song and Shade

A King of Masks and Magic

A Duet of Sword and Song

~

ABOUT THE AUTHOR

Lisa is a self-published fantasy author by day and book nerd in every other spare moment she has. She's a self-confessed coffee snob (don't try coming near her with any of that instant coffee rubbish) but is willing to accept all other hot drink aficionados, even tea drinkers. She lives in Australia's capital city, Canberra, and like all Australians, is pretty much in constant danger from highly poisonous spiders, crocodiles, sharks, and drop bears, to name a few. As you can see, she is also pro-Oxford comma.

A 2019 SPFBO finalist, and finalist for the 2020 ACT Writers Fiction award, Lisa is the author of the young adult fantasy series *The Mage Chronicles,* and epic fantasy series *A Tale of Stars and Shadow.* The first book in her latest series, *Heir to the Darkmage,* released in April 2021. She has also partnered up with One Girl, an Australian charity working to build a world where all girls have access to quality education. A world where all girls — no matter where they are born or how much money they have — enjoy the same rights and opportunities as boys. A percentage of all Lisa's royalties go to One Girl.

You can follow Lisa on Instagram and Facebook where she loves to interact with her readers. Lisa also has a Facebook group - The Writing Cave - where you can jump in and talk about anything and everything relating to her books (or any books really).

lisacassidyauthor.com

Printed in Great Britain
by Amazon

77946198R00231